ADRENALINE

(2002)

THE YEAR'S BEST STORIES OF
ADVENTURE AND SURVIVAL

ADRENALINE

2002

THE YEAR'S BEST STORIES OF ADVENTURE AND SURVIVAL

EDITED BY CLINT WILLIS

Thunder's Mouth Press
New York

ADRENALINE 2002: THE YEAR'S BEST STORIES OF ADVENTURE AND SURVIVAL

Compilation copyright © 2001 by Clint Willis
Introductions copyright © 2001 by Clint Willis

Adrenaline ® and the Adrenaline® logo are trademarks of
Avalon Publishing Group Incorporated, New York, NY.

An Adrenaline Book®

Published by
Thunder's Mouth Press
An Imprint of Avalon Publishing Group Incorporated
161 William Street, 16th floor
New York, NY 10038

Book design: Sue Canavan

frontispiece photo: © Bobby Model/National Geographic

Library of Congress Cataloging-in-Publication Data is available.

ISBN: 1-56025-413-0

Printed in the United States of America

Distributed by Publishers Group West

For Ava and Eloise,
the world's best girls

c o n t e n t s

introduction

When you are gathering a collection of adventure writing, you need a definition of adventure. Our current culture provides an off-the-rack definition: An adventure is a life-threatening experience—preferably on Mount Everest, but the ocean or Antarctica might do.

That definition is of course too narrow to be useful. An adventure doesn't need to be life-threatening. Such threats tend to sharpen our focus and hence our awareness; they sometimes awaken our deepest intelligence, providing opportunities to live our experience more fully. But we can summon such intelligence in any context: We can live fully in conversation, in a concert hall, in a hospital, at a party.

Adventure is what we experience when we live with at least some awareness of the way things are. Such experiences connect us to the world through our senses and our minds; they wake us up from the daze of mindlessness and the torrent of worry that ordinarily distract us from what is important, what is beautiful, what is real. Adventure may or may not threaten to kill us, but always it threatens to shift, at least temporarily, the quality and the rhythm of a life that is not entirely lived.

x

Adventure is in that way seditious. Modern commerce and its offshoot—corporate power—aim to reduce us from creators to consumers. They encourage us to be absent; to sleepwalk through our lives, to take our cues from television, movies, theme parks, advertisements, pornography, video games. At work, we often subordinate our human designs to the motives of ambitious superiors, faceless institutions and anonymous shareholders. At school, we often learn to follow orders and instructions that will, if we are lucky, help us to become above-average getters and spenders.

Adventure reminds us that we are here; that we are in some sense God's creatures; that what we do matters. It reminds us that our life is important, that at any given moment something sacred is at stake. Such reminders might arrive when our lives are threatened. But they can as easily occur when we come upon a place that has itself been preserved— so far—from commerce. They can occur when we take on a challenge that demands our utmost effort and focus—or when we are unpacking the car for a picnic or reading a good story. Adventure reminds us that we are alive, that any moment lived in awareness makes our lives worth living, that death and other inevitabilities pale in the light of such moments.

We are drawn to adventurers and to adventure stories because they tell us what we forget: that each of us is on an adventure, that our lives are filled with opportunities to wake up and do the right thing—that we'll know that right thing when we allow ourselves to see it. The adventurers you'll encounter in this book include climbers and sailors and Antarctic explorers; they also include amateur boxers and soldiers and travel writers and office workers. Their stories are good ones—and, as such, they remind us that we have our own stories, that those stories are waiting for us to live them, and that they won't wait forever.

CLINT WILLIS
SERIES EDITOR, ADRENALINE BOOKS

The Numbers
by Bryan Charles

At 8:45 a.m. on September 11, 2001, Bryan Charles was starting his workday at Morgan Stanley on the 70th floor of Two World Trade Center.

Here was a morning like any other. I got up at 6:40, took a shower and got ready for work. I hadn't slept well the night before. My eyes burned. Walking to the bathroom required tremendous energy. I blamed my new neighbors. Their surround-sound TV was set up just a few feet from my head. The first two times I ever talked to them was to tell them to turn down their TV or stereo or whatever. Last night, I didn't have the heart to complain. I just lay in the dark and accepted it.

For several minutes after my clock radio had clicked on to Howard Stern, I contemplated calling in sick. It was a Tuesday. Nothing happens on Tuesdays. Whatever I was working on could wait. What harm could come from my sleeping in a few extra hours and enjoying the rest of the day? I could go out to breakfast, get some writing done, maybe take a walk.

But my boss was in Italy, on her honeymoon, and the more lucid I became, the more I reasoned that it would look bad, like I was trying to take advantage of her absence. I threw off the covers and got out of bed. As I dressed, I half watched-half listened to *Good Day New York*, with Dave Price, the wacky weather guy, and Jim Ryan, the straight man. I went to the kitchen, opened the window and leaned out. My apartment was on the third and top floor. Laundry lines crisscrossed the little lawns and patios below. The tip of the Chrysler Building gleamed across the river. The sun was out, the sky was cloudless, the wind blew a little. It was a perfect day.

Outside, I took the B48 bus to Metropolitan Avenue, in Williamsburg, and caught a Manhattan-bound L train. At Union Square, I transferred to the N\R line which stopped right in the World Trade Center, where I worked as a copywriter in the Morgan Stanley marketing department. On this day, my commute was fast. The bus came right away, and both trains. I was walking along the concourse in the trade center by about 8:15.

Usually, I'd buy the *Daily News*, but not that morning. I was engrossed in a new biography of Kurt Cobain and wanted to finish it before nine. I was right at the suicide part, where the author reconstructs what Cobain might have been thinking before he pulled the trigger, what music he might have been listening to, et cetera. I did that sometimes. If I was near the end of a book, I'd sit at my desk and keep reading, reaching for random papers in an attempt to look busy whenever I heard footsteps.

I put my ID badge on the scanner, pushed through the turnstile, and got in one of the big cattle-car elevators that shuttled back and forth between the forty-fourth floor. A fact of working in Two World Trade that never quite became routine was that it took two elevators to get there. On forty-four were several other elevator banks, the second of which led to the seventieth floor, where I worked.

So much of life there was transport: the perpetual, maddening bling of elevators coming and going, escalators whose silver ridges approximated the façades of the towers themselves. Each day was a series of small surrenders to vast hidden systems of cables and electrical wiring and computer chips. Once, last winter, one of the elevators malfunctioned and either dropped a few floors or slammed into the ceiling. I think there were some broken bones. It made the news the next day.

Before heading up to seventy, as was my routine, I went down yet another flight to the cafeteria for a bagel and coffee. On my left as I descended was a new waterfall installation, two planes of thick glass pressed together as water illuminated by colored lights flowed between them. The whole thing probably cost twice my yearly salary. Above me was a mounted TV tuned to some all-Morgan Stanley channel. The screen was cluttered with graphics, stock tickers and boxes from which the faces of analysts and other market experts telegraphed their daily predictions.

"Well, clearly this has been a rough couple of quarters for technology. But these kinds of shake-ups are all part of the game. We're in this for the long haul."

Each day I tried my best to ignore the looming presence of this TV. It reminded me of where I was, that I had gone to college to study creative writing and literature and now spent my days cranking out cheesy copy advertising about the need for careful planning in the pursuit of one's financial dreams. It reminded me that the short stories I labored over on evenings and weekends went unpublished while the brochures and newsletters I wrote enjoyed print runs in the thousands and millions. It reminded me that at an earlier time in my life I had played punk rock music and sometimes went weeks without washing my jeans, but was now outfitted in a corporate casual wardrobe purchased largely at Banana Republic, a wardrobe that rendered me indistinguishable from the thousands of other young men I saw pouring in and out of the World Trade Center every day.

That TV reminded me of a lot of things, mostly my own sense of failure. One thing it could not detract from, however, was the view.

On a clear day, walking past the cafeteria windows was like witnessing a live slide show. The Hudson River, the harbor, the Statue of Liberty, Governor's Island, Ellis Island, the tall ships on the Fourth of July. People spent their life savings and traveled from around the world to see what I saw every morning, five days a week.

Working for a multinational, multibillion-dollar financial institution may not have been my dream job, but being in that building every day sure was cool.

Out of the cafeteria, back up the escalator, into an elevator.

I had a whole car to myself, which was rare. I pushed seventy. The doors closed. The car went up.

By 8:30, I was at my desk, reading about Kurt Cobain killing himself.

When I was a senior in high school I wanted to be Kurt Cobain. A long time before that I wanted to be Jim Morrison. Both of these guys died when they were twenty-seven. Sometime during my Jim Morrison phase, I told a teacher at my school named Ms. Schade that I wanted to die when I was twenty-seven.

"Why, because Jim Morrison did?" she said.

I said yeah. I was fifteen when I said that. Later, when Kurt Cobain killed himself, I thought, "Ah, twenty-seven, that's a good life. He must have been in pain." I was nineteen when I thought that.

On August 2, a little over a month earlier, I had turned twenty-seven.

I put peanut butter on my bagel. At work, I ate a lot of peanut butter. It was a cost-cutting measure. New York is an expensive town. Sometimes I'd have it for breakfast and lunch. In my cupboard, there were about ten empty peanut butter jars, all Skippy brand. I never threw them away. I always thought that one day I'd take them home and recycle them.

In the book before me, Kurt Cobain got ready to put a gun barrel in his mouth. I looked at the clock on my desk phone display. It said 8:45 exactly. I thought about changing into my work shoes and decided against it. (I wore sneakers to work because of all the walking I do. Kind of girlie, I admit. But New York is not the place to live if you don't like walking. Comfortable shoes are a necessity.)

A couple minutes later I heard a series of muffled booms. The floor trembled. It sounded like thunder, but closer. From where I sat, it had the odd effect of being both loud and not loud. One thing felt certain. It was very near. In fact, at that instant, I thought something was happening down the hall. I thought it was a bank of file cabinets falling over. Then a man from accounting named Leo Kirby started yelling. He didn't stop. "Oh my God! Oh my God! Oh God! Oh dear God!"

He was yelling so loudly that my next thought was, "Someone down by Leo Kirby is hurt. The file cabinets fell over on someone and crushed them." For the first time that day, I got scared. I stood up. Two guys I work with named Mark Sanford and Brian Whelan were by John Warner's office, staring out the window. I sat in a cubicle, gray walls, no window. I walked over. All I saw were thousands of papers flying through the air. Some of the papers were burning. My stomach dropped.

Mark cocked his head like when a dog hears a high pitch. "Hey", he said. He was looking out at One World Trade. "That building's on fire."

Whelan and I went to another window. There was smoke. He and I looked at each other. I could see over the cubicles, across the office, down the hall. I sensed the chemistry of the air changing. It went from stale, recycled, artificially cold office air to something different, something I can't describe except to say it was alive. It buzzed like a high-tension power line.

Without realizing what I was doing, I went to my desk, got my backpack and walked to the hallway near the elevators, where people had already congregated. I knew a lot of them. Whelan was there, but the only other person I saw from my department was Lauren Wohl. A lot of people from the sales department were there. My friend Leslie was there. She had her arm around her boss, a woman named Zobeida. Zobeida was crying. Not very long ago, she had a baby. I saw another woman named Gail who also just had a baby. A woman from our department named Joanna just had a baby. I looked around and didn't see her. So there we were, standing around, not knowing what had happened. I thought of Leo Kirby's screams. We waited for an announcement but none came. The security guy didn't know anything. He was just standing up from his desk when I saw him.

"What?" he said when he heard the news. "Something happened to the other building?"

I looked at everyone but didn't register more than a blur of scared faces. A few minutes passed. Someone said, "Shit, the fire warden's not here. Where's the fire warden?"

But what difference did that make? The fire warden was just some cubicle worker. It's an arbitrary title they give out during fire drills. I could have been the fire warden for our floor and at that moment probably couldn't have recited my address.

More people rounded the corners and fell in with the group. I don't remember any one person suggesting that we get in the stairwell. I know I didn't say it. Probably it was a collective decision. All I know is that the door opened and we filed in. It was packed, two lanes, shoulder-to-shoulder with workers from the higher floors already making their way down. I looked at the sign by the door that said Seventy and took my first step. For a few minutes I was next to Julie Lin, from sales.

"Are you scared, Bryan?" she said, like she was asking if I were hungry.

I said yes and wondered if she was scared. She didn't seem like it. She said, "I've never seen you like this. Usually you always have something to say."

It's true. I was always joking, always goofing on having a big corporate job. But right then I couldn't speak. My legs were crazy. My breath came in quick little gasps.

Then Julie disappeared and Whelan was on my right. Whelan was my best work buddy. He sat in the cubicle next to me and we spent whole days quoting from our favorite movies. *Fast Times at Ridgemont High, A Few Good Men, Just One of the Guys,* vintage Chevy Chase like *Fletch* and *Vacation*. We even quoted from *Kramer vs. Kramer*. He and I had a running joke about spending our days at a place that was ground zero for a terrorist attack. But that had already happened. The building had been bombed before. I was a freshman in college then. My mom picked me up one day and was driving me home to do laundry when it came on the radio.

What goes on in the World Trade Center? I wondered. *Who works there?*
I glanced up and saw Leslie walking with Zobeida. Zobeida was still crying, clinging to Leslie. I heard stories. People said that a plane had hit the side of the other tower. A plane? I pictured a tiny ten-seat propeller plane with a guy who'd just had a heart attack at the controls flying into One World Trade. A freak accident. A woman behind me

was crying hard. Her red eyes radiated shock, sadness and terror. She talked to herself, and what she said was that she'd seen people jumping from the broken windows of the other building.

Around the fifty-ninth floor, there was an announcement. The whole line of people up and down stopped to listen. From behind the stairwell door we heard a voice on a loudspeaker. "There is a problem in building one," the voice said. "Building two is secure. I repeat, building two is secure. Please go back to your desks and wait for further instruction."

The voice repeated this message. Hearing that kind of comforted me, but not a lot. It comforted other people, I guess, because some of them turned around. I heard one guy say, "Well, fuck it, I'm walking all the way back up," like the whole thing was a big drag and he was annoyed.

You couldn't reenter every floor from inside the stairwell, so Whelan and I got out at fifty-five, I think it was. Lauren was there, in a big crowd. It was a weird floor, just white walls, no offices. It looked like a maintenance area, or some kind of telecommunications hub. People everywhere, roaming the halls. Tension and dread flowed through every look, every verbal exchange. A black guy came walking over, shaking his head, looking sad and tired. He said he'd just seen bodies, dozens of bodies, falling from the other building, workers in the other tower leaping. "What?" someone said. "No."

A bunch of guys ran to look. By then I was almost as confused as I was scared. These people appeared to be telling the truth, but I couldn't believe it. I couldn't believe that anyone had jumped. It was too horrible to think about. Over the year and a half that I'd been working in the trade center, nearly everyone in my department had made at least one joke about jumping or falling out of the window on the seventieth floor. It wasn't possible to get through a work day without achieving at least a moment of consciousness about being that high up. And again, there was the view, always the view. From the corner boardroom where we had our status meetings you could see straight into midtown: the Empire State Building, the Chrysler Building, the Met Life building on one side; on the other was the Brooklyn Bridge, the East River, all of Brooklyn, on into the haze forever.

Whelan and I trudged past a cluster of people waiting to take elevators either up or down. I saw Lauren, but we got separated. Back into the stairwell.

A few floors later, maybe ten, maybe less, came another explosion. This one was loud. It was a sonic boom. The tower shook. I slipped down the stairs. People screamed and gripped the railing to keep from falling. The building, this enormous skyscraper, this national landmark, swayed back and forth like a child's toy, like a ride at the fair. A slow violent unreal rocking. This is it, I thought. Get ready to go down with the ship. My body and mind went numb. I didn't start praying, I didn't have visions of childhood, I didn't see my life flash before my eyes. I went into this white arctic zone of either acceptance or resignation or preparedness. I don't know what it was. I was blank. I was nothing. People screamed, they prayed. The screams and prayers merged into one.

"What the fuck is happening, Whelan?" I said. "Are we being bombed?"

"No," he said, "that was just the fuel tank exploding from the plane that hit the other building."

The building must not have moved like that for very long, maybe fifteen or twenty seconds, but it felt like forever.

There was a heavyset black lady about three people ahead of us, babbling an endless prayer. "Oh, please God," was all it consisted of. "Please Lord." She moved slowly, heaving her body from side to side, and I saw that she wasn't wearing shoes.

Whelan's face was tight and pale. Had he felt what I had a moment earlier, that we were experiencing our last seconds of life? I reached over with my right hand and squeezed his shoulder. The woman behind me sobbed. I turned around and touched her shoulder. I ran my hand down her back, over her sweat-soaked shirt. She didn't acknowledge me.

Sometimes the line stopped cold. Congestion on the lower floors.

We'd be standing in the stairwell, not moving forward, with voices above us screaming, "No! Don't stop! Go down! Keep moving!" A moment or two of waiting, of agony, of wondering whether or not the people below were crushing each other to get out of the building, and then we'd go again.

Every few minutes I called out the words, "It's gonna be okay." I didn't believe myself, but kept saying it anyway. One time when the line was stalled, I turned to the guy behind me. We smiled weakly at each other and shook hands. The line started again. It was very hot, either from the fire above or body heat or both, and you could smell smoke.

After the explosion, life became a matter of watching the numbers on the signs in the stairwell get smaller. It was a long, slow process. Forty. Thirty-nine. Thirty-eight. Thirty-seven. Thirty-six. And so on. I couldn't tell how long we'd been in there. Time had vanished. There was no time. There was only descent. There was only counting and waiting and counting, circling around again and again. There was only concrete walls painted a grimy flesh color. Then we wound down the last ten floors. We came out on the plaza level and I looked through the big windows. Everyone did.

It was then that I realized something had happened that was far more terrifying than any of us had thought being blind and dumb in the stairwell. It was then that I realized the whole world was probably watching this on television.

The plaza with the fountain and the big gold sculpture and stage for summer concerts still set up was filled with large chunks of jagged burning metal and smoke and ash and debris. That was all you could see. It covered every inch of the ground and was still raining down. Car-sized hunks of the building, that famous sleek silver, lay burning twenty feet away. There were police and rescue workers there, guiding us. We circled around by the TKTS booth, past posters for famous Broadway shows. I saw Leo Kirby, the guy I'd heard screaming on the seventieth floor. I said, "Did you see that?" He nodded but didn't say anything.

There was a long line for the inoperable escalator but we finally made it down into the mall area, with stores like Banana Republic, the Gap, J. Crew, Ben and Jerry's, Sbarro's and Borders. Everything was dark. There were no people except rescue workers and police and firemen. We filed past a jewelry store called the Golden Nugget. The girls who worked at the Golden Nugget wore tight clothes, a lot of make up and had bleach-blond hair. Where were they right now?

Whelan and I shook hands by the PATH train escalators. He gripped my shoulder and said, "You're pretty cool under pressure, there, Bry." I wondered what he meant. Had I been cool? Did I seem panicked? Should I have stayed behind and tried to help women, old people and the disabled? Could I have done more?

We took a right at Sbarro's. Another line at the escalator leading up to Borders, where I went every day at about three o'clock to read books and magazines for as long as I felt like it. When I looked down I saw Melissa Murphy, from sales, and Lauren Wohl and Julie Lin. I waved and smiled. Lauren waved back. The line kept moving. We went outside. The rescue workers shouted to turn off all cell phones. They shouted, "Don't look up! Whatever you do, do not look up! Just keep moving! Do not look up!" But I couldn't help it. I had to see. I turned around and looked up and there were the two towers of the World Trade Center burning. Fire and smoke poured from enormous black holes in both buildings. Real fire, giant lapping tongues of flame. The sky in the background was very clear and very blue. Crisp. Kodachrome. A postcard of someone's nightmare. It was the most terrible thing I had ever seen. Not even the movies had prepared me.

"Keep moving," the rescue people said. "Go up to Fulton to Broadway."

Dust and white ash blanketed the pavement. Fire engines, police cars, sirens coming from all around, a thousand displaced office workers. I saw bright red blood splattered in the street but not where it came from. A guy ran up with a little spiral notebook and said, "Hey, buddy, were you in there?" I nodded. He said, "Would you talk to me?" I shook my head and waved him away. The guy behind me started telling his story.

As I walked, I kept looking over my shoulder. It was all still there, still real, still happening. I never thought I'd live to see something that horrific, but there it was. I was talking to myself, saying, "Oh my fucking God, holy fuck, Jesus fucking Christ."

On Broadway, among the throngs of spectators, I found Lauren and Julie. The three of us went north. When we got to the Staples by Park Row Julie crossed the street and Lauren and I couldn't because there were firetrucks going by. I put up my finger to say to Julie wait a minute but she kept going. We lost her. Whelan was gone too. It was just Lauren and me.

Up by City Hall, I asked her what she wanted to do. She said all she wanted was to get away from the trade center. Her dad worked in the city, on West End and Sixty-fifth. She said she wanted to go there. I didn't want to be alone and I didn't want her to be alone so we kept going together. We stopped a minute later and asked this lady if Lauren could use her cell phone. She said yeah, but good luck because all the circuits were jammed. She was right. The phone didn't work. The lady was nice and smiled and said good luck as we walked away. I wanted to stop to try and calm down, and also look at the buildings because I still didn't believe what was happening, but Lauren said no. "Let's get out of here," she said.

By then we were at a weird angle and the towers were hidden. All you could see was the smoke. Soon we were on Canal Street, China-town, my least favorite part of town. It's always so crowded and dirty. We started east on Canal, in a futile effort to avoid the crowds. I saw the little storefronts with I (heart) NY T-shirts and pirated CDs and a bunch of other junk that I don't know why anyone makes or buys. All the pay phones had long lines. We stopped and waited. There was a woman in front of me speaking Chinese into the receiver. She kept going on and on while I stood there. She didn't seem panicked or weepy. It sounded more like she was just shooting the shit. So I tapped her on the shoulder and said, "Look, I was just in the World Trade Center and I need to use the phone right now." She hung up and she and her friend gave me dirty looks and disappeared. Lauren was on the other phone, talking and crying, with her hand on her face. I think she was telling her dad or her mom that she was okay. I tried making a credit card call but the signal went dead. Lauren came over. She helped me dial and this time it worked. I punched in my credit card number.

My mom answered the phone in Galesburg, Michigan, in the house I grew up in. Her voice was very grave. "Hi, mom," I said. She started sobbing. I pictured the living room, the kitchen, our dog. I tried to imagine what my parents were seeing on their brand new big-screen TV. "Honey," she cried.

"Honey, it's Bryan." My stepdad got on the phone and he couldn't talk because he was so choked up. It was the first time I'd ever heard him like that. I'd only seen him cry once, about seven years ago. We were sitting out on the deck and he said he loved me and that he'd try his best to help me pay off my student loans. My parents were on the other line breaking down, freaking out, and I couldn't react to it. I was switched off. A part of me was still in that cold place I'd entered when I thought that Two World Trade was going to break in half and plunge into the street. I said, "Hello? Hello?" My stepdad said, "Yeah, I'm here, I love you."

Then my mom got back on and I said I had to go, there were other people waiting to use the phone. Lauren stood next to me, talking to a group of women, telling them about how she'd been in the building. I hung up.

We started walking again and I noticed for the first time that it was very sunny and hot. I had on a blue short-sleeved shirt and gray khaki pants and Nike sneakers. I had a backpack. We walked through some dirty, vacant side streets where there was nothing but workers loading restaurant supplies into greasy buildings. We went into a deli and bought water and I contemplated buying a beer.

Outside were thousands of Wall Street refugees walking north. It looked like the city was being evacuated on foot. It looked like a pilgrimage. It looked like a crusade. There were men carrying suit jackets who had sweated entirely through their shirts, ties loosened and fluttering in the breeze.

We came up through Astor Place. People were stunned and crying, wondering what had happened.

On Tenth Street we walked west and paused in the middle of Fifth Avenue, right on the center line. Two women asked Lauren for directions to West Fourth Street. They were like lost tourists who didn't know the city was burning. We looked south. There was the arc in Washington Square Park with One World Trade rising above it, burning in the distance. I thought that my building, Two World Trade, was behind the smoke.

Everyone stood in the street, numb and staring, and then it happened. One World Trade collapsed. A chorus of screams rose from the street. I reached for Lauren's hand and found it. A last glimpse of the antennae coming down and then nothing, no sound, just smoke and dust rising as it fell in on itself. It looked as perfect as if it had been wired with dynamite by a team of demolition experts. What had taken all those years to build was gone in seconds. How many people had just been killed?

Lauren and I thought our building was still there, hidden in the smoke. I turned my head, in shock. A woman took my picture. When she lowered the camera I saw her tears. There was another woman standing next to me. I said, "But the other building's still there, right?" She shook her head and said, "No, they're both gone."

What? When the hell did that happen? And how long had I been out? Again I wanted to stop. I wanted to lay down on the sidewalk. I wanted to rest. I wanted to think. Or Maybe I didn't want to think. I don't know what I wanted. But at least I wasn't alone. I was with Lauren. She was beautiful. Everyone I saw was beautiful in their grief and fear, in their just being alive.

We kept walking.

from Four Corners
by Kira Salak

Just before embarking on a new adventure, Kira Salak suffered a minor panic attack, brought on by the memory of her 1992 trip to Mozambique. Here she recalls her Mozambique experience.

lantyre, Malawi. Dr. Banda keeps me company. Everywhere I look, a picture of him flutters in the wind. On every street lamp, on every overpass, Dr. Banda. Dr. Banda. His scathing eyes, the incongruously friendly expression. A formidable man. Except for him, the streets are completely deserted. Only my footsteps give voice to the silence.

I'm twenty years old and my age feels comical. What do I know about anything? And more to the point: What is this place that I've reached now? Two summers working in a factory packaging croutons to get myself dumped off here, in yet another dark, dusty African town. Nowhere to sleep. The towns endlessly coming before me. My feet, as usual, keeping me in motion so I won't panic and stop moving. Stopping is when I question the sanity of it all, and tonight more than any other night, I must keep going.

I head resolutely out of town, my backpack heavy, the sweat like oil upon me. Dr. Banda smiles benignly as I approach another of the distant street lamps. I tell the Malawian president that I know about him. So many Malawians have come up to me and secretly told me about their sons or daughters disappearing in the night. I'm American, and so they think there is something I can do. I haven't had the guts to

tell them otherwise. I have all these people's names—people probably
dead now—and I don't know what to do with them. From the banners, Dr. Banda's face snickers.

Around me is the Malawi most visitors don't hear about. If there are
visitors, they can usually be found in the old resort town of Monkey
Bay on Lake Malawi, though Malawi isn't the tourist destination it
used to be. The large country of Mozambique with its civil war is an
inconvenience for overland tour buses from South Africa and Zimbabwe. Now there's no safe way to get to Malawi except by air or
through Zambia, and all I ever hear about is what a corrupt, exhausting
pain-in-the-ass Zambia is, all of one's money going for customs officials' bribes.

I spent a few days in Monkey Bay with some South African tourists.
It was from them that I first learned of the insanity of Mozambique,
woeful Malawi sounding like an Eden by comparison. Think of the
worst thing one human being can do to another, I was told, and I'll
find it in Mozambique. Worse than anything Dante could have
thought up and all of it honest-to-God reality. Babies used for target
practice. Little girls kidnapped and made into sex slaves. Torture. Muti-
lation. Killing sprees. The army, on both sides, composed mostly of
adolescents conscripted into one side or the other after their families
were butchered. You name it.

And I was only twenty, I reminded myself. I was nearly as old as
Mozambique's war. The entire situation there had sounded nearly
inconceivable.

The South Africans said they hadn't wanted to get near Mozambique and had flown into Malawi. When I told them I was interested
in crossing through the country to Zimbabwe, that I'd heard it was possible to do so along the "Tete Corridor"—a single road used by con-
voys of trucks transporting goods from the east of Africa to the
south—they shook their heads: not possible. That route was too dangerous now, was always being sabotaged by rebel soldiers. But I had
never been more serious in my life. I wanted to try to get across, see
that other world.

It was hard for me to understand the idea of a civil war. I'd glimpsed such wars on the news, but the images never seemed to gel in my mind as being *real*, reality. I wanted to see what was actually taking place. And in the process, I would see if I could actually get through such a place. If I could, then maybe I would have proof that I could do anything, that I could change as a person. Maybe I could believe in myself for the first time. I would just try to avoid getting embroiled in the politics of it all; I would stay as neutral as possible, focusing instead on the crossing itself, on the idea of making such a trip on my own.

I headed to the Malawian capital of Lilongwe to try to get the elusive transit visa to cross Mozambique. The South Africans had said I'd never be able to get one, but uncanny luck intervened on my behalf: When hitchhiking in town, I was picked up by a man who claimed to be best friends with the Mozambican ambassador to Malawi. As everything in Africa seemed to depend on who you knew, I received my visa in a miraculous five minutes. Suddenly there was nothing stopping me from crossing the country, except finding someone to take me through.

And so the town of Blantyre now. I search for a truck depot, and the chance of finding someone going across the Tete Corridor. I continue up the highway under Dr. Banda's watchful eye and arrive at a lit area, which is filled with parked trucks. As I approach from out of the dark, I must look like an apparition. An Indian manager in an office stops talking mid-sentence. The truck drivers standing near him fall silent. I'm profoundly conscious of being the only woman among them, and they struggle to account for me.

"Yes, Miss. What can I do for you?" the manager asks, with hints of curiosity and alarm in his voice.

"I'm wondering if there are any more trucks leaving tonight for Mozambique."

"You want to go through Mozambique?"

This news is passed on to the rest of the men, and everyone gapes at me and laughs. Why would I want to do such a thing? Has anyone told me that Mozambique is in the middle of a war?

The manager shushes everyone and beckons me to him. "Please tell me," he says politely, "why you want to do this."

I can't tell him the real reason. I would sound insane. So I tell him, "I want to know what's happening there . . . maybe write about the place."

He takes a deep breath and examines his feet for a moment. "What is happening there is very bad. Three drivers were ambushed last week. Killed. I think you should know this. Also, forgive me, but it's not a place for a young girl like you. Forgive me. But I think you should reconsider."

The manager bows his head and looks on with gentle, curious eyes.

I explain that I've set my mind on it already. I want to see Mozambique. I want to know what's happening there.

The other drivers, I notice, have grave faces and are now silent.

The manager sighs. "I believe you are a brave girl," he says, "but this is the wrong decision. Now is a very bad time. But I cannot stop you." He raises his hands and looks at the night sky. "If you must go, God willing, you will be safe. My friend will take you to the trucks that may leave tonight. I am sorry to tell you that a group already left for the border. Maybe, though, you will find one or two who were lazy and have not left. You can ask."

His friend leaves the building and starts walking down a hill. I follow. Soon we arrive in the midst of rows of trucks. Most of them are parked, deserted, but there are a few with their engines being revved, and work being done under the hoods.

"Follow me, Miss," my guide says. "There are a few trucks that may leave tonight. We'll ask. Do you have money?"

"Yes, I can pay the driver something."

"Good. Good."

We walk past the trucks and my guide makes inquiries. Refusal after refusal.

"Simmias?" My inquirer asks a man seated in a far corner of the lot.

Simmias is a little man, much shorter than my five foot seven, with a plainly sincere and trusting face. He has tiny mahogany-colored eyes hidden beneath the front of a brown pilot's hat, which is too large for him and engulfs his head. I can't help smiling at it and when his quick little eyes register why, he laughs.

"I would take you," he says, "but my company forbids carrying passengers. I could get fired." The crowd of men around me has dispersed. Simmias seems my last hope; I see no one else preparing to leave.

"I'll pay you," I say to him.

"Yes, but others will see you and tell my boss." Suddenly he holds up a finger. "We will ask Jerry. Jerry is my best friend."

Jerry, a tall man in khaki shorts doing work under the hood of a truck, appears indifferent to all the commotion I've caused.

"Jerry," Simmias says.

No response.

"Jerry, hello!"

His friend finishes some adjustments and looks slowly down at us. He doesn't seem the least bit surprised to see me. "Yes, what is it?" he says to Simmias.

Jerry is somewhere in his mid-twenties, and he's definitely not Malawian. His eyes are dark, his features more pronounced. His cheek bones reign strongly over a wide face with a flat, shapely nose. An attractive man, he seems clearly of Zimbabwean descent.

"Jerry, will you take her through Tete, to Zimbabwe?"

He sighs, irritated, and jumps down from the truck. He rubs his oil-smudged hands together and shakes his head.

"She shouldn't go," he says to Simmias. "The fuel injector is broken. There is a chance the truck will break along the way." And to me, "There is a chance the truck will break, do you understand?"

"Yeah. But you're still going, right?"

"Yes, yes. This is my job."

"I still want to go," I tell him.

Simmias now speaks to Jerry in a tribal language, and I hear the tone of their conversation crescendoing.

"You'll pay me something?" Jerry suddenly says to me.

"Yes."

"How much?"

"I have eighty kwachas left." About thirty U.S. dollars—a great deal of money for a Malawian or, I figure, a Zimbabwean.

"But do you have a visa for Mozambique?" He thinks he's got me now.

"Yes. I've got one."

" 'Yes. . . .' "

"Jerry," Simmias is pleading, "take her, okay?"

"You know there is a war in Mozambique?" he asks me.

"Yeah."

"Trucks get attacked, blown up. All the time. I been in two ambushes in the past month. Bullets hit my truck." He points to the steel frame of his truck, to a scattering of small dents. "It is real, you know."

"I know." But I realize I'm lying—both to him and myself.

He sighs and shakes his head. He doesn't ask me why I want to go through the country. It doesn't seem to matter. I can tell this is a man who has already learned to avoid the tediousness of asking questions and pondering answers. For him, life has become one great game of getting from one place to another in the quickest time, and with the highest monetary reward. This is the truck driver's game, this is what he's paid for. His life is worth only as much as his wealthy South African boss will pay him to deliver his cargo through Mozambique's war.

"Get in. I will take you through, but if she breaks . . ." He clucks his tongue. "She could break, you know."

He opens the passenger door of his truck, and hoists himself inside behind the wheel. He starts clearing away garbage.

"She's really not meant for you," he says. He points to a sign on the dashboard: LONELY LOVER.

When he starts the engine, it catches roughly. He gets out to do a few last-minute adjustments under the hood. He isn't carrying any cargo in back, and explains that he's anxious to get the truck back to a country with better repair service and cheaper parts than Malawi has: a wasted trip, then, but a necessary one. And if, in this dangerous truck driver's game, Jerry's life is worth as much as the cargo he's carrying, then it has now depreciated in value to almost nil, to the thirty dollars I'll be paying him. He accepts this as a matter of course, jumping into the driver's seat with an eagerness to get started. His only concern, his only reason for pause, is for his truck. "She is sick," he says of it, shaking his head.

It's an old truck, dirt matted in the rubber floor covering, the numbers worn off of the gearshift knob. Garbage is still strewn about, and I push some aside with my foot as I lean back in the seat and look in front of me. My eyelids droop. I feel hypnotized by the idling of the engine.

The Lonely Lover climbs up behind the wheel. He looks at me and his stern face releases a faint smile. I realize, as he does, that this is my last chance to change my mind and get out of the truck.

I don't move.

He puts the truck in reverse. "Ready? We go!"

It is one in the morning, and I sit with Jerry and Simmias outside the truck as they boil flour over a portable gas heater. We're parked on the side of the road behind a long line of trucks, all of us waiting for the border crossing into Mozambique to open in the morning. Most of the other drivers are asleep, but Simmias and Jerry are wide awake and chatting in Chichewa as they prepare our dinner of *mili-mili*—boiled balls of flour filled with tomatoes and chunks of beef.

As we eat, I open my journal and, by the light of the gas flame, begin writing.

"What you writing?" Jerry asks.

"A journal entry, in case I'm killed tomorrow."

"Before, they did not kill the white people they ambushed. They were frightened of your embassies." Jerry slides some dough into his mouth. "But now they kill everyone. Especially white people."

"Oh."

"When I first became a driver, my boss said I must go through Mozambique or not get the job." Jerry rearranges himself Indian-style.

"That was a few years ago, when they did not have soldiers to escort the trucks. I was young and poor, so I said, 'Okay, I will go.' I was almost through the country, almost through the Bone Yard Stretch—"

"The first half of the road we travel on tomorrow. The worst part of the road through Mozambique," Simmias explains as he washes out his plate.

"Yes, the worst. The most dangerous. So anyway, I was almost through, almost into Malawi when *pptt! pptt! pptt!* Ambush! The rebels kill the driver in the truck before me, and they stop my truck and they tell me to get out."

"You saw a man get killed?" I ask, incredulous.

"Oh, yes," Simmias says, "it's no lie."

"They shot him in the neck," Jerry says. "So anyway, I get out and the rebels steal everything from my truck. They steal the radio and my food, my shoes, my clothes. Everything I have. I only wore underwear, and they wanted to take that too! But they didn't. Then they hold their guns at me and laugh and say they will shoot me. Very funny for them. But the leader, he says, 'Run! Run!' He wanted a game. So I run very fast, you know, and they shoot at me until I run into the bushes and they cannot see me anymore."

"And Jerry was close to Malawi, and he walked the whole night and most of the next day, very frightened."

"No! I wasn't so frightened!"

Simmias slaps him on the shoulder. "You were too, my friend."

"And I crossed the border into Malawi. A week later, my company sent me through again."

"You should have quit!" I say. "You were almost killed."

"Well, I was too smart for them."

"Doesn't it scare you that the same thing could happen tomorrow?"

"No, I am not scared of death. I been in many ambushes, and I seen many men who were shot. I seen trucks blown off the road, the drivers burned to death."

"Oh, yes," Simmias says, his tiny eyes peeping out at me from under the pilot's hat.

"Perhaps you will see it tomorrow and you can write about it in your little book."

Jerry sighs now, obviously sick of talking, and gorges himself on more *mili-mili*. When I finish writing and close my journal, Jerry turns the flame off. Simmias says good night to me, and we head to the trucks.

I curl up in the front seat of Jerry's truck under my Maasai blanket while Jerry lies on the pallet in back.

"Good night," he says. There is no further formality and he is soon asleep.

I'm too exhausted to think about anything and close my eyes. I can't even think about what might happen tomorrow.

As if a moment later, dawn arrives, the stark orange light from the east promising another hot day. My uneasy sleep is shattered by the sounds of revving truck engines. Drivers walk quickly toward the customs house, impatient to get their passports stamped and the paperwork out of the way so they can be one of the first trucks to leave Dr. Banda and his country behind. Jerry and I join them.

We have only just entered Mozambique, yet the signs of the war are immediately upon us. I can see the front of our snakelike convoy of trucks curl around land-mine craters in the road and dive in and out of potholes. We pass a blown-up jeep or two. An occasional truck.

Jerry has explained to me that the Mozambique National Resistance (MNR), known as Renamo, plants the mines at night for the incoming trucks to hit during the day. If the rebels had the chance to do some work on the roads last evening then someone will die today. That simple.

Jerry pops in a mix tape, and Bob Marley starts singing. *". . . vi-bra-tions, oo-oo . . ."*

Marley wails out our open windows. I wonder if there are any rebel soldiers out there who can hear the music and recognize it.

Mozambique seems a scorched country compared to Malawi. I'm

reminded vaguely of Arizona. Somewhere hot and dry, with parched soil and scant brush. There was once potential here, though. Jerry said people used to come to this region of the country to vacation. I notice that it's rather hilly by this Bone Yard Stretch, and the mountains' higher elevations are covered with vegetation. They're not very high mountains, but they're appealing enough with their gentle slopes and mix of autumnal shades. Hiking used to be quite popular.

Our truck starts to climb, groaning in a low gear.

"That's where an ambush happened two weeks ago," Jerry says, pointing to a growth of trees nearby where I see a charred metal truck frame.

I realize that Renamo soldiers could be out there right now, hiding in the brush. The dark shadows under the branches could conceal a machine-gun nest. They could be anywhere, the rebels. They could be right at the bottom of this hill, near that stream that curves so peacefully across the arid landscape.

We reach the bottom of the hill and I see the remains of four more trucks beside the road.

"This part of the road, in Chichewa, means 'Makes Many Cry,'" Jerry says.

We pass a few deserted villages. Round mud houses with thatch roofs in disrepair, the mud chinking in the walls having crumbled to reveal gaping holes. What were once small vegetable gardens behind the houses are now tangles of shriveled weeds and debris.

It's strange to see no sign of life here. Having gone across East Africa, I'm used to seeing an abundance of animals. But here in Mozambique there is nothing. No antelope, wildebeest, lions or giraffe. Not even a mangy dog, a scavenging bird. Not even a human being. Nothing.

A few buildings are left behind where there were once villages of some kind. Most of them have been reduced to rubble, the white stucco walls lying in chunks about the yellow grass. The bullet holes that litter the still-standing sections tell of days scourged by shooting matches.

Our convoy travels now on a flat plain. The area within fifty yards of either side of the road is newly burnt. All trees—except the baobabs—have been crudely cut, three-foot-high stumps scattered about the charred terrain.

"Why did they burn everything?" I ask Jerry over the beat of Marley's band.

"This is the best place to ambush trucks, so the soldiers burn everything down. Burn, burn, burn. Now the rebels have nowhere to hide."

"Then why did they leave the baobabs?"

Jerry looks at them and shrugs. "I think, maybe, because they are special trees. They take a long time to grow." He hums loudly to Marley.

"They care about that?"

Jerry shrugs again and turns up the song.

I look at the thick trees with their stubby gray appendages and tough, ringed trunks of smooth bark. They are the only things left to posterity, yet they're of the perfect width to conceal soldiers with their grenade launchers. Is it possible that a people so concerned with killing could be, at the same time, sentimental about their trees? The idea is too strange, too daunting. I listen, as Jerry does, to the Bob Marley beat.

A jeep of government soldiers passes us on the right. Five young men sit inside while a sixth man stands behind a machine gun. The red bandanna he wears around his neck flaps wildly in the wind. They're all almost identical in appearance: tall, emaciated-looking figures with taut faces flashing a hint of perverse delight. Their dark skin glimmers with a film of sweat. Their camouflage uniforms hang loosely on them like shedding snake skin, red berets falling down to their brow. I stare at them, these men ordained my Protectors, the ones guarding our convoy from rebel soldiers. They're mere fledglings to the job of death. Most of them look to be fifteen, sixteen. The oldest seems eighteen. He's the one with a sweaty hand lounging over the stock of the machine gun, and it's he who spots me first.

He points at me. The other soldiers lean on their AK-47s to take a look. Through my open window I hear Portuguese utterances.

Jerry turns his head and sees the jeep keeping pace with his truck.

Usually nothing seems to faze him, but here is an exception. His face tightens and he puts on the brakes. The jeep sails past and he makes sure it's long gone before he presses on the accelerator again. Trucks pass on the right now, but he doesn't seem to care.

"One time," he says suddenly, turning down his music, "I was crossing on this road, and there was an ambush. The soldiers with us shot back at the Renamo soldiers. *Pptt! Pptt! Pptt!* Then it stopped. Very quiet. The rebels were killed and some soldiers and drivers went to collect the dead bodies. When they saw the bodies," Jerry laughs hysterically, "when they saw the bodies they saw that the dead were government soldiers. The soldiers had shot their friends!"

"I don't understand. Was it a mistake? What, were they traitors? Deserters?"

"Oh no," Jerry laughs. "There is no difference. They are both, you see. During the day they fight for the government. At night they take off their uniforms and join Renamo."

"I still don't understand. Isn't there loyalty or anything?"

"You are not meant to understand things in this country. There is no loyalty, no rules. If the soldiers are hungry, they ambush a truck, kill the driver, steal his food and his money. Then they say Renamo did it. Or," he adjusts his mirror so he can see Simmias behind him, "they just join Renamo because the killing is easier. No pretending."

"Chaotic."

"Yes." He looks at me with impatience. "Of course."

Jerry goes on to say that every once in a while, a bus full of Mozambican civilians will attempt a crossing down the Bone Yard Stretch. They leave from the city of Tete—controlled by President Joaquim Chissano's government soldiers—and make an exodus through Renamo's domain. Perhaps they'll migrate further south into their country or, more likely, they'll illegally enter Malawi or Zimbabwe as refugees. But the idea is just to escape. They'll risk everything not to become a victim of Renamo. They've seen or heard of the torture, the massacres: innocent villagers burned alive, asphyxiated, maimed, gang-raped, gunned down by bored soldiers taking potshots.

These refugees fleeing in their buses know, of course, what kind of a chance they're taking. Completely unprotected, their single crammed bus rumbles down the gutted road with heavy black exhaust marking the passage as blatantly as would a bellowing loudspeaker. I picture them in my mind, see them as some sick animal left behind by the herd, prey to the whims of the hunger-driven predators.

I'm now looking at the result of their being discovered. I'm looking at a land-mine crater easily four feet deep. What's left of the bus— some singed metal bits and an axle—is scattered about in the surrounding grass. Shards of window glass cover the asphalt and reflect the sunlight like glitter. Sun-bleached clothing flutters in the breeze. The bodies are gone, but a book lies open, its pages flipping back and forth as if moved by invisible hands.

"Here last week," Jerry explains, "nineteen people died."

I shudder and put my backpack up against the window as if it could protect me from rebel fire, exploding mines—whatever. But I put it down again. The hell with it. If I get shot I get shot. I'm starting to understand how Jerry can do this job for a living.

I look at the bits of clothing: Those people had almost made it. Bob Marley finishes his song and the tape turns over. Silence. I feel, strangely, just as I felt when I visited Auschwitz. A heavy nausea for the human race. Yet here, in the Bone Yard Stretch, in the midst of such an inescapably horrible reality, I begin to feel a profound change coming over me. I'm surprised at how suddenly it occurs—not in days, months or years, as one might think, but in a single moment. Suddenly, *now*, it happens: I unwittingly grow up. My innocence abandons me, and I'm left only with a fear of the world that I know to be irrevocable. Mozambique greets me soberly. I wonder what the hell I'm doing here. What self-centered foolhardiness led me here? It's as if I just woke from a dream, and I want to tell Jerry to turn around, take us back to Malawi before we go any further. I made a terrible mistake. I'm not ready for a war.

But I say nothing. Some Kenyan music starts—lively chords and jovial whoops of Swahili. I roll my window up and lean my head against it, my sweatshirt a pillow. Our truck's wheels plummet down and out of the crater and we leave the wreckage behind. Jerry takes a swig of orange drink and starts tapping his fingers on the dashboard to the beat of the music.

"This place really doesn't scare you?" I ask him.

"No, no. People fall dead going to the toilet. I do not ask when my turn will come. I do not care."

"Fate. You believe that if it's meant to happen, it will."

Jerry looks at me and shakes his head. "You are funny," he says. "You sit with me in a broken truck, on the road to Tete, in the middle of land controlled by Renamo, and you talk about death. You are a funny girl. Do you know where you are, Kira?"

It's the first time he's used my name and I sit up.

"I know where I am," I say. But I have never felt more lost. I have only the truck and its rough, coughing hum of momentum to orient me.

I watch a truck pass us, roaring by in a race to the front of the convoy. Jerry scoffs as a second and third truck pass. Embarrassed, he explains that if his truck were in full-working order he wouldn't keep losing his place like this.

I start to understand that the truck drivers have made crossing Mozambique into a macabre game of machismo, the object of which is to be the first truck in the convoy to reach Zimbabwe. Jerry tells me he's been first five times already. *Five* times—a distinction not to be taken lightly as the first truck in the convoy usually discovers any newly planted mines.

"I have a reputation now," Jerry says.

"What reputation?"

"They say my luck is very good."

The city of Tete. The end of the Bone Yard Stretch.

I'm halfway to Zimbabwe and smile, having gotten through what I think is the toughest part of the journey. The side of the tape with Bob Marley's pleasant reggae beat is playing again, as though to congratulate us.

"Are we safe now?" I ask Jerry.

"No. There are still ambushes, but not as many. We still need to go with a convoy or Renamo will—*pppttt*—kill us easy. Easy, if they are by the road."

But I'm less concerned because life has returned to the landscape. To my right is the Zambezi River flowing from Zimbabwe, and I see a few women about to start their washing. They walk along the mud-covered banks, baskets balanced on their heads. They're the first women I've seen since entering Mozambique, and the lackadaisical way they go about their work has me confused: I wonder where the war has gone.

The bridge over the Zambezi has been blown up and repaired so many times that it can only take one truck at a time. Our convoy idles in a long, single-file line, awaiting passage. Some local peddlers try to sell the drivers their wares as we wait, and items are passed in and out of truck windows.

Jerry inspects a yellow baby shirt handed up to him and asks the price. What interest he, the Lonely Lover, could have in a baby shirt, I'm not sure, but the man points to the shirt Jerry's wearing—a green cotton one—and gestures that he'd like to swap.

"Ha! This is fine quality." Jerry pinches his shirt and speaks to the man in English, aware that he doesn't understand. "This was bought in Johannesburg. Jo-han-nes-burg. Ha! Stupid man. South Af-ri-ca."

Jerry tosses the baby shirt out the window. The man catches it, babbles in Portuguese, and moves on. In the truck's mirror I see Simmias behind us, buying the baby shirt for his little girl back home.

It is now almost our turn to cross the Zambezi. The truck before us is halfway across the bridge and as soon as it exits on the other side, Jerry starts to roll forward, pressing on the gas. I watch the river pass below, shrunk to half its normal size from a drought that has struck much of south central Africa. I remind myself that these same gray, dismal waters once flowed down the mighty Victoria Falls.

We enter downtown Tete now, which looks to all appearances like a typical African city with its gray and white stucco buildings and high-rises and grid work of streets. Yet, strangely, no one is out on those streets, and there are no cars. Some stores advertise different services or products—groceries, auto repair, Coca-Cola—but they're all closed, and appear to have been closed for some time, the storefronts guarded by padlocked iron shutters. Graffiti mars the sides of buildings. Scrawny dogs wander and sniff about garbage piles. It's possible to believe that the city of Tete was, at some point, a thriving place, but now everything looks unkempt or abandoned, weeds sprouting from the grime covering the roads. Tete reminds me of one of those Armageddon cities in some sci-fi movie. Abandoned. Left to the vermin.

"We will leave Tete, now," Jerry is saying.

"Good."

The engine lurches and the hand of the tachometer flickers. Jerry downshifts, but the engine gains no more power.

"Shit. The fuel injector."

We're creeping along now. I watch the back of the truck we've been following sail away from us down the road. The trucks behind us start passing on the right. One. Then another. Another. *Oh, God, three more . . . four more. . . .* Two jeeps of government soldiers zoom past, the men inside looking back at me. When Jerry pulls over onto the side of the road, a couple of passing trucks honk at us in pity.

Simmias, of course, is still directly behind us, and he pulls over, too. Jerry stares at the tachometer as though he can fix the problem with his gaze. I bite my lower lip and remain silent. Outside is a wasteland of rocky soil. The baobabs are gone, and the sun is oppressively hot. It must be easily over 100 degrees, and there is no wind. Sweat runs into my eyes, burning them.

Simmias pokes his little head through Jerry's open window. For such intense heat, he still wears that pilot's hat.

"Hi," he says to me, smiling.

Jerry frowns at him. "Fuel injector. What did I say to you?"

They speak in Chichewa for a moment, and Jerry gets out of the truck. He opens the hood and examines the engine, shaking his head.

More trucks roar by with honks of condolence. These passing trucks are getting fewer, I notice. The convoy must be almost past us.

I've been so concerned about the trucks leaving us behind that I don't notice we've got visitors: A jeep of government soldiers has parked behind our truck, and some soldiers are walking toward Jerry and Simmias. One man sees me in the passenger seat and whoops, pointing excitedly. The others come by to see what he's pointing at, and their excitement is evident in their eyes and laughs. They taunt me in Portuguese, and one soldier cups his hands at his chest and makes obscene gestures.

I crouch down in my seat and lock the door, remembering what Jerry had told me about their dual loyalties, their brutality. From my backpack, I pull out my Swiss Army knife and open it to the largest blade. Little comfort, though: Each soldier carries an AK-47 over his shoulder. I stick the knife into the pocket of my jeans, and watch with relief as Jerry and Simmias walk up to them. Jerry speaks some fractured Portuguese, smiling as though there's nothing wrong.

But Jerry never smiles.

From their gestures, the soldiers are determined to know whether Jerry realizes that he has a young white woman in his truck—as if I were Jerry's property, as if he might consider loaning me out. Jerry slams down the hood. He puts his fingers to his mouth to tell them that we've stopped to eat lunch. That's all. When one of the soldiers points to me again, Jerry says "American," waving me aside, blatantly directing them toward their jeep. To my surprise and relief, they leave.

Jerry walks over and climbs into the truck. When he sees my fright, he sighs and shakes his head. "They are animals," he says. He pulls out his bag of flour and gas stove, saying only, "We will eat lunch now and I will think what to do about my truck."

The convoy has completely left us now. A few stragglers, delayed for whatever reason, grind up the road toward us. They also have no way of catching up with the "herd" and so park to make lunch with us: strength in numbers. We are nine trucks now and have no jeep escort to protect us (if, of course, we *would* get protection from such soldiers).

I unlock the door and hop down onto the dusty soil of Mozambique as if into a pool of murky water, the depth of which is beyond my ability to comprehend. This is the first time in my life that I've set foot in this country, excitement the last emotion I'm feeling. I hate the idea of leaving the truck. I see a single, rather bushy shrub and head to it. I hope it's not my fate to be blown up while I take a piss.

There must be a village close by because, just as I finish, a congregation of young boys gather on a nearby slope. One of the drivers making *mili-mili* chucks a stone at them and they scatter, only to return again with hesitant steps, their eyes following our actions.

The drivers ignore them, talking in Chichewa or Shona while they prepare the porridge and pour themselves cups of water from huge plastic jugs.

The boys, I notice, wear nothing but strips of filthy rags. They're skinny, and the younger ones all have swollen bellies that they touch lightly—almost tenderly—right above the belly button. They're dirt-smeared, their eyebrows gray with dust, and they squint at us in the sunlight with crusty mouths held open.

Another driver throws a stone at them and the pack disperses, regrouping at a safer distance.

"They *steal*," the driver says to me after he's thrown another stone. "They grab at you—*grab grab grab!* Then you look and everything is gone."

"They're starving."

"Yes, Miss, but in another year most of them will be given a gun and they will hide out and wait for me to pass in my truck!"

He throws a handful of rocks at them now, but they're too far away for any of his missiles to hit.

"Humph!" The driver digs a hand into the large ball of dough Simmias has removed from the flame. The others dive in, but not before my little friend has removed a large portion for me and placed it in a separate plate with some mashed tomatoes.

I eat it all, not wanting to waste any in a country like this. Simmias makes another batch for the drivers, while the boys look on with longing. I pity them, not so much because of what they endure now, but because of Tomorrow, of what this war will do to them when they're old enough to be given a gun. I don't want to believe that what he said is true, that they're destined only for war and killing. Yet, I'm aware that a good part of the world is preoccupied in the same way. Angola, East Timor, Guatemala, . . . It feels strange for me to be here in their country, in the midst of their chaos, because I'm only an observer. I can always leave them behind, return to three meals a day, air-conditioning, clean clothes. Safety, sanity.

And they cannot.

The meal ends quickly, and Simmias is left with a plastic plate of leftover porridge and a few chunks of meat. Jerry takes the plate from his friend and, amid the other drivers' protestations, marches out to the skittish group of boys. He stands at the top of the slope. Hand resting impatiently on his hip, he extends the plate. One of the braver boys drifts toward him and, with a ravenous lurch, grabs the baseball-sized ball of dough and struggles to shove it in his mouth before the other boys can get to him. Too late. The others reach him, and they pull at the dough between his lips. The smaller boys grab for any morsels still left on the plate, practically ripping it from Jerry's hand. Food flies everywhere. The boys scramble for the scraps in the dirt, scratching, punching, clawing each other aside.

Jerry calmly watches it all, seeming to care only when the plate may be taken from him. Finally, he yanks it away and heads back toward us. The drivers, long since bored with the spectacle, are busy washing their hands.

Simmias takes the plate from Jerry and rinses it off.

"Let's go," Jerry says to me as he hoists the bag of flour to his shoulder and hands me the gas heater. "The sun will soon start to leave, and my truck, she is very sick now. If Renamo is out there, we may die tonight."

I want to believe that this is more of his machismo. "But is the truck as bad as—"

"She is bad. She can only drive very slow."

I suggest, if the situation is so grave, we leave his truck behind altogether, go with Simmias to the border.

He scoffs, glares at me. "I will not give my truck to Renamo."

I bow my head, chastised.

"But we must all go now. It is safer to travel in a group. We cannot wait anymore because the sun is going. I need you to watch the right side of the road. I will watch the left."

"Watch for what?" I ask him.

He sighs impatiently. "Anything that moves."

I stop him before I climb into the truck. "Jerry, how bad is it?"

"You are a funny girl," he says.

It's only Simmias and us now. We've been doing a pitiful twenty kilometers an hour. Without a military escort for protection, we're as much a pair of sitting ducks as that busload of refugees blown up a week ago. The other trucks of our small pack all waved good-bye to us more than an hour before, when our speed started to drop. They were anxious to reach the border and live to see Zimbabwe the next day.

"If Renamo is by the road, we're dead," Jerry says, speaking in an unusually low tone. He squints from one side of the road to the other as though reading small print.

I study every thick growth of vegetation, trying to discern soldiers-in-waiting. What they would look like—or even what I'm supposed to be looking for—is unclear. My heartbeat is loud, my senses acute. I'm conscious of the adrenaline rushing through my body like a thick sap, and I would give anything to be safely at the border right now.

I keep scolding myself for being here, doing this. *This is for real, no joke. You're in the middle of Mozambique, in the middle of a war, in the middle of country controlled by rebels, in a faulty truck that could completely go at any moment. There is absolutely no form of military protection and the sun's going down.*

I nod. I know. But beyond all this is the part that hurts the most: There is no waking from this nightmare.

I glance at the tachometer, and I will the truck to pick up speed.

Simmias, in his blue-striped truck, is pacing us on the right, his little eyes frisking the countryside. Occasionally, he looks steadily at Jerry and they nod at each other: best friends—literally—to the death.

But perhaps some kind god has more in mind for us in life because in the distance are the mountains of Zimbabwe. Beautiful wonderful Zimbabwe. I smile because it is so close, and my ordeal, I think, is over.

Then our truck dies.

One thing you don't want to do in Mozambique is stop. Not ever, for any reason. We have already stopped once, and Jerry is wary about doing it again. Simmias has stopped with us and has been trying to get Jerry to abandon his truck. This is a futile business, though, because Jerry doesn't want to leave "her" behind. He's fond of the broken old thing, and so am I: Though it's been like riding a lame horse, we've gotten this far. We're only a few miles from the border, and Jerry hopes to fix it and get it across.

The alternative, Jerry explains, is to leave it behind for Renamo or the government soldiers to find that evening, or perhaps the next morning. They'll take it, of course. Or, if they can't get it working, they'll pick it apart. Steal his spare, the parts under the hood—everything worth any bit of money.

"They are animals," he says. It is a familiar refrain.

Simmias doesn't seem to hear him because he points down the road. From the direction of the border, we see a distant vehicle approaching.

"The animals are coming," Jerry announces, not moving.

Simmias grabs my hand. "Quickly," he says, his English disintegrating in his frenzy. "Your rucksack, take, take! Bring to my truck!"

I follow his orders in a panic, Jerry still standing in a state of indecision by the side of his truck. From the small size of the vehicle coming toward us, and from the speed, it appears to be a jeep of government soldiers. Jerry isn't ready to surrender to them. He stands with his hands clenched, glaring with obvious disdain for Mozambique and its war.

Simmias hurries me into his truck, and I sit on his pallet in back. With a composure that surprises me, as if someone else has taken over my actions, I find myself shoving my passport and money pouch down the front of my jeans. It's hot, but I throw on a black pullover and stuff my journal into the front pocket. There's spare money and traveler's checks in my backpack that I've forgotten about. Quickly, I take them out of their various hiding places and shove them down my hiking boots.

Simmias starts his engine and squints outside. I can hear the vehicle pulling up beside us.

"Not Renamo," he says. "Government soldiers." He motions with his hand for me to get down, and I press myself into the corner, to hide.

Simmias has his hand on the gearshift knob. The truck is idling fiercely. Yet we don't leave: not without Jerry.

It's dim in back, and I feel as if I'm watching a play from behind the scenes. I try to assure myself that I won't have to participate, that Mozambique is someone else's show. I lose this feeling of immunity when I hear voices outside and Simmias abruptly leaves the truck.

The minutes pass. I hear arguing, but know better than to make an appearance. I wait, listening to my heart thumping away. With my black pullover on, the heat is overwhelming.

The passenger-side door suddenly opens and Jerry swings himself inside.

"They want me to leave my truck. They want to take us to the border," he snarls, dumping some things beside me.

Given the circumstances, this seems like a good thing. "Are we going to do that?" I ask.

"You are a very silly girl. They won't take us to the border."

I look at him in silence. My hands have started to shake and I order myself to be calm. "What do we do?"

Jerry sighs and glances outside. "I am thinking. Don't leave this truck."

The truck door slams. More waiting. More snatches of conversation drifting in from outside. The driver's-side door opens now and I think it's Jerry again. Then I see the red beret and a dark, sweaty, excited face. When it sees me, it smiles broadly, white teeth beaming.

"American?" it asks. This young man can't erase the smile from his face. Something is extraordinarily funny or ironic to him.

It occurs to me that I've seen this face before: It's one of the government soldiers who had earlier passed us when we were eating lunch.

Now the moronic-looking soldier, still smiling, reaches back for me. I feel his damp, eager fingers on my wrist and strike them away. His smile breaks into a wide grin. He reaches for me again. I punch him away.

"Get the fuck away from me!"

He reaches, I punch. Again and again. I wonder how long this game is going to go on. The soldier, though he looks directly at me, doesn't seem to see me or to know what's happening. Such vacuous eyes, and that shit-eating grin.

Another soldier climbs into the passenger seat. He is older, maybe in his mid-twenties, and looks angry and impatient as his eyes settle on me. I have also seen this face before, recognize that one eyeball lolling off to the side, sickly and invaded by a brown patch of infection. I sense he is the leader, if indeed there is such a thing in this ragtag army. But a dream now, surely not reality: his rifle trained on me and my life sitting before me. That it is such a minuscule life, so easily done away with, shocks me.

The rifle goes down. This man's hand is gummy and strong on my arm as it pulls me from the back of the truck. I try to wrench away, and succeed, only to be promptly grabbed again and reprimanded in Portuguese. My stubborn actions amaze me, for we never really know how we will act when faced with a real threat. We can speculate. We can be certain we'll remain calm or scream, will fight with vigor or curl up helplessly. But when it comes down to it, there is no way to know until it happens. And then it is simply too late.

And now I discover myself punching and squealing at this man who won't let go of my arm. He grabs me by the hair, and so does his still-smiling friend, and I know only that I must get their goddamn hands off of me. Nothing in the world matters but freeing myself from them. My hand pushes at the face of the moronic boy and he stops smiling and lets go of me. The other pulls harder on my hair, and the pain is intense. I'm certain my scalp will be ripped from my head, and as I reach out to strike him, the moronic boy grabs my arm. Again, the gun in my face. My body is shaking uncontrollably. I cry out, and discover myself calling for Jerry over and over again. I sound like some wretched creature torn from its mother. To my amazement, Jerry responds from outside the truck. He is pleading with them to let me go.

They do. They let me go.

"Come out," Jerry says to me. "Don't make them angry."

I wait till the soldiers leave the truck then slowly get out, a certain buoyancy to my movements from the adrenaline rushing through me. Jerry stands near me while I get down, though the soldiers surround us now. Simmias is some distance away, kneeling on the ground, pleading with the soldiers who nudge him with their feet. I suddenly understand how I have endangered Jerry and Simmias by traveling with them. If only I could take back the events of the past two days! If only I could put myself back in Malawi when I was making this stupid, selfish decision to cross Mozambique, and decide not to do it. Why didn't I realize the added danger my presence might cause? The soldiers knew I was traveling in a broken truck, and they knew we fell behind the others in the convoy. I wonder if there is anything I can do now—but I see that it's too late. Much too late.

Jerry's eyes are focused on some point down the road. "Listen," he says to me. "These soldiers, they want to do something with you, do you understand?"

I don't understand. I don't want to understand.

One of the soldiers, a boy scarcely older than fifteen, harshly reprimands Jerry for talking, but Jerry ignores him. "They say they will take you to the border, to a rest house. But this is a lie."

"Just me? Where are they going to take me?"

Jerry's eyes are still locked on some point in the distance. "Listen to me—when it is dark, *run*. We are close to the border."

I feel weak all of a sudden, physically sick from this news.

"Where are they going to take me?" I ask him again.

He shakes his head slowly. "I don't know."

The building is crumbling, reeks of piss. It's empty but for the bench where I've been sitting for the past half hour, watching two young boys playing soccer with baobab pods in the dusty yard out front. But watching isn't the right word. My eyes refuse to focus on anything. I'm numb, and can't seem to move. It is a strained kind of numbness, though, as if I were on the verge of snapping.

Though we left the main road, we're near the border. I know that much. Jerry and Siminias were left behind, and I've not seen them since. They were trying to convince the soldiers to let them go to the border. Maybe they succeeded. I don't know. I hope they succeeded. As I was being driven away, I saw Jerry standing next to Simmias. Jerry was flashing phony smiles, and I noticed that the soldiers' rifles were shouldered. I suspect the soldiers were just interested in me.

The soldiers refuse to let me leave this building. Someone has brought beer for them, and they are—for the moment, at least—busy getting drunk outside on the veranda. When they need a diversion, which is often, they come inside to bother the American girl. These diversions have gotten predictable, and take one of two forms.

They may try to hit me on the head with various objects. They've thrown everything from plastic water bottles to stones, though they prefer baobab pods—hard, yellow-skinned objects the size of a tennis ball, which often shatter on the wall above me and shower me with seeds. They've hit me twice already, to the accompaniment of hysterical, wheezing laughter.

The second diversion is to walk up to me and demonstrate what they intend to do with me. The drunker the man, the worse the demonstrations. Knives imitating copulation. Putrid breath as the leader with the sickly eye stands an inch from my face and asks me lewd questions in a smattering of bad English or reaches for me. My legs are clamped together till the muscles strain. As stupid and terrifying as these games are, I know what's supposed to happen when they're over.

Strange: They don't do anything with me yet. Just taunt. But it can't go on like this much longer. I don't know if they're waiting for someone—another leader, maybe—or are drinking away any hesitation. They've probably never had a foreign woman in their possession before, and perhaps they're nervous. Not nervous about raping someone—God, no. But repercussions. Maybe they fear some kind of political outcry, something they haven't anticipated. I don't know.

What I do know is that I'm pretty close to Zimbabwe. All of this beer had to come from somewhere, after all, and when they brought me here I could see the mountains of Zimbabwe in the distance. It's nearly dark outside, and I know I have to run. Still, new soldiers and even some plain-clothed Mozambican men, seem to be coming all the time, and they swarm around the building. Inside, I know I'm the main attraction, that a back room is being cleared out for me.

I can't wait much longer. I struggle for the necessary courage, all the while keeping the blank expression on my face. When they nudge me, I move like a rag doll. I want to bore them, make them think I'm lifeless though I watch everything now. I watch soldiers going into a small toilet room across from me to take a piss. When one of them suddenly throws a beer bottle at me, I dodge my head just in time and it misses. Beer splatters on me, glass litters the floor, and another sharp smell is added to the stench of the room.

A perfect moment is not going to come, I tell myself. *Now. Right now.*

It takes all of the willpower I have, but I get up.

"Toilet," I say to the looks of surprise. I point at the toilet. "Toilet," I repeat. My hands are shaking wildly and I press them against me. I wonder if they can hear my heart beating, it's so loud in my chest. I'm terrified that they can somehow sense what I'm about to do and will stop me before I can even try.

But just as I had hoped, the soldier with the sickly eye waves me permission from where he lies on the veranda outside.

I walk to the toilet and close the flimsy wooden door behind me. There is a small, grimy window in front of me. Through it, all is blackness but for a single light far off in the night. A lone light that seems to be in the direction of the border.

I feel this drive in me now, so strong, so ready for anything. I haven't a plan, but a plan seems unnecessary. All I need to do—all that matters— is getting past the soldiers hanging around the front of this building. I don't doubt myself at all after that. I know how hard I'll run.

I turn around, push open the door. I head slowly across the room, as if returning to the bench. The soldiers speak to me in Portuguese and try to get my attention by pssting me as if I were a dog. To my left is the way out of the building. I turn as if to face the soldiers, then, in a rush, I run as hard as I possibly can.

I'm out of the building! I run past men on the veranda, certain my heavy steps will cause the whole structure to cave in. *Faster, faster, faster!* I'm on the ground now. Soldiers are getting up, but too slowly. I'm leaving them behind. Only the dark ground before me. I tell myself not to trip over anything. *Watch where you're going, keep up the speed.*

Here is what all of those years of competitive running were for. Here is where it all matters. I run toward that distant light, barely able to see anything else. Behind me, shouts. The voice in my head starts to get cocky. *You can run faster than them! Keep up the speed.* I feel as if I'm running in the State meet again, listening to that inner voice which is like a drill sergeant's urging me to the win. The only thing I'm scared of now are their guns, of a bullet in my back. Yet, I haven't heard a shot. This gives me hope—I must not be a target. I must have eluded them. Each move of my legs feels mechanical, like a piston moving, and the sounds of my pursuers start to fade. I don't hear shouts anymore. Nothing but my own heavy breaths and the thudding of my hiking boots on the ground. The money shoved down my socks pricks my feet and wads under my heels.

Now I slow down, but only a little. I have to pace myself. I keep running toward that distant light. As my eyes adjust to the dark, the stars above seem abnormally bright. I glance over my shoulder for signs of pursuers. No one. Just scraggly bushes and a dull moon. I know the night has a new meaning for me now. I grew up with the requisite tales of bogeymen and ghosts, but those tales dim by comparison to the darkened landscape before me, and bushes that might not be bushes at all, rocks that might be anything but. I could be running straight toward a rifle aimed at me, a return to that stinking house. Is there even an American embassy in this wretched country? No one knows where I am. (Such a sinking feeling now.) No one at all. If I died here, no one would ever know.

At last, I decide to stop. That once distant light is close, shining dimly by a few buildings in the distance. The border crossing? Or am I already in Zimbabwe? I'm afraid of going any further, of being seen or heard by someone in the night, and decide to wait out the dawn to try to figure out where I am.

I see a large bush nearby, and settle down beneath it. I'm exhausted and spend my time trying to discern the causes for the myriad sounds about me. When it at last seems as if my mind is making them up, I rest my head on the ground, ready to give up. I look above me. To watch a night spread out in constellations, moving in an ordered pace across the sky, is to learn the nature of loneliness. I measure the progress of time by tracking the stars through the tangled branches of the bush that hides me. Nothing in the world could make the evening pass faster. I know this. Yet I try to convince myself that time can get away from me, mercifully pulling the stars farther than they should go. A slight wind rattles the brittle leaves of the bush. A bird sweeps by. Now, for the first time, the tears. They wash over my face, down my chin, staining the dirt beneath me. I ask myself: Is this what you were looking for? Are you glad you came, Little Girl?

Are you glad you came?

I see that I was looking for a journey that wouldn't require any responsibility on my part. A journey that wouldn't require me to become invested in the horrible reality of the situation and the people around me: Jerry's and Simmias's safety, the cruelty of a country ravaged by civil war, the politics of the situation and the way my own incongruous presence complicated that picture. In short, I didn't expect there to be any ramifications to such a self-indulgent, foolish trip across the Bone Yard Stretch.

And, to top it off, I haven't become anyone new. And if I'm any different—and I know I am—it's not in the way I might have hoped. Instead, provided I can somehow get to Zimbabwe, I must live with the guilt and terror of this entire experience.

It's impossible to sleep, though I feel utterly exhausted. The questions stay with me, mock me, as the eastern horizon grows into clarity, revealing my ghosts and monsters of the night to be bushes, termite mounds, rocky earth. The questions stay as I get up to see the road to Tete surprisingly close to me. The electric light is still on in the distance, marking the border post into Zimbabwe. Rows of parked trucks, having arrived too late and stuck in Mozambique for the night, sit in silence before the border, their drivers asleep inside. The trucks, I know, are my way out. As I cautiously approach them, I recognize two: one without cargo in back, the other with a telltale blue stripe across it. And now I see my two friends. I smile and start to run. The sun is reaching out, gaining the momentum of day.

from Selkirk's Island

by Diana Souhami

Fearing that his ship, the Cinque Ports, was unseaworthy, Alexander Selkirk implored his captain to remain at a small island long enough to make repairs. Fearing mutiny, the captain sailed without him. Here Diana Souhami (born 1940) describes Selkirk's life on the island. Daniel Dafoe drew upon Selkirk's story for his 1719 novel Robinson Crusoe.

elkirk watched as the small boats prepared to leave the shore. He lumbered over the stones and tried to get on board but was pushed back. He waded into the water, pleading. He watched as the anchor was drawn and the ship towed to the open sea. The sound of the oars dipping into the water, the calling of orders, the little silhouettes of men as they made fast the cables and unfurled the sails, all imprinted on his mind. There was a light breeze from the west. The ship slipped behind the cliff face and from his view. Against this abandonment the rest of his life had the comfort of a dream.

All courage left him when the ship was gone. The sea stretched out. The line of its horizon was, he knew, only the limit of his sight. The sea that had beckoned freedom and fortune now locked him in.

Thomas Jones, James Ryder, William Shribes, John Cobham . . . He thought they would come back for him. He stayed by the shore, scanning the ocean. Whatever their fate he now wanted to be with them. If their ship sank he would choose to go down with it. It was his ship too.

Laurence Wellbroke, Martin Cooke, Christian Fletcher, Peter Haywood . . . they defined his world. The voyage they had made together was for more than gold: it was to show courage, to have a common purpose, to be men. Without them The Island was a prison and he a mariner without a ship, a man without a voice.

The day grew cool, the wind ruffled the water and for a moment a rogue wave or a cloud looked like a sail. His hope was that someone would persuade Stradling to think again. They would come back for him. He would welcome them with fires and food.

He waited outside of time, like a dog. Prayer, he had been taught, had a controlling force. He invoked God, to sort this mess out. He prayed in a cajoling way. He felt rage at Stradling. Even Dampier, mad and drunk, marooned Huxford in the company of men. But Stradling had marooned him, Selkirk, with calculated malice and mocked him as the boat rowed off.

He did not leave the shore. He clambered over the stones to the western edge of the bay, wanting the wider view of the ocean. The fur seals bottled and dived, surf broke over the rocks. He was trapped in the bay by sheer cliffs. He clambered back to the eastern edge by the fast-flowing stream where trees grew close to the water's edge.

The sun dipped down, the air cooled, the mountains loured. Dark came and the moon cut a path across the ocean. All night the seals howled. These were monsters of the deep. He feared they would encroach and break his limbs with their jaws. He fired a bullet into the air. For a minute the bay seemed quiet. Then it started again, a croak, a howl. This Island was a place of terror.

In his argument with Stradling, he had seen The Island as a place of plenty and comfort. The safe bet. He had reasoned that survival would be possible, even pleasurable. That rescue would soon come. But there was fear in the dancing shadows of night. There was malice focused on him. A hostile presence sensed his every move. He feared cannibalism. That he would be taunted and devoured.

The wind surged through the valley, the wind, he was to learn, that was strongest when the moon was full. It uprooted trees. They swished and crashed. The sound merged with the breaking waves, the calling seals and the cries of creatures preyed on at night.

It was early spring and around him life regenerated, but he hated The Island, its inaccessible terrain, ferocious waterfalls and gusting winds. A faint breeze at night would stir to whirlwind. It was as if the wind was born in these mountains.

Time passed. 'He grew dejected, languid, scarce able to act.' He stayed by the shore, drank rum, chewed tobacco, and watched the sea. He stared so hard and long he only half remembered he was searching for a sail. Often he was deceived by the blowing of a whale or the refraction of light.

There was a makeshift hut by the shore, of sailcloth, sandalwood and rushes. He put his possessions in it and envied those who had built it. They had got away.

He had with him his clothes and bedding, a pistol, gunpowder, bullets, a hatchet, a knife, a pot in which to boil food, a bible, a book of prayers, his navigation instruments, and charts on how to read the imprisoning sea. He had two pounds of tobacco, and a single flask of rum. He had bits of food, enough for three meals—quince marmalade and cheese—but no bread or salt. He suffered when his liquor flask was empty. Liquor brought oblivion.

'At first he never eat any thing till Hunger constrain'd him, partly for grief and partly for want of Bread and Salt; nor did he go to bed till he could watch no longer.' He drank from the streams when thirsty, splashed himself with water if he itched, or stank or was hot. He pissed where he stood, shat on the stones, ate turnips and watercress pulled from the earth, picked up turtles and lobsters that crawled the shore and scooped out their flesh with his knife.

He became thin and weak. He wanted death and to be gone from this fate. It calmed him to suppose that if no ship came his gun to his temple would end his life. He thought of drowning, of swimming toward the horizon until exhausted. But he had seen sharks devour the corpses of men buried at sea. He had seen a shark tear the leg from a boy who fell from the masthead.

And then it seemed The Island would kill him, would do the deed. The turtle flesh 'occasion'd a Looseness' that twisted his guts like knives, his shit was liquid, he retched and vomited and supposed he would die. He crawled into his bedding and forgot to hope for the ship's return.

The pain abated, he survived. Survival was all. He collected twigs and branches of sandalwood, started a fire with the flint of his gun, boiled water in his kettle and infused it with mint that grew in the valley and with Malagita pepper which he thought to be good for Griping of the Guts.

Selkirk supposed in time a ship would come, fatigued by the sea, needing a harbour, but time for him might stop. He had seen bleached human skulls on deserted islands, abiding proof of the marooned.

Other men had survived The Island: the two who escaped the French. In six months they suffered no extravagant hardship though they did not linger when dubious rescue came. And Will, the Miskito Indian—it was twenty years since his rescue. The remains of his hut and hearth were high in the mountains, engulfed by ferns. Like Will, Selkirk could forge harpoons and lances from the metal of his gun, strike fire from sticks, survive on seal and cabbages and fashion clothes from animal skins.

And Dampier had told of a shipwreck, before Will was abandoned, in the Great Bay where only one man reached the shore alive. 'He lived alone upon this Island five years before any Ship came this way to carry him off.'

Marooned men fended until rescue came: Pedro de Serrano, stranded on a barren Pacific island, drank the blood of turtles and survived seven years without fresh water, though he went insane. Philip Ashton, captured by pirates in 1700, then abandoned on Roatan Island in the Bay of Honduras, was attacked by snakes and a wild boar, but did not die. In the manner of counting blessings Selkirk might deem himself fortunate. There were worse scenarios than his own. He was as strong as any man. He could endure The Island for months or even years.

He thought of escape, of a raft with branches bound with the entrails of seals, of a hollowed canoe. But the nearest land was Valparaiso, six hundred miles north. Were he by fluke to survive the treachery of this ocean, its capricious currents, the violence of its waves, the appetite of sharks and the heat of the sun, if the *guarda-costa* caught him they would show no mercy. They made it a rule never to allow an Englishman with knowledge of these seas ever to go free. Were he to reach the mainland he would be consigned to the workhouse or the mines, put in leg irons, tortured for information about his fellow privateers. At best, murdered.

If a French ship came to The island he would surrender and hope for mercy, but never to the Spanish. He would make a lair, a hideaway, high in the mountain forest, in case they came.

So he hoped for rescue and feared dying uncomforted in this overwhelming place. He looked out over the ocean thinking Dampier, Clipperton, Funnell, Morgan, Bellhash might return him to the world he knew. Their misfortune was his hope. The *Cinque Ports* might limp back, leaking like a sieve. He supposed there would be further mutinies on both ships. More men would turn on Dampier. He was an adventurer, a seasoned navigator, but he could not manage men. Mutineers would leave him, take prize ships, fly the bloody flag and try their luck. The two ships might now be six.

Selkirk's Island was the best to careen, to water, to eat fresh food. Here was good anchorage. Whoever came, he would give them greens and goat broth to cure their scurvy. His fire would dry their clothes and warm their bones. They would restore in the mountain air. He would welcome any of the men, except Stradling. He would be marooned forever sooner than see Stradling again.

And so he became a watchman by occupation. His obsession and abiding fear was that he would miss a ship that passed or be surprised by an enemy. He watched in the first light of the morning, at noon and at dusk. Behind the bay he climbed to his lookout, his vantage point. He scanned the encircling sea. He surveyed The Island, its tormented forms, its peaks and valleys, the islet of Santa Clara, the forests of ferns. Day after day he did not see his ship of rescue. He saw no ship at all.

Here was a paradox of freedom: he was free from responsibility, debt, relationship, the expectations of others, yet he yearned for the constraints of the past, for the squalor and confinement of shipboard life.

Hunger and thirst were diversions. He ate roots, berries, birds' eggs. He shot seals and sea birds. A goat stared at him with curiosity. He killed it with a cudgel, boiled it with turnips, flavoured it with pimento. Rats scuttled in the undergrowth, waiting their share.

Days elided into weeks and months. Whatever The island had, he could use, whatever it lacked, he must do without.

He pined with 'eager Longings for seeing again the Face of Man'. He was alone on a remote piece of land surrounded by ocean. Chile was 600 miles away, Largo 7000. He was an unsociable man, but disagreement and provocation were preferable to this. Had Stradling left him with a Negro slave, they might have built a boat, farmed goats. Had he left him with women prisoners, he would have peopled The island and been served.

This fate seemed like a curse. His father had warned that his temper would cost him his life, and opposed his going to sea with the privateers. If he returned to Largo he would make amends, work as a tanner, find a wife.

His mother, he supposed, would pray for him. Texts from the Bible. All that happened was God's will. God acted with surprising vengeance, but good intention. The Bible was the word of God. It was the Truth. God created all things, owned and controlled the lot. He made the world in seven days and man in his own image. He was benevolent. He had a purpose, a grand design.

'It was Selkirk's manner to use stated hours and places for exercises of devotion, which he performed aloud, in order to keep up the faculties of speech, and to utter himself with greater energy. Sometimes as the sun rose lighting the woodland of sandalwood trees and huge ferns (*Blechnum cycadifolium*), their fronds unfurling like wakening snakes, the mountain he called the Anvil rising three thousand feet behind him, cloud trapped on its peaks, he read from the Bible, the only narrative text he had. He read of Sodomie and Beastialitie in Leviticus and of Heaven and Redemption in the Gospels. He mumbled the psalms and appeals of his church: 'Hear O Lord my Prayer, give Ear to my Supplication, hear me in Thy Justice, I stretch forth my Hands to Thee; my Soul is as Earth without Water unto Thee, Hear me speedily O Lord; my Spirit hath fainted away. Turn not away Thy Face from me.'

Such lamentations yielded no change in his circumstances, but had a consoling force. He did not care too much about the sense of what he intoned. It was vocabulary he would not otherwise have used and feared to lose. He hoped that God was halfway human enough to get him out of this hole. Only God and Stradling knew he was marooned.

Withdrawal from tobacco left him light-headed. It had been an addiction for fifteen years. He wondered if there was some substitute opiate on The Island, some other leaf to chew. But he did not experiment. Foxglove and hemlock he knew could kill. Dampier had warned against eating plants that birds rejected.

Activity dispelled depression. He kept busy. And on a day when the sky was clear and the valley still, his mood lifted. He felt vigorous, reconciled. He grilled a fish with black skin in the embers of a fire, ate it with pimentos and watercress and forgot to deplore the lack of salt. Around him hummingbirds whirred and probed. Mosses, lichens, fungi and tiny fragile ferns, epiphytes, *Hymenophyllum* and *Serpyllopsis*, covered the trunks of fallen trees.

He resolved to build a dwelling and accrue stores. He chose a glade in the mountains a mile from the bay, reached after a steep climb. Behind it rose high mountains, wooded to the peak. This glade had the shade and fragrance of adjacent woods, a fast, clear stream, lofty overhanging rocks. From it he had watched mist fill the valley and dissipate with the morning sun. White campanulae grew from the rocks, puffins nested by the ferns. A little brown and white bird, the rayadito, swooped for insects. Clumps of parsley and watercress grew by the stream.

The random yield of the island became his tools, weapons, furniture and larder. By the shore he found nails, iron hoops, a rusty anchor, a piece of rope. With fire and stones he forged an axe, knife blades, hooks to snare fish, a punch to set wooden nails. He carved a spade from wood and hardened it in glowing embers. He hollowed bowls and casks from blocks of wood. He turned boulders and stones into larders for meat, a pestle and mortar, a hearth and a wall.

He liked goat meat, but often the goats he shot crawled to inaccessible rocks to die. When his bullets and gunpowder were finished he felt undefended, on a par with creatures that scurry for cover at a sudden sound. Without gunfire, he caught goats by chasing them. Out of their horns he carved cutlery.

On either side of the stream he built huts of pimento wood. He thatched their roofs in a lattice of sandalwood. The cruder hut was his larder and kitchen, the larger was his dwelling. On a wide hearth of stones, he kept a fire burning night and day, its embers banked high. His wooden bed was on a raised platform, his sea chest held such possessions as he had. He scraped, cleaned and dried the skins of the goats he killed, in the way he had learnt from his father. With a nail he made eyelets, then joined the hides with thongs of skin. He lined the walls of the hut with these skins. The place smelled like a tanner's yard, it smelled like home.

Home shielded him from squalling winds and the threat of night. From his bed he saw the ocean lit by stars, the morning sun above the eastern mountains. The seals were quieter when they finished breeding. Other sounds amplified: the clamour of birds, the waterfalls.

This glade defined where he felt safe, but 'his habitation was extremely pestered with rats, which gnawed his clothes and feet when sleeping'. Their forebears had jumped from European ships. Pregnant at four weeks, they gave birth after three weeks gestation, had litters of eighteen, became pregnant again immediately, and lived for two years.

They ate bulbs, shoots, carcasses, bones, wood and each other. They left spraints of urine wherever they went and their fur was infested with lice and fleas. Their appetites were voracious and their most active time, the pitch of night. The island housed them in millions, white, grey, black and brown. As he slept they gnawed his clothes and the bone-hard skin of his feet. He would wake to hissing fights. He slung pebbles at them, but in seconds they resumed.

Equally fecund were the feral cats. They too came from Spanish, French and English ships. He enticed them with goats' meat wanting them to defend him against the rats. Kittens in particular within days were tame. 'They lay upon his bed and upon the floor in great numbers.' They purred to see him, settled in shafts of sunlight, curled round his legs. To them he was a gentle provider, a homemaker.

In the face of this feline army the rats kept away. Instead he endured the cats' territorial yowls, their mating calls and acrid smells. He talked to them, they made him feel less alone. 'But these very protectors became a source of great uneasiness to him.'

> For the idea haunted his mind and made him at times melancholy, that, after his death, as there would be no one to bury his remains, or to supply the cats with food, his body must be devoured by the very animals which he at present nourished for his convenience.

To ensure his meat supply, he lamed kids by breaking their back legs with a stick. He then fed them oats gathered from the valley. They did not equate their pain and curtailment with him and were tame when he approached them with food.

So he became The Island's man. Monarch of all he surveyed. He swam in the sea, washed in the streams, rubbed charcoal on his stained teeth. His beard that was never cut merged with the tawny hair of his head. His shoes wore out but he did not try to repair them. The soles of his feet became as hard as hooves. He ran barefoot over rocks. 'He could bound from crag to crag and slip down the precipices with confidence.'

The seals and sea lions ceased to be a threat:

> merely from being unruffled in himself he killed them with the greatest ease imaginable, for observing that though their jaws and Tails were so terrible, yet the Animals being mighty slow in working themselves round, he had nothing to do but place himself exactly opposite to their middle, and as close to them as possible, and he despatched them with his Hatchet at will.

Their fat was cooking oil, their fur his bedding, shared with pale fleas and ticks that burrowed and blistered under his skin. He gouged these out with a wooden pin.

As time passed he ceased to imagine threat from monsters or cannibals. Nor was he troubled by the moan of the wind, the calling seals, the chirps and screechings of The Island. His hut, cats and goats created a semblance of home. He adapted to The Island's ways.

Selkirk viewed The island as his, though he did not paint it, or describe it. A rainbow arched the sea, the night was lit by stars, the morning sun coloured the sky, and all for him alone. The island had offered itself to him and made him safe. He carved the days of his banishment on a tree in the grove of his home. The past might not have existed, he had so few mementoes of it.

Sandalwood burned light and fragrant. In his lesser hut he stored food: turnips, cabbages and pimentos, dried oats, parsley and purslain and little black plums, gleaned from an orchard high in the mountains. He kept his food in boxes he had made, secured with stones and goatskins. On his improvised table with the knife he had honed he prepared his meals each day: a broth of goat and cabbage, flavoured with herbs, a roasted fish, baby seal fried with turnips, boiled lobster with oatcakes. He drank water and infusions of herbs, simmered plums for their juice, turned them into a kind of jam.

His shirt and breeches got torn to tatters in the forest foliage, the rasping tree ferns, and giant roots. He tailored himself a skirt and jerkin out of goatskin and sewed these garments with thongs of skin. 'He had no other Needle but a Nail'. Out of the bale of linen in his sea chest he fashioned shirts, 'and stitch'd 'em with the Worsted of his old Stockings, which he pull'd out on purpose'.

He was, he thought, a better cook, tailor and carpenter than before, and a better Christian too. Whatever he did on The Island seemed neither right nor wrong. He killed seals, bludgeoned goats, masturbated against palm trees, picked puffins' eggs from their nests and intoned psalms: 'I am become like a pelican of the wilderness; I am like a night raven in the house. My days have declined like a shadow and I am withered like grass. Hear O Lord, my prayer. Turn not away Thy face from me.'

Apart from such borrowed incantations he had no use for words. He learned The Island the way a child learns language, its moods and reiterations, the meaning of its hills. He tutted at the cats and kids and grunted as he pursued goats. Deceived that he was one of them, they turned to greet him until they smelled his sweat, heard his mumbling and saw the cudgel he wielded.

His exercise and lust of the day was hunting and fucking goats. 'He kept an Account of 500 that he killed while there, and caught as many more which he mark'd on the Ear and let go.' His tally was of their size and agility and the quality of the chase; a chart like those kept of the variations of the tide, the phases of the moon or the days of his captivity on The Island.

Goats worked out at about five a week. Most days he had a go. He devised various ruses for catching them. He would crouch on a concealed rock by their watering hole. As they drank at the stream he would leap on one and cudgel its head. Or he would pursue a herd down the mountain to the shore. In confusion and fear they jostled together and made easy prey. Or he would tie a looped thong with a circle at its centre across the path they took. One would catch its horns or neck in the loop. As it panicked and twisted the thong tightened.

Fucking goats was perhaps less satisfying than the buggery and prostitution of shipboard life, the black misses of heathen ports. It lacked fraternal exchange. But Selkirk was an abandoned man. On The Island, at the day's end, he would have liked a woman to cook for him and provide. He might have preferred it had the goats been girls.

> His Agility in pursuing a Goat had once like to have cost him his Life; he pursu'd it with so much Eagerness that he catch'd hold of it on the brink of a Precipice, of which he was not aware, the Bushes having hid it from him; so that he fell with the Goat down the said Precipice a great height, and was so stun'd and bruis'd with the Fall, that he narrowly escap'd with his Life, and when he came to his Senses, found the Goat dead under him. He lay senseless for the space of three days and was scarce able to crawl to his Hutt, which was about a mile distant, or to stir abroad again in ten days.

He computed the time that had passed from the waning moon. He supposed he might die on The Island, lie unburied and be food for the cats.

It was July when he fell. There was a light fall of snow. In the voyages he had made death was all that many booty seekers found. But it was death in the company of men, not alone in an implacable place like this.

The fire went out and he scarcely ate. When he was able to limp from his hut, he thanked God for not taking his life. He gathered a mound of dried grasses as tinder, crouched over it and on his knee rubbed together two pieces of sandalwood. The effort seemed endless, the sticks got warm and worn, his body ached, the cats sat around. A desultory spark hit the tinder and expired. He rubbed on. It had worked for Neanderthal man, it must work for him. He rubbed until it happened. The elemental change. Showers of light, grey smoke then flames.

He vowed never again to let this fire die, to guard it night and day, feed it, bank it. It gave him light and heat, it was a symbol of hope, a focus of rescue, a beacon to the seas that he might be saved.

As the days passed, day after day after day after day, he got inured to solitude. Company was not essential. His relationship was to The Island. He was a rough man but it seduced him. He had so much time to observe the sunlight on the sea, the mist in the valley, the shapes of the mountains, the shadows of evening. He came to know The Island's edible plants, its thorny shrubs, scented laurels and palms, its useful animals and freshwater springs, its natural shelters, birds and fishes, its lizards that basked in the sun, its rocks covered in barnacles. He carved a map of it on a piece of wood.

Things he had thought essential he found he could do without: salt, liquor, tobacco, shoes. He built a walled enclosure, drove a few kids in, their mothers followed, he turned the kids out and started a small herd. He churned their milk to a kind of cheese. He made a raft from the trunks of palm trees, carved a double-ended paddle and keeping close to the shore on a calm day explored the bay between what he called Great Rock and Great Key, around what he called Rough Point and Rocky Point. He came to a cave and thought it a place where a man might shelter. He fished from this raft and from the rocks and kept a few clawing lobsters at the brink of life in a barrel of seawater. In all that he did he thought ahead, in case the weather turned foul, in case he again was ill, in case an enemy came.

He carved a little flute, blew a few notes and imagined his tamed animals listened and moved to his tune. He was afraid of nothing on his island. Only of who or what might come to challenge his hegemony.

• • •

Selkirk saw the irony of his fate. He had crossed the world in search of fortune and ended up with nothing. Less than when he began. He was marooned and penniless and resembled a goat.

Such treasure as he had was The Island. Such music as he heard was the wind in the mountains, the sea, the noises of creatures who cared for each other and nothing for him. The Island imposed a terrible boredom. He yearned to leave it. It was the death of ambition. It tested him to the edge of endurance. And yet in surviving it he found a strength.

He had times of anger, when the goats eluded him, when the fire smouldered and could not be coaxed to flame; times of satisfaction when turnips sprouted and there was an abundance of plums. He found repose in the glade of his home when he had fished and hunted, stoked the fire, fed the cats, milked the goats, done all that he had to do to stay alive.

But it was not the frustration and rewards of practical things that informed and changed him. Nor was it The Island's scenic views, its turquoise ocean, pink horizon, tints and hues; rather it was the way it defeated everything that visited it, gave it food, provided shelter, dished out death. There were times when the intensity of the place overwhelmed him. Times that had nothing to do with the incantation of prayer, or of fear or danger. It was the sheer stretch of the mountains, the fact of the trees. It was as if The Island claimed him with its secrets, its essential existence, made him a part of its rhythms, turned him fleetingly into more than he was. In his piratical soul he knew that he would die in this place, whether he was rescued from it or not.

Stooping to drink, Selkirk saw a distorted reflection—a tangle of beard and hair, a weathered skin. He became immune to the bites of insects and to the ferocity of the sun. He tied his hair with a goatskin thong, used his nails as claws. He kept his knife and cudgel strapped to his waist.

He swung from lianas with the grace of an ape, ran faster than any creature on The Island, got the fruits of the cabbage palms by climbing.

No creatures preyed on him. No scorpions or tigers. Only once he thought he saw a snake. It startled him in the long grass.

Though he looked like a goat there were times when he thought like a man. With the mind of a mariner, he thought of the forces and laws of nature by which the world might be understood. He had among his navigational instruments a glass that made the stars seem near. He observed the phases of the moon and how these influenced the tides. He watched the constellations of Orion and Andromeda, the light of the planets—Mercury, Venus, Saturn, Mars. With the hope that he might help to 'find the so-much-desired longitude' he tried to chart the movement of the moon against the stars.

It occurred to him that the stars he saw, like the horizon of the ocean, were also only the limit of his vision. He had learnt from Nicolaus Copernicus that illusion was delusion, that the sun was not moving across the sky. The truth held secrets and paradoxes. It occurred to him that time might move in the opposite direction from what was supposed, that the beginning of the world was in fact its end, that the men on the *Cinque Ports* were probably dead, washed by the ocean to the start of their lives.

On days when Selkirk did not scan the south side of The Island, he feared he might have missed the ship of rescue or the manoeuvres of an enemy sail. High at his lookout above the Bay, the air was cool when the valley was humid, there was shade from the *luma* and *gunnera* and the huge ferns. Away from the enclosing valley, he could see the fracture of the archipelago, Santa Clara, the little broken islets, the peaks and ridges of mountains stretching out.

It occurred to him that England might have been defeated in the war, that no friendly ship might again come to these seas, that the whole of the South Sea might now be occupied by Spain. Three times from this vantage point he saw a ship, far out, circle the island then traverse the bay from west to east. It was as if it was the same ship. He saw its sails. Each time he ran to the bay. He dragged a burning branch to the shore and stoked a fire until it blazed. The ship sailed by.

Then one dawn he went to the shore's edge and a ship was there. Flying the red and yellow flag of Spain. Anchored in the bay with boats heading in. There were men like him on the shore. For a moment he stared, then turned and ran for the protecting trees.

His retreat was an admission. They pursued him, firing pistols and shouting in Spanish. *Salvaje* he heard, and *perro*. Had they been French he would have surrendered and hoped as a prisoner for transport to Europe. But he would rather die alone on The Island than fall into the hands of the Spaniards. They would murder him or use him as a slave in the silver mines.

Fit as he was, and sure of the terrain, escape was hard. There were many of these men, all armed. They pursued him, shooting, yodelling, as if he were indeed a goat.

He made for thick woodland at the eastern mountain, where he had fashioned a hideout, high in a tree. 'At the foot of the tree they made water, and kill'd several Goats just by, but went off again without discovering him'. He feared they would smell him, sense his presence, flush him out. But they gave up. He was not big game. He was of no more consequence than a wolf or deer that got away.

Again The Island protected him. Its darkness and concealing woodland. At night he drank water, ate birds' eggs and plums, saw other creatures that like himself searched cautiously for sustenance, scrabbled for cover and sniffed at the air.

His enemy stayed two days. Their sounds of departure reached him, then a palpable silence. When he returned to his glade his lamed kids were dead, the fire out, his hut burned to the ground. But again he had kept his life and again The Island, the shimmering sea and the hills.

They had destroyed his sea chest, kettle, bedding, bible and books, the tools he had forged and nails he had whittled. He had few possessions when he arrived. They left him with even fewer.

It was a clear day. Hummingbirds fed on purple flowers

(*Rhaphitchamnus venustus*). Shearwater skimmed the sea, on which for once he was glad that no ship sailed. Cats came out of the undergrowth mewling. A kitten chased a leaf.

His visitors had left traces: picked bones and footprints in the sand. He scoured the shore for their debris: a gold coin, three arak bottles, a rusty anchor, a broken cask, a piece of sailcloth, a short length of chain, a coil of worn rope, discarded lumber. Their garbage became tools and materials with which to refurbish his home.

Once again he lit a fire, the long friction of wood on wood. He improvised a forge. Over days and weeks he hammered iron, hacked timber, rebuilt his huts, caught goats, herded kids into a walled enclosure, stored food, rendered seal fat into tallow, ground ears of corn, wove a basket from twigs, made string from rope, moulded pots from mud and burned them hard in the fire. With patience he restored what had been destroyed.

His new bed was an improvement, raised higher from the ground. The stone pots he used to cook his food were still intact, so was the raft from which he sometimes liked to fish, his knife he kept strapped to his side. As a precaution he built another tree house in the mountains, high in the forest on the southern side. An enemy might again arrive.

And so his life resumed, the habits of the day, the intelligence of survival. It occurred to him that there were worse scenarios than rescue. The Island calmed his mind. He had no bible now, but he thanked some notional God who might have brought him to this special place.

Selkirk was cooking food by his hut in the late afternoon, when the ship of rescue came. He judged the month to be late January. He scanned the sea and there, on the horizon, was a wooden ship with white sails. He knew that it was his ship. It was so much the ship of his dreams.

In the moment of seeing it time stopped. There seemed no interval between the point of abandonment and this promise of rescue. The same wide bay, the straight line of the horizon, the high cliffs and wheeling birds. Nothing had happened between then and now. Only the inchoate process of his mind. Uncommunicated. Lost. He had been nothing to anyone. A shadow of self.

A second ship came into view. It seemed that here again were the *Cinque Ports* and the *St George*. He felt in conflict, fearing the ships would pass, wanting them to pass, fearing the fracture of his solipsism, the sullying of The Island. He supposed that the same men had come back for him, that Stradling was the captain of the smaller vessel. He hated him as acutely as the day they had quarrelled. He would rather die alone in the mountains than see him face to face.

The ships were heading east. He thought they would miss The Island, it was such a small block of land. Even Captain Dampier with his legendary navigational skills had sailed past, supposing it to be somewhere else.

Selkirk dragged a burning log to the beach. It was meant as his beacon of welcome. He wanted to show that his was the bay of safety, that here were warmth, food and water. He wanted to steer his brothers away from the sheer cliff face.

He was with them again. The cold sea air at night, the drenching rains, the misery of sodden clothes. Many he knew would be near death from scurvy and hunger. Like Will before him, he killed three goats, skinned and butchered them and roasted the meat on embers. He gathered turnips and herbs for a soup. Guests were coming to his Island. Rescue was near.

He knew he must not let this ship elude him. Here was a task at which he must not fail. He threw wood on the beach fire until it blazed. He made The Island bright with flames.

At seven in the morning on the last day of January 1709 Woodes Rogers saw a ridge of land, fringed with cloud. It was The Island.

Locating it had been hard. Dampier 'was much at a loss,' though he said he had a map of it in his head. He had to return to the coast of Chile to get his bearings. The ships sailed east, located Valparaiso, then again headed due west.

Rogers was uncertain of a safe route in to the Great Bay. The wind blew in squalls. Fearing shipwreck against the cliffs he kept about twelve miles out. At two in the afternoon, Captain Dover took the *Duke*'s pinnace and its crew to explore the shore and find the road into the bay. It was a dangerous distance for a small boat in turbulent waters. By dusk the pinnace was within three miles of the shore. Plying the lee of The island the men saw Selkirk's fire. They took it as evidence of an enemy. Woodes Rogers dimly saw the fire's light too. At first he thought it to be a signal from the pinnace, but as the sky darkened he decided it was too large for that.

He gave a signal for the boat to return:

> We fir'd one Quarter-Deck gun and several Muskets, showing Lights in our Mizen and Fore-Shrouds, that our Boat might find us. About two in the Morning our Boat came on board, having been two hours on board the Dutchess, that took 'em up a-stern of us: We were glad they got well off, because it begun to blow. We are all convinced the Light is on the shore, and design to make our Ships ready to engage, believing them to be French ships at anchor, and we must either fight 'em or want Water &c.

So, because of Selkirk's bonfire, the men prepared to fight. They feared there might even be a Spanish garrison to defeat. They were in dire need of water, food and land. They could not sail on. Dampier advised that they make for the south of The Island, then go in to the bay with the first southerly wind close to the Eastern Shore.

At ten next morning the ships reached the Great Bay. Heavy flaws from the shore forced them to reef their topsails. The *Dutchess* flew a French ensign. They expected sight of the enemy, but there was no sign of human life, or in the next bay, three miles to the west. 'We guess'd there had been Ships there, but that they were gone on sight of us' Rogers wrote.

At noon he sent the yawl ashore with Thomas Dover, Robert Frye and six other men all armed. On the ships all hands were told to stand by the sails, 'for fear of the Winds carrying 'em away'.

Selkirk could not believe that the pinnace had come so close to the shore, then turned. That his fire of welcome had been misconstrued. It was *déjà vu*: waves breaking against the shore, a boat moving away toward a waiting ship, while he stood powerless at the water's edge. Only this time he was in goatskin and had spoken to no one for four years and four months.

Reason told him they must investigate more and check at dawn for enemy ships. That they would long for a harbour and know there was no other land nearby. But he was not sure. He saw the lights go out in the Mizzen and Fore-Shrouds and knew the pinnace had returned. He banked the flames of the fire and stared across the starlit water. He saw the ships glide to the east and felt his chance of rescue wane. He would die on The Island as ships passed by.

It was intolerable to do nothing, but he could do no more than wait. If he lit another fire they would assume an enemy. Without a fire, they would not know of his need. He ran to his lookout, up the pass he had carved. He had not slept or eaten for twenty-four hours. At the mountain's ridge, when the sky lightened and the forest clamoured with sounds of life, he stared at the surrounding sea. As ever there was no ship in view. Only a grey sea with a white hem. Cliffs and silence.

Descending the mountain he saw the yawl and its crew. He believed them to be English but he was not sure. The men's stature, the shape of the boat were familiar. He waved a piece of white rag on a stick. The men called to him to show them where to land. He ran to the eastern edge of the shore where the rocks were manageable, the water deep and a boat could be secured. He stood on the rocks. Eight men pointed guns at him. He raised his hands above his head. He tried to speak, he said, 'Marooned.'

He was clearly unarmed, but only because he was on two legs did they think him human. They feared he might be some hybrid of the forest, of a cannibal tribe, a primitive beast like in Dampier's journals, a thing for dissection, or to be put on show. If you left your home and crossed the seas this was the kind of curiosity you found.

They butted him with guns and fired questions. Who was he? Was he alone, why was he there, what was his name, where was his ship. He stood with his palms spread and said again, 'Marooned.' He turned his hands to the hut by the shore, the quenched fire, the broth he had prepared for them, the mountains, and then he wept.

The men laughed. Their need was for water and food. They turned their attention to the clear streams, the cooked food, the lobsters that clawed the stones. He showed them The Island's larder, where to bathe under running water, the herbs that were a salve to wounds. Robert Frye went with him over the rocks and through the thickets to the clearing in the mountains where he had built his huts and tamed cats and goats. He showed another man his home.

The ships stayed outside the bay. The yawl was gone so long Woodes Rogers feared it had been seized. He sent more armed men in the pinnace to investigate. It too disappeared for an unconscionable time. He fired signals for the boats to return.

On shore the men quizzed Selkirk. He was a trophy, a curiosity. He became agitated and incoherent. 'He had so much forgot his Language for want of Use, that we could scarce understand him, for he seem'd to speak his words by halves.'

They invited him to the ship. He tried to say he would not leave The Island if a certain person was on board. They did not know what he meant. He said it again. There was someone whom he could not meet, a man whom he hated, who had consigned him to a living death. He told them it was Stradling, Thomas Stradling. They assured him Stradling was not among the officers, that the only men from the previous journey were William Dampier and John Ballett. He could come with them to the ship and see for himself. If he was not satisfied, they would leave him on The Island.

'Our Pinnace return'd from the shore' Woodes Rogers wrote in his journal, 'and brought abundance of Craw-fish, with a Man cloth'd in Goat Skins who look'd wilder than the first Owners of them.'

Barefoot, hairy and inarticulate, Selkirk boarded the *Duke*. He shook hands with men: Woodes Rogers, William Dampier, Thomas Dover, Carleton Vanbrugh, Alexander Vaughan, Lancelot Appleby, John Oliphant, Nathaniel Scorch. They said his name, welcomed him and put their arms around his shoulders.

Woodes Rogers in particular asked many question: Where was he from, What voyage had he been with, What was his rank, How had he survived, How long had he been alone. Selkirk found it hard to answer. His thick Fife accent, this overwhelming rescue, the unfamiliar company of men, the incoherence of his punishment, the severance from a place that at times had seemed a paradise . . .

So he told them what they perhaps wanted to hear. He was Alexander Selkirk. He came from Fife in Scotland. He had been alone on The Island four years and four months. Captain Stradling from the *Cinque Ports* had left him there. He had built a hut of pimento wood, and sandalwood, made a fire, stitched skins for clothes, tamed cats and kids, chased goats, picked little black plums from high in the mountains. He told them of the arrival of the Spaniards and of the day when he fell down the mountain precipice and nearly died. He told them of how, because he was a man, he had survived.

They offered him liquor. It was hard to drink, it so burned his throat. They gave him food so salty he could not eat it. They gave him clothes and he felt constrained, shoes that made his feet swell and which he felt obliged to discard. They arranged his hair and shaved his beard. On Dampier's recommendation he was appointed Second Mate on the *Duke*.

Woodes Rogers called him the Governor of The Island and its Absolute Monarch. Selkirk could not explain that it was not like that.

That The Island had governed him and was its own Monarch. That it would erupt again. That he had been subdued by the enfolding mountains and the unrelenting winds. That the true experience of being marooned was elusive, noumenal, that it was in his eyes perhaps, but not his words. That The Island had cast him in on himself to the point where no time had passed, except for the silence between breaking waves.

Bit

by Mark W. Moffett

In September, 2001 ecologist Mark Moffett accompanied his friend, Joe Slowinski, an eminent herpetologist, on a biological expedition to a remote part of Myanmar.

That morning I woke at dawn and crawled from my tent into the big unpainted schoolroom where the members of our biology expedition slept. We were in Rat Baw, a village in the far north of Myanmar. Outside, expedition leader and herpetologist Joe Slowinski and his best friend, photographer Dong Lin, stood wearing matching green T-shirts stenciled with one of Dong's photos of a cobra, poised to strike. I walked up as Joe's Burmese field assistant, U Htun Win, held out a snake bag. "I think it's a *Dinodon*," he was saying. Joe extended his right hand into the bag. When it reappeared, a pencil-thin, gray-banded snake swung from the base of his middle finger. "That's a fucking krait," Joe said. He pulled off the snake and kneaded the bitten area, seemingly unmarked, with a fingernail. Other scientists have been known to cut off their finger at such a moment. Joe sat down to join the rest of us for breakfast at a long wooden school table, joking about his thick skin. It was 7 a.m. on September 11, 2001.

I'd known Joe for two years, seeing him most often when he drove over to Berkeley for evening herpetology seminars at the University of California. A 38-year-old field biologist with the California Academy of

Sciences in San Francisco, he had published papers on evolutionary theory, systematics, and the origins of biological diversity—but mostly he was the man to talk to about cobras. For years, Joe had been concentrating on the rich biological triangle of Southeast Asia where Myanmar—still commonly known as Burma—and Laos meet southwestern China. He was conducting a comprehensive survey of the herpetofauna of Burma; on ten expeditions since 1997, he'd found 18 new species of amphibians and reptiles, including a new spitting cobra, *Naja mandalayensis*—which he considered "the ultimate discovery." He hoped to help the country establish a biodiversity museum; eventually he wanted to write the definitive book on the area's natural history.

Before a seminar, Joe, Dong Lin, and I would share beers at La Val's Pizza. Dong, now in his midforties, told me how, after surviving Tiananmen Square with 60 stitches, he had escaped China in 1990 and made his way to a position in photography at Cal Academy. There, Joe helped guide him through the book *English as a Second F**king Language,* and soon after, Dong started to join him as expedition photographer. Over Coronas, Joe would describe his upcoming trips, slapping me on the back and telling his best adventure stories to entice me to "come along this time, bro."

As an entomology researcher at Berkeley, I recognized in Joe someone like myself, someone who in earliest childhood fell hard for a disrespected creature—in Joe's case snakes, in mine ants—and managed to retain that fascination into adulthood and even build it into a career. He had a boy's sandy hair and freckles, and his habitual expression of sheer uninhibited wonder was matched by a precise and agile mind. His fieldwork had the same old-fashioned sense of exploration I'd grown up admiring in 19th-century scientist-explorers like Charles Darwin and Alfred Wallace.

Time and again, Joe's schedule and mine had conflicted. Then one night in La Val's he described a trip coming up in September. He'd recruited colleagues from different disciplines to conduct a broad species inventory of Burma's remote northern mountains. Perfect.

• • •

The expedition would take us into the foothills of the Himalayas; it was scheduled to last six weeks and span 200 miles. Our group of eight American and two Chinese scientists and four Burmese field assistants gathered on September 3 in the village of Machan Baw—the dusty remnant of an old British outpost—and started walking, accompanied by along line of porters. Machan Baw sits at 1,400 feet; the plan was to climb above 10,000 feet, surveying a range of habitats from subtropical forests to temperate highlands, and traveling eventually into the new Hkakabo Razi National Park.

Adventures are made mostly in the recollecting mind; the doing is generally more drudgery than drama. It was monsoon season, and our path, more mud trough than trail, was hard slogging. Leeches emerged in droves. We tried to keep them at bay by spitting tobacco juice onto our legs or wearing panty hose but Joe, trekking in shorts and sandals, simply put up with them, as did many of the porters. At times I'd look down and see the rain puddles along our route were red with blood.

The first week took us through farmland and villages. Houses with roughly stacked pole walls were raised on stilts so that pigs and chickens (and their legions of fleas) could sleep in the slightly protected muck below. Each evening sandflies speckled our arms with welts, while mosquitoes threatened us with a malaria resistant to most prophylactics—one reason we zipped ourselves into tents even when sleeping under a roof.

In patches of rainforest between rice paddies we found enough species to keep us moving eagerly toward richer territory. The sonic duet of gibbons and two huge-beaked hornbills passing overhead indicated more pristine habitat nearby. After each trek, Joe would gather bags with the day's specimens from his Burmese team and from our frog specialist, Guin Wogan, one of his graduate students at Cal Academy. Dong Lin would video the most unusual individuals. If venomous snakes were involved, Joe would wrangle them so Dong could get the best footage, shooting from inches away—greatly impressing the inevitable crowd of Burmese onlookers. Joe was careful with snakes;

he'd chased them since he was a boy in Kansas City, Missouri. He was also famous for close calls. Bitten by a copperhead in college in Kansas, he'd gone back the next day to catch another, left-handed. On a previous trip to Burma, a spitting cobra had struck through the bag Joe put it in, stabbing his finger. He waited calmly for the venom to take effect. Luck of the draw, he would say, telling the story: Sometimes a snake bites without injecting its toxins. On a later Burma trip, a cobra squirted venom into his eyes. After a few hours the excruciating pain passed. Joe never paused much over these incidents. He seemed to embody the understanding that a fully natural world includes the possibility that nature can kill us—and afterward glide freely away into the wet grass it came from. That love in any form involves an element of risk.

It was good to see Joe at work in the country he'd described so often. He was proud of his Burmese field assistants, on permanent loan to him from Myanmar's Department of Forestry. In a country with few scientists, Joe saw these young men and women as an essential resource for the future. Species inventories are a big part of conservation, and his assistants caught, preserved, and documented specimens year-round. Joe had struggled hard over the past five years to build government contacts—research in heavily militarized Burma is no simple thing.

Returning late at night by headlamp, Joe would unload his catch of snakes and frogs and sit with whoever was still awake, usually Dong Lin and me. During those conversations I began to see the different sides of my friend. Some nights it seemed he felt invincible. Downing Burmese rum, he knew he would rise high enough in the hierarchy of science to put a stop to the "political bullshit" he saw all around him. Much of what he imagined seemed possible: He'd just been awarded a $2.4 million grant from the National Science Foundation, already a sponsor of his ongoing Burma research, to study biodiversity in China's Yunnan province. He confided a thousand ambitions, certain he'd realize them all.

Other times Joe raged into the night, once about another biologist working in Burma who he believed had blocked the original funding for this trip. Joe had hastily cobbled together funds from his other grants and gone anyway. His tirade explained something. I'd wondered why our expedition had come during the rainy season, when (as was evident once we started walking) we could have taken jeeps along much of the route any other time of the year. Remembering how discovery breeds rivalry and how scientists can turn research into races, I sat in a small dry spot surrounded by what seemed a world of mud, an understanding comrade to Joe's fury.

Still other nights Joe grew melancholy. For years he'd focused only on science, he said; he'd been too single-minded, traveled too much, even for love. Now, though, he'd started a relationship with an ornithologist back home. He wondered if he should devote less time to snakes.

Managing the people and logistics along with his research on this trip was clearly taking a toll. There was a lot to worry about. Among the multitudinous supplies we'd brought were drying ovens and pounds of newspaper for the plant specimens, snap traps and mist nets for the mammals and birds, gallons of alcohol to preserve reptiles and insects, a generator and its gallons of fuel to recharge batteries for cameras and computers and to run the blacklight for attracting insects. Ninety-odd porters hauled the equipment of ten academics. Many of the inevitable problems were handled by a Burmese guide, but Joe had to think about them all. In addition, he'd paid $44,000 to a well-connected expedition coordinator to cover the in-country expenses, yet somehow such basics as rice and bottled water were in astonishingly short supply, so Joe kept spending more, out of pocket. Nor was there any sign of the two military doctors and radiophone the government had promised. Joe guessed the real cost of the trip was probably a tenth of what the expedition had put down.

Then there were the scientists. Each of us wanted to work at our own pace and had our own agenda. Personalities often clash in the field, and for Joe, feeling responsible for the group's harmony must have been one more stress, along with our long daytime treks and his own additional nocturnal collecting. I noticed the accumulating effect on him during a walk on September 10, the seventh day of the trip. Joe was moving sluggishly, and each time he paused to pull a leech from his leg, his fingers were visibly shaking.

After it was over, we'd all wonder why Joe had reached into the snake bag with barely a glance inside. As with any pivotal moment, the exact words exchanged beforehand would be endlessly debated. Snakes of the genus *Dinodon* are harmless, but some are near-perfect mimics of the multibanded krait (*Bungarus multicinctus*), a cousin of the cobra and much more deadly. As field team leader, U Htun Win should have known the difference—but he told us he'd been bitten by the snake the day before and nothing had happened. Joe, however, was the authority. Possibly simple exhaustion brought his guard down; perhaps he failed to heed the uncertainty in U Htun Win's tentative identification.

Following breakfast, around 7:30, Joe lay down. At 8 he noticed a tingling in the muscles of his hand, and asked Dong Lin to call the group together. By 8:15, two Burmese assistants started the run of eight miles to Naung-Mon, the nearest town with a radio. Joe calmly told us what would probably happen and what we should do. He described the effects of a slowly increasing paralysis, eventually requiring mouth-to-mouth respiration until he could be taken to a hospital. If he lived, the neurotoxins would work their way out of his system in 48 hours. He would be conscious, he told us, the whole time.

As the morning went on Joe had to reach up to open his eyelids. His breathing grew raspy; his voice was reduced to a slur. In time he could only write messages: "Please support my head, it's hard for me." "If I vomit, it could be bad." "Can I lean back a little." By noon he could no longer breathe on his own. "Blow harder," he wrote. In his final message, minutes later, Joe spelled out "let me di." We won't let that happen, Guin Wogan said. Kick butt, Joe, I added.

At 3 p.m. our runners returned alone, and told us the military had requested an update before they would send an air rescue. Two fresh assistants were sent back, again insisting that a helicopter be sent. By evening the weather turned from the best we'd seen in a week on the trail to a renewed downpour; low clouds would impede the rescue again the next day. That night soldiers arrived on foot with an ancient field radio and a young Burmese doctor with two nurses and a little equipment, including an old respirator no one could get to work. Throughout that long night, we all helped out as we could, but much of the time was spent in simple exhausted witness. From time to time, Dong would put his arm around various members of the group and say, "I love you." In one long moment of vertigo, as someone who's had his own close calls with snakes, I looked at Joe in the torchlight and saw how alike we were in build, complexion, even our features, and I felt I was somehow watching myself die. Looking at Dong, Guin, and U Htun Win standing silently nearby, I wondered if they felt something similar.

By 3 a.m. Joe could no longer signal us except with his big toe. His final communication occurred when ornithology assistant Maureen Flannery, whose strength had been keeping us all going, asked if she and Guin could stop doing mouth-to-mouth and let the guys take over. Joe's toe signals indicated a preference for the women.

During the 26 stifling, sandfly-infested hours that the artificial respiration continued, four airliners plowed into their final destinations in New York, Washington, and Pennsylvania. The only one of us who knew was David Catania, a Cal Academy ichthyologist so unobtrusive I often forgot he was there. Dave had listened to his shortwave radio after collapsing briefly in his tent late in the night. Keeping the news to himself, he came out and gave Joe mouth-to-mouth for hours, his face showering sweat. He refused to let anyone else take over, even long after Joe's heart had stopped.

At 12:25 p.m. on September 12, the doctor told us Joe's pulse was gone. We began three hours of CPR, in anticipation of a rescue helicopter that was never able to land.

Joe's body was cremated in a small Buddhist ceremony two days later in the town of Myitkyina, and Dong Lin and some of the team brought his ashes back to San Francisco, along with many of the expedition specimens. Other members made their way home as best they could. It was not until two months later that I returned from Asia and visited Ground Zero in New York. Compared to the devastation before me, Joe's tragedy had been such a small, intimate drama. For everyone in Rat Baw but our team, September 11 had seemed an ordinary day. It was a place where death from such natural causes as snakebite was a common event—there are more snakebite deaths in Burma than almost anywhere else in the world. Children played in the field within yards of the room where our small circle performed CPR. Elders sat on benches outside, talking softly and watching the rain, as one supposes they always had.

One of Joe's gifts was the way that for him the ordinary always seemed to yield to the extraordinary. The day before the bite Joe had returned from a walk in Rat Baw flushed with excitement—he'd found a pair of entwined kraits. "It was beautiful. Goddamn beau-ti-ful! Courting like that, right in the middle of the trail. I've never seen anything like it." His arms sliced arcs in the soupy air. The weight of all our petty concerns had vanished from his face, and his eyes seemed to glow, as they always did at moments like this, with the love of snakes.

Thirteen Ways of Looking at a Void
by Michael Finkel

Michael Finkel (born 1969) ventured to the middle of the Sahara desert to spend time in a place called the Ténéré—154,000 square miles of emptiness.

H ell," says Mousaka. He raises a forefinger and circles it in the air, to indicate that he is referring to the whole of the void. I am sitting on Mousaka's lap. Mousaka is sitting on Osiman's lap. Osiman is sitting on someone else's lap. And so on—everyone sitting on another's lap. We are on a truck, crossing the void. The truck looks like a dump truck, though it doesn't dump. It is 20 feet long and 6 feet wide, diesel powered, painted white. One hundred and ninety passengers are aboard, tossed atop one another like a pile of laundry. People are on the roof of the cab, and straddling the rail of the bed, and pressed into the bed itself. There is no room for carry-on bags; water jugs and other belongings must be tied to the truck's rail and hung over the sides. Fistfights have broken out over half an inch of contested space. Beyond the truck, the void encompasses 154,440 square miles, at last count, and is virtually uninhabited.

Like many of the people on board, Mousaka makes his living by harvesting crops—oranges or potatoes or dates. His facial scars, patterned like whiskers, indicate that he is a member of the Hausa culture, from southern Niger. Mousaka has two wives and four children and no way to provide for them, except to get on a truck. Also on the truck are Tuareg and Songhai and Zerma and Fulani and Kanuri and Wodaabe. Everyone is headed to Libya, where the drought that has gripped much of North Africa has been less severe and there are still crops to pick. Libya has become the new promised land. Mousaka plans to stay through the harvest season, January to July, and then return to his family. To get to Libya from the south, though, one must first cross the void.

The void is the giant sand sea at the center of the Sahara. It covers half of Niger and some of Algeria and a little of Libya and a corner of Chad. On maps of the Sahara, it is labeled, in large, spaced letters, "Ténéré"—a term taken from the Tuareg language that means "nothing" or "emptiness" or "void." The Ténéré is Earth at its least hospitable, a chunk of the planet gone dead. Even the word itself, "Ténéré," looks vaguely ominous, barbed as it is with accents. In the heart of the void there is not a scrap of shade nor a bead of water nor a blade of grass. Most parts, even bacteria can't survive.

The void is freezing by night and scorching by day and wind-scoured always. Its center is as flat and featureless as the head of a drum. There is not so much as a large rock. Mousaka has been crossing the void for four days; he has at least a week to go. Except for prayer breaks, the truck does not stop. Since entering the void, Mousaka has hardly slept, or eaten, or drunk. He has no shoes, no sunglasses, no blanket. His ears are plugged with sand. His clothing is tattered. His feet are swollen. This morning, I asked him what comes to mind when he thinks about the void. For two weeks now, as I've been crossing the Sahara myself, using all manner of transportation, I have asked this question to almost every person I've met. When the truck rides over a bump and everybody is jounced, elbows colliding with sternums, heads hammering heads, Mousaka leans forward and tells me his answer again. "The desert is disgusting," he says, in French. "The desert is hell." Then he spits over the side of the truck, and spits again, trying to rid himself of the sand that has collected in his mouth.

"Faith," says Monique. "The Ténéré gives me faith." Monique has been crossing and recrossing the void for four weeks. We've met at the small market in the Algerian town of Djanet, at the northern hem of the Ténéré. Monique is here with her travel partners, resupplying. She's Swiss, though she's lived in the United States for a good part of her life. Her group is traversing the void in a convoy of Pinzgauers—six-wheel-drive, moon-rover-looking vehicles, made in Austria, that are apparently undaunted by even the softest of sands.

Monique is in her early 70s. A few years ago, not long after her husband passed away, she fulfilled a lifelong fantasy and visited the Sahara. The desert changed her. She witnessed sunrises that turned the sand the color of lipstick. She saw starfish-shaped dunes, miles across, whose curving forms left her breathless with wonder. She heard the fizzy hum known as the singing of the sands. She reveled in the silence and the openness. She slept outside. She let the wind braid her hair and the sand sit under her fingernails and the sun bake her skin. She shared meals with desert nomads. She learned that not every place on Earth is crowded and greed-filled and tamed. She stayed three months. Now she's back for another extended visit.

Her story is not unusual. Tourism in the Ténéré is suddenly popular. Outfitters in Paris and London and Geneva and Berlin are chartering flights to the edge of the void and then arranging for vehicles that will take you to the middle. Look at the map, the brochures say: You're going to the heart of the Sahara, to the famous Ténéré. Doesn't the word itself, exotic with accents, roll off the tongue like a tiny poem?

Many of the tourists are on spiritual quests. They live hectic lives, and they want a nice dose of nothing—and there is nothing more nothing than the void. The void is so blank that a point-and-shoot camera will often refuse to work, the auto-focus finding nothing to focus on. This is good. By offering nothing, I've been told, the void tacitly accepts everything. Whatever you want to find seems to be there. Not long after I met Monique, I spoke with another American. Her name is Beth. She had been in the Ténéré for two and a half weeks, and she told me that the point of her trip was to feel the wind in her face.

After a fortnight of wind, Beth came to a profound decision. She said she now realized what her life was missing. She said that the moment she returned home she was quitting her Internet job and opening up her own business. She said she was going to bake apple pies.

"Money," says Ahmed. "Money, money, money, money, money." Ahmed has no money. But he does have a plan. His plan is to meet every plane that lands in his hometown of Agadez, in central Niger, one of the hubs of Ténéré tourism. During the cooler months, and when the runway is not too potholed, a flight arrives in Agadez as often as once a week. When my plane landed, from Paris, Ahmed was there. The flight was packed with French vacationers, but all of them had planned their trips with European full-service agencies. No one needed to hire a freelance guide. This is why Ahmed is stuck talking with me.

Ahmed speaks French and English and German and Arabic and Hausa and Toubou, as well as his mother tongue, the Tuareg language called Tamashek. He's 27 years old. He has typical Tuareg hair, jet black and wild with curls, and a habit of glancing every so often at his wrist, like a busy executive, which is a tic he must have picked up from tourists, for Ahmed does not own a watch, and, he tells me, he never has. He says he's learned all these languages because he doesn't want to get on a truck to Libya. He tells me he can help tourists rent quality Land Cruisers, and he can cook for them—his specialty is tagela, a bread that is baked in the sand—and he can guide them across the void without a worry of getting lost. Tourism, he says, is the only way to make money in the void.

Inside his shirt pocket, Ahmed keeps a brochure that was once attached to a bottle of shampoo. The brochure features photos of very pretty models, white women with perfect hair and polished teeth, and Ahmed has opened and closed the brochure so many times that it is as brittle and wrinkled as an old dollar bill. "When I have money," he says, "I will have women like this."

"But," I point out, "the plane landed, and you didn't get a client."

"Maybe next week," he says.

"So how will you make money this week?"

"I just told you all about me," he says. "Doesn't that deserve a tip?"

"Salt," says Choukou. He tips his chin to the south, toward a place called Bilma, in eastern Niger, where he's going to gather salt. Choukou is on his camel. He's sitting cross-legged, his head wrapped loosely in a long white cloth, his body shrouded in a billowy tan robe, and there is an air about him of exquisite levity—a mood he always seems to project when he is atop his camel. Often, he breaks into song, a warbling chant in the Toubou tongue, a language whose syllables are as rounded as river stones. I am riding another of his camels, a blue-eyed female that emits the sort of noises that make me think of calling a plumber. A half dozen other camels are following us, riderless. We are crossing the void.

Choukou is a Toubou, a member of one of the last seminomadic peoples to live along the edges of the void. At its periphery, the void is not particularly voidlike; it's surrounded on three sides by craggy mountains—the Massif de l'Aïr, the Ahaggar, the Plateau du Djado, the Tibesti—and, to the south, the Lake Chad Basin. Choukou can ride his camel sitting frontward or backward or sidesaddle or standing, and he can command his camel, never raising his voice above a whisper, to squat down or rise up or spin in circles. His knife is strapped high on his right arm; his goatskin, filled with water, is hooked to his saddle; a few dried dates are in the breast pocket of his robe, along with a pouch of tobacco and some scraps of rolling paper. He is sitting on his blanket. This is all he has with him. It has been said that a Toubou can live for three days on a single date: the first day on its skin, the second on its fruit, the third on its pit. My guess is that this is truer than you might imagine. In two days of difficult travel with Choukou, I saw him eat one meal.

If you ask Choukou how old he is, he'll say he doesn't know. He's willing to guess (20, he supposes), but he can't say for sure. It doesn't matter. His sense of time is not divided into years or seasons or months. It's divided into directions. Either he is headed to Bilma, to gather salt, or he is headed away from Bilma, to sell his salt. It has been this way for the Toubou for 2,000 years. No one has yet discovered a more economical method of transporting salt across the void—engines and sand are an unhappy mix—and so camels are still in use. Camels can survive two weeks between water stops and then, in a single prolonged drink, can down 25 gallons of water, none of which happens to be stored in the hump. When Choukou arrives at the salt mines of Bilma, he will load each of his camels with six 50-pound pillars of salt, then join with other Toubou to form a caravan—a hundred or more camels striding single file across the sands—and set out for Agadez. In the best of conditions, the trek can take nearly a month.

Choukou occasionally encounters tourists, and he sometimes sees the overloaded trucks, but he is only mildly curious. He does not have to seek solace from a hectic life. He has no need to pick crops in Libya. He travels with the minimum he requires to survive, and he knows that if even one well along the route has suddenly run dry—it happens—then he will probably die. He knows that there are bandits in the void and sandstorms in the void. He is not married. A good wife, he tells me, costs five camels, and he can't yet afford one. If he makes it to Agadez, he will sell his salt and then immediately start back to Bilma. He navigates by the dunes and the colors of the soil and the direction of the wind. He can study a set of camel tracks and determine which breed of camel left them, and therefore the tribe to which they belong, and how many days old the tracks are, and how heavy a load the camels are carrying, and how many animals are in the caravan. He was born in the void, and he has never left the void. This is perhaps why he looks at me oddly when I ask him what comes to mind when he contemplates his homeland. I ask him the question, and his face becomes passive. He mentions salt, but then he is quiet for a few seconds. "I really don't think about the void," he says.

• • •

"Cameras," says Mustafa. "Also videos and watches and Walkmans and jewelry and GPS units." Mustafa has an M16 rifle slung over his shoulder. He is trying to sell me the items he has taken from other tourists. I am at a police checkpoint in the tiny outpost of Chirfa, along the northeastern border of the void. I've hired a desert taxi—a daredevil driver and a beater Land Cruiser—to take me to Algeria. Now we've been stopped.

Mustafa is fat. He is fat, and he is wearing a police uniform. This is a bad combination. In the void, only the wealthy are fat. Police in Niger do not make enough money to become wealthy; a fat police officer is therefore a corrupt police officer. And a corrupt officer inevitably means trouble. When I refuse to even look at his wares, Mustafa becomes angry. He asks to see my travel documents. The void is a fascinating place—there exist, at once, both no rules and strict rules. To cross the void legally, you are supposed to carry very specific travel documents, and I actually have them. But the documents are open to interpretation. You must, for example, list your exact route of travel. It is difficult to do this when you are crossing an expanse of sand that has no real roads. So of course Mustafa finds a mistake.

"It is easy to correct," he says. "You just have to return to Agadez." Agadez is a four-day drive in the opposite direction. "Or I can correct it here," he adds. "Just give me your GPS unit." He does not even bother to pretend that it isn't a bribe. Mustafa is the leader of this outpost, the dictator of a thousand square miles of desert. There is no one to appeal to.

"I don't have a GPS unit," I say.

"Then your watch."

"No," I say.

"A payment will do."

"No," I say.

"Fine," he says. Then he says nothing. He folds his arms and rests them on the shelf formed by his belly. He stands there for a long time. The driver turns off the car. We wait. Mustafa has all day, all week, all month, all year. He has no schedule. He has no meetings. If we try to drive away, he will shoot us. It is a losing battle.

I hand him a sheaf of Central African francs, and we continue on.

"Beer," says Grace. "Beer and women." Grace is maybe 35 years old and wears a dress brilliant with yellow sunflowers. She has a theory: Crossing the void, she insists, seeing all that nothing, she posits, produces within a man a certain kind of emptiness. It is her divine duty, she's decided, to fill that emptiness. And so Grace has opened a bar in Dirkou. A bar and brothel.

Dirkou is an unusual town. It's in Niger, at the northeastern rim of the Ténéré, built in what is known as a wadi—an ancient riverbed, now dry, but where water exists not too far below the surface, reachable by digging wells. The underground water allows date palms to grow in Dirkou. Whether you are traveling by truck, camel, or 4x4, it is nearly impossible to cross the void without stopping in Dirkou for fuel or provisions or water or emptiness-filling.

Apparently, it is popular to inform newcomers to Dirkou that they are now as close as they can get to the end of the Earth. My first hour in town, I was told this five or six times; it must be a sort of civic slogan. This proves only that a visit to the end of the Earth should not be on one's to-do list. Dirkou is possibly the most unredeeming place I have ever visited, Los Angeles included. The town is essentially one large bus station, except that it lacks electricity, plumbing, television, newspapers, and telephones. Locals say that it has not rained here in more than two years. The streets are heavy with beggars and con artists and thieves and migrants and drifters and soldiers and prostitutes. Almost everyone is male, except the prostitutes. The place is literally a dump: When you want to throw something away, you just toss it in the street.

Grace's emptiness theory has a certain truth. I arrived in Dirkou after riding on the Libya-bound truck for three days. Of the 190 passengers, 186 were male. Those with a bit of money went straight to Grace's bar. The bar was like every structure in Dirkou: mud walls, palm-frond roof, sand floors. I sat at a scrap-wood table, on a milk-crate chair. A battery-powered radio emitted 90 percent static and 10 percent Arabic music from a station in Chad. I drank a Niger beer, which had been stored in the shade and was, by Saharan standards, cold. I drank two more.

My emptiness, it seems, was not as profound as those of my truck mates. In the Ténéré, there exists the odd but pervasive belief that alcohol hydrates you—and not only hydrates you but hydrates you more efficiently than water. Some people on the truck did not drink at all the last day of the trip, for they knew Grace's bar was approaching. Many of these same men were soon passed out in the back of the bar. There is also the belief that a man cannot catch AIDS from a prostitute so long as she is less than 18 years old.

One other item that Dirkou lacks is bathrooms. After eating a bit of camel sausage and drinking my fourth beer, I ask Grace where the bathroom is. She tells me it is in the street. I explain, delicately, that I'm hoping to produce a different sort of waste. She says it doesn't matter, the bathroom is in the street. I walk out of the bar, seeking a private spot, and in the process I witness three men doing what I am planning to do. This explains much about the unfortunate odor that permeates Dirkou.

"Spirits," says Wordigou. He is sitting on a blanket and holding his supper bowl, which at one time was a sardine tin. His face is illuminated by a kerosene lamp. Wordigou has joined us for dinner, some rice and a bit of mutton. He is a cousin of Choukou's, the young salt trader who told me that he does not think about the void. Choukou allowed me to join his camel trek for two days, and now, in the middle of our journey, we have stopped for the evening at a Toubou encampment. Wordigou lives in the camp, which consists of a handful of dome-shaped grass huts, two dozen camels, an extended family of Toubou, and a herd of goats. In the hut I've been lent for the night, a cassette tape is displayed on the wall as a sort of curious knickknack. Certainly there is no tape player in the camp. Here, the chief form of entertainment is the same as it is almost everywhere in the void—

talking. Wordigou, who guesses that he is a little less than 30 years old, leads the mealtime discussion. He is a sharp and insightful conversationalist. The topic is religion. The Toubou are nominally Muslim, but most, including Wordigou, have combined Islam with traditional animist beliefs.

"The desert," says Wordigou, "is filled with spirits. I talk with them all the time. They tell me things. They tell me news. Some spirits you see, and some you don't see, and some are nice, and some are not nice, and some pretend to be nice but really aren't. I ask the nice ones to send me strong camels. And also to lead me to hidden treasures."

Wordigou catches my eye, and he knows immediately that I do not share his beliefs. Still, he is magnanimous. "Even if you do not see my spirits," he says, "you must see someone's. Everyone does. How else could Christianity and Judaism and Islam all have begun in the very same desert?"

"Work," says Bilit. "It ties me to the desert." Bilit is the driver of the overloaded truck that is headed to Libya. He has stopped his vehicle, climbed out of the front seat, and genuflected in the direction of Mecca. Sand is stuck to his forehead. The passengers who've gotten off are piling aboard. Only their turbans can be seen through the swirling sand. Everyone wears a turban in the void—it protects against sun and wind and provides the wearer with a degree of anonymity, which can be valuable if one is attempting a dubiously legal maneuver, like sneaking into Libya. Turbans are about the only splashes of color in the desert. They come in a handful of bold, basic hues, like gumballs. Bilit's is green. I ask him how far we have to go.

"Two days," says Bilit. "*Inshallah*," he adds—God willing. He says it again: "Inshallah." This is, by far, the void's most utilized expression, the oral equivalent of punctuation. God willing. It emphasizes the daunting fact that, no matter the degree of one's preparation, traveling the void always involves relinquishing control. Bilit has driven this route—Agadez to Dirkou, 400 miles of void—for eight years. When conditions allow, he drives 20 to 22 hours a day. Where the sand is firm, Bilit can drive as fast as 15 miles an hour. Where it is soft, the passengers have to get out and push. Everywhere, the engine sounds as though it is continually trying to clear its throat.

His route is one of the busiest in the Ténéré—sometimes he sees three or even four other vehicles a day. This means that Bilit doesn't need to rely on compass bearings or star readings to determine if he is headed in the correct direction. There are actually other tire tracks in the sand to follow. Not all tracks, however, are reliable. A "road" in the Ténéré can be 20 miles wide, with tracks braiding about one another where the drivers detoured around signs of softness, seeking firmer sand. Inexperienced drivers have followed braided tracks and ended up confounding themselves. In a place with a blank horizon, it is impossible to tell if you're headed in a gradual arc or going straight. Drivers have followed bad braids until they've run out of gas.

Worse is when there are no tracks at all. This happens after every major sandstorm, when the swirling sands return the void to blankness, shaken clean like an Etch A Sketch. A sandstorm occurs, on average, about once a week. During a storm, Bilit stops the truck. Sometimes he'll be stopped for two days. Sometimes three. The passengers, of course, must suffer through it; they are too crowded to move. The trucks are so crowded because the more people aboard, the more money the truck's owner makes. The void is a place where crude economics rule. Comfort is rarely a consideration.

One time, Bilit did not stop in a sandstorm. He got lost. Getting lost in the void is a frightening situation. Even with a compass and the stars, you can easily be off by half a degree and bypass an entire town. Bilit managed to find his way. But recently, on the same route, a truck was severely lost. There are few rescue services in the Ténéré, and by the time an army vehicle located the truck, only eight people were alive. Thirty-six corpses were discovered, all victims of dehydration. The rest of the passengers—six at least, and possibly many more—were likely buried beneath the sands and have never been found.

"War," says Tombu. Where I see dunes, Tombu sees bunkers. Tombu is a soldier, a former leader of the Tuareg during the armed rebellion that erupted in Niger in 1990. Warring is in his blood. For more than 3,000 years, until the French overran North Africa in the late 1800s, the Tuareg were known as the bandits of the Ténéré, robbing camel caravans as they headed across the void.

The fighting that began in 1990, however, was over civil rights. Many Tuareg felt like second-class citizens in Niger—it was the majority Hausa and other ethnic groups, they claimed, who were given all the good jobs, the government positions, the college scholarships. And so these Tuareg decided to try to gain autonomy over their homeland, which is essentially the whole of the Ténéré. They were fighting for an Independent Republic of the Void. Hundreds of people were killed before a compromise was reached in 1995: The Tuareg would be treated with greater respect, and in return they would agree to drop their fight for independence. Though isolated skirmishes continued until 1998, the void is quiet, at least for now. This is a main reason why there has been a sudden upswing in tourism.

Tombu is no longer a fighter; he now drives a desert taxi, though he drives like a soldier, which is to say as recklessly as possible. I have hired him to take me north, through the center of the void, into Algeria—a four-day drive. We were together when the police officer forced me to pay him a bribe. During rest stops, Tombu draws diagrams in the sand, showing me how he attacked a post high in the Massif de l'Aïr and how he ambushed a convoy of jeeps in the open void. "But now there is peace," he says. He looks disappointed. I ask him if anything has changed for the Tuareg.

"No," he says. "Except that we have given up our guns." He looks even more disappointed. "But," he adds, visibly brightening, "it will be very easy to get them back."

"Speed," says Joel. He has just pulled his motorbike up to the place I've rented in Dirkou, a furnitureless, sand-floored room for a dollar a night. Joel is in the desert for one primary reason: to go fast. He is here for two months, from Israel, to ride his motorbike, a red-and-white

Yamaha, and the void is his playground. Speed and the void have a sto-ried relationship; each winter for 13 years, the famous Paris-to-Dakar rally cut through the Ténéré—a few hundred foreigners in roadsters and pickup trucks and motorbikes tearing hell-bent across the sand. The race was rerouted in 1997, but its wrecks are still on display, each one visible from miles away, the vehicles' paint scoured by the wind-blown sand and the steel baked to a smooth chocolate brown.

Joel reveres the Paris-to-Dakar. He talks about sand the way skiers talk about snow—in a language unintelligible to outsiders. Sand, it turns out, is not merely sand. There are chotts and regs and oueds and ergs and barchans and feche-feche and gassis and bull dust. The sand around Dirkou, Joel tells me, is just about perfect. "Would you like to borrow my bike?" he asks.

I would. I snap on his helmet and straddle the seat and set out across the sand. The world before me is an absolute plane, nothing at all, and I throttle the bike and soon I'm in fifth and the engine is screaming and sand is tornadoing about. I know, on some level, that I'm going fast and that it's dangerous, but the feeling is absent of fear. The dimensions are so skewed it's more like skydiving—I've com-mitted myself, and now I'm hurtling through space, and there is nothing that can hurt me. It's euphoric, a pure sense of motion and G-force and lawlessness, and I want more, of course, so I pull on the throttle and the world is a blur and the horizon is empty, and it is here, it is right now, that I suddenly realize what I need to do. And I do it. I shut my eyes. I pinch them shut, and the bike bullets on, and I over-ride my panic because I know that there's nothing to hit, not a thing in my way, and soon, with my eyes closed, I find that my head has gone silent and I have discovered a crystalline form of freedom.

"Death" says Kevin. "I think about dying." Kevin is not alone. Everyone who crosses the void, whether tourist or Toubou or truck passenger, is witness to the Ténéré's ruthlessness. There are the bones, for example—so many bones that a good way to navigate the void is to follow the skeletons, which are scattered beside every main route like cairns on a hiking trail. They're mostly goat bones. Goats are common freight in the Ténéré, and there are always a couple of animals that do not survive the crossing. Dead goats are tossed off the trucks. In the center of the void, the carcasses become sun-dried and leathery, like mummies. At the edges of the void, where jackals roam, the bones are picked clean and sun-bleached white as alabaster. Some of the skeletons are of camels; a couple are human. People die every year in the Ténéré, but few travelers have experienced such deaths as directly as Kevin.

Kevin is also on the Libya-bound truck, crossing with the crop pickers, though he is different from most other passengers. He has no interest in picking crops. He wants to play soccer. He's a midfielder, seeking a spot with a professional team in either Libya or Tunisia. Kevin was born in South Africa, under apartheid, then later fled to Senegal, where he lived in a refugee camp. His voice is warm and calm, and his eyes, peering through a pair of metal-framed glasses, register the sort of deep-seated thoughtfulness one might look for in a physician or religious leader. Whenever a fight breaks out on the truck, he assumes the role of mediator, gently persuading both parties to compromise on the level of uncomfortableness. He tells me that he would like to study philosophy and that he has been inspired by the writings of Thomas Jefferson. He says that his favorite musician is Phil Collins. "When I listen to his music," he says, "it makes me cry." I tell him, deadpan, that it makes me cry, too. This is Kevin's second attempt at reaching the soccer fields across the sands. The first trip, a year previous, ended in disaster.

He was riding with his friend Silman in a dilapidated Land Cruiser in the northern part of the void. Both of them dreamed of playing soccer. There were six other passengers in the car and a driver, and for safety they were following another Land Cruiser, creating a shortcut across the Ténéré. The car Kevin and Silman were in broke down. There was no room in the second Land Cruiser, so only the driver of the first car squeezed in. He told his passengers to wait. He said he'd go to the nearest town, a day's drive away, and then return with another car.

After three days, there was still no sign of the driver. Water was running low. It was the middle of summer. Temperatures in the void often reach 115 degrees Fahrenheit and have gone as high as 130 degrees. The sky turns white with heat; the sand shimmers and appears molten. Kevin and Silman decided they would rather walk than wait. The other six passengers decided to remain with the broken vehicle. Kevin and Silman set out across the desert, following the tracks of the second Land Cruiser. Merely sitting in the shade in the Sahara, a person can produce two gallons of sweat per day. Walking, Kevin and Silman probably produced twice that amount. They carried what water they had, but there was no way they could replace a quarter of the loss.

Humans are adaptable creatures, but finely calibrated. Even a gallon loss—about 5 percent of one's body fluid—results in dizziness and headache and circulatory problems. Saliva glands dry up. Speech is garbled. Kevin and Silman reached this state in less than a day. At a two-gallon deficit, walking is nearly impossible. The tongue swells, vision and hearing are diminished, and one's urine is the color of dark rust. It is difficult to form cogent thoughts. Recovery is not possible without medical assistance. People who approach this state often take desperate measures. Urine is the first thing to be drunk. Kevin and Silman did this. "You would've done it, too," Kevin tells me. People who have waited by stranded cars have drunk gasoline and radiator fluid and battery acid. There have been instances in which people dying of thirst have killed others and drunk their blood.

Kevin and Silman managed to walk for three days. Then Silman collapsed. Kevin pushed on alone, crawling at times. The next day, the driver returned. He came upon Kevin, who at this point was scarcely conscious. The driver had no explanation for his weeklong delay, He gave Kevin water, and they rushed to find Silman. It was too late. Silman was dead. They returned to the broken Land Cruiser. Nobody was there. Evidently, the other passengers had also tried to walk. Their footprints had been covered by blowing sand. After hours of searching, there was no trace of anyone else. Kevin was the only survivor.

"History," says Hamoud. Hamoud is an old man—though "old" is a relative term in Niger, where the life expectancy is 41. I have hired a desert taxi to take me to a place called Djado, in eastern Niger, where Hamoud works as a guide. Djado is, by far, the nicest city I have seen in the Ténéré. It is built on a small hill beside an oasis thick with date palms and looks a bit like a wattle-and-daub version of Mont-Saint-Michel. The homes, unlike any others I've seen in the void, are multistoried, spacious, and cool. Thought has been given to the architecture; walls are elliptical, and turrets have been built to provide views of the surrounding desert. There is not a scrap of garbage.

One problem: Nobody lives in Djado. The city is several thousand years old and has been abandoned for more than two centuries. At one time, there may have been a half million people living along Djado's oasis. Now it is part of a national reserve and off-limits to development. A handful of families are clustered in mud shanties a couple of miles away, hoping to earn a few dollars from the trickle of tourists.

Nobody knows exactly why Djado was deserted; the final blows were most likely a malaria epidemic and the changing patterns of trade routes. But Hamoud suggests that the city's decline was initiated by a dramatic shift in the climate. Ten thousand years ago, the Sahara was green. Giraffes and elephants and hippos roamed the land. Crocodiles lived in the rivers. On cliffs not far from Djado, ancient paintings depict an elaborate society of cattle herders and fishermen and bow hunters. Around 4000 B.C., the weather began to change. The game animals left. The rivers dried. One of the last completed cliff paintings is of a cow that appears to be weeping, perhaps symbolic of the prevailing mood. When Djado was at its prime, its oasis may have covered dozens of square miles. Now there is little more than a stagnant pond. Hamoud says that he found walking through Djado to be "mesmerizing" and "thrilling" and "magnificent" and "beautiful." I do not tell him this, but my overwhelming feeling is of sadness. In the void, it seems clear, people's lives were better a millennium ago than they are today.

"Destiny," says Akly. He shrugs his shoulders in a way designed to imply that he could care less, but his words have already belied his gesture. Akly does care, but he is powerless to do anything—and maybe this, in truth, is what his shrug is attempting to express. Akly is a Tuareg, a native of Agadez who was educated in Paris. He has returned to Niger, with his French wife, to run a small guest house. Agadez is a poor city in a poor nation beset by a brutal desert. It is not a place to foster optimism.

Akly is worried about the Sahara. He is concerned about its expansion. Most scientific evidence appears to show that the Sahara is on the march. In three decades, the desert has advanced more than 60 miles to the south, devouring grasslands and crops, drying up wells, creating refugees. The Sahara is expanding north, too, piling up at the foothills of the Atlas Mountains, as if preparing to ambush the Mediterranean.

Desertification is a force as powerful as plate tectonics. If the Sahara wants to grow, it will grow. Akly says he has witnessed, just in his lifetime, profound changes. He believes that the desert's growth is due both to the Sahara's own forces and to human influences. "We cut down all the trees," he says, "and put a hole in the ozone. The Earth is warming. There are too many people. But what can we do? Everyone needs to eat, everyone wants a family." He shrugs again, that same shrug.

"It has gotten harder and harder to live here," he says. "I am glad that you are here to see how hard it is. I hope you can get accustomed to it."

I shake my head no and point to the sweat beading my face, and to the heat rash that has pimpled my neck, and to the blotches of sunburn that have left dead skin flaking off my nose and cheeks and arms.

"I think you'd better get used to it," Akly says. "I think everyone should get used to it. Because one day, maybe not that far away, all of the deserts are going to grow. They are going to grow like the Sahara is growing. And then everyone is going to live in the void."

from The Last Kilometer
by A. Preston Price

*A. Preston Price (born 1921) was a young lieu-
tenant in late 1944 when he was sent to Belgium to join the First Infantry Division. The
division, known as the "Big Red One," advanced
from Belgium towards Czechoslovakia during the
final months of the war.*

mmediately after arriving at my unit's assembly area, I am summoned to the company commander's post, a hole like any other, to receive the attack order. We attack at dawn, tomorrow, the twenty-fourth of January.

A sleepless night in a hole, and then off to join L Company for the attack. I like this because the company commander, Captain Ritter, is the best. First the long march from Elsenborn to Butgenbach, then the long delays caused by action at the Dom Butgenbach. In Butgenbach the men are freezing, and suddenly they decide to do something about it. A group in front of me gathers in the ruins of a house and builds a fire in the bathtub. The smoke is terrible, but some are so cold that they brave the smoke and huddle over the tub. I see Sherman tanks skating down the ice-covered highway, tons of steel with brakes locked, sliding with ever-increasing momentum down the hill, one after another, looking like brown toys in the distance. Some end up in the ditch, others miraculously survive, pointed in the right direction at the hill bottom.

The order comes to move out again. The column stretches a mile in front of me and a mile behind me. Now we are passing Dom Butgenbach, just one or two buildings in rubble, with Jerry's barbed wire just beyond. One of our tanks hits a mine and one of its tracks is blown off. The rumor passes that it hit our own mines buried before the snow fell, and just now thawed to the extent that the pressure of the tank treads could explode them.

We turn off the road to the right and start across a wide field about three feet deep in snow. We follow in the tracks of the men ahead of us. Blazing the trail must have been hell on the leading scouts. My load is almost intolerable. I am carrying my extra radio battery under one arm in addition to all of the other equipment and my trench coat. Finally we leave the field and start up a high series of hills, all densely forested. An occasional mortar round hits far ahead of us. Up and up we go through the deeply drifted snow, stumbling, unable to see the logs, sticks, and rocks under the snow. It is sometimes necessary to crawl over fallen trees. The company I am with now turns slightly left toward the north and begins to attack toward a crossroad, somewhere to our front. For some reason, the crossroad is known as Paratroop Cross Roads. I later discover that we are attacking the 1st Battalion of the 1055th Volksgrenadier Regiment, a distinctly nonparatroop outfit.

Now I have fallen slightly behind the men in front of me and seem to be out of touch with the men behind me. I am alone following a trail in the snow. Where is everybody? Suddenly I hear a sound to my left. A German soldier is crawling toward me. He is saying something, over and over. He is wounded, and he is saying, "Wasser! Wasser! Wasser!" A sort of panic overtakes me at this sight of my first German at close range. "No, no, no!" I say in German. "Go back, go back, that way!" I point back down the trail. The German reaches out with his hand, pleading with me and making motions as if he is drinking from a canteen. I brush past him, swearing, and shout at him to go back down the trail. I pass on without looking behind me. I know that the first-aid men are at the rear of the column. They will take care of him. Thus, I clear my conscience. Now I catch up with the file in front of me.

Suddenly we are in a clearing with a main road cutting through the woods in front of us. The men in front of me have flushed up a German. He runs across the road. The men shout, "There he is! Get him! Get him!" The German is joined by about ten other Germans running across the road to the forest on the other side. Now the firing is general, as every rifleman is taking potshots at the Germans. Some are firing as fast as their rifles can fire. The sound of the empty clips pinging into the air as the last round of eight is fired makes a musical sound strangely at variance with the harsh echoing sound of the rifles firing.

Some of the Germans are hit and fall. Others run a little farther then kneel with their hands in the air. The firing continues for a few seconds, then the Germans are quickly rounded up. We find that we are at a small crossroads and just a few yards from it is a German command post bunker. In almost no time, our soldiers, who have fanned out and crossed the road, begin to appear back on the road with prisoners, and about fifteen are collected. I walk over to them. One is sitting on a stump, keening to himself and rocking back and forth. He is shot through both thighs, and the blood is beginning to seep through his white camouflage uniform pants.

Now a German aid man points to the wounded man with his fingers, which are clasped across the top of his helmet, just as are the hands of all of the prisoners. The aid man points to his medical kit, and then to the man, several times, until finally he walks over to the wounded man, helps him pull his trousers down, and inspects the wounds. He begins to put first-aid dressings on the legs, and some of the other Germans watch. It is a tableau of men, German and American, standing in the snow, looking at each other, with no motion, and no words. Only the aid man is doing something. Now another German prisoner begins to point at his backside, with downward shoveling motions. Everyone knows what this means. He has to defecate. I nod my head. The German man immediately drops his pants and squats. Yes, it is diarrhea. Now others make motions requesting to do the same or to urinate. This they do.

I notice one prisoner is as white as a ghost and leans more and more against a comrade. He slumps to the snow, and we see the blood running down his hand from under his jacket sleeve. One of our sergeants places two men in charge of the prisoners, and I turn to go on into the forest on the other side of the road. We hear firing again to our front.

I come to an edge of the forest and gaze across a small valley that is cleared of all trees.

A horse-drawn military vehicle is attempting to flee across the opposite hillside on a small road. Our soldiers have opened up on the wagon with rifles and automatic rifles. Suddenly someone shouts, "Cease fire! Don't shoot! Ambulance! Don't shoot." But the vehicle is riddled. The horses scream, a sound that carries easily through the clear of the beautiful snow scene, even though the wagon is about two hundred yards from us. Our soldiers swear horribly—no one wanted to hurt the horses, although men are a different story. A sergeant takes his squad on the run toward the wagon. He shouts something about "putting them out of their misery." A few minutes later several shots ring out. The horses have stopped screaming.

Now the business of consolidation of the position we have seized begins automatically. We take up positions at the edge of the cleared field, and most of us find German foxholes, which are immediately taken for our own use. It is impossible to dig in the frozen ground, and later we hear blocks of TNT being detonated by some of our men who try to break up the frozen topsoil. My hole contains the usual quota of litter—old letters, ration cans, and the like—left by the previous occupants.

I walk back up the hill to the crossroads to see what assistance I can be to the company commander. At the crossroads I find that the large bunker was also used as a first-aid station, and that nearby in the woods there is a stack of at least twelve dead German soldiers. I see some of our soldiers breaking the German rifles against pine trees in order to render them useless in case a German counterattack retakes this position. This looks like fun, so I too step over and pick up a German rifle and proceed to bend it as much as possible around a sturdy pine. I find that it is easy to break the wooden stock but another matter to try to bend the barrel. As I am engaged in this task I look up to find my platoon leader, Lieutenant Ciccone, watching me with a camera in his hands. He asks me to pose for him, and I oblige, holding one of the German rifles in my hands.

A heavy snow begins to fall, and when I leave the bunker a few minutes later, after finding out the general direction from which the company commander feels the Germans will counterattack, I find that the body of a German soldier who was killed in our attack is now half-covered with snow. I know I shall not easily forget the sight of the skyward staring eyes and gaping mouth, now filled with snow, and the body rapidly disappearing from sight under the huge snowflakes.

I have only been gone from the new company command post for a few minutes when I hear the sickening crump of mortar shells falling very close to it. I pay no attention to the shelling, which ceases as quickly as it began, and proceed to my new observation post. A few minutes later a messenger from the L Company commander arrives and tells me that one of the mortar rounds hit and killed Capt. Seth Botts, the battalion operations officer. Captain Ritter wants to know if I can do something about the German mortars. I tell the messenger that I was unable to hear the German mortars fire, but that I will certainly bring them under fire if I can locate them. As usual, I cannot hear the enemy weapons fire.

I get my radio going and find out that my mortars are set up several hundred yards behind me on the other side of the crossroad. I go through the registration of fires procedure that I will employ after every attack or advance from now until the end of the war. I have one of the mortars fire at various points to our front, which appear to be the most likely avenues of approach of a German attack. I "walk" these mortar rounds in toward me, until a round lands only seventy-five yards in front of our line. Over the radio I tell my mortar crew, "Mark that one as Concentration One." I mark about six such concentration points, placing their numbers and locations on my map. Now I am in business.

Shortly after dark I am in my foxhole—which, incidentally, is coated top, bottom, and sides with about three inches of ice from the breath condensation of the previous occupant—when a runner comes from the company commander requesting my presence immediately. I am up and out in the snow in a matter of seconds, since the only clothing I have removed is my boots. I walk back up through the trees to the bunker and notice that the dead German on the path is now completely covered, although the snow ceased in the late afternoon.

The company commander tells me that his listening posts have heard sounds in a small clump of tall trees located in the open field. I immediately recognize the feature, as I zeroed one mortar concentration on that point during the afternoon just in case. A few minutes later my radio operator and I are back at the edge of the clearing, and I order the mortars to fire a twenty-seven-round concentration, which covers an area one hundred yards square, directly into the clump of trees. Because of the previous registration, it is not necessary for me to fire a registration round at all, and the Germans, if there are any there, suddenly, and without warning, have twenty-seven rounds of mortar fire dropping on their heads. I soon receive a report that all sound from that target has ceased. A patrol the next day reports finding a few foxholes started in the clump, but nothing else of interest.

The next morning, after finishing my breakfast, which is a C-ration can of baked beans heated rather inadequately over a small German field stove, I walk back up to the company command post. Here I notice for the first time that the main highway we captured the day before is literally covered with large pine trees that the Germans felled using explosives tied around the tree trunks. The highway is covered with fallen trees for approximately 150 yards to the right of our position.

As I arrive at the command post, a large engineer bulldozer comes thrashing up the trail over which we attacked and appears at the command post. The driver is a giant of a man, and he calls out as soon as he arrives, "Are these the trees you want moved?" Captain Ritter tells him that all the trees must be moved so our tanks can get through. "Watch out for mines!" Ritter adds. "We haven't cleared the road under these trees."

The bulldozer operator, who is chewing gum, replies, "I don't give a damn about mines." He turns his bulldozer toward the giant trees and begins to throw the blade of his vehicle against first one and then another. When I leave to go back to my observation post a few minutes later, I see that the bulldozer operator has made good progress in pushing the fallen trees to the side of the road and has already cleared about one-fourth of the trees from the highway. I leave with his curses, directed toward his giant machine, ringing in my ears.

During our wait at Paratroop Cross Roads we are issued the new "snow-pacs." These are felt-lined boots with an additional half-inch felt insert to go under the foot. We are told that they are guaranteed to keep our feet warm. We hasten to put them on and turn in our leather combat boots, which are carefully collected and hauled to the rear for use in the spring. I find that the snow-pats keep my feet much warmer than the combat boot when we are in a stationary position.

On the twenty-eighth of January we receive our orders: the battalion will attack the town of Büllingen. I am pleasantly surprised to get this order as I am fully aware that the main German defenses of Büllingen were on the northern side of the town facing Elsenborn Ridge, which we defended for so long. This attack will come from the south, and we will be able to enter Büllingen by the back door, so to speak. We all devoutly hope that the defenses on the south side will be much weaker. Another bit of good news: L Company will not lead this attack.

We begin the approach march just after dark. The battalion assembles on the highway, and there are long delays before L Company finally begins its march. The snow reflects enough light so that we can see for approximately two hundred yards. It appears that the attack will be made with no artillery preparation. Just in front of L Company I can hear some of our tanks moving in the column.

We march down the highway for about half a mile and then leave the highway, turning right into alternating forest and fields. Now the most grueling part of the attack begins. First march. Then we stand and wait. We find that the new snow-pacs make our feet sweat excessively and that the sweat saturates the felt inserts. Then when we stand, often for half an hour without moving, in snow that ranges from knee to waist deep, the sweat freezes and our feet become unbearably cold. Now we move again; then once more we wait.

Once we leave the highway it is necessary for each man to follow in the tracks of the man in the front of him. Much of the delay is caused by the fact that the leading men in each single-file column must be alternated frequently as they become exhausted in just a few minutes. The mutter of artillery in all directions continues without abatement, as it has ever since I came to the front.

We have marched perhaps a mile and a half; it has taken us hours. Now we hear firing at the head of the column. The leading company is catching it. Soon we can hear rifle and machinegun fire. Then we hear heavier explosions of mortar and artillery shells. Every few minutes I turn to Potts, who follows me five yards behind, and ask him to test the radio. Something is wrong. Probably the mouthpiece is frozen or else some other part of the radio has become frozen in the intense cold. We are unable to raise anyone by radio. We move on.

Marching directly in front of me is a heavy-machine-gun squad from M Company, which is attached to L Company for this attack. Now we move into a forest. Suddenly a German "burp gun" fires a staccato burst to our left. The German submachine gun has such a rapid rate of fire that the bursts sound almost like someone tearing canvas. Bullets snap through the trees above our heads. We dive into the snow the moment we hear the firing, and fortunately, no one is hit. The riflemen and machine gunners in the snow stare up to the left through the trees. "Where is he?" "Do you see him?" "Where is that bastard?" The burp gun is silent, and slowly the long single-file column arises and moves steadily forward again.

I notice an officer breaking his way through the snow about five yards to my left. He seems in a hurry to get to the head of the column. As he comes closer I recognize him as Lieutenant Colonel Murdoch, the new 3d Battalion commander. I wonder to myself what he is like. He will have a hard time replacing Colonel Corley, who has finally been rotated to the States. Now, nearer, the German burp gun again opens fire on us. As I dive for the snow, it is with satisfaction that I see the battalion commander doing the same. There is some pleasure in finding that even high-ranking officers have the same reactions as the rest of us. I notice, however, that Colonel Murdoch is up and moving forward long before the rest of us.

Shortly after we begin moving again, German mortar shells begin to hit our column. Now the small-arms fire ahead reaches a crescendo. We continue to move forward in single file. Now we are out of the forest and in open fields. We move through gaps in barbed wire fences that surround the small fields. The lead men have cut a path through the barbed wire. I step on an unseen object beneath my feet in the snow. My foot turns under me and I find myself thrown heavily into the snow. I have sprained my ankle badly. There is nothing to do but get up, which I quickly do. I find that after a few yards the pain begins to subside. Potts is asking me if I am all right. I reassure him.

Now the mortar shells exploding around us begin to afford us better illumination. Those striking in the hedgerows, which border the fields, are tree bursts and spray their hot fragments of metal in all directions. Behind me and in front of me from time to time I can see men being hit. They crawl a few yards out of the path into the snow. The cry "Medic!" is passed up and down the line, but the line continues to move forward. In the illumination of the bursting mortar shells, I see that there is another single-file column marching parallel to us on the other side of the field. Again I trip over something in the snow and am thrown heavily to my knees. Again I struggle to my feet. The snow is soft and yielding. This time Potts seizes my arm and assists me. There is no chance to stop or to take cover from the shelling; we must move on.

The attack takes on all aspects of a nightmare. I lose all track of time. In the middle of the field to my right I see something, or someone, crawling. In my imagination it is a German. The object that I see points a rifle in my direction. I call to the soldiers in front of me. "See that German out there! There! There! Don't you see him! Shoot him! Shoot him!" The soldiers look in the direction I point but appear to see nothing and continue to trudge straight ahead through the snow. Again I look to the right, but this time I see nothing moving in the snow.

A few minutes later I see what appears to be an antitank gun in the snow to the right. As I come closer to it, I realize that it is the tongue of a wagon protruding from the snow. My imagination is playing all sorts of tricks on me. Now the mortar fire on the column increases. A few soldiers ahead of me I see a soldier drop to the snow by the side of the path. He is sitting up. When I draw abreast of him, I see that it is Father Bracken.

"What's the matter, Father?" Are you hit?"

"I can't make it, Lieutenant. I want to go on, but I can't make it." I can see in the illumination of bursting shells that his face is pale under the usual grime that covers it. I plead with him to get to his feet and get back in the column. But I can stay here no longer. I can see by the blank look in Bracken's eyes that threats or cajolery will not move him.

"You'll be all right, Corporal. Just rest here a few minutes. You'll be okay."

Potts and I struggle through the deep snow, at the side of the path, trying to catch up with our place in the column. Once again my weakened ankle gives way beneath me and I am thrown head-first into the deep snow. Once again Potts assists me to my feet. And still the radio will not work. Now a faint light appears over the distant horizon. Dawn is beginning to break, and in a few minutes it will be light. If the Germans catch us in the fields they will be able to mow us down. The column quickens its pace, and soon we can make out the first building on the edge of the town.

Now our column moves through a gap in a hedgerow at the end of a field. Just in front of us we see the first building of the town. The field beyond the trees is under intense mortar fire. I hear Potts, directly behind me, calling to me. He shouts, "We can't go in there!" I immediately reply, "Oh, yes we can, Potts. Come on! We're too exposed here. It'll be better in the buildings."

We move on. It gets lighter each minute. I find a large number of riflemen huddled around the walls of the house. Captain Ritter is standing outside it, giving rapid orders to his attacking squads. The men around the house are from the leading company, which has suffered heavy casualties from German machine-gun and mortar fire. From inside the house I hear pitiful shrieks and moans. Someone tells me that the leading company caught hell.

Captain Ritter seems to realize that we must push on before daylight or we will suffer more casualties. And so L Company continues the attack into the town. As the attacking squads disappear on each side of the main street running through the town, the sound of small-arms and machine-gun fire increases.

Potts follows me as I move toward the left-hand row of houses. In front of me, moving toward me, is a stretcher with a wounded man on it carried by four stretcher bearers. In the half-dark I can see that they are slipping in the snow. Suddenly there comes the slithering swish of an incoming shell. It strikes the snow about ten yards to my left and about fifteen yards from the stretcher. Everyone hits the ground and I instantly feel a tremendous blow as a fragment of the shell slaps into my boot. It is as though someone has hit me on the leg with a hammer. Once again the deep snow has slowed the fragment down and I am not wounded. As I get to my feet I see the stretcher bearers working the wounded soldier back on to the litter. Now I break into a limping run for the first house on the left. More shells continue to come in. As I move from house to house, rushing rapidly from one sheltering wall to another down the long street, I realize that it is daylight.

In crossing a vacant lot between two houses I am brought up short by an unusual sight. There appear to be five piles of snow equally spaced in a straight line across the lot. I move closer to the first pile and discover that it is one of our riflemen wearing his snow camouflage sheet. He is crouched on both knees—dead. Bright red blood has congealed on the side of his face. It is the same with the next four riflemen. They have been hit by machine-gun fire and stopped in their tracks. All of them are kneeling or crouching. None are out flat on the snow.

I realize I have outdistanced Potts, who is carrying the heavy radio. I rush into a large barn and run to the center of the room. There in front of me, at the corner of two walls, stands a German soldier. Both his feet and arms are spread apart slightly as though he is trying to push himself back into the corner of the barn. He stares straight at me. I grab for my pistol but do not draw it as the German makes no move whatsoever. Then in the dim light I make out the saffron-colored skin that indicates death. Now I see the hole in his forehead just between his eyebrows from which a small trickle of blood drips down one side of his face. He is frozen in his standing position.

This German shocks me. I begin to think I am dreaming. I rush back out of the barn in time to see that Potts has come up. We make our way from house to house, moving always toward the sound of the firing ahead of us. Now the sounds of machine-gun fire on the outskirts of the town cease. Evidently we have broken the line of German resistance.

I pass the door of a large stone house. Some L Company riflemen are standing there. Over the sound of the shell fire and small-arms fire I can see that they are listening to the shrill ringing of a German telephone. "There's a Jerry phone in there ringing, Lieutenant," they say. "Why don't you answer it?" I think rapidly. If an American answers the phone this may bring German artillery fire on the town in immediate answer. I tell the riflemen, "Better leave it alone. Let it keep ringing." Potts and I move on.

In the center of the town I find Captain Ritter. He has taken over the cellar of one of the large houses as his command post. In all directions we see our soldiers herding in small groups of German prisoners. Once L Company penetrated the town, resistance collapsed. Because of the occasional incoming artillery shells, prisoners and captors alike huddle close to the sides of the houses.

Up the main street I see several white phosphorus rounds land. They fill the street, first with their vivid streak of orange fire, then with billowy stinking clouds of white smoke. Some of the soldiers in front of us scream out as the white-hot phosphorus burns their skin. Captain Ritter rushes forward to see that the burned men are given aid. I rush after Captain Ritter, telling him that I will move on to the front of the town to see if I can find any retreating Germans to shell as they pull out of town. He nods agreement.

Potts and I move steadily forward, and when we reach the far end of the town we find that the small-arms fire has ceased. German artillery shells continue to burst in and around the town. I discover that the front end of the town ends just before the railroad embankment. From the end house, which stands in ruins, as does almost every other house in the town, I find a window that overlooks the entire northern landscape. Again I have Potts try the radio, and this time we are able to make contact with the mortar platoon.

Now I begin my observation of the hills rising in front of me in the direction that the Germans are retreating. At first I see nothing moving, but I continue to scan the terrain with my glasses. I have a funny feeling about this observation post because the house stands so high and isolated. Worse, it has no cellar. Sure enough, as soon as I think this, several artillery rounds land around the house in quick succession. Potts and I throw ourselves to the floor against the front wall of the house. Looking up, I find myself staring through an enormous hole in the ceiling through which the beautiful blue sky is visible. One round hits the back side of the house with an enormous explosion. We are covered with dust but otherwise unhurt. As soon as the shelling stops, I am back at the window again, scanning the terrain.

At a distance of about a mile, to my left front, I begin to see signs of movement. Some Germans are digging in a hedgerow on a hillside. They have evidently only just begun to dig, as I can see that their bodies are still above the surface of the ground. I take them under fire with the mortars and have the satisfaction of seeing some of my rounds fall in or extremely close to the hedgerows. I report this target by radio to the mortar platoon and continue to shell the hedgerow for about an hour until there is no more sign of digging there.

A runner comes to my position and tells me that Captain Ritter wants me to come to the command post to question some prisoners. I move back through the village smelling the unmistakable stench of town fighting. There is the smell of burning wood, the disagreeable, pungent odor that white phosphorus gives off, the smell of high explosive, and feces and manure. After questioning several German noncommissioned officers and privates I realize that they probably know nothing of the general situation. All are in agreement that things look very bad for Germany. Our attack through the back door of the town took them by surprise. Captain Ritter releases me. He looks dead tired.

On leaving the command post I see the long column of German prisoners gathering to march out of the town to the rear. I count two hundred of them in the column. A real bag! I walk over to one prisoner who is wearing the usual German snowsuit. It consists of a beautifully quilted, warm jacket and pair of quilted trousers. The pieces are reversible, a mottled camouflage design on one side, white on the other. I direct Jerry to take off his snow trousers, as I very much want them for the warmth and camouflage they will give. He obliges me, and I see that he has on his regulation greenish grey woolen trousers under the snow trousers. I get into the snow trousers and walk around the building looking at the numerous pieces of German field equipment lying on the ground. I am attracted to a German helmet and so take off my helmet and put the German helmet on my head. Without thinking, I now stroll of the building into the main street.

Instantly several riflemen point their rifles at me and yell "Halt!" I freeze in my tracks and begin to call loudly that it is me, Lieutenant Price, not a Jerry. The men recognize me and begin to laugh. I throw the German helmet from my head, determined never to make such a mistake again. One of the enlisted tells me that I looked exactly like a Kraut. An incoming German shell makes a little more rubble out of the rubble of a nearby house. This puts an end to the fun for a while.

I walk back down the cellar stairs of the ruined house being used as the command post. The room is crowded with the company headquarters personnel: the runners, the radio operators, the first sergeant, and messengers from the platoons. Captain Ritter lies on one of the bunks scattered around the room. He seems very happy; the attack was a success. He motions me over to him. "Better get some of this Jerry pork," he says. "It was cooking when we took the place." He motions to large quart-sized cans of pork meat on a table. Several of the cans are being heated on a stove. I pull out my spoon, which is always present in the breast pocket of my field jacket, and dig in to the steaming contents of a can. The pork is delicious, and fat runs down both sides of my chin. I suck the juice from the tips of my mustache and remember that in both attacks I found myself chewing the tips of my mustache. Just a nervous habit.

Captain Ritter speaks to me again. "Price, I'm saving you a bunk here where you can sleep. Say, have you seen the mess of stuff that the 99th left in this town? *Beaucoup!*" A sergeant speaks from behind me. "We found a whole field desk full of reports. Switchboards and *beaucoup* stuff." The sergeant pulls something out of his field jacket pocket. "Here, Lieutenant, have a Combat Infantry Badge courtesy of the 99th Division." He hands me the gleaming blue and silver badge. "Why, merci, Sarg." I unbutton my field jacket top and pin the badge over my left shirt pocket. Over my shoulder I add, "Well, Captain, I'll just head back to the OP. Thanks for the chow." I clump up the steps. The cold air stings my face as I reach the top.

As I start back down the main street I see that our phone lines now stretch along the sides of the street in all directions, and that the colorful red-and-green Jerry telephone wire lies just beneath our brown-colored wire. On arriving at the observation post, Potts informs me that we now have a telephone line to the mortars. We can turn off the radio and save the battery. He reports that all is quiet to the front, but in all directions we still hear the mutter of the guns. Their bass melody never seems to end. Potts and I stay at the observation post that night, just in case of a counterattack. The night passes slowly as the cold creeps deeper into our bodies, and we stamp our feet to try to bring back some feeling. All is quiet.

The next morning I send Potts back for breakfast and examine a propaganda leaflet I picked up on the snow back at Paratroop Cross Roads. It is one of ours, dropped on the Jerry position either by our aircraft or by artillery rounds especially equipped to carry packs of leaflets instead of high explosive. On one side is a map of Germany. The extent of the advances of the Russians to the east and the Allies to the west is clearly depicted. I have a little trouble but finally translate the German text below the map:

THE RUSSIANS ARE HERE!

The above map shows the advance of the Red Army until 12 noon 24 January. In the next 24 hours the Russians will attack in the direction of Berlin. And before this pamphlet comes to you, the Russian flood will have completely engulfed Eastern Germany—the last dam is broken!

On the reverse side it says:

THE FRONT IS BROKEN! THIS IS THE END!

The day of the war criminals . . . stands now in front of the door!

What does the last line mean? Still, it sounds good. I hope Jerry reads them instead of using them for toilet paper as we do.

I look up from my letter to see Lieutenant Womack. He is one of the rifle platoon leaders of L Company. I have grown very attached to him, as he is extremely friendly and always wears a happy grin on his broad face. He is built like a wrestler, short and powerful.

"Hi, Price. Been looking for you. What say we don't shave until we get through the Siegfried Line?"

"Okay by me, my friend. Whiskers stay until we crack it. It's about one mile beyond tomorrow's objective, so I don't think we'll have to wait very long."

The same morning I hear the tremendous sound of firing to the east. Other units of the 26th are attacking Mürringen, the last Belgian town before the border of Germany. I wish them luck. During the next two days, I notice that the town of Büllingen begins to fill with more and more rear-area units: signalmen, engineers, and higher headquarters. This can only mean that we are going to push on soon.

And just as I predict, on the thirty-first of January, the 3d Battalion receives its attack orders. After we have been given our assignments at the company command post, I decide that it is time for me to write home. I borrow some cheap sheets of German paper from one of the runners and sit down at the German field desk to compose a letter. As usual, I feel most urgently the need to allay my mother's fears, and at the same time I curse the censorship rules that do not allow us to give details of where we are and what our plans are:

> First let me say that I haven't had any more mail since the letter saying Dad had gotten to Atlanta, so I don't know how his operation was, or anything.
>
> About the only thing that sounds good to me recently is the news of the Russian advances. Really very heartening. We have been pushing recently and ought to be in Germany pretty soon. We are beating the snow and the Germans at the same time. I am writing from a cellar in a small Belgian town that used to be German back in 1918. We took it recently and probably will leave soon. I am unwounded, safe, and healthy, though tired as hell . . . Funny how things work. A few days ago I was blasting this place with mortars, and now I'm here. We finished the meal that the Jerries had been preparing.

I am wordy today, writing five pages in all. On the back of the letter I draw a crude sketch of my face and helmet, taking extreme care to draw my mustache exactly. Underneath the sketch I write in capital letters "SEMI ANNUAL MUSTACHE REPORT!"

The next morning, the first of February, we move out at dawn. We hear reports that a large number of Germans are around Krinkelt to the northwest. Our mission is to attack into Krinkelter Forest to the north of Mürringen and seize an important crossroad in the forest. If the attack is successful, we will be in Germany. I remain attached to L Company, and L Company will lead the attack.

The company moves out to march the two kilometers to Mürringen. There is a single-file column on each side of the narrow, snow-covered road. The strange-looking white sheets on the men flap in the breeze. Potts and I march with the company headquarters men, behind the leading platoon. We reach Mürringen without incident and see the usual signs of the recent capture of the town. It lies in complete ruins from our artillery and mortar fire.

"You'll be sorry!" The customary taunts flow from the men of our regiment who have captured the place. They are happy to be spectators rather than participants. Our men grin self-consciously; some reply with profanity. We march on east through the ruined town, and after another kilometer cross a small stream and enter a dark, forbidding forest. Once in the forest, our alertness increases. The leading platoon spreads out with flankers in the forest on each side of the road, which is nothing more than a trail. It turns sharply north, and we are now heading directly for our objective, about two kilometers ahead. Our marching speed decreases as the leading scouts now move with extreme care through the forest. I mentally note that if we are going to hit anything, it will be soon. Our radio is working perfectly with the mortar platoon in the rear. We are ready.

Now it comes. Ahead of me we hear a few rifle shots, then the sound of a German machine gun firing long bursts. One of our automatic rifles joins in. Captain Ritter comes back to me. "The leading squad has hit Jerries," he says. "This side of the objective. Can you get some 81s in there?" I listen to the firing intently. Sounds are extremely deceiving in the dense forest. "Without observation, about all I can do is shell the area just beyond the crossroads, Captain." I turn to Potts and tell him to alert the mortars for a firing mission.

Captain Ritter says, "Merci" and starts back toward the firing. I plot the coordinates of the crossroad on my map and quickly encode them into letters, using the proper codeword. I add about two hundred yards of range to my fire command as I don't want to hit our attacking troops. Soon I hear my mortar rounds hitting several hundred yards ahead. Some of the bursts are louder and clearer than others. Tree bursts. A messenger from the company commander runs back to me. "Your firing's good," he says. "Keep it up!" I continue to fire at the same locality. The firing ahead grows louder, and I can see riflemen rushing forward from tree to tree. I signal Potts to follow and move forward myself. The snow on the ground between the trees lightens the scene, which is now covered with the light blue smoke of the firing.

As suddenly as it began, the firing ceases. I move on to the cross-road, just in time to see our leading squads disappear into the woods across the road, which runs vertically across our route of march. On my left, about twenty yards into the woods, I see a German soldier lying dead across his light machine gun. A dead American lies nearby. A soldier standing nearby points to the American. "He got the machine gun! Rushed right at it."

Now I hear the sound of our soldiers digging in, their small folding shovels clanging loudly against the earth and rocks as they form a defensive perimeter around the crossroads. A few minutes later I hear an armored vehicle rumbling up the road behind me. It is one of our tank destroyers. It drives straight to the crossroads, stops, then backs and turns so that its gun points straight down the road coming into the crossroads from the left. I see our engineers laying mines across the same road, about fifty yards from the crossing. I am puzzled for a minute, then remember that this side road leads to Krinkelt, and if the Germans there try to break out, this will be the route they will use.

With a shock I notice that it is getting dark. Potts and I move forward across the crossroads to the platoon positions to the right front. There are several German bunkers in this area. In a few minutes it is totally dark. A squad leader, covered with mud, is moving from one German bunker to another, swearing. "These lousy holes are collapsing. Don't try to get in this one, Lieutenant; the damn thing damn near buried us." Although there is snow everywhere, the warmth of the day has melted enough snow to soften the frozen dirt into mud. "They're all leaking like sieves," the sergeant adds.

After walking from bunker to bunker for awhile, looking for a place to bed down, Potts and I are invited to sleep in the bunker of one of the rifle squads. The hole is a large one, covered with a thick layer of logs and dirt and holds about one half of the rifle squad. "Ain't got much room, but you're welcome," we are told. Potts and I squeeze into the hole. There is barely enough room for all to sit with our backs propped against the dirt walls. After eating a D-ration, which is an extremely hard chocolate bar, for our supper, Potts and I try to get some sleep. The hole stinks of dirty, smelly men and is full of smoke from the burning of the wax-coated cardboard K-ration boxes. We have found that the boxes burn extremely well, and the men often heat their rations over this blaze. Tonight they are burning them to keep warm. The roof of the hole drips water everywhere, and the water drops make a metallic clink as they strike the tops of our helmets. Finally I doze off.

Sometime during the night we are awakened by a tremendous explosion about two hundred yards to our left. The ground shakes with the concussion of one detonation after another in quick succession. We can hear yelling and small-arms fire to our left. It ends abruptly. The whole noise has lasted no longer than three minutes. Potts and I collect our gear and begin to crawl out of the hole. We find the rifle platoon leader just outside the hole. The blackness of the night is broken on our left by flickering fires, dimly visible through the trees. The platoon leader has been talking to the platoon on the left. "It's all over," he tells me. "Some Jerries tried to break out of the pocket over there. We got 'em all. Now maybe we can get some sleep." Potts and I crawl back into the hole, spread the news around, and then once again fall into a fitful sleep.

The next morning at daybreak, we walk back to the crossroad. I notice that there are several empty shell cases around the tank destroyer. The crew of the tank destroyer are cleaning their gun. They are elated. "Beautiful!" one of them says. "First they hit the mines, and then we opened up on them! They never had a chance to fire a shot!" Just behind the tank destroyer I notice two German graves, with the occupants' helmets hanging on two wooden crosses. The graves look neat and strangely geometrical. Probably killed during the earlier fighting in the breakthrough.

As we walk down the road toward the scene of the action, we see many of our soldiers milling around. The scene is ghastly. There are dead Germans everywhere. From the trees bordering the trail hang bits and pieces of clothing and human flesh. On the trail stand two smoldering German self-propelled guns. I can reconstruct the scene with no difficulty. About a platoon of German infantrymen were marching on the road into our position, one self-propelled gun just ahead of them and one following them. The self-propelled guns—we call them SPs—are heavily armored tracked vehicles with a gun protruding from their sharp, prowlike nose. The gun does not rotate from a turret like a tank gun, but can fire only to the front.

The leading SP hit a mine. Immediately our tank destroyer opened fire, scoring direct hits. The infantrymen behind must have hit the ground, and in the darkness the second SP rolled forward over the men on the road. From under the tracks of the second SP protrude the heads, torsos, and legs of a dozen German soldiers. Their bodies are black, and their clothing is still smoldering. Bluish smoke comes from the crushed chest of one. The most horrible expressions are on the burned faces of the soldiers. Their mouths are open as though they were screaming when they felt the heavy vehicle roll over them.

The ditch on either side of the trail is full of the dead. Some have had their clothing blown from their bodies by the mine explosions and the fire from the tank destroyer. Others were caught and killed by the deadly small-arms and machine-gun fire of the nearby rifle platoon. Many of the bodies are cut in half or lack a leg or an arm.

I see that our soldiers have already rifled the pockets of the dead, and I am nauseated when I see a soldier start through the breast pockets of one of the dead Germans whose body lies half under the SP. The trail is covered with the litter of war. Pieces of German equipment, rifles, gasmask canisters, and letters and personal documents lie everywhere. I pick up one of the letters lying in the trail. It begins "Lieber Anton" and is signed by his sister. I cannot read the letter as it is written in German script, which is illegible to me. There are the usual photographs lying in the mud: proud parents, girlfriends, a kid brother in his new uniform.

I am sickened by the sights and smells and walk away. I head to the company command post, which is a shell hole about one hundred yards behind the crossroad. Already I hear soldiers beginning to refer to our location as "SP Crossroads." As good a name as any, I reflect, and there is no name given for it on any of our maps.

At the command post everyone is talking about the destruction of the German unit and the large number of enemy soldiers captured in the action. I am amazed that such activity could have taken place in such a short amount of time. Across the hood of a jeep at the command post I see a blanket covering one of our soldiers; only his brown hair and boots are visible. Captain Ritter is telling someone to notify battalion to have the body moved to the rear as soon as possible.

The next day, other units have attacked beyond us, and all is quiet. Although snow still stands on the ground, the roads and trails in the forest are now solid mud. The dirt that I have gotten all over me by sleeping in the muddy hole begins to irritate me, so I go to the command post and fill my helmet with hot water from the galvanized can in which we dip our mess gear after washing it in other cans. I borrow a mirror, soap, and a razor from someone. I prop the helmet in the snow, and hang the mirror from a tree limb.

I unsling my field glasses case and my gas mask, then take off my harness, which holds my canteen, first-aid packet, entrenching tool, trench knife, compass, pistol, and ammunition clips. Next I take off my woolen scarf, my field jacket, the brown woolen knitted sweater, my OD woolen shirt, and the long woolen underwear shirt. Under it, against my skin, I am wearing a sleeveless woolen sweater; I remove this: The sun warms my naked back, and I proceed to wash the upper part of my body. I smell better already. Using the borrowed gear, I proceed to shave the dirty stubble that covers my face, taking care not to injure the beautiful mustache. As I look in the mirror I am amazed at my pale, fleshy reflection, which seems to stand out from the dirty skin I can see through my hair and on the sides of my neck. I swish the razor around in the now-filthy water and hear someone come up behind me.

"Damn, Price!" says Lieutenant Womack. "What did you do that for? You shaved! You broke our bargain!"

"Oh God! I forgot!"

Later this day we get the news: we will attack through the Siegfried Line tomorrow. L Company, thank the Lord, will not be the leading company. Once again I feel the urge, like so many others, to write a letter home. I scrounge around for a piece of paper. "Here, lieutenant. I took it off one of those dead Krauts this morning." The soldier hands me a single sheet of extremely poor grade paper and a soiled envelope. I thank him and begin to write on the hood of the jeep. After writing the date, 3 February 1945, I write the single word "Germany," under-lining it twice:

> DEAREST MOTHER AND FATHER,
>
> I wrote you a few days ago from the cellar of a small vil-lage in Belgium that our battalion captured. Since then in another push we crossed the border and are now . . .

What shall I say? Better make them feel we have already passed the Siegfried Line.

> . . . well into Germany. Tough sledding behind us, and ahead of us.

I decide to write about my feet being dry and warm, then about the fact that I have still received no mail since the letter telling me that my father is home. Now, about the weather:

> The weather has been a little warmer lately, enough to turn the roads to mud, and make the dugouts leak like sieves, but the snow is still here and it won't be Spring for a long time.

I write about the Russian advance, and then the urgings of my empty stomach turn my thoughts to food:

There is really nothing that you can send me, as we have all
we need including cigarettes. But when you do send something make sure it's food.

Like cans of sardines, and peanut brittle or peanuts.

I end up writing about the brave soldiers with whom I am serving and
express the wish that the war will end quickly. I seal and address the
envelope, write "Free Mail" in place of a postage stamp, and sign my
signature on the upper left hand corner, to show that I have censored
my own mail—an officer's privilege.

A few minutes later, two artillery jeeps arrive, bringing the field
artillery forward observer party that will accompany us in the attack
tomorrow. I greet them and we start talking about the Siegfried Line. The
artillerymen bring good news: some self-propelled 155-mm artillery
pieces are being brought forward through the woods to place direct fire
on the German pillboxes. Suddenly, we all dive for the ground, as
though we are puppets and attached to the same string. At the same
instant there is the tremendous whishing sound of an incoming shell,
and then the explosion just on the other side of the road. I crawl behind
a mound of earth and hardly notice that two others have piled on top of
me in their effort to get shelter. Now another round swishes overhead
and lands fifty feet beyond us. No one moves. I notice that the eyes of
one of the artillerymen are glassy and open extremely wide. He stares at
the ground beneath him without moving a muscle. Now a salvo of shells
passes over us, all hitting in the trees about one hundred yards beyond
us. We wait. There is no further shelling. From a distance I hear a
rifleman in the company headquarters group. "Why doesn't somebody
get those bastards?" We all get to our feet. No one is hurt.

The next morning we wait for a column of trucks to arrive. They will
take us another two miles forward to a point just short of the Siegfried
Line. I climb in the front seat of the two-and-a-half-ton truck loaded
with riflemen. Just beyond SP Crossroads we see the remains of a
German horse-drawn artillery battery that has been shelled. Dead
horses lie on and by the side of the road.

Excited murmurs come from each of the trucks as they pass a dead mare, still in harness. The hind feet and body of a foal protrude from the womb of the mare. The shelling has caused her to bring forth her foal in death. I listen to the men on my truck. "Them dirty, lousy, sneakin' bastards!" A hundred feet farther on we pass two of our Sherman tanks. There are large holes in the turrets and sides from German tank fire. They have been sitting there since the sudden German breakthrough in December.

We unload from the trucks about one kilometer from the Siegfried Line and form on the road. Just ahead of us we can hear the sound of artillery fire, and the echoes of explosions rattle through the fire-breaks in the forest. We move forward a little way, stop, then move forward a little more and stop again. I am surprised that there is no incoming artillery fire. Surely Jerry knows we are using this road. Ahead I can hear German mortar rounds falling—but no artillery.

Now L Company is at the edge of the forest, and I get my first look at the Siegfried Line. First are the lines of barbed wire, then come the dragon's teeth—rounded humps designed to make a tank expose its soft belly as it attempts to roll over them. Interlaced in the teeth is more barbed wire. I can see the dragon's teeth stretching to the horizon on either side. Behind the dragon's teeth I see German pillboxes spaced about two hundred yards apart and in great depth. I am happy to see that the leading company has been making steady progress through the defenses. Through my field glasses I see that almost every pillbox has suffered direct hits from our artillery. The only defense the Germans can mount is counterfire from their own artillery. Evidently they have very little in this sector. In the distance to my right I can hear the artillery firing. The 16th Infantry, which breached the Siegfried yesterday, is mopping up in the town of Ramscheid. Our objective is Hollerath, a small town about one kilometer to our front.

The engineers have been busy. We march through the dragon's teeth, being careful to stay in the narrow lane, marked on both sides by white tape, which indicates the area that has been cleared of mines. Already a bulldozer is at work pushing dirt up over the dragon's teeth to make a roadway for our tanks and other vehicles. Ahead of us we hear sporadic small-arms fire and the explosions of grenades as the leading company continues to seize pillbox after pillbox. Maybe the intelligence reports are right: that the Germans have manned this line with cripples and second-class soldiers.

A heavy rain begins to fall. The road we are on is a great quagmire, and we sink up to our ankles even on the sides of the road. We stop long enough to slip our heads through our ponchos. Now L Company is ordered to seize the right side of Hollerath. Captain Ritter gives his orders, pointing out the location of the pillboxes on that side of Hollerath. Resistance seems very light, and I follow one of the platoons as it moves to attack a large pillbox built in the side of a steep valley. The platoon attacks from the blind side of the box. Rifle and automatic rifle fire is placed on the embrasures of the pillbox. I can hear a tremendous explosion as TNT is detonated against the steel door of the pillbox. Soon a squad of Germans are filing from the pillbox, their hands in the air.

Potts and I move forward and enter the pillbox. I am amazed at the ingenuity of its construction. Inside there are tiers of bunks—enough for a whole platoon—and even a built-in bathroom. Every entrance has double baffles made of heavy steel, as do the machine-gun embrasures. The pillbox stinks of stale sweat and smoke and the fumes of high explosives. I look out the main machine-gun firing slit. From it I have a beautiful view of the valley, but there is no possibility that the Germans could have fired up on the plateau over which we advanced. It becomes apparent that every pillbox depends on the fires of other pillboxes to protect its blind spots. Once one fortification is captured, you have knocked a hole in the defenses of several others.

It is rapidly growing dark. Over our radio, we hear that our mortars are now in a position behind us, and Potts and I go up above the pillbox to begin registering defensive fires. The occasional bursts of small-arms fire in the town have ceased. I find that Hollerath is almost surrounded on the south and east by an extremely deep valley and begin to understand why it was so lightly defended. Jerry would have a hard time supplying it from the east. I begin to plot and fire white phosphorous rounds in a semicircle around our position until I am satisfied that I can bring fire on any of the danger areas.

Potts and I walk back up the hill in the dark to the road leading into the town. We stumble through deep ruts filled with water in the road, and in some low places the entire roadbed is covered with water. We also stumble over boxes and pieces of equipment lying in the road. I can see that about half of the houses are in ruins from our artillery fire. About halfway down the main street we find a house with its roof still standing, and I tell Potts to report our location to the command post and then return.

I enter the living room of the house alone. There are blackout curtains on the windows, and so, using my flashlight, I search for a candle. Finding one in a drawer, I light it and place it in the center of a table. Outside the night is quiet. I begin to examine some books lying on the floor. One is a small volume of Goethe's *Faust*. I sink into a chair and begin trying to read it. But I find that I am tired and can scarcely keep my eyes open. I lie down on a couch and fall asleep. I am instantly awakened when Potts enters the room. Seeing who it is, I wish him pleasant dreams, and go right back to sleep.

At the company command post the next day, I get the wonderful news that we are being relieved by the 99th Division, and that we, wonder of wonders, will go back into a rest area in Belgium. During the morning we stand in the doorways of the houses and watch the double file of infantrymen from the 99th stream through the town, moving forward to take over the positions of our men. Their black-and-white checkerboard shoulder patches stand out against the drab color of their field jackets. Our men greet them with the usual cry of "You'll be sorry!" Some have more uncomplimentary things to say. Most of the men look like new replacements, and I noticed that they do not take their eyes off the mud and water in which they are walking. Our jibes die away. The 99th caught hell during the Bulge.

In the middle of the afternoon we form in the muddy main street and begin to march out of Hollerath to the rear. There are the usual delays, halts, and starts, and hours later we reach the place where we are to entruck. We have marched back through the Siegfried Line and are about one kilometer beyond it. Darkness falls as we stand around the roadside waiting for our trucks, which have been shuttling troops back into Belgium. It is bitterly cold, and a heavy wind is blowing.

Just before dark I noticed a side road coming into our main road. I decide to walk down this side road. I will be able to hear our trucks when they arrive. The road I am walking on goes through a patch of heavy forest and turns sharply across a small open field. There is suffi-cient light in the sky reflected on the snow to see about ten or fifteen yards. As I walk through the field, I begin to notice objects in the field to my left. I leave the road and walk toward them.

As I come closer I can make out a man on the ground—a German. He holds both arms out toward me above his body. I am shocked and draw back. Now I see on each side of him other Germans. As far as I can see in all directions there are others. Dead Germans, half-uncovered by the melting snows, in every conceivable position. There are dozens of bodies, all laid out in neat rows. I shiver, more from the eerie sight than from the cold. I slowly walk along the front row of bodies. Some lie on their backs with their legs elevated, some hold their arms up, many hold their heads up off the ground in their frozen positions and seem to be staring at me. It seems that everyone is frozen into the posi-tion he held when he was killed. Many are squatting or sitting.

As my night vision improves, it dawns on me that the entire small field is covered with these bodies. It is a German collection point for the dead killed during the breakthrough fighting. I feel a strong desire to run and walk hastily back through the trees to the main road. I say nothing about my discovery, and soon our trucks arrive.

We drive through the night, with only the tiny blackout lights to guide us. I fall asleep several times, only to be awakened as the truck lurches through a hole in the road. We drive back through Krinkelter Forest, and then through several small towns standing in ruins, and finally arrive in the familiar town of Butgenbach, the site of Colonel Corley's command post during our defense. Stiffly we crawl from our trucks and move into some of the less-damaged houses. We are grateful that there is hot chow waiting for us, and then we all find a space on the floors of the houses and fall asleep.

Early the next morning everyone is talking and laughing. The relief of being in the rear manifests itself in jokes and boisterous behavior. Looking around, I discover that almost all the snow has melted and decide to rid myself of the German snow trousers I have been wearing. I take them off and leave them hanging on a hook on the back of a door. Many of the riflemen in the room joke about my "Jerry britches;" others tell me how much they wished that they had a pair during the fighting in the snow. Later in the morning our trucks arrive, and we gladly mount the vehicles, which are taking us back deeper into Belgium for the long-awaited rest.

from Hunted
by David Fletcher

At the beginning of a solo expedition in Alaska's Hayes range, British climber David Fletcher encountered a bear. He panicked and threw his ice axe at the animal—then realized that it was a grizzly cub. The vengeful mother followed Fletcher for more than a week before catching up with him on the West Fork glacier.

All the previously hidden features on the glacier now come into sharp focus in the early morning sunshine as I bound on my way. Most worrying are the numerous avalanche cones, another good reason to drive on relentlessly in anticipation of a decent meal down at Ravine Camp 3. Unfortunately, the clouds and mist have returned once more. The sun has never stayed out for long enough on this expedition. A few hours here and there, this has so far been the pattern of my holiday. But the lack of any real sunshine is not the main reason for my complaints about the weather. These misty cloudy conditions will make it very difficult for me to find the correct ice slope that will take me off the glacier. If I'm not careful I could lose my way here completely and find myself climbing up the wrong ice slope, leading down into the wrong valley. I try to put this terrible thought to the back of my mind as I confront my first serious crevasse, deep and narrow, so I can easily jump across. I land well in control on the far bank.

I'm suddenly stopped dead in my tracks by something lying on top of a raised bank of snow directly in front of me. It's a single black object in a great expanse of white. I fantasize about it being some other climbing party's discarded food parcel. Dumping surplus food and equipment to lighten the load isn't at all unusual. And if they don't need it, I do. A decent meal to eat at last. But I only manage to take another ten steps down the glacier before I'm brought to a knee-jarring stop, paralyzed with an awful fear. This black object on top of a raised bank of snow is no food parcel, it's the long black snout of a grizzly bear. Surely it can't be Scar Face? But I can clearly see the jagged scar cutting down through its nose now. How on earth did it manage to escape from the lake surrounded by nine-metre-high walls of ice? But the question becomes somewhat academic when faced with the awful reality of the bear confronting me, its eyes boring into me. I'm sure it is playing a game with me. It's the kind of game that a hunter might play with his quarry when he knows that there's not the slightest chance of his victim ever escaping.

"I'll jump inside the nearest crevasse! Do you hear that? No bear will ever get the satisfaction of killing me!" I scream across at Scar Face. "Fuck you! Bastard!" That's what I'll do. I'll simply take my chances inside the nearest crevasse. If I get injured jumping in, too bad. Anything is better than being eaten alive by a bear.

I begin to run back up the glacier, my rope, still tied into the back of my waist belt to relieve the weight on my shoulders, trailing behind me.

I can only hope that it doesn't get caught between any of the rocks on the way. Ten steps to go! The bear is fast behind me now. I can almost feel it breathing down my neck! Just a few more steps to go . . . The jaws of the narrow crevasse loom in front of me. The ice shakes as the bear comes bounding up behind me. But it won't get me now. There's no hesitation. I jump inside the crevasse.

I come to a sudden stop, spinning around on the end of my rope. One of the knots must have caught on the lip of the crevasse. Has a single knot saved me, jammed inside the crack that the rope itself must have created as it sawed through the lip of the crevasse? Who knows the answer to that question? I'm only glad that I'm still alive.

I still can't quite see where my rope has jammed, and in trying to peer upwards at the thin strip of white light high above I start spinning around on the end of my rope again. I quickly reach out with my hands. I'm fortunate that I can touch both walls of the crevasse at the same time. I stop myself from turning.

The bear knows where I am. It towers over me now, with its huge rear legs on either side of the crevasse, looking for all the world like some monster from a bygone age. I can't help but wonder what it is going to do next. I am not kept long in suspense. With a vicious deep-throated growl it reaches deep inside the crevasse with its long forelegs, trying to hook me out. But I'm far too deep down to be within its reach. When it works this out and gives up trying to hook me out, it prowls back and forth across the top of the crevasse. Large pieces of ice, dislodged by its paws, begin to fall down on me. Whether or not this is a deliberate act by Scar Face, I don't know. But it keeps roaring down at me each time it steps over the top of the crevasse and each time it does this more large pieces of ice fall down in my direction. I try my best to dodge the heaviest lumps but this starts my rope oscillating wildly.

The bear spots this movement and begins pounding on the walls of the crevasse above me in a fury of pent up anger and frustration at not being able to reach me. My rope begins to oscillate even more wildly and it's not long before the bear is attracted to this movement. It reaches down to grasp my rope in its two huge hairy paws. The bear has it firmly in its grasp now. I've got to act decisively if I'm to save myself from being pulled out of the crevasse. I quickly stab the pick of my ice-axe deep into the wall of ice in front of me. At least I can offer some resistance now if the bear tries to pull me out but what chance do I have in a tug-of-war with a grizzly? It is already pulling quite strongly on my rope which comes tight at my waist. Then the bear begins to lift me slowly up the wall of the crevasse.

Suddenly my rope comes free of the bear's claws. I fall past my ice-axe. My full weight hits the end of my rope with a tremendous force. My ice-axe pulls out of the wall of the crevasse. I fall even further down inside the crevasse, landing on a small crumbling ledge of snow. I instinctively stab the pick of my ice-axe back into the wall. The snow collapses beneath me. I'm left jammed tightly in between the two enormous walls of ice once more, with my rope falling smoothly around my head and shoulders. But my complete rope has come down now. I'm not secured from above anymore but the bear can't reach me now. However, only the pick of my ice-axe placed into the wall of the crevasse in front of me and the straps and buckles of my rucksack, digging hard into the ice behind me, are preventing me from falling further into the depths.

I've only got my ice-axe left to hold onto. But it's no use. The ice is proving to be far too brittle in this section of the crevasse for it to stay in place for very long. I'm bound to fall further down sooner or later, unless I can jam myself tight. But I still can't exert enough pressure to prevent myself from slowly sliding down. There's no substitute for a sharp pair of crampons here. Unfortunately my snowshoes are still strapped onto my boots. I continue to slide down inside the crevasse, slowly at first, then faster, in a screaming-screech of rucksack straps and buckles scraping along the ice behind me. I've got to increase the pressure on the pick of my ice-axe. But it's no use, it continues to cut a neat useless groove down through the ice in front of my face. I'm brought to a temporary stop as it strikes a rock embedded in the wall of the crevasse. But relief is short-lived as my ice-axe suddenly pulls out of the wall, taking the small rock with it, and I instantly plunge down into the darkness, with the noise of the clattering rock echoing loudly in my ears.

I come to a bone-shattering stop some eight metres down inside the crevasse, landing on my snowshoes which are still tied onto my boots. My snowshoes are side by side now, jammed tightly between the two walls of the crevasse. My knees come up to hit my chest hard. I fight to regain my breath. I can hardly breathe at all now. But I'm still in a position to realize, even in my shocked and battered state, that my snowshoes have most probably saved my life. They have formed a very effective bridge between the two walls of the crevasse, with the front ends embedded deep in the wall of ice facing me, and the back edges wedged even tighter in the wall behind me. At least I've got something to sit down on now. I'll never complain about having to carry heavy and cumbersome snowshoes again. John lent me this pair back in Anchorage. Where on earth he got such an old pair from I don't know. All I know for certain is that I'll take them back to Anchorage with me if it's the last thing that I do. That's the very least I can do for John if they save me from a slow death in the bottom of the crevasse.

But I can't remain kneeling on top of my snowshoe bridge forever. I'm going to need my crampons strapped onto my boots if I'm ever going to climb out of here. The bear continues to observe me. It seems fascinated by every move I make. It watches me put my crampons back on. Our stalemate continues and I begin to grow very cold on my snowshoe perch. But there's nothing that I can do about the cold. There's nothing that I can do about the bear either. All I can do is wait for it to go away. Bears don't have a monopoly on patience.

What I need are some warming up exercises. The trouble is that there's hardly enough room in this part of the crevasse to turn around in, let alone do any exercises. However I notice that it does become wider further along in the direction of a large snow plug. I can't see the bear now. I'm tempted to climb out. The bear might have gone away. Bears have to eat sometime. Then I think, on balance, it would be better if I stayed down here a little while longer. I begin to feel a bit warmer now with my arms wrapped tightly around my knees, lying back against my padded nylon rucksack on my snowshoe bridge. I feel sure that I can wait here for as long as it takes.

Unfortunately, the bear soon returns. I didn't think it would stay away for very long. But what on earth is it doing now? The bear is actually pissing on me! I can't believe it! The bear is urinating into the crevasse directly above me. This can't be happening? That dirty stinking bear! The bright yellow piss showers down all around me. I try to shelter beneath my cagoule. I've got to cover my nose. Bear piss stinks like hell. I watch it fizz each time it strikes the icy cold walls of the crevasse. The ice looks like it's on fire. Is the bear trying to show its utter contempt for me? Or is it trying to mark me with an extra strong scent to give a clear message to any other creatures in the area that I'm spoken for? Well, I've got news for you bastard, I'm not spoken for! I don't belong to anyone!

My usual good humour has somehow deserted me.

Perhaps the bear thinks that the smell will drive me out of the crevasse? But it will have to think again. This is my crevasse. I'm staying here for as long as it takes for the bear to go away. It may be smelly down here. But at least I'm safe. I wonder what people back home would think of a bear pissing on someone? I bet they've never heard of that one before. But home seems a long way off now: somewhere across the vast empty wilderness, somewhere across the other side of the world. The sleep of exhaustion on the other hand is a lot closer.

I feel momentarily confused by my surroundings. I can see that I'm deep inside a crevasse. But which expedition is this one? And which glacier am I on? I must somehow piece together the events of the last few days. What on earth has been happening to me. Very slowly and gradually the awful reality of my situation dawns on me.

I still feel stiff and sore from sitting in the same cramped position on top of my snowshoes all night. The one good thing is that, amazingly, I've had a good night's sleep. But I ache all over. My legs in particular seem to have been stretched to new lengths by the weight of my heavy climbing boots, left on during the night to keep my feet warm. It's clear to me now that I've got to make a move while I'm still in a position to do so. Whether I ache all over now or not doesn't come into this equation. A thin layer of ice has already begun to form on the outer layers of my clothing. This ice adds an even greater emphasis to my thoughts. But where on earth can I possibly go inside my crevasse to get warm? Any move that I make now is obviously fraught with danger and the only place I can realistically move to is the great wedge of snow blocking the crevasse to my right. I can always run up and down on top of the snow plug. But herein lies the real danger. The crevasse becomes wider in the area of this huge snow plug, and this is bound to increase the possibility that the bear may be able to get inside. I'll just have to take a chance here. If I don't make a move soon I'm simply going to freeze. The need to take some warming up exercises and make a warm drink is proving to be a far greater incentive than my fear of the bear. I can always turn around and run back inside the narrowest part of the crevasse if it does come down.

I reach the relative safety of the snow plug after bridging across between the two walls of the crevasse, and feel a great sense of relief at having something solid beneath my feet at last. I must get some exercise now as a first priority. I begin to run up and down the snow plug, some thirty paces out and back. At least I'm starting to get warm again, and thirsty. It's not long before I have my gas stove burning red hot beneath my pan full of ice, to provide me with a large amount of warm drinking water.

There's still no sign of the bear. But I'm beginning to feel a lot warmer. The final drops of water pour down my throat. I even begin to feel quite optimistic about the future. Perhaps the bear has gone off in search of easier prey? If it has gone away this could be the opportunity I've been waiting for. It does seem to be very quiet above. The only way that I'm going to find out is if I go up and look for myself.

I start to front-point my way up the wall of the crevasse. I must move fast if I'm not to become too tired and fall off. The faint strip of light at the top of the crevasse gradually turns into a blaze of brilliant white sunlight. I place an ice-screw into the wall just a short distance below the surface of the glacier. Then I clip a short tape ladder into the eye of the ice-screw. I step very carefully up each rung of the ladder in turn. I can only hope that the ice-screw doesn't squeak when my full weight finally comes onto the top rung. But it makes no sound. I raise myself higher, then peep out over the glacier. There's still no sign of the bear though there are plenty of huge paw prints in the snow. My heart pounds in my chest as I look all around me once more. I'd like to think that I'm fully in control of this situation but I'm not.

I've got to lure Scar Face over into some kind of trap. I can't possibly continue with my journey down the glacier until I've taken care of the bear. But what kind of trap would be able to contain such a monstrous creature? I know full well that if I try to run for it the bear will soon catch me up. Any plan that I formulate now is obviously fraught with danger. The best idea I can come up with is to try and lure the bear over into an unstable area of depression I remember passing on the way up, and hope that the bear following me, being far heavier than I am, will break through into a crevasse before I do. I can think of no better plan of action.

I push down with both my hands, mantelshelfing over the well defined edge of the crevasse into daylight in all its complexity. However the moment I pull my snow-goggles down over my eyes everything comes back into focus. I must untie the rope from the front of my sit-harness. I'm never going to be able to run flat out across the glacier dragging it behind me. Why on earth do I have to tie the knots in my rope so tight? I must hurry up. I must be in full view of the bear. I push and pull on the knot in a desperate attempt to spring it loose. But I can clearly see the bear now! Scar Face is only a short distance away from me on the other side of the crevasse.

The bear has definitely seen me! I quickly spin around. The hot stinking breath of the bear suddenly envelops me. It's the most disgusting smell imaginable. The bear lunges forward towards me, catching me a glancing blow on the side of my climbing helmet, as I jump back inside the crevasse. My rope slips from my fingers, but I'm fortunate in that I fall cleanly through space without hitting the sides and my rope suddenly comes tight at my waist. I'm left hanging upside down from my top runner just a few metres above the snow plug, with the biggest headache imaginable. How on earth did the bear get behind me so fast? It continues to watch me from high above me out on the surface of the glacier. But I'm far too stiff and sore in my head, neck and shoulders to give a damn what it is going to do next.

I remain sitting on the snow plug for some time. I still feel dizzy. The bear has definitely caught me a glancing blow on the side of my climbing helmet. But I must remain conscious at all costs. There's no telling what the bear might do next.

A deathly silence continues to hang over the area of the crevasse. I could sit here forever listening to the silence. But the sound of water pouring over the sides of my cooking pan suddenly spurs me into action. It is full to the brim. How could I have forgotten that I'd left it beneath an icicle to fill up with water? I find I have an enormous thirst. I'll drink till I drown, after warming it up on my gas stove. As I drain the last drops I close my eyes in ecstasy. What a fabulous drink of water this has been. I'll collect some more from beneath another long icicle and have another huge drink later on.

But the bear is inside the crevasse! I can't believe it! Scar Face has somehow managed to gain the far side of the snow plug. I've got to get back inside the narrowest part of the crevasse before it reaches me. I drop my pan in my haste to escape. It lands on top of my gas stove I kick them both over, snatch up my stove—can't survive without that—and hook one of the prongs of the burner through a hole in the aluminium deadman belay plate on the side of my waist-belt. There's a sizzling noise as the hot metal contacts the webbing. But there's no time to stop to deal with that as I scramble along. I don't get very far. I'm brought to a sudden stop by my rope coming tight at my waist. It is still tied into the ice-screw at the top of the crevasse. I find myself being pulled slowly backwards into the snow. I'm never going to make it back to my snowshoe bridge now.

The bear, seeing me in difficulties, makes towards me faster. I'm sure it is about to throw itself at me. I cut the rope at my waist with one decisive blow of my ice-axe, and run back down the full length of the crevasse with the bear almost breathing down my neck. It must surely be within striking distance of me now. The bear lets out a terrible high-pitched scream as it prepares to sink its fangs into the back of my neck. I've had it! I'm never going to make it back into the narrowest part of the crevasse alive. My snowshoe bridge is so close. I can almost see it from here. However it's already too late to reach the safety of the narrowest part of the crevasse. I turn around to face the bear. I'll stab the pick of my ice-axe into its chest. This is going to be a last defiant gesture.

But the bear has stopped running towards me. It has stood on my hot cooking pan and forgotten all about me. All I can hear is my cooking pan being stomped into the ground.

I reach the safety of my snowshoe bridge still jammed between the two enormous walls of the crevasse, test it is still secure, and sit down to take stock in a state of near collapse. The bear is still pounding my cooking pan into the snow plug. That's one pan that's never going to be used to melt snow into water again. There are going to be some thirsty times ahead for me if I get out of here alive. My chest still heaves like hell. At least I'm safe inside the narrowest part of the crevasse. But the bear has got me trapped again now. All I can do is sit here and wait.

The bear remains crouched at the end of the snow plug just metres away. We continue to observe each other. Scar Face must hate me for what I've done. All I know is that I feel so afraid. Even the glacier seems to be holding its breath. Could this be the proverbial calm before the storm? *Please go away! Great bear!* I feel so helpless when faced with such a powerful creature. After taking care of my cooking pan the bear seems intent on taking care of me.

It begins to pound its two massive front paws into the snow close to the edge of the snow plug. I look on in horror as it repeats its actions. I can only hope that the snow plug will collapse under its blows. But it remains firm. The bear is working itself up into a fury. It stops moving, and I can see it is actually foaming at the mouth. Vile green saliva dribbles over its jaws. It must be utterly mad now, driven crazy by the hatred that it feels for me. The look on its face has only one meaning—that I must be wiped off the face of the earth!

My axes are already hooked into the walls of the crevasse, one on either side of me. Their downward sloping picks should be sufficient to hold me in place on top of my snowshoe bridge should the bear decide to charge. The bear continues to wait. I continue to hold my breath.

Then suddenly, without any warning at all, the bear charges forward towards me, tearing into the narrowest part of the crevasse with its claws, hooked into the walls of ice on either side, acting as effectively as any crampons I have ever seen. The shoulders of the great bear strike the walls of the crevasse just where they begin to converge. The force of the impact is enormous. A huge shock wave is sent racing down the full length of the crevasse. My snowshoe bridge begins to shake. I shake. Then some large pieces of ice begin to fall down from somewhere high above me near the top of the crevasse. The bear gets the full force of all this snow and ice upon its head and shoulders. But it simply shrugs this debris off as if it were of no consequence at all. It continues to squeeze forward towards me until it can advance no more.

The bear is now jammed tightly in between the two converging walls of the crevasse just a short distance in front of me. It begins to heave and strain with all the strength and determination at its disposal, trying to force the two walls of the crevasse apart. Surely the bear is never going to be able to succeed? But I begin to have doubts about the end result of this great trial of strength. All I know for sure is that if it does manage to squeeze any further forward towards me, even by a small amount, I can't retreat any further back inside the crevasse. The section behind me is too narrow to admit anything. The bear's eyes begin to bulge with the effort of trying to force the two walls of the crevasse apart. I still can't believe that it will be able to squeeze any further forward towards me.

You'll never reach me inside here! Bastard!

My snowshoe bridge begins to slip very slowly further down inside the crevasse. I move down with it. *Jesus Christ!* The two walls of the crevasse are moving apart! This movement is not very much, perhaps a few centimetres at the most, but my snowshoe bridge is definitely slipping further down inside the crevasse.

I know what I must do next. I need to find my matches. (I'm sure I left a box inside one of the pockets on the outside of my rucksack.)

I've no wish to harm you great bear! Just leave me alone!

I back off to the very edge of my snowshoe bridge. I can't possibly move any further back now. The bear doesn't wait for a single moment. It suddenly reaches out with its long forelegs, claws at the ready, in a frenzied attempt to hook me off the top of my platform. Surely it will get its claws into my clothing at any moment now? I watch helplessly as the bear begins to squeeze even further forward towards me. This is the most amazing show of strength I have ever seen. I would never have believed that it could have got so close. There must be a look of absolute horror on my face now. The eyes of the bear continue to burn into me.

I pull my ice-axe out of the wall of the crevasse and stab at the bear's hairy forelegs in a desperate attempt to keep it at bay. But the pick of my ice-axe isn't long enough to have any real effect. The thick mat of hairs acts like a spongy armour plating to absorb my blows. I finally give up trying to fend it off with my ice-axe. I let go of my ice-hammer, still hooked into the wall of the crevasse beside me. I need both my hands free. But I won't be beaten here. I reach down for my gas stove, still hooked into a hole in the deadman plate on my waist-belt.

I'm truly sorry great bear! I've got no choice in the matter of what I must do next!

I slowly unscrew the burner on top of the gas cylinder. The liquid propane gas begins to squirt upwards out of the hole in the top of the cylinder the moment I expose it. It's now or never! I strike the match. The bear instinctively pulls back at the first sniff of this explosive mixture. But its reactions are too slow to save it. The mixture ignites. I hurl my gas stove like a flame-thrower into the face of the screaming bear. Its entire upper body is instantly enveloped in a red hot flaming fireball.

The heat is intense. But my head is already turned away. I cover my face with my arms. My eyes are closed. But I don't need to see anything to know what is happening to the bear. A long wailing sound follows in its wake as it runs back down the full length of the crevasse. I turn around to look the moment the heat from my exploding gas cylinder dies down. The bear is still clawing at its face. The metal prongs on top of my gas stove have somehow caught on its claws with the flames still licking up the full length of its left foreleg. It's a terrible sight to behold. The bear gradually retreats from view.

Water continues to run down the walls of the crevasse, melted by the heat of the explosion. I take a drink of water from an icicle close to hand. I think that I'll always hate myself for what I've just done. But I had no choice in the matter.

There is still no sign of the bear.

I'll never have a better chance of escaping from here. I must climb out of the crevasse now, while the bear is still occupied with its burns and trying to remove my gas stove from its claws. Then I must put my earlier plan into action. I have got to get rid of the bear. I must try to lure it to its death.

I'm left gasping for breath after front-pointing my way up the wall of the crevasse in one long pitch. I haven't a moment to lose. The bear could return at any moment, and once I stand upright on the surface of the glacier there's no hiding place. What I have to do is take advantage of some nearby dodgy ground I noticed on my way up. It forms a crater-like depression which probably held a lake at some time in the past. The floor must be riddled with crevasses to drain the water. In the centre there's a tower of ice. If I can get to that tower without going through the surface myself, I can climb it, lure the bear into the crater after me and wait for its body weight to do the rest.

I hesitate over jumping into the huge crater. But I don't really have any choice in the matter of what I must do next. I jump down onto the floor of the depression. My heart pounds in my chest. Whatever I do I mustn't lose my nerve here. I arrive at the base of the tower sweating with fear. I'm sure the ice moved beneath me on several occasions as I ran across the floor of the depression. But I must climb up on top of the tower now before the bear comes back. I literally throw myself up at the wall of ice, front-pointing my way up towards the top. I glance behind me. There's still no sign of the bear.

The top of the tower is as flat as a billiard table and not much larger. I lie back in the snow and close my eyes for a moment. I must rest before I do anything else. I ache all over now. Where has Scar Face got to? It definitely isn't inside the moat-like depression surrounding me. At least I'm safe up here on top of the tower. I sit down on top of my rucksack to wait.

What a marvellous view I've got of every feature on the surface of the glacier from up here. I can see for several kilometres in all directions. If only the sun would appear. Unfortunately there's nothing but a thin blanket of grey cloud drifting past low over my head. No sun, no chance of a decent meal to warm me either. I've only got three small pieces of white candle wax left to eat. They are meant to last me for three days, half a candle per day.

There's no reason why I shouldn't eat today's ration now. The small piece of wax tastes wool in my mouth. Now I've only got two pieces left to eat. All I can do is dream about food perched on my rucksack on top of my pillar. My right hand is moving. It reaches inside my trouser pocket. I can't seem to stop my hand from lifting the two remaining small pieces of candle wax out of my pocket. But if I eat them now I'll have nothing left. I squeeze the two pieces together in one wedge. I seem mesmerised by the sight of food. I mustn't eat tomorrow's candle wax! *For God's sake don't do it, David!* I begin to plead with myself. *Please don't eat it!* But my right hand refuses to obey and places the wax in my mouth. Any claim I've had of strong willpower simply evaporates. I bite hard into the soft white candle wax. It seems to taste of anything that I've ever dreamed of eating. But my willpower has been broken. Two small pieces of white candle wax have managed to do to me what nothing has ever succeeded in doing before. The effect on my morale is shattering.

Self-discipline is what I have always prided myself on. It has helped me not to give up in tight corners in the Alps as well as Alaska. It has helped save other lives than mine. I have never given up the struggle before. My survival to this day has all been the result of discipline! The ultimate test is here and now! If I swallow this candle wax, I tell myself, I will be finished! I will simply die out here! Perhaps I've waited all my life to be tested in this way. The candle wax is still in my mouth. I have a clear choice. I can simply eat it now and choose to die out here in the mountains. Or I can spit it out of my mouth and choose to live.

I watch mesmerized as the sweet-tasting candle wax falls straight down the side of the tower. Tears form in my eyes now. I'm crying because I've got nothing left to eat. There are tears in my eyes also for a smouldering grizzly bear. But they are a small price to pay for the return of my willpower. I was once told that wherever the mind goes, the body follows. In spitting the candle wax out of my mouth I have decided to go all the way to Anchorage and beyond.

I can see the bear now and it is definitely coming towards me. All I've got to do is blow my whistle in order to attract it over into the moat. But I'm still far too afraid to blow it. I'm still fearful what the bear may do next. My whistle remains frozen in between my lips. No sound comes out of the end.

The bear continues to lumber forward towards me. Then it comes up against the edge of the crevasse that was the scene of our last encounter. The bear stops just once to sniff the air, as it pads along the rim, and to run a huge paw in a cat-like way over its burnt face. It is still too far away from me for me to see the real extent of its injuries. Then it begins to roll over and over in the snow. It must be trying to get some relief from the burns inflicted by my flaming gas cylinder. I can see the damage to the bear's upper body now. It doesn't look to be too severe. Its thick shaggy coat has obviously saved it from far worse injuries. I'm glad in a way, part of me has never wanted to harm it and still recoils at having to do so.

The bear remains lying down in the snow for some time, still unaware of my presence on top of the tower. I must somehow entice it over into my trap, but I still can't pluck up the courage to blow my whistle. Then the bear stretches and continues to prowl forward along the edge of the crevasse, getting closer to me all the time, stopping occasionally to look down into the darkness within the crevasse itself, staring intently down into the icy cold depths below, sniffing the air, looking for me.

The bear still hasn't noticed me on top of the tower. I'm still the silent observer trying to plot its downfall. I'm going to have to use myself as live bait in order to lure it over into the unstable area of the crater. I can only hope that it breaks through into a crevasse quickly, because if it does get across the floor of the depression unscathed, it might, I now realize, just be able to reach up to the top of the tower. But that thought is too awful to contemplate. I must act now before I lose my nerve here completely. I raise my plastic whistle to my lips. I take a long deep breath. But no sound comes out of the end.

At this point the bear comes across my trail in the snow, leading away from the edge of the crevasse in the direction of the depression. Its coat literally begins to bristle. Then the bear lets out a tremendous roar. Scar Face sniffs the air once more before bounding off along my trail towards me until it finally spots me on top of the tower and stops dead in its tracks on the very edge of the moat-like depression to stare up at me.

I can clearly see the bear's face now. It has been completely distorted by the fierce heat of my exploding gas cylinder. Small puffs of smoke can still be seen coming out from beneath the bear's smouldering bodily hair to shroud its melted facial features. It's a terrible sight. The bear has not been mortally injured, but it has been even more disfigured. There's nothing more that I can do now but wait.

The bear begins to prowl up and down the far edge of the moat and I, needing to do something to ease the tension, begin to walk around the top of my tower. Before I know it I find we are tracking each other, each prowling round in perfect circles, with me walking a small one on my tower and the bear having to cover a far larger distance around the edge of the crater—and yet still striving to keep up with me. The bear is very determined in its efforts. We remain locked together, with only the width of the moat separating us, until I start to slow down. The bear starts to slow down also. So it is definitely trying to compete with me. As if mesmerized by this horrific game we are playing, I break into a run, just for the hell of it. The bear is having to move extremely fast now in order to keep up with me.

The bear is definitely trying to race me. But if there is a race, there has to be a winner, and I hold the initiative in this race. Whoever holds the initiative in any race usually wins. "You're never going to be able to keep up with me now, bastard!" I shout across at the bear as I run even faster, with the bear having to take great bounding leaps in order to keep up. But this bizarre race can't go on forever. As if acknowledging the fact, the bear brakes to a furious halt, screaming at me with its two huge front paws slamming into the ice on the edge of the depression. It seems to be going absolutely crazy now. It backs off and charges back to the edge of the moat. Though it can't possibly jump the gap separating us, I take several quick steps backwards, almost falling off the top of the tower in my fright. I never expected it to move so fast. It's a good job that this charge was only a bluff.

This is one game that is definitely over.

I'm left with a terrible feeling that all hell is about to break loose. I must put my plan into action before I lose my nerve completely. I begin to taunt the bear. I sit on top of my rucksack with my legs dangling down over the edge of the huge block of ice. "Come on, bastard! Get my legs if you dare!" The bear continues to prowl up and down the edge of the depression, completely ignoring me now. It must be able to see my legs dangling down so invitingly. "Come on, bastard! Do something!" But it still refuses to leave the relative safety of the glacier.

I've a terrible feeling that my plan is not going to work. If the bear stays where it is on the glacier, I'll be the one that's trapped on top of the tower. I think I'll have a drink of water while I'm waiting. I turn round to look for my water-bottle inside my rucksack. I'm sure that I placed it inside one of my woollen jumpers in order to stop it freezing. The moment I turn my back the bear moves. I'm sure I heard it drop down into the moat. But I mustn't turn around yet. I've got to keep my nerve here. I must give it a clear chance of falling through into a crevasse. I can still hear it moving across the floor of the depression. It must be getting close to me now. Then suddenly the bear is directly beneath me.

It hurls itself up at my legs dangling down temptingly over the side of the tower. I only just manage to lift them up in time. The bear's claws slam into the wall of ice beneath me. The tower shakes. I drop my water-bottle in sheer fright. The bear falls backwards into the depression. But it hasn't fallen through into a crevasse. My plan to trap it is clearly not going to work. The bear slowly regains its feet. But where has it got to? I throw myself flat on top of the tower. Scar Face is nowhere to be seen. I drive the pick of my ice-axe deep into the ice on top of the tower. I don't want to be thrown off when it makes its next move. But I must find out which side the bear is trying to climb up. I must be ready for it when it appears over the top of the tower. I grasp the head of my ice-axe even tighter now. I hardly dare look down into the depression. But I've got to do that if I'm to find out which wall of the tower the bear is trying to climb up. It is definitely not beneath this one. But there are three others. I crawl slowly across towards the opposite side of the tower after changing hands on the head of my ice-axe. The bear's not beneath this one either. It could even be moving around in order to confuse me.

The bear's claws suddenly appear over the edge directly in front of my face. I immediately stab the pick of my ice-axe into one of its paws. It lets out a scream and falls backwards into the depression, fortunately not taking my ice-axe with it. I must see where it has landed before it has a chance to recover. But the bear is far too quick for me. It is already on its feet and immediately throws itself up at the same wall. There's a tremendous crash as it strikes the iron hard ice. The tower shakes once more. My water-bottle slides off the top of the tower. But I'm already braced lying down and far too slow to save it. I'm left hanging onto the pick of my ice-axe as if my very life depended upon it.

My legs begin to swing over to one side of the tower as it starts to lean over at an alarming angle to the wall of ice surrounding the depression. I pull myself back towards the centre of the top of the tower, using the picks on both my axes. There's another loud crash as the bear strikes the tower and its huge hairy paws suddenly reappear. My heart pounds in my chest as I bring the pick of my ice-hammer slicing down into one of the bear's forelegs this time. It screams out loud. Blood spurts everywhere. Then it falls backwards off the side of the tower with another reverberating crash. My ice-hammer is torn from my grasp, caught up in the thick mat of blood-stained hairs on the bear's left leg. It flies across the full width of the moat, landing somewhere on the glacier. That's done it now! I'm going to need my ice-hammer if I'm ever going to climb out of here. I grasp my ice-axe even tighter. If I lose them both I'm never going to be able to escape from here. I could find myself trapped inside the depression forever.

The tower is clearly moving beneath me. The bear is trying to push it over. It roars up at me, a terrible high pitched scream as it pushes against the side of the tower, causing it to rock ever so gently back and forth. I dig the front-points on my crampons deeper into the ice. I must stop my legs from swinging over the edge of the tower. But the huge block of ice suddenly stops moving. It is left tilted over at a frightening angle. Why has the bear stopped pushing? It suddenly goes very quiet. But not for long. The bear suddenly starts to pound on the side of the tower with its two massive front paws. The vibrations pass up the full length of the huge block of ice until I can feel each individual one in my knees and forearms which are pressed hard into the ice. There are some terrible noises coming from deep within the base of the huge block of ice now. It groans and starts to lean over even further. I begin to realize that it's only a matter of time before I'm tipped off the top. There's nothing that I can do about it other than to hang on to the head of my ice-axe and hope for a miracle to occur.

The bear goes quiet once more. What is it up to now? Then I hear a very definite droning coming from somewhere lower down on the glacier. The bear must be listening to this same noise. The droning becomes louder. Then louder and louder still. The complete valley floor is filled with the noise of an aircraft coming directly up the glacier towards me. I can see it approaching the top of a barrier of séracs lower down on the glacier now. It has got to pass directly overhead. I must signal to the pilot. I begin to wave my rucksack, holding it in my one free hand. I still daren't let go of my ice-axe. I'm sure that the pilot will land on the glacier if he sees I am in trouble. He can then shoot the bear. He is bound to have a rifle with him as part of his standard survival kit. So I continue to wave like hell, as the aircraft approaches me through a small gap in the clouds, wings glistening in the bright sunlight. There's the distinct possibility that John could be the pilot. He could be looking for me now. "I'm over here, John!" I begin to shout futiley up at the aircraft.

The aircraft passes directly over the top of my head and enters the clouds once more. The pilot has obviously had to gain altitude in order to clear the summit of Mount Deborah at the head of the glacier. I doubt he will be coming back in my direction today. The noise from the aircraft gradually fades into oblivion, and I return to guessing from which direction I am next going to be attacked by the bear.

The bear starts to pound on the side of the tower once more and large cracks begin to appear in each of the four corners, then radiate towards me. The tower is definitely starting to fall to pieces. The top of the huge block of ice is no longer the safe haven that it once was. I've simply got to take my chances in the depression. I'll jump down at the first opportunity and run for it. But there's no point in kidding myself either. I know full well that I'm never going to be able to outrun the bear. As the tower begins to tilt over even further, there's hardly any time left to put my plan into action. I'm left hanging from the shaft of my ice-axe with my legs dangling very close to the ground. I must climb up onto the highest corner of the tower before the bear gets its claws into my legs. Scar Face is already directly beneath me. I fancy there's a horrendous expression of triumph on its snarling face as it reaches up for my legs. But the bear misses them at its first attempt. I lift them higher up towards my chest now. Scar Face doesn't hesitate for a single moment before leaping high into the air once more. This time the bear hooks its claws into the edge of the tower close to my legs. I've got to stab the pick of my ice-axe into its skull the moment it appears on top of the tower. I'll use the pick like a knife. I'm never going to get another opportunity to kill the bear. This is my only chance of staying alive.

The bear lets out a victorious roar as it pulls up over the side of the tower to confront me. I raise the pick of my ice-axe high above my head. But the weight of the bear is already proving to be too much for the tower, leaning over as it already is in the most dramatic manner possible. I have to let go of my ice-axe to grasp the edge of the tower with both my hands as it slowly begins to topple over, landing on top of the screaming bear. Scar Face must surely be crushed beneath the tower now. I slide slowly backwards, down the sloping side of the tower, landing safely in the snow, next to my water-bottle. There's a long hideous wail coming from the bear. The ground begins to shake. Then the main bulk of the tower itself begins to tremble. I hardly dare open my eyes as I shelter beneath one of its toppled walls.

The noise of falling debris gradually subsides. There's a new equilibrium in the depression now. There's a new order around the base of the tower.

I feel an immense sense of relief with the bear at last destroyed under what must be one of the world's largest tombstones. If only I had the time to carve out an epitaph on this monstrous block of ice, I'd write the simple words, "In memory of a great bear!"

from Above the Clouds
by Anatoli Boukreev

Russian climber Anatoli Boukreev (1958-1997)

climbed 11 of the world's fourteen 8,000-meter

peaks during the last decade of his life. This story

from a collection of his writings describes a 1993

climb on the notoriously dangerous K2, the

world's second-highest mountain.

I arrived in Moscow on May 28. The cumbersomely ineffective bureaucracy seemed to be the only thing left operating normally from the Soviet era. After spending a week resolving the numerous problems associated with my passport and obtaining visas for the trip, I took a train to Bremen. The ticket cost a little more than $100. That was a relief. I had $500 in my pocket. I changed trains in Warsaw, and leaving behind the last outlines of hills or mountains, I watched perfectly flat North Sea coastland fly past the window for hours. On June 13, I arrived in a charming German town. Crowded, spotlessly clean streets were full of people going about their business on bicycles. The monument in the Bremen town square honored fabled animal musicians, not war heroes.

The time that had passed since our previous meeting had not changed Reinmar Joswig. Though fifty years old, his physique would have caused envy in someone thirty. In Bremen he religiously avoided any kind of motorized transportation, preferring to ride his bike from place to place. A dedication to fitness had allowed him to make it to the top of several 8,000-meter peaks: Gasherbrum I, Broad Peak, and Nanga Parbat. Many of our expedition's logistical details fell on Reinmar's shoulders. He managed them all with typical

German precision. In the final days before our departure, I helped pack the equipment that had not been shipped earlier with our main baggage. Undisturbed by a thousand last-minute details that would have driven me crazy, Reinmar found the time to train every day.

His climbing partner on Nanga Parbat and longtime friend Peter Metzger was our expedition coleader. After meeting Peter, I was confident that our leadership was strong and wholesome. The personalities of these two good men complemented each other: Metzger was charismatic and possessed boundless energy, while Reinmar had a quiet strength and calmness that was reassuring.

On June 18 we took a train to the Frankfurt airport. There we were joined by the fourth member of our group. Though lacking his friends' depth of experience on 8,000-meter peaks, fifty-four-year-old Ernst Eberhardt's success on a hard, high peak in India's Himachal Pradesh had inspired him to try K2. I found Ernst easy to talk with; he had a wonderful full beard that gave him a genial look. His mild manner and patience proved to be blessings, helping to solve the many problems that confronted us during our sojourn in Pakistan.

After a six-hour flight, the four of us stepped off the plane into the sweltering heat of the Islamabad night. Foul-smelling city air fell on us like a blanket. When we claimed our baggage, Ernst's pack containing all his climbing gear was missing. Mishaps would not end there; they were only beginning.

We settled into the Holiday, a pretty good hotel in Rawalpindi, the old city next to Islamabad. The next morning our expedition agent, Ashrif Aman, welcomed us with more bad news. He had been unable to notify our government liaison officer that Reinmar had changed our arrival date. We were stuck. Foreign expeditions are forbidden to travel in the sensitive border regions around K2 without an army officer to report on expedition progress and assist in solving problems with the local citizens. Peter and Reinmar spent the next four days at the Ministry of Tourism lobbying for a new officer.

I laid out my financial situation for Ashrif. Being a mountaineer (he was the first Pakistani to summit K2), he was sympathetic. He convinced me the most interesting way for me to return to Almaty was overland through the Hunza region and Sinkiang. Land transportation was cheap. The Chinese controlled Sinkiang, so I spent my time in their consulate trying to obtain a transit visa for my trip home to Kazakhstan. Ernst made daily visits to the airport until he recovered his backpack and equipment.

Andy Locke, the last member of our expedition, joined us. At the last moment Reinmar had included this pleasant, muscular Australian policeman on our permit. At thirty, he was the youngest person on the team. I had become acquainted with Andy during my time at Everest Base Camp in 1991. He arrived in Rawalpindi straight from his second unsuccessful attempt to climb Mount Everest. Though he was tired, several nights at the South Col had given him the advantage of excellent acclimatization. As events unfolded, we had plenty of time to rest before there was any work to do.

After five days in Rawalpindi, we breathed a sigh of relief when an official at the Ministry of Tourism assigned us a new officer, only to be disappointed that he could not arrive in the capital until June 26. With that problem partially resolved, none of us had any desire to wait in the city suffering the heat. Peter volunteered to stay to meet the officer.

His sacrifice liberated the rest our party to fly to Skardu, the last refuge of civilization on the trail to K2. There the countryside and traditional Moslem culture was reminiscent of the pleasant villages in Tajikistan in the southwestern Pamirs where I had done a lot of climbing. Eternal snows on an embrace of high peaks made the air clean and cool. Our roomy accommodations at the Sehr Motel were simple and comfortable. Peter called to confirm that he and our new officer would arrive on June 28.

We settled down and made the best of the delay. The next portion of the journey was by jeep over a rough dirt track to the village of Askole. There everything would be loaded on the backs of porters for the trip to Base Camp. All supplies and equipment had to be repacked into 25-kilogram loads for the porters. Thanks to Reinmar and Peter's lists of what, where, and how much to put into each load, we finished that job quickly in Skardu.

During our stay, a helicopter arrived, evacuating from K2 Base Camp a doctor and two Slovenian climbers who had bad frostbite. Their black, shriveled feet appeared all too familiar; it was clear to me that most of their toes would have to be amputated. These men had reputations as excellent mountaineers, so their predicament increased my motivation to stay in shape. Each morning I ran for an hour along the banks of the Indus River, which flowed by the edge of town. In the evenings, I climbed to the rock ridges of the nearest mountains. Reinmar continued his training routine as well. The delay did not tell on our physical readiness, but our vacation would haunt us in other ways throughout the expedition.

Toyota jeeps loaded down with us and all our supplies left Skardu for Askole on the twenty-ninth. Bad weather had caused all the flights from Islamabad to be canceled. Peter and the new officer raced to catch up with us by car. Finally joining us in Askole, the officer assembled sixty-seven porters. Each man was assigned a load and a ration of food, and at last we set off on the trail to Base Camp. Given our earlier experiences, things went pretty smoothly on the trek. Enjoying the hot, sunny weather, our small army traveled seven days through the mystical countryside. It is impossible to do justice with words to the grandeur of the mountains along Baltoro Glacier. Nothing compares to that place; the stone towers and rocks are mysterious and wonderful. By day six we arrived where two great glacial rivers, the Godwin Austen and the Upper Baltoro, flowed together. As we camped at Concordia, the imposing pyramid of K2 dominated the view and our imaginations.

Following the Godwin Austen glacier another eight miles, we arrived at the site that would serve as home for the next six weeks. Though most of expeditions camped on the glacier had been working for several weeks before we arrived, only two groups had managed to climb higher than Camp II.

In two days of sunny weather when we were setting up camp, three members of a Canadian-American team summited. Tragedy did not pass them by; one of the Canadians fell to his death descending the slopes above the snow-burdened bottleneck couloir. The members of the Slovenian team were descending from the summit. In addition to the men who had suffered frostbite, they lost one member of their group to complications from cerebral edema. A Dutch team aided by expensive high-altitude porters and a well-equipped Swedish group had gotten no farther than camp at 6,500 meters. With satellite communication to their homeland, the Swedes had the advantage of accurate weather information for the area. Three friends from Great Britain, Victor Saunders, Julie Clyma, and Roger Payne, had established their first camp. Like us, all those expeditions were climbing K2 via the Abruzzi route. My American friend Dan Mazur was leading a big team of international climbers attempting the West Ridge. Other, smaller groups were trying harder routes. About one hundred mountaineers were camped below K2 with us. Its history had nothing to recall like that. The permit fee in 1994 was going to cost three times more than what we had paid; that was the reason for the invasion.

We spent July 6 and 7 setting up a kitchen and dining area and sorting out supplies. Separating gas, equipment, and food into high-camp loads occupied my time, but I made a special effort to locate Dan Mazur in the maze of tents around us. For almost a month in the fall of 1991, Dan and I had lived together on the Khumbu Glacier in Nepal. High-altitude mountaineers are a small group. Our friendships are formed under unusual circumstances. It seems there are no foreigners among us. Men and women are judged not for what they have or where they come from, but who they are in hard circumstances. We meet in remote camps, a community of individuals with strange, difficult ambitions and a peculiar appetite for mountaineering life. For me the opportunity to reacquaint with old friends is important. The positive emotions I experience in these encounters give me an unusual charge of strength and energy.

Eager to get started, on July 8 we were up at 2 a.m. We left camp at three-thirty after eating breakfast. On our backs were the supplies we needed to set up Camp I. We crossed the glacier in two hours, following a trail well marked by members of previous expeditions. Like the other teams on our route, we climbed to Camp I having been spared the effort of fixing line on the steep section above the glacier. We had the Slovenians and the Americans and the Canadians to thank for that.

Peter and Andy climbed ahead of me. When Peter stopped to make radio contact with our Base Camp, I went ahead, trading places with Andy. Working in the lead is slow and tiring. Every step you must kneel into the loose snow above you to compress it, so there will be some traction for your crampons when you step up. That day the snow was not too deep and we shared the work. At about nine-thirty we arrived on a flat snow-plain where the other expeditions had set up their first high-altitude camp. All the level areas were occupied. After locating a suitable gentle slope, we worked together digging out tent platforms. Ice underlay the fresh snow, and the work was tiresome. The weather steadily deteriorated until we were working in horizontally blowing snow. Julie Clyma and Roger Payne, who were acclimatizing in their tents at Camp I, decided to head down. Rapidly securing our supplies, we followed them back to Base Camp. The weather got much worse before it got better.

In the night, a heavy accumulation of new snow and the force of the gusting wind collapsed the roof of our kitchen. From 5 until 10 a.m. we worked rebuilding it. Snow fell continuously for four more days. That delay weighed heavily on Peter's and Reinmar's nerves. The clock was ticking; we had a limited time to accomplish our goal. Reinmar was scheduled to leave for Germany on August 18. Because of his work, that date could not be changed. Confined to our tents, we passed days restlessly inactive. Occasionally, the monotony was broken by a visit from climbers on other expeditions. Hospitality would prompt us to move to more comfortable surroundings in the mess tent. For a time the delay would be forgotten in the diversion of our stories and conversations.

At eleven in the morning on the thirteenth, the weather improved. Carrying a load of supplies, we decided to forge a new trail to the beginning of the fixed rope. The glacier was covered in deep new snow that lay like icing on a treacherous cake. No trace of the many crevasses marked the smooth surface; our progress had to be slow and deliberate. I worked first, testing the snow, cautiously probing with my ski poles to reassure myself that the next weighted step would not be into a frozen abyss.

We returned to camp about dinnertime and accepted an invitation to dinner from the Canadian-American team. Though three members of their expedition, Phil Powers, Dan Culver, and Jim Haberl, had summited, there was no mood of victory or celebration in their tents. Dan Culver had paid for the summit with his life. He was remembered fondly by Phil Powers and his other teammates. In conversations that night we listened to the questions mountaineers ask in such times: "Do we need to return to the summits above the clouds?" "Is this risk of life necessary?" We said good-night to those companionable men. A jar of honey and a part of the grief over the death of their friend were the gifts we took back to our tents. Each of us had new feelings and a clear awareness that danger awaited us as well, somewhere at the top.

At 3:30 a.m. we were at the breakfast table, after which we shouldered heavy loads of supplies for our high camps and crossed the glacier on our newly broken trail. Ascending the next steep section where before we enjoyed the fixed rope was difficult. Sinking with a heavy pack through waist-deep snow, the leader had to wade forward, compress a new step, liberate the frozen, buried rope, and pull it up to the surface. By noon we had made it up to Camp I and set up two tents. The weather was excellent, clear and calm, and our spirits were high.

After lunch and a short rest, I asked Peter and Reinmar if I could carry an eight-kilogram load with two tents up to 6,700 meters. They gave me permission, though they were mystified why after such a long, hard day I wanted to go higher. I was aware that my capacity for work would drop dramatically for the next two days while my body adjusted to a higher elevation. My rationale was that if I could accomplish the work in good spirits that afternoon, I should not delay until the next day when the same job would feel much more difficult. Thanks to the time on McKinley, carrying a regular load to 6,500 meters had not bothered me. Our many days of forced inactivity left me feeling I had rested enough for a month.

I set out from camp at four o'clock, enjoying a hard crust on the névé snow that made climbing easy. In two hours I reached a band of steep, yellow rocks. Phil Powers had advised me that above those yellow rocks at 6,800 meters we would find the best location for Camp II. I secured my load in a protected place, and one-half hour later I was back in camp. My teammates had eaten and were comfortably resting in their sleeping bags. I drank some tea and ate a little food. Sleep came quickly without problem.

After years of self-analysis, I know that the ability to fall asleep after hard work is an indication that my body is properly adjusting to the altitude. Difficulty falling asleep indicates that I must reduce the stress on my body and slow down the rate of my ascent. In general, I am so accustomed to exercise that I cannot sleep if I do not work hard enough during the day. Though the process is different for each individual, I think that if you maintain a normal pulse rate and can rehabilitate by sleeping well, you should work until you feel a pleasant tiredness, even at high altitude. Then the body accepts rest as a joy.

Of course, this rule does not apply to anyone who is ill in the mountains. It is crucial for an athlete and especially a mountaineer to listen to his body, to feel it intuitively. Though it is possible to overcome fatigue with inner motivation in the early stages of an expedition, too much work is unnatural and can affect resilience. Serious fatigue can go unnoticed by someone who is physically fit. No dramatic effect from overwork will be appreciated until it is too late. I know from personal experience that fatigue subtly accumulates in the body, only to manifest at the most stressful moments, usually up high. Insidiously it can leave you without strength and the ability to perform. In mountaineering, much that happens and many decisions depend on external factors over which we have no control, such as the weather and the conditions on the route. The most important individual responsibility on an expedition is balancing personal needs so you maintain your strength and health while still performing in accord with the group's desires and objectives.

The next morning after a leisurely breakfast we left our tents at nine o'clock. True to my intuition, my load felt heavier and I could not maintain my previous day's speed. The weather was no help. We unloaded our supplies at Camp II in the kind of gusting wind that comes before a squall. That afternoon the trip down to Camp I took an hour instead of thirty minutes. Everyone was moving slower.

I arrived at the tents ahead of my friends. Ernst and I began fixing dinner. Not feeling well, he had turned back halfway to Camp II. At his age it was natural for him to require a longer period to adjust to increases in elevation. Andy reported that he was not experiencing problems with the new altitude, not surprising since he had recently camped at eight thousand meters on Everest. When they arrived, looking really fit, Reinmar and Peter said they felt well. They were not novices and knew what to expect of their bodies, thanks to a good foundation of experience at high altitude. Judging from the huge supply of food we had carried up, I could see that they had no problems with digestion.

Appetite at high altitude is an individual thing. For me it is generally best to consume as little as possible, and then only those foods that are metabolized quickly. That night I tried to joke with Reinmar, saying that if we ate half the store of provisions we had carried up, our bodies would be so occupied digesting that we would have no ambition to make it to the summit. That was taken as a criticism. Because of nuances in languages, it was easy for us to misunderstand one another in subtle ways. We used English to communicate, which, except for Andy, was not anyone's native tongue. Reinmar was comfortable speaking it, but my English is far from good. The effort we each had to make to understand one another created a fatigue of sorts.

The sixteenth greeted us with miserable weather. I made hot chocolate for breakfast. Certain we were going down, I wanted to hold out for flat-bread chapatis and eggs at Base Camp. Reinmar and Peter were ready to carry up another load of supplies to Camp II. I thought we would be better off waiting out the bad weather in Base Camp. At the lower elevation our bodies could recuperate from the previous days of hard work. When the weather improved and we were rested, a big supply carry to Camp II would be easier. Then, after one night sleeping at Camp II, we would be acclimated well enough to go up the next increment of elevation. Offhand, I remarked that if we exhausted ourselves carrying loads high in bad weather, we could be compromising our ability to climb when the weather improved.

Reinmar had a short answer to that: "If you are feeling tired, then you should go down and rest, but the team is going up."

I did not think I felt any weaker that anyone else, so I gave up trying to make my point of view understood. I broke trail for them in fresh falling snow. Behind me, Reimnar and Peter were slow; the days of work without respite had affected their pace. My intuition and experience were telling me we needed time for rehabilitation after carrying so much weight to 6,800 meters.

Despite my concerns, I sympathized with their point of view. Peter and Reinmar had committed great effort and energy to organizing the expedition for all of us. Certainly I had contributed nothing in those areas. The bad weather ate up many of our days. It would have been unfair if after so much work they did not have time for an assault on the summit. Reinmar's departure deadline hung over us and influenced all our decisions. Willingly, I cooperated with them. They were my leaders and were responsible for our climbing plan. I wanted to work for them and for our success.

Initially, I presented a completely different acclimatization strategy for their consideration. Appreciating the problems that the delays in Islamabad and the weather had cost our expedition, I suggested we focus on achieving a good acclimatization. I thought we should make a schedule of trips to allow our bodies to adapt to each new level of altitude before beginning to carry up the heavy supplies. I suggested we should carry minimum food and equipment to Camp I, spend the night, and go on to Camp II at 6,800 meters, sleep one night, and descend to rest at Base Camp. Then subsequent trips to 6,800 meters carrying weight would be easier for our bodies. We could ferry up summit-day supplies to Camp II before going on with minimum supplies to acclimate at 7,300 for a night, come down again, and move the loads up to 7,300 when we went up for the final acclimatization trip to 7,900 meters. That way we would have preliminary acclimatization at the level of our last camp, and we could climb lightly loaded to 7,300 meters on the summit bid.

I did not invent this scheme. It was tested and proven by many men on tens of Soviet expeditions to 7,000- and 8,000-meter-high peaks. From my first steps as a mountaineer in the Almaty club, our experienced coaches taught me that formula.* It had worked for me on every expedition. Our experience proved that multiple nights at progressively higher altitudes without descending for the body to recuperate was a less effective method. Actually, that kind of advance diminished the body's ability to perform work. In prolonged oxygen-deprived circumstances, working to capacity, lactic acid and other waste products build up in the muscles, which produces weakness and fatigue. Sleeping and eating at high altitude, one cannot replenish the body's energy stores or eliminate waste. Digesting complex food at high altitude, the body actually spends energy, and many foods cannot be digested in that atmosphere. A fit body is naturally resilient and responds to rest at lower altitude.

Properly acclimatized, like me, Peter, Reinmar, and Andy were able

---

* The heart of the Soviet school's scheme for climbing high was a pattern of acclimatization and rehabilitation. A plan was developed relevant to the height of the peak and the speed those climbing could travel at different elevations. Speed of ascent depended on the physical condition of the climbers, adaptation to altitude (acclimatization), and the conditions on the route. Everyone knew his personal variable, but in general the higher you go, the slower you go. After proper acclimatization and carrying a load of twenty kilograms, I can ascend 300 vertical meters an hour on normal terrain up to 7,000 meters. Between 7,000 and 8,000 meters carrying ten to fifteen kilograms, I gain 200 vertical meters an hour. Above 8,000 meters my rate of ascent with

to climb one hundred meters an hour above 7,500 meters. The summit of K2 is 8,611 meters high; I outlined a schedule that would have prepared our bodies to work ten hours above 7,900 meters on summit day. There was no guarantee that in adhering to my schedule we could summit. In the forbidden zone, fate and luck play their hand. But the commitment of time and effort to adequate acclimatization improves personal performance and decreases the odds of developing acute mountain sickness. Proper acclimatization is the most important variable of safety an individual can affect when climbing at altitude. Ignoring that responsibility, a climber raises the risk to himself and his team.

Reinmar listened to all I had to say, as well as I could explain it, and made a good-natured response to my ideas and concerns. I understood from his gentleness that he did not want to offend me. He conceded my plan might be correct if we were attempting a "sports climb," but countered that our group had variable physical conditions and we were climbing the normal Abruzzi route. For our purpose he felt that the demanding acclimatization would not work, that it might even be dangerous, exhausting us before the summit bid.

My friends' good judgment had brought them success on Nanga Parbat, Broad Peak, and Gasherbrum, all about 8,100 meters high. My reservations were based on my experiences climbing Everest and Kanchenjunga. K2 is 8,611 meters high, and performing above 8,500 meters, especially without bottled oxygen, is different from climbing lower 8,000-meter peaks. I did not feel it was my place to argue about

minimal weight is 100 vertical meters an hour. Generally, I can go down twice as fast as I can go up on the same terrain.

The altitude of the last camp and last elevation for acclimatization on an 8,000-meter peak is derived by a simple formula. Subtract the vertical height one can ascend and descend in ten hours from the mountain's summit height. You make trips to acclimatize at 500-to-1,000-meter intervals up to that height. Each acclimatization trip is two to four days long, depending on the altitude to be achieved. Following each trip there is a two-to-five-day rest period. The rest period depends on the time spent on the previous trip.

our tactics because I was just a member of the expedition, not the leader. Also I respected that the Russian scheme was not the only way that high mountains were successfully climbed.

Peter and Reinmar had confidence in their plan. During the summit bid we were going to acclimatize to 7,300 meters and to 7,900 meters as we ascended. Now I am certain, given the turn of events, that my concerns were well-founded. Any climb higher than 8,500 meters without the use of supplemental oxygen is a major athletic under-taking, and there are rules you cannot break in the mountains. That day I had no wish to see my reservations validated by the high price we paid. My hope was that we would make it to the top and back to Base Camp without tragedy.

On the sixteenth we made our deposit at 6,800 meters and returned to Camp I exhausted. The weather left us wishing for better. Peter gave Andy and me permission to descend to Base Camp. Our absence would spare the food supplies we had struggled to carry up. To avoid the problems of crossing the glacier at dusk, Reinmar and Peter chose to stay the night at Camp I. Going down, we met Ernst coming up with a load from Base Camp. We told him Peter and Reinmar planned to descend the next day. Finally feeling good, Ernst wanted to spend the night at an elevation higher than Base Camp and went up.

To my surprise our descent took only two hours. The temperature on the glacier was so much warmer than above, we were able to remove our outer layers of Gore-Tex clothing. Back at Base Camp, Andy and I headed straight to our mess tent. Our Pakistani cook, Rastam, cooked up a stack of delicious chapatis. We ate with the gusto of men who had been on high-altitude rations for several days. Our evening radio con-tact with Reinmar and Peter confirmed that Ernst had arrived with his load. Weather permitting, they decided to ferry it to Camp II the next day. We were instructed to bring more supplies to Camp I.

Snow was falling heavily when we woke on the seventeenth. With pleasure Andy and I rolled over and went back to sleep. By late morning, like a broom, a sudden wind swept away the clouds. About 11 a.m. we learned by radio that Peter, Reinmar, and Ernst were starting for Camp II with supplies. Since it was late, Andy and I decided to rest a day and carry double loads up the following morning. Anxious to spend my first night at 6,800 meters, if the weather did not confound my plan, I thought our rest would make it possible for us to climb directly to Camp II in one day.

Toward evening, men and women emerged from their tents, escaping from another day of tedious confinement. We said our farewells at the Canadian-American camp. The porters for their expedition had arrived, and their equipment was being dismantled for transport down the glacier. The next morning, Phil Powers, the genial mountaineer from Wyoming, and his friends departed for civilization. Behind them they left a sad remembrance of their experience. A plaque engraved with the name of Dan Culver was fixed to the rocks in a place below Base Camp—the site of the memorial cairn for all climbers who die on the slopes of K2.

Under a clear sky Andy and I got an early start from Base Camp. Alone on the route, our silent progress was suddenly interrupted by Rastam's shouts. He came running after us to deliver my forgotten thermos. After the day's rest, even with a double load of supplies, I moved easily in the knee-deep snow, breaking trail and pulling the ropes up to the surface. I imagined many climbers would follow us, happy not to be trapped in their tents. Due to the continuous storms, many teams who had arrived as early as May had only reached 6,800 meters. After ten days of work our team could expect to spend the night at that elevation.

About eight-thirty I joined my German friends for breakfast at Camp I. After the previous day's hard work, they weren't moving very quickly. With the double load I had carried, I had no pangs of guilt about my contribution to our effort. I felt strong; my only problem was a cough caused by breathing the dry, thin air. Thanks to Rastam I had my preferred remedy—mint tea. About ten o'clock Peter, Reinmar, and Ernst were ready to go. Andy arrived; stomach problems had slowed him down. Carrying about fifteen kilograms of group equipment and five kilograms of my personal gear, I set off and was soon ahead of Reinmar and Ernst, catching and passing Peter below the yellow rocks. He looked stronger than his comrades and was feeling quite good at that elevation. I used a jumar on the fixed rope to climb up a steep section of rock and arrived on a snowy ridge.

Camp II was located in an inconvenient place on the ridge completely exposed to the prevailing winds. Flapping flags, the shredded remains of many tents littered the area, their debris a testimony to the hurricane-force winds that ripped across this slope and the trouble those tents had caused their owners. I began to cut ice bricks from the snow as I cleared level platforms in the slope. Peter, Reinmar, and Ernst arrived later and immediately began to help me. Andy, not feeling well, had turned back to spend the night at Camp I. By radio he said that he would join us the following day. Peter and Ernst set up our three-man dome tent. Carefully, Reinmar and I secured my two-man North Face in the lee of an ice-block wall. The evening weather was beautiful and the air was still. Far to the south, the ridges of the mountains were painted with the splendid reds and purples of sunset. After making ourselves comfortable in our sleeping bags, we cooked a wonderful supper. That night I had no complaints about the delicacies we had hauled up the mountain.

Though I slept soundly through the night, the next morning I felt the increase in altitude for the first time. I had no appetite. My teammates were none too joyful either. The multiple nights above 6,000 meters and the hard work were telling on them. That morning we discussed a plan for setting up the next camp. I suggested that we ascend carrying minimal equipment and supplies and spend a night at 7,300 meters for acclimatization at the new elevation. Peter and Reinmar were totally opposed to my idea. They decided we would transport heavy loads of gas, food, and equipment, which would be needed in the future, and that we would return to Camp II for that night. The next day we were supposed to carry another load up and overnight at the new elevation.

I tried to reason with them, explaining why I thought it was important to spend one night without the stress of heavy work at the new elevation. Also, the ropes on the steep section ahead of us were the unstable remnants from old expeditions, and descending tired later in the day along this precipitous terrain without the benefit of a well-secured trail was an added risk. I lobbied for the night of acclimatization at 7,300 meters because I thought it was necessary for my German friends, more so than for Andy and me, who had spent the spring climbing high. I knew this safety precaution would improve our performance later on. Given the energy level that morning, I seriously doubted we would be in form to make another carry to Camp III the next day. My plan was dismissed out of hand. Peter and Reinmar pedantically insisted I return with them to Camp II after our carry. They had a confidence in their physical resilience and energy stores I could only admire.

As we waited for Andy to arrive, we sorted the loads for our last two camps. Ernst felt unwell in the night; he was tired. After bringing up the load he had left below the yellow band the day before, he decided to descend to Camp I to spend the night. In my professional assessment, Ernst was adjusting fairly well by taking interim days of rest. Many times I had seen older mountaineers in the Soviet Union succeed on peaks higher than eight thousand meters by taking more time to acclimate.

I left camp following Peter and Andy up the fixed rope. Reinmar came behind me. By his pace, I could tell he was fatigued. Reinmar, with his strong soul, looked fully ten years younger than his fifty years. Twenty- and thirty-year-old men would envy his physical condition. Though fluent in German, English, and French, he was not a man of many words. His inner strength and his rational mind impressed me. When climbing, he was disciplined, motivated, and always good-tempered. Whenever I found myself ahead breaking trail, Reinmar was close to me, ever ready to exchange leads, to help me, even if he was tired. Though sometimes we found it difficult to comprehend what the other was saying, mainly due to my poor command of English, Reinmar and I always reached a common understanding. I never heard any tone of reproof from him, even if he was not happy with me. If things were not going according to plan, he would simply spread his arms and say in a way that sounded like English, "Yeah, yeah."

We had interesting discussions about the political problems that had beset our countries since the Second World War. Germany and Russia share a common history, and not much of it was good. Because of men like Reinmar, I learned it was possible for Russians and Germans to respect one another despite the dark experiences of our recent past. Reinmar's determination had taken him to the top of many mountains. I watched him moving surely toward his goal, the summit of K2. He deserved to succeed. He had earned that victory. The summit was within his physical and mental grasp, but so many things in our expedition worked against him. We had lost valuable time in Islamabad and were haunted by bad weather, and there were personal details, which depend on fate and luck, the significances of which are magnified by the circumstances up high.

At the beginning of the steep part of the route to Camp III, I went ahead of Peter and Andy. The weather was weird. Tiny snowflakes were blowing around, and occasional gusts of wind were strong enough to push a man with a heavy load off-balance. When the sun broke through, the wind calmed and our windproof Gore-Tex suits were instantly hot and stuffy. The rocks became less steep and I searched for the location of the third high-altitude camp. After a section of rocks, we came to an icy slope with a veneer of deep, dry snow. I sank up to my knees. The dry powder flowed like a river from my steps down the steep slopes. There was no traction between my crampons and the snow. It was so bad that, two hundred meters below, Reinmar, moving persistently, had trouble ascending, though I had just compressed the snow with my weight.

Across a crest of ice that dropped away abruptly to rocks, I emerged onto a steep, snowy slope. The wind calmed down, the sun came out, and the snow stopped falling. I moved up, pulling out pieces of old fixed line from under a thick covering of snow. I came to a huge waterproof bag; it belonged to two Swedish climbers. Somewhere under the new snow was the cave Phil Powers had told me about. The Canadian-American team had built it for their Camp III. I did not stop to look for this landmark. Two hundred meters higher there was a flat place; an obvious route lay ahead of me through the new snowdrifts that had piled up on the bergschrund. I decided that establishing a camp on the flat area would require half the effort needed to dig out a platform on the windy slope where I was standing. It was 2 p.m. I plunged ahead, soon sinking up to my chest in powder. It was impossible to extricate the fixed rope. I worked with my hands and elbows in a swimming motion, shoveling the loose snow aside and ramming it into walls with my shoulders. Then I brought up my knee and searched for a spot that would support my next step up. Reinmar followed the trench I had created and caught up with me plowing through the snow. I explained my rationale for moving ahead. He agreed it was a good idea. Fifty meters away just behind the bergschrund, I could see wind-hardened névé, which would provide perfect traction and stable support for walking. Completely exhausted by this hellish work, we stopped for a drink of hot tea. I was so tired that I could no longer lift my backpack. Reinmar went ahead of me and worked for about fifteen minutes before exhaustion forced him to stop. Peter arrived at the level of the Swedish dry bag. I saw him try to move up in the trench we had made. Quickly, he gave up, deposited his load, and began his descent.

I gathered the last of my strength and switched places with Reinmar. With clenched teeth I swam through the final meters of bottomless powder that overlay the ice crevasses of the bergschrund. Finally after forty minutes more work, my crampons found traction in hard snow below. As I moved forward, the depth of powder decreased to two feet, then to the top of my plastic boots. On the level ground ahead I saw the abandoned remnants of a camp—a Russian Primus stove, a few abandoned oxygen bottles, and an orange shovel with the name Ed Viesturs written clearly on the back. I had found the site used by members of the 1992 Russian expedition led by Vladimir Balyberdin.

Ed Viesturs and two other American climbers, Scott Fischer and Charlie Mace, had been on that expedition. Ed Viesturs I knew and respected as a strong mountaineer. I had first met him in Kathmandu when the Americans and the Russians were celebrating their ascents on Kanchenjunga in 1989. We had succeeded on different sides, as usual. After that our paths crossed many times, on Lenin Peak, once in the Caucasus, and again in 1991 after our ascent of Dhaulagiri and his success on Everest. With an impressive ascent of K2, Ed Viesturs became the seventh person in the history of mountaineering to climb the three highest peaks in the world. It was my turn to add my name to the short list. Judging by the determination of my German friends that day, I felt the opportunity would not be lost.

About five in the afternoon Reinmar and I dropped our load of supplies and gear at the hard-won site for Camp III. We started down. The weather became pleasant toward evening; the wind that had worried us all day ceased, and the air was still during our descent. Reinmar was ahead of me until he decided to rest for a moment. I passed him at the beginning of the steep portion of the route where the fixed lines began. It was difficult to say which of us was more exhausted, Reinmar after four nights and days steadily working above six thousand meters or me after struggling all day long through the terrible snow. After rappelling down the first section of rope, I turned to locate my friend; he was moving down steadily as well. After I saw him past the worst section, I turned to continue my descent. The route below us all the way to the tents was protected with fixed line and was not so difficult.

Peter and Andy were fortifying their tent when I arrived at Camp II. I removed my crampons and climbed into my tent. I fired up the Primus stove and melted a pot of water from the snow I had prepared before leaving that morning. Drained by my day's efforts, I drank the water and sank into sleep, comforted by the warmth of my sleeping bag. Shouts awakened me. Judging from Peter's and Andy's voices, I knew something unexpected had happened, and that it must concern Reinmar.

Rushing out of the tent, I found Andy standing next to Reinmar, who was covered in blood. Fifty meters above the camp, he had unclipped from the fixed line at a juncture of rope. He had relaxed his guard too early. Believing the snow was stable névé, he had misstepped his crampons onto ice and slipped. Collision with a ridge of rocks that jutted out of the snow was all that had kept Reinmar from falling over the rocky south wall into bottomless space. A head wound was bleeding profusely, and he had cuts over his face. He said he felt that he hit his head and chest pretty hard.

We were concerned about a concussion, and because of his pain when breathing, it seemed likely he had broken ribs. All his extremities were functioning fine, and only time would reveal if he had serious internal injuries. Reinmar settled into Peter and Andy's big tent, where we cleaned and bandaged his wounds. I boiled water all night long and carried it to their tent thinking because of the head injury we needed to rehydrate him. The night was terribly cold. I did not sleep until just before dawn.

July 20 I awoke tired and groggy from the night's ordeal, but I immediately began preparing tea. We decided it was best to descend to Base Camp. It took us a long time to get ourselves ready. We helped Reinmar into his clothes and harness and at about 10 a.m. started down. Andy went first, Reinmar next, belayed on Peter's rope. After securing the tents, I left camp with my backpack full of Reinmar's extra belongings. I caught up with my friends at Camp I.

Many climbers were ascending the fixed line and settling into their tents while we enjoyed a good lunch and drank more tea. Ernst, who had been informed of the accident by radio, had prepared everything for us. The weather had stabilized and was perfect for working on the route. We warmed ourselves in the sun, enjoying the food and tea. Reinmar was upset when I told him that I had his personal gear. Embarrassed or uncertain of his plans, he insisted he could carry his things. I did not say so, of course, but I thought the climb was over for him. When he'd left the higher camp, I believe he, too, harbored serious doubts that continuing was possible. At Camp I with only side pain to remind him of the accident, giving up on the insidiously dangerous peak was no longer a certainty.

Under the blazing sun, we began a lethargic descent from Camp I. Heavy, wet snow stuck in our crampons and our boots got heavier. Tired bodies were forced to work a little harder. As we finished negotiating the last section of fixed rope, fortune smiled on us from the face of a cute, young British doctor. Thoughtfully she had hiked across the glacier to help us. From the first sight of her, our fatigue disappeared. Suddenly we were laughing and chatting amiably. Sitting on the rocks, we drank tea and watched as she cleaned and examined Reinmar's wounds. She led us back to the British camp, where she skillfully put six stitches in his scalp. Although she confirmed our suspicion that he had a broken rib, his other injuries were superficial. Reassured by her diagnosis, Reinmar would go back up the mountain.

We slept late the next morning, and no one was in a hurry for breakfast. The day was sunny, without wind. One could only envy those men who were working up higher in such perfect weather. After eating, I stripped down to my underwear to spend fifteen minutes sunbathing on a cot. My stomach was full and the warmth of the sun was intoxicating. I fell asleep instantly and came to my senses three hours later. The result was a vivid red sunburn, which became so painful that it kept me from sleeping that night.

On July 22 the weather changed and another storm enveloped the mountain. Tired climbers from the other expeditions returned from their high-altitude camps. I heard the clank of their equipment and the rhythm of their tired steps as they passed our tents. The day evaporated; we visited other camps or entertained friends in our mess tent. Dan Mazur and I had time to catch up on the events in our lives since 1991.

Reinmar felt better. Again I watched him put aside the adversities that fate had dealt him. Perhaps it was that ascent that makes me superstitious. How does a man escape his destiny? Now as I look back and analyze events, I am certain that if we had made a proper acclimatization, we could have avoided the tragedy that awaited us. Every setback and difficulty conspired to keep pushing us up the mountain. Each difficulty forged a link in the chain of events that would cost my friends their lives.

That night we sat in the mess tent discussing our tactics. We had news from the Swedes that a window of good weather would begin on the twenty-eighth. Calm conditions were predicted to last for about forty-eight hours, then a major storm would follow. We decided to leave Base Camp on the twenty-fourth for Camp I, move to Camp III by the twenty-sixth, establish Camp IV at 7,900 meters on the twenty-seventh, and go for the summit early on the morning of July 28. We had one or two days of leeway, but if success eluded us during that window of opportunity, there would be no time for a second chance.

When asked for my opinion, I said we did not have adequate acclimatization to 7,300 meters, much less 7,900 meters. I cautioned Reinmar and Peter that our bodies were ill-prepared for those heights, that an attempt on the summit would be dangerous. As a team, I felt we would run out of power at or near the top, but that it would be difficult to turn around so close to our goal. The descent could be treacherous. But I added that I was ready to go with their decision. They were my leaders. Peter and Reinmar insisted they had never experienced difficulty above eight thousand meters. I pointed out that the last five hundred meters on K2 should not be compared to the difficulty of other mountains. Still, if they were going, I was ready to accept the risk. The discussion ended on that stark note, and we did not come back to the topic. By unanimous consensus, we were going up.

To provide a diversion from the bad weather, Reinmar and Peter sent out invitations to members of all the other expeditions to join us on the twenty-third for the "Baltoro Rock Olympics." Wet, falling snow did not deter one hundred climbers of every nationality from abandoning the comfort of their tents to participate. The entry requirement was a team song and introductions. The main event required marksmen to knock a small rock off a bigger one from one hundred paces. There was no end of ammunition in the endless store of rubble around us. I do not recall which team won; the opportunity to laugh and talk was more important. Socializing went on late into the night. For a day, humor and friendship relieved us of the burden of our ambitions. Reinmar's organizational skills and Peter's unfailing energy and enthusiasm presented us with those gifts.

On July 24, Peter, Ernst, and Reinmar climbed to Camp I: the Canadian-American team had started out this way—slow, with a night at the lower camp. They had hoped an easy day would compensate for the long one that came at the end. Andy left at five in the afternoon, so the climb to Camp II would not be as long and hard for him. For me it would take seven hours to reach II. Traveling light, I left Base Camp on the twenty-fifth at five-thirty in the morning. Two members of the Swedish expedition, Rafael Jensen and Daniel Bidner, followed in my tracks. I arrived at Camp I as my friends were finishing breakfast. There I brewed tea and rested awhile before setting out with Andy. Reinmar was in no hurry to move; it appeared to me that his ribs were bothering him. He did not move with the same ease he had in the days before his fall. What could I have said to him? How could I have helped him? In those situations, each person makes his own decision to go up or to end the risk and go down. I watched Reinmar begin to ascend, just as sure, but slower on the ropes. There was still time for him to change his mind.

I passed Andy and Ernst and arrived at Camp II with Peter only to find the big dome tent broken and torn by the wind in the last storm. Another adversity; they fell on us one after the other until they no longer surprised me. Peter's down suit and sleeping bag had blown out of the tent. Unable to conceal his emotions, he said the climb was over for him. Fate seemed to be giving him the opportunity to abandon the effort. He began to descend. Sitting there alone, I felt relief in my soul. Deep in my heart, I believed that without proper acclimatization our attempt was too risky. I gathered the remaining things from the broken tent and put them aside in a place protected from the wind. Then I climbed into my tent, set up my stove, and began melting snow into water for tea.

Later I heard the voices of my teammates, Peter's voice as well. I understood from their conversation that Ernst had given his down suit and sleeping bag to Peter. Ernst was giving up the summit attempt. This was wise of him, because in our situation, given his age and without better acclimatization, he had little chance of succeeding.

We set up the three-man tent we had stored for Camp IV. Then we lit up the stoves, cooked dinner, and quickly settled in for the night.

Later we heard the two Swedish climbers arrive. They elected to follow our plan of assault. Like us, Daniel and Rafael found their tent broken. They radioed Base Camp and asked permission of the British team to use their tent. Roger Payne, the leader of that expedition, kindly agreed.

After breakfast on the twenty-sixth, as Reinmar and I dressed to leave for Camp III, a foul wind began to blow. I thought the force of the blast would sweep away the tents and us as well. I was silently grateful for the snow wall that we had built days before, which afforded the only protection from the gale. The sun was shining through the clouds that flew over us, but no one started out. We contacted Base Camp for a weather report and learned the window of good weather was predicted to move in on the twenty-ninth. We had to wait. The storm was relentless and blew with hurricane force all day and all through the night. The Swedes, like us, endured the gale in their sleeping bags protected by the thin walls of a buffeted tent.

When we awoke on the twenty-seventh, it seemed that the tempest had passed. Reinmar and I broke down my hard-tested North Face tent and packed our backpacks. Loathe to move from their shelter, Peter and Andy watched us and the weather. Like the Swedes, they were not in a hurry to leave that refuge.

As if lying in wait, the wind increased as Reinmar and I started out. Weighing the effort it would take for me to reconstruct the tent against the effort of climbing, I chose the latter. It was possible to balance my body against the direct pressure of the gale; I leaned over into the slope and moved up, secured by my jumar on the fixed line. Everything necessary for the night was in my backpack. Our instructions were that if anyone ascended to Camp III that day, they should wait for the team there. I needed no further permission. Seeking relief from the wind, I stopped in a crack, pressed against the rocks, and looked down. Below me, Reinmar was climbing. Andy moved into the squall, but gave up and rejoined Peter, who prudently observed our efforts from the tent. In that moment huddled against the rocks, I felt the wind begin to abate.

It took four more hours of climbing to arrive at the loads we had dropped for Camp III. I selected a place for the tent in the lee of an ice wall above the site of the old Russian camp. I shoveled away snow, making a hard, flat surface for the tent. Reinmar arrived about two hours later. He informed me that Peter and Andy had decided to wait at Camp II until the next day.

I felt pretty well during the night, but the next morning I was much less energetic. That was normal for the first night at 7,400 meters. After the sun hit the tent, I stirred from my sleeping bag and slowly prepared water for tea. The air was still. Protected from the wind by the ice wall, the sun-warmed atmosphere in the tent reached tropical comfort. The heat and altitude made me feel sluggish, and I had no appetite. I knew that I was better off moving around to stimulate circulation. So after eating some dried fruit and drinking tea, I decided to dig a snow cave to compensate for our lost tent, knowing it would save Peter and Andy some effort when they arrived. Reinmar watched for a while. Despite complaining of pain in his ribs, he ate a hearty breakfast. I advised him against working with the shovel. The weather appeared to be clearing, and wind had decreased. Reinmar went down to the load dropped previously by Peter and brought it up to camp. After five hours of work, a cave big enough for three people was finished. Reinmar decided to settle into the comfortable space with me. We moved our things from the tent, freeing a place for Peter and Andy who finally arrived later that evening.

After breakfast on the twenty-ninth we loaded our packs in clear, calm weather and started out for our assault camp. Last to leave, I packed up the food in the cave and covered the entrance with the dry bag we had found, securing the cave for use on our descent. Above me Peter and Andy moved up really well, and Reinmar was ascending easily. The route was in perfect condition: the hard névé snow was easy for climbing. I felt worn-out from the digging the day before and caught up with the group only after they'd stopped to rest before a steep section. Above the rest spot we could see the terrain flatten out, and we knew that there we would find where previous expeditions had made their assault camps. There were two routes to the flatter ground: up a steep, icy slope or around through the deep snow. We chose the second alternative. I climbed about one hundred meters and passed Andy and Peter. For another hour I took the lead, breaking trail in the deep snow up to the gentler slope. The weather was perfect: the sky was cloudless, the wind mild. Mercifully, the forecast of good weather proved true.

The remains of a tent and some equipment abandoned by the Slovenian expedition littered the site of Camp IV. The summit was clearly visible, and from that perspective the final distance did not look too difficult. In one hour we were in our tents, two men in each. We prepared dinner and climbed into down sleeping bags.

From the security of our tents, the clank of equipment was heard as the Swedes approached camp. Like us, they had minimal acclimatization: Rafael and Daniel had spent only one night at 6,800 meters. In favor of light loads, they carried only a tent, thinking they would sleep without bags and leave for the summit just after midnight. They counted on the warmth of their excellent down suits and state-of-the-art gear to protect them. I wondered if that was enough to compensate for the lack of acclimatization. I surrendered a down sleeping bag to them that I had found abandoned in the tangled equipment remains around camp. The night was bitterly cold.

On July 30 Reinmar and I woke up to five centimeters of hoarfrost on the inside walls of our tent, a lace of ice condensation from our breath in the night. Peter and Andy departed for the summit about 3 p.m. Reinmar and I waited for better visibility. I moved sluggishly and had a poor appetite—the negative effects of altitude. Though Reinmar said he felt okay, I believe he had the same symptoms that I experienced. He managed to eat more breakfast than I could choke down. I was only thirsty and forced myself to eat some muesli. Judging by Andy and Peter's early departure, I thought they felt better than we did.

We packed up, and each of us put forty meters of rope into our backpacks. The Slovenian and American-Canadian groups had reported they had not used fixed line above this camp. It was later in the season, and storms had continuously swept the route. One man had fallen above us, and we wanted to avoid that. We would fix line on the infamous "bottleneck," providing some security for our descent.

At 4 p.m. Reinmar and I left camp. Our crampons found good traction in the névé-covered slope. The cold penetrated my Gore-Tex jacket and down clothes and freshened my step. I was more energetic, though I was aware that my speed was slower than normal. With the dawn light, we could see Peter and Andy ahead of us. After moving for one hour, I noticed the distance to the summit did not appear to change. Distance in the mountains can be deceptive; the perspective from Camp IV was misleading. Ascending, I understood that the summit of K2 was a long way off.

About ten-thirty I caught up with Peter and Andy at the bottleneck. There the slope became much steeper. Peter asked for the rope and two ice-screws, and I pulled them out of my pack. We decided to traverse to the left. The sunlight caused a stifling heat. At high altitude, nights are as cold as deep space, and the sun has an intensity that parches the skin; its heat robs one of ambition. The air was motionless. We had dressed for the morning cold, and in the blazing sun we became hot and stuffy in our clothes. On any other day that would have been perfect, but at that altitude the heat made us sluggish. Our speed was catastrophically slow. Seven hours of climbing for Reinmar and me, and eight hours for Peter and Andy, had brought us only one-third of the distance to the summit! Reinmar was two hundred meters below, but catching up to us since we had stopped.

Andy and Peter stripped off and stored their down gear. I sat on my backpack secured to the fixed line, musing on our plan while sipping tea. My throat was dry. It felt dehydrated from the effort of breathing. Periodically, I moistened my throat with small amounts of mint tea to relieve my discomfort. Ascending to the assault camp the day before had made my chest hurt, and the pain had become more noticeable. I was certain we should fix the rope on the bottleneck and descend to rest in our tents for the night. I thought we could make another attempt on the summit early the next morning.

Peter, Andy, and I discussed how to cross the insidious bottleneck. Fresh, knee-deep snow was on a steep slope, but when testing the snow, one hit a thin, brittle crust of hard ice that broke away in layers and slid down the mountain. The powder underneath did not compress into reliable steps. I suggested we wait for Reinmar. Rafael and Daniel were following close behind him. I thought it would be safer for us to negotiate the traverse together. Andy was standing secured to a well-fixed ice-screw.

Near me an abandoned ice ax lay among the rocks and ice. I picked it up. After testing the snow conditions on the section ahead of us, I thought I would need it. Ignoring my warnings, Peter moved up and across the slope, trampling down steps in the rotten snow. He fixed one section of line, moving cautiously but without protection. I thought of Phil Powers and recalled his summit-day recollections. Only a little higher on that ridge, Dan Culver had fallen while descending. More than twenty days had passed since they were in our position; the snow conditions and temperature were now different. Gazing at the section ahead of Peter, I thought that area looked quite treacherous, and I knew that we needed to fix it with rope. Late in the day the sun-melted snow would turn to solid ice. I looked at the sheer rock walls of the south face; it would be impossible to stop if you started to fall in that place.

Reinmar joined me and wanted to know what our plan was. I asked for his forty meters of rope. Leaving my backpack with my down jacket, my thermos, and my extra gloves attached securely to the end of the fixed rope below the bottleneck, I went up along the line, caught up to Peter, and went ahead to secure the next section. As I suspected, under the unconsolidated snow was hard ice. My crampons scratched it. I adjusted to that condition by relying more on my ice axes. My fortuitous acquisition of the second ax now provided a measure of safety as I ascended: kicking my crampons into the ice with all my strength, driving in the two ice tools, one after the other, and moving up a step. Every ten meters I stopped to rest, breathing hard. Belayed by Peter, slowly but surely I moved up and to the left, fastening the rope along the slope with ice-screws. Finishing the job left us so short of breath we were unable to speak. We looked at one another and asked only with our eyes, "What next?" The air passed whistling and wheezing through our dry throats. My watch said 2 p.m. Reinmar and Andy were sitting on their packs at the bottom of the fixed line talking to Rafael, who in the interim of our work had caught up with us. Peter called down to tell them the route was secured.

As we rested, trying to catch our breath, I asked, "What are we going to do about the time?"

Peter replied that a little higher up the slope would flatten out and from there the summit was close. I could see he was tired but feeling well. The nearness of our goal was energizing him. I was worn-out by the effort of fixing the rope. I told him that I had left my backpack with my warm clothes at the beginning of the fixed line, and that I was tired. "It will be better to go down to the tents and try again tomorrow," I said. "We can start earlier than we did today, and using our work on the lines, we will move faster. The summit will not take so long."

Peter would have none of it. "Anatoli, the weather may be stormy tomorrow; today is our last chance. We must endure a little."

True, the weather was finally in our favor, but our pace frightened me. Never on any previous ascent had I felt so weak. But I knew Peter might be right. The next day I might not feel stronger, and the weather was supposed to get worse. Some intuition told me we should not go up. I sensed danger waiting for us at the top of the mountain. It was not exactly fear, but some kind of alertness possessed me. I felt as if we were crossing the border of what is allowed and what was forbidden—as though we were going into foreign territory. Peter and I did not argue. We spoke quietly. That venerable fifty-year-old man with his beautiful black mustache went on ahead to continue up, and I was left on the snow slope leaning over my ice ax, struggling to keep my equilibrium.

I felt empty inside, probably because I was so tired. At that altitude inner emotions and moods change at a different speed: both movement and thinking slow down. I watched as Reinmar and Andy ascended the fixed line, moving in slow motion like characters in a film. I could feel the emptiness in me slowly being replaced by a feeling like anger. It was not anger at Peter, but at this whole situation, and at myself. At that moment, I was without self-esteem or pride. My brain was asking, "Why is it so important to go to the summit, what is the meaningfulness of our effort?" Perhaps some inner instinct of self-preservation was working, prevailing over my ambition. I cannot tell even now what changed in me as I watched Peter moving off. I can only recall that this jumble of emotions generated new energy in me . . . some force that challenged me to move.

Perhaps this energy had been passed to me from Peter, because he was a man who could inspire people in that way. First I followed after him like a robot. Then I experienced the same feeling one has during a marathon, when older people pass you by. That does not make you angry, you do not wish to get even with them in a bad way. It makes you turn inside to see what is wrong with yourself. The example that Peter set was like a push, and some internal engine that had been out of order in me started to work, producing energy.

When I caught up with him, he let me go in front without saying a word. He had probably known that his example would influence me in such a way. This man had a shining virtue and a boundless energy that were infectious. He put himself to a task honorably and inspired others by his standards. His social grace allowed him to tackle problems easily, and he knew how to influence people and lead them. If the situation was difficult for him, he never showed it. Such inner strength in a human being always generates respect.

After the fixed line, we crossed another hundred meters of steep ice and snow; then finally the slope became flatter and it was easier to move. The crust of snow was hard. Occasionally a slab would slide out from under my step, skittering toward the abyss that was the drop over the South Wall of K2. That was a warning to us not to relax too soon.

We moved that way, with Peter ten meters behind me, for two more hours. Then again, totally worn-out, I sat down in the snow. Peter approached me, took out his thermos, and poured a drink of hot tea. Without a single word he offered the cup to me. The hot drink passed down my dry throat, and the energy of that gesture slowly penetrated my tired muscles. The summit appeared to be no more than fifteen minutes away. I gathered all my energy and all my soul into one bundle and moved toward the peak. It was terribly difficult. In the late-afternoon shadow an invigorating coolness settled on the southeast slope. I was unable to think. I felt only a primitive awareness to go forward.

During my years of training as a ski racer, and then as a mountaineer, I had learned how to wring out the last of my energy for a finish. But this is dangerous in mountaineering, because the summit is not the finish of your competition with a great mountain. To survive you must be able to get down from the forbidden zone. There is no pausing in this place, no possibility to recover. If you have spent all reserves of power, and you are required by circumstance to fight for your life, you reach into a dry well. That moment, on K2, I was in just such a condition. I could think of nothing. The summit before me became the finish line. That was bad.

Perhaps Peter, Andy, and Reinmar, and those two Swedish mountaineers, felt exactly the same way. Maybe they were not thinking beyond the finish line—about the descent. I do not know. Instead of fifteen minutes, I climbed for exactly one hour more before I reached the summit. When I crossed that imaginary line, I did not feel joy or satisfaction at my achievement. I did not care that I was standing on the summit of the second-highest mountain on earth. The only pleasant thought that came to me was that the tortured effort of placing my feet one higher than the other was over.

I could see the whole length of the glacier running from K2 to Concordia. Across the glacier, opposite me, the top of massive Broad Peak was lit by the last rays of the sun. There was no strength to admire the colors of the sunset as I half-sat, half-lay on the snowy slope in a dreamlike state. I felt like a squeezed lemon. As soon as the sun slipped beyond the ridge, the stifling warm air was replaced by a cold that instantly penetrated my gloves and boots. Like a robot I removed my camera from the chest pocket of my bib and took photos of the surrounding mountains. I was unaware of the time passing, but Peter came up sometime before 6 p.m. Andy arrived right behind him. Everyone was tired and slow. I cannot remember what we talked about while taking photos of one another on the summit. I put my camera away and became aware of the cold in my hands and feet. My old Koflach boots were the ones the Soviet team had been issued for Kanchenjunga. Looking down, thinking of the long descent ahead, I wished I were wearing the One Sport boots that had protected me on the last two expeditions. Those I had sold to pay bills.

Peter and I left the summit simultaneously. Andy waited for Rafael, who was climbing the presummit ridge. I could not see Reinmar. About two hundred meters lower, we met him moving slowly and steadily; he was two hours climbing distance from the summit. I stopped ten meters away on easy ground and asked how he was feeling. I looked at my watch. It was six-thirty, with only ten to fifteen minutes more light in the day. Reinmar did not answer my question. When Peter came up, they discussed the situation in German. I thought that Reinmar would turn back, knowing that in the dying light, it would be safer for him to negotiate the dangerous section above the bottleneck with us. Though I wanted him to descend, at that moment it would not have been right for me to intrude; only he could make the decision. Even Peter did not have the right or authority to order his friend to turn around. Now I think it most likely that he could not consider the dire possibilities hidden in his choice. He was determined to go to the summit. K2 was the goal of all his years of climbing in the Karakoram. Daniel was behind him, two hundred meters lower. Slower than Reinmar, he would need more time to reach the summit. Peter removed Ernst's down jacket and a headlamp from his pack and gave them to Reinmar, who continued up the slope, while Peter and I went down.

I still wonder if I could have helped in that situation. My clothing for the cold was in a backpack at the end of the fixed line. As darkness was falling, I knew I had about one hour before my hands and feet would begin freezing. Descent for me would then become impossible. If I did not move and get to my clothing, I would shortly be in a fatal situation. How could I have changed the chain of events? I do not know the answer even now. I continued my descent, using the two ice tools. As on the climb to the summit, when there was only one thought in my mind, I could not contemplate the possibilities hidden in our situation. I had to focus on my every move to descend without losing my balance or misjudging the conditions of the snow under my boots. If I fell, I would not be able to stop myself. The darkness obscured our trail and made judging the relief difficult. I turned to face the slope and descended down randomly.

At one point, intuition alone inspired me to move fifty meters to the right. There I felt a ridge of hard ice and snow. I drove my ice axes into the slope and stepped down, kicking into the snow and ice with my crampons. At times, snow fell on me from Peter's steps above. In places of poor traction, big chunks of the névé snow slipped from under my feet, falling into the black emptiness. I arrived at the beginning of our fixed line, clipped a carabiner onto the security of the rope, and descended. I was working on autopilot; there were no thoughts. It had been fifteen hours since I'd left our camp. It would be more than an hour in total darkness before I could hope to reach the tents. I was at the end of my strength and on the brink of failure.

Ten meters before the end of the fixed rope, a crampon came off my boot. I lost balance and fell to the anchor point at the end of the rope, crashing into my backpack. Removing my gloves to replace the crampon, my fingers froze numb while I struggled with the metal. Unsuccessfully I tried to warm them against my body, then continued down the route below the bottleneck in the dark, moonless night. I had no sensation in my toes or my fingers. The cold penetrated my body, and my heart did not have the energy to pump my thickened blood into my feet and hands. Almost every ten meters the crampon came off my boot.

In one such moment I fell again and slid slowly down the slope. Automatically I turned onto my stomach and with my entire strength drove the ice tools into the snow. By some miracle I stopped. That extra ice ax, a gift from some unknown climber, had been like an invisible hand of help, assisting me all day. After that fall, I lost my orientation to the route. I was unhurt but more alert. There was no visibility. I had no headlamp. I fastened my crampon on my boot once more and moved randomly down. When the slope started to flatten, I chose a direction. Luckily it proved to be right. I fell again and again, clumsy with fatigue, but the slope near the tents was less steep, and it was not difficult to arrest my falls. At last I made out the dark silhouettes of the tents. When I could finally see them, they were fifteen meters away.

I staggered to the tent with one crampon on my boot. With effort, I liberated myself from my equipment. After falling into the tent, I found my headlamp and turned it on, so the tent would be a reference point for those who were coming down the mountain. It was 8:30 p.m. when I lit my stove and put the pot of compressed snow on the burner to melt. That was all I could manage to do. I could feel nothing inside my plastic boots, but I had no strength to do anything to warm my feet. The heat of the stove raised the temperature in the tent. I dozed off cradling the pot in my hands while attempting to thaw out my frozen fingers. Hot water spilled on me; it burned my hand and startled me to my senses. I checked my watch; I had slept forty minutes.

Only after I had warmed up by drinking the hot water did my mind go beyond the primitive needs of my survival. Then I focused on the critical situation forming on the mountain. Obviously, something had happened to Peter; he should have arrived. Like me, he was not well equipped for cold or darkness. Three hours had passed since I'd last seen him two hundred meters above the beginning of the fixed line. I thought, even with the down jacket, Reinmar did not have enough warm clothing. Andy was better off with his down suit. The Swedish mountaineers were dressed really well and could survive the night out. But with what kind of aftermath? My thoughts were interrupted by steps outside the tent. It was Andy.

He had seen nothing of Peter during his descent. If Peter had made it to the fixed rope, he should have been in camp by now. If Andy had not seen him, he might have fallen, as I had, on the relief below the fixed line. It would be impossible to find a person on that slope in the moonless night. I understood that brutal fact clearly. Outside events were unfolding chaotically. My mind told me to go out, to look for Peter, to help someone, but I had no strength at all. What could I have done in those hours but add one more name to the list of victims? Andy and I did not discuss going back up the mountain. Exhausted, we had no options. I did not sleep, but spent the night semiconscious, aware only of the cold.

At 4 a.m. I looked out of the tent. The relief of the slope was still unclear. I saw a slow-moving red dot. Who was it? Dressed in red, it could only be one of the Swedish climbers. When Rafael came up to the tent, tears were streaming down his cheeks. Tears of grief . . . his friend had been lost. Daniel had developed altitude sickness, cerebral edema; he had become disoriented and fallen while descending. Rafael had no news of Peter or Reinmar. He believed they had descended ahead of him to the safety of the tents.

I did not cry. Slowly I reckoned with what had happened. I did not want to accept Peter's and Reinmar's deaths. I wanted to change something in the situation, to find some peg on which to construct a scenario for their survival. I could find nothing that gave me hope. Finally it was clear to me that they were dead. For two hours I sat staring at the tracks we had made in the snow on the way to the summit the day before. The mountain was lit harshly by the sun, and in the shade it was cold blue. K2 looked like a monster. I suggested to Andy that we should go up. He shrugged his shoulders as if he could not understand. In reality, I had no strength to go up. Around 11 a.m. Andy and Rafael started down the mountain. I spent three more hours in camp, just sitting, looking at the mountain, as if hypnotized.

I left camp at 2 p.m. and caught up with Rafael and Andy. They were talking to the British mountaineer Victor Saunders. He offered to help Rafael down to the snow cave below Camp III where the other members of Rafael's expedition were waiting. Andy and I stayed in the cave I had built, and on August 1 we descended to Base Camp. That day the wind came up again and destroyed all the tents at Camp II.

Writing this now, there is no joy in my achievement. I only look at life and value it a little differently. It is easy to lose in the mountains if you step over the border of what is possible. Where are those borders? For four months since my return, I have searched my soul for answers. Why were Rafael, Andy and I allowed to come down alive, after crossing into that no-man's-land, the forbidden zone? Why was the door of return closed to Daniel, Peter, and Reinmar? I feel my participation in these events acutely. What more could I have done that day to help my friends? Is it wrong that I lived, that I did not die with them?

I Cried Aloud for You

by Jeff Rennicke

In the middle of a hike in Wyoming's Wind River
Range, Presbyterian minister Mike Turner slipped
on an unstable boulder. The boulder shifted, pinning Turner's legs against another rock. Writer
Jeff Rennicke reconstructed the events that followed for Backpacker's June 2002 issue.

The nameless lake sits at 11,400 feet in Wyoming's Fitzpatrick Wilderness, tight up against a ridge known as the Brown Cliffs. This high in the Wind River Range, there is no gentle fringe of trees, no sprigs of wildflowers to soften the sharp angles of the rocks, nothing but a few wind-blasted banks of snow. The blue eye of water stares straight up from a cracked bowl of boulders into a remote, seldom-visited land of wind and rock and sky.

At 1 o'clock in the afternoon on August 2, 1998, a lone hiker with a black dog was making his way through the chaos of boulders along the eastern shore of the unnamed lake. He was a tall man with a gait that was used to eating up the miles, but here he was moving slowly under the weight of his pack, picking his steps carefully and sweating under a chocolate-brown floppy hat. It was day 4 of a 9-day hike, and the going was tougher than he had hoped for. Snow and ice in the passes had rubbed the dog's paws raw, slowing the pace. And now all this rock.

Nearing the lake, the hiker stepped onto a large boulder that shifted precariously under his weight. Instinctively, he leapt. The rock ahead was solid but tilted up at an awkward angle. His boots hit, and slid. The boulder behind kept coming, closing the gap. Just as his legs slipped off the edge, the boulders slammed together, catching the man above the knees, pinning him as if in the jaws of a trap.

There would have been pain, panic rising hot in the back of his throat, a swirl of dust in the air like smoke. There would have been the gunpowder smell of cracked rock and the ricochet of smaller pebbles clattering down the slope and splashing into the lake. And then nothing. As suddenly as it all had started, the rocks stopped rolling. The deep silence of the wilderness flowed back in like the water that closed around those few small stones settling without a sound on the bottom of the unnamed lake.

In the first moments following the rockslide, Mike Turner lay stunned. His breath came in ragged gasps choked with dust and fear, his heartbeat thumping against the rock. The dog, a Labrador mix named Andy, pricked up his ears at the commotion, waiting for his master to get up and move on.

Turner checked himself for injuries. Miraculously, his legs were trapped but not broken. With his bare hands and then using his tripod as a lever, he heaved against the tremendous weight of rocks, trying to pull himself free. At first, the boulder moved enough to ease the pain, though not enough to free him. A flicker of hope rose in him like a flame. He tried again, the tripod nearly snapping under the strain. Nothing. And again.

For more than an hour, he pried and shoved. But caught facing away from the boulder that pinned him, legs dangling in midair, even a big man like Turner could not gain enough leverage to move a piece of granite the size of a small car. The flicker of hope began to fade.

Exhausted, he rested, mind racing. This didn't make sense. People don't get trapped this way. How many thousands of times before had he stepped on boulders that wobbled? Perhaps he could dig himself out. He couldn't reach the ground. Maybe he could yell for help. The wind swatted the sound from his throat.

He looked around. His view was nothing but rock, sky, and a glimmer of lake. He had almost made it; a dozen more steps and he'd have been at the lake's edge, resting, filling his water bottles, the dog lapping happily at the water, nudging him to move on around the lake. Below, he noticed a few scant pockets of snow in the shadows. He needed to calm down, take his time, and think this through rationally. And so the Reverend Mike Turner reached for his journal and began to write.

"About 2 hours ago a large rock rolled upon me and trapped my legs," the journal entry reads in scrawling, jagged letters. *"I was very careful, be sure of that, but I hurt . . . I am in your hands Lord . . . I don't know what I face."*

For 10 years, Mike Turner had been the pastor at Boone Memorial Presbyterian Church, a pleasant brown brick building on a quiet, tree-lined street in Caldwell, Idaho. At 6'6", the 48-year-old Turner could, at times, seem larger than life, yet parishioners say they were drawn to his open face and ready smile. They describe him as "an inspirational pastor" who was active in all aspects of his congregation's life. "I had five operations in the last few years," one church member says, "and Pastor Mike was always with me, making the long drive whenever I needed him."

The seemingly opposite joys of both leading a 500-member congregation and witnessing the solitary beauty of wild places peacefully coexisted in Turner's life. "Mike saw God's hand everywhere," his wife, Diane, says, "in church just as much as in the backcountry." Childhood hikes took him deep into the cathedral-like light of the Sierra. He celebrated his ordainment as a minister in 1976 with an 18-day hike in these same Wyoming mountains. The first time he held hands with Diane was in Rocky Mountain National Park; vacations with the kids were hiking trips, and he enjoyed long theological discussions with friends on the trail. "Mike was drawn to the high country," says friend Mark Smith. "It was where he felt closest to God."

So in the summer of 1998, when Turner wanted to cap off a 3-month sabbatical with something that would challenge both his body and his spirit, he naturally looked to the high places. The Wind Rivers rise out of western Wyoming like a crest of waves gone to stone—100 miles long, with 48 peaks above 12,500 feet. They are the highest and wildest mountains in the state. The 60-mile hike Turner planned, much of it off-trail, would begin and end in the 428,169-acre Bridget Wilderness. It would cross the Continental Divide twice, traverse a glacier, top 12,000-foot passes, and take him deep into the 191,103-acre Fitzpatrick Wilderness, one of the most remote places in the lower 48.

He wanted to do it solo. Hiking alone, Turner reasoned, would let him travel at his own pace, linger over his photography, and enjoy some quiet retreat time with God. It was to be the trip of a lifetime. In big letters across the top of his itinerary, he called it his "Wander in Wonder."

On the morning of July 30, 1998, Turner loaded his gear and his dog Andy into his blue Honda Civic. Before he drove off, he gave his wife of 20 years a bouquet of flowers. "Thank you for letting me live this adventure," the card read. "Know wherever I am and whatever doing, I am thinking of you!"

With that, Mike Turner walked into the Wyoming wilderness.

He spent his first night alongside Eklund Lake, 6 miles into the Bridger-Teton National Forest. A few birds sang. A breeze stirred the pines.

". . . so quiet, so perfect. Is it all just as you want it, God? Or like skeptics say . . . is it just random events and we are nothing before the beneficence and destructiveness of nature? You send the winds and rain and yet even amidst the deep savagery and destruction of life, I sense your hand. In threatening my comfort, even my life, you challenge me to cope. In beauty and peace you refresh me. And all of it I need . . . God bless this trip. May it fulfill your holy purposes."

Turner wound his way to Island Lake, the beautiful, sky-blue heart of the Winds with its *"amazing beauty that fills my soul,"* then up 12,150-foot Indian Pass. The rocky notch is the border between the well-traveled Bridger Wilderness, with its web of maintained trails, dayhikers and sport climbers, and the virtually empty and trail-less Fitzpatrick Wilderness.

Atop the pass, Mike Turner took a few photographs, checked his map, then stepped over the Divide onto Knife Point Glacier, an immense ice field rippled with crevasses. To cross it, Turner had to negotiate three increasingly steep pitches. On the second pitch, Andy, whose paws were tender on the ice, began to slide and whine. On the third pitch, it was Turner who slid. Without crampons or an ice axe to stop himself, all he could do was point his feet downhill and ride it out. *"What a tough time."*

Although he downplays it in the journal, that "tough time" may have had a role in what would turn out to be a fateful decision. If he had kept to his intended route, Turner would have veered south from the bottom of the glacier back up into the snow of Alpine Lakes Pass. Or he could have moved north through the grassy valley of the North Fork of Bull Lake Creek, a longer but lower and even less-traveled route. *"We decided to take a longer route"* is all the journal says of his divergence from his "Wander in Wonder" itinerary.

At first, the place seemed almost magical. They *"entered an enchanted valley of wildflowers and grasses. Beautiful."* In a dimming, golden light, he set up his tent and heated some soup. Andy sat licking sore paws while Turner opened the journal to write.

"Tiredness is the fruit of one thing I love about wilderness, the chance to be fully committed to something. We worked hard today, faced danger and risk, played it safe though, too, where wisdom was called for. I will remember this day. It is filled with the ecstasy, the essence of life. By it, the Lord will fill me with strength, conviction, wisdom and trust. Thank God we made it down that hill."

He closed the journal and stood to stretch, feeling his body tingle with the mix of exhaustion and exhilaration that comes from hard work in wild country. Then he crawled into his tent, snapped off his flashlight, and drifted to sleep beneath a blanket of stars twinkling like ice chips in the blue-black mountain sky.

The next day, a sliding boulder would change everything.

• • •

After the terror of the rockslide, the panic of realizing he was trapped, and the initial struggle with the immovable boulder, Turner turned his thoughts away from getting free and toward surviving the coming darkness. He passed a fitful night with his sleeping bag jammed awkwardly around his legs for warmth. Surely in the morning he'd figure a way out of this.

The journal passage for the next morning shows him listing his concerns as if thinking things out on paper:

"I am concerned about first losing my legs, second running out of snow to melt for water, and fuel, third hypothermia. My biggest concern is water. I have only 2 quarts left. The irony is that the lake is only 30 feet away . . . I am drinking 1 quart today, saving a quart for tomorrow. I am also saving my urine. I wonder how it will taste with Crystal Light?"

Emptying his pack, Turner set up a makeshift "camp" around him. He had his stove, sleeping bag, and food for a week or more. Careful not to let anything slip out of reach, he took stock of each piece of gear, pondering how it could be used to free him or signal for help. His camera became a wedge to pry the rock. The rainfly to his tent became a sun shade and a means to catch rain, a possibility he didn't know whether to pray for or dread.

"On one hand, a rainstorm could save my life, giving me the water I need. I've got plans to catch every available drop . . . but then the rain is also my worst enemy because if I get soaked my legs will get very cold . . . A rain . . . would be very hard to survive."

As if the writing of the words sparked another thought, he added, *"I just had an idea about using the tent poles that just might work"* and signed off to try it.

"I know one of the reasons he didn't write even more in the journal," says Turner's friend Mark Smith, "is that he was busy trying to think of ways to get himself free, or at least survive until someone found him. That's the kind of person he was. There is something honorable in the way he fought every way he could think of to survive."

That first full day in the rocks, of all that were to come, was probably the best. Turner had enough water, at least for a day or two. There was no intense pain or significant bleeding. And he still had hope.

"I had dreamed of a special time alone with God, facing the elements, the passes, thinking about my life, the direction of the church, about my family. Indeed this has been all of those things only magnified 100 times. Thoughts about life, God, people, risk, filling my time. When I think about it this way, I believe I will survive, smarter or wiser, more thoughtful, more aware of my limits . . . I do feel confident in my Christian hope. God will make a way either earthly or heavenly. My only dread is not seeing my family and being present with them in body. That's what I think about."

He even found the strength for a bit of humor, writing to Diane, *"If I make it, you will hear a lot about this time, details you are probably not that interested in but I know you will listen."*

And Turner himself was listening, straining for any hint of hikers approaching. A single hiker could get him water and go for help; a pair of them might be able to pry the rock free. A group from the National Outdoor Leadership School (NOLS) had gone through just 2 days before the boulder pinned Turner's legs. But now, there was no one. Once, there did come the whoop-whoop of a helicopter out of sight behind the ridge. At first the sound must have seemed like a miracle, yet it came no closer. After a time, Turner realized the helicopter was not for him. Despite his own predicament, his heart went out to who-ever was in trouble. *"Hope they find that lost person too,"* he wrote, in a weakening hand.

Eventually, the sound of the chopper faded. The solitude that Mike Turner had longed for was beginning to tighten around him like a noose.

Danny Holgate, search commander for Tip Top Search and Rescue, pressed his hand against the cold plexiglass window of the Bell 206B3 Jet Ranger helicopter to blunt the vibration and stared out at the jumbled landscape of rock and ice passing below. His eyes peeled back every shadow, untangled every knot of fallen trees, searching for any movement or flash of color that might be a hiker in trouble.

According to the "Wander in Wonder" itinerary, Turner was to complete his hike in 9 days and meet his family and friends at the Big Sandy trailhead on Saturday, August 8. When he didn't show up at noon as planned, Diane at first felt little worry. "Honestly, I just felt irritated," she says. "I figured he was out there taking pictures, leaving the rest of us to carry the gear to the first lake, our 'plan B' if we didn't meet up at the trailhead."

As Saturday afternoon dragged on and the party set up camp at Dad's Lake to wait, questions began to creep into Diane's mind. What was slowing him down? Was it the knee he had injured skiing 4 years ago, or a dog with sore paws? "Before Mike left," Diane says, "Katie, our youngest, had asked him what we should do if he didn't show up. We laughed, then thought it would be a good idea to set a deadline." If he didn't arrive by Sunday at 4 p.m., they would seek help. But as that second deadline neared, Diane found herself re-reading the words printed on her map: "You will be charged for the rescue costs (i.e., helicopter time or horse rental)."

"I knew Mike wouldn't want us to make a big deal over nothing," Diane says. And so they waited.

By the time the moon rose that Sunday night, casting the peaks in an eerily beautiful silvery light, Diane knew something had gone very wrong. Her husband was missing. They would go for help in the morning.

The call came in to the Sublette County Sheriffs Office in Pinedale at 10:06 a.m., August 10, and the dispatcher notified Danny Holgate. A strong, compact man with a cop's direct gaze, 42-year-old Holgate has been working search and rescue for 18 years, the last 6 as search commander. He's helped build Tip Top Search and Rescue from a "jeep and beer operation" ("jump in a jeep, drive to a remote spot, and drink beer until the guy walks out") into one of the best all-volunteer units in the country. Yet every instinct told him this one was not going to be easy. The search area was immense: two national forests, two sides of the Continental Divide, two counties, three designated wilderness areas, and the Wind River Indian Reservation. As one volunteer claimed, "You could have every volunteer in Wyoming link arms and never cover a quarter of it."

As the helicopter banked for another pass, Holgate strained to make out new footprints on Gannett Glacier and thought, "Hell of a place to get lost."

"I feel so foolish taking this longer pass," Turner wrote on the Wednesday after he was trapped. *"So lonely, more than I imagined . . . Who would have guessed that 4 days would have gone by and no one has come this way?"*

Although the loneliness was difficult, the weather was his most immediate threat. Records from the weather station at nearby Big Piney show that temperatures during that time broke 100°F during the day and dropped to 39°F at night. Five thousand feet higher in the mountains, the cold nights would have seemed endless, the midday sun brutal. The merciless cycle of cold and heat wrings the water from a human body. At rest, a human male loses about 2 ½ quarts every day through sweat, urination, and respiration. Heat, exposure to sun and wind, and physical exertion such as struggling with a boulder can double the loss. Thirst begins at just a .8 percent drop in body weight from water loss. A 3 to 4 percent loss, which can easily occur in just 24 hours of exposure, can cause fatigue and confusion. At 10 percent, physical and mental deterioration begins. A 15 to 25 percent drop causes death.

At first, Turner melted snow, but the few pockets he could reach soon ran out. Once, he tied a length of cord to the lid of his water bottle and tried tossing it into the lake. It jammed in the rocks just a few feet short.

Another night. The dead cold of the boulders sucked the warmth from his body. He woke again and again, shivering.

Another day, hours on end with nothing but the sound of the wind shoving against the mountains, an occasional whistle from a pika in the talus. Without water, exposed to the elements, Turner soon began feeling the effects, hallucinating once that he could see Diane and Katie standing nearby.

"They had been on the rock. I cried out aloud for you. The rock seemed to have moved . . . [I]t is like others are present, only it is Andy and then I am doing something because 'they' suggested it."

But there was no "they." Every moan of the wind must have seemed like a human voice, every clatter of rock like an approaching footstep. Still, no one appeared. Mike Turner was alone, almost.

"God is with me but I am angry with him. Why this terrible injustice, or is it the product of pride? This sense of wrestling against God or the angel of God is distressing. What can I do against God? . . . I don't want to be fighting against God's will. How am I failing him or what does he need me to teach? What is the purpose of this ordeal? Will I ever know, or continue to be puzzled, angered, and feel quite abandoned by the one I serve?"

To a man who had spent most of his adult life teaching others the joys of God's eternal presence in their lives, the sense of abandonment must have been gut wrenching. Steeped in biblical teachings, he could not help but recognize the parallels between his entrapment and the imprisonment of Paul or the Old Testament sufferings of Job. He understood that even a lifetime of faith and obedience did not keep a person from pain and suffering, but this was more than even he could have imagined.

"Last evening I was getting my bedding set around my feet, my bedding can't get down there normally, when I noticed something like a cast on the front of my leg. It was my leg without feeling. I felt like I had to get out and began working from 9 p.m. to 12, slowly levering the rock. Now it is tighter. I cried out and cried out to God who doesn't seem to care about my suffering, struggling, and pain, and the loss of my left leg. I begged and prayed for some help in moving the rock but none seemed to come."

He was, in a sense, living out his own parable deep in the wilderness, alternately wracked by guilt, anger, hope, betrayal, and yearning. The question of faith must never have seemed so stark, so simple, and yet so difficult. Alone in a way few people experience, Turner had only the biblical promise that nothing, "neither death, nor life, nor angels . . . nor height, nor depth, nor anything else in creation will be able to separate us from the love of God."

Sometime after the 5th day, as Turner shifted his body or struggled against the boulder, the journal slipped out of his reach. In the time he had been trapped, the notebook had kept his voice and hopes alive, providing him with a thin, frayed connection to his family and friends, to a life beyond the pile of rocks. Now it was gone. Frantically, he dug for anything to write on. In his first-aid kit he found a pocket New Testament, and over the next few days he filled the blank pages at the front and back. When those were full, he used the margins of the only piece of paper he had left, the instruction sheet for his one-burner camp stove.

These notes are less organized, less legible. *"Shutting down,"* he wrote as he passed a week trapped in the rocks. *"Getting low. Thought I would be found yesterday . . . Many thoughts, most of church, future for kids, some friends . . . I love you Diane, terribly sorry for stupid [unreadable word]."*

Even with the scrawled, undated entries in the Bible and on the instruction sheet, it is impossible to imagine what the last days of Mike Turner's life were like—the burning dryness of his throat, the cramping muscles, his mind losing track of time and place. "3," he wrote, and then circled it. *"Journal, the Bible, and this,"* clues to be sure all his notes would be found. *"Fading to nothing. So skinny."* He removed his wedding ring and set it on a rock nearby so that it would not slip off his finger and be lost.

As a pastor, Mike Turner had been called upon hundreds of times to comfort others in the face of death. At funerals and in the hushed living rooms of mourning families, he had overseen the passing of others. Now, alone in one of the wildest places on the continent, he was, in effect, overseeing his own.

"Fill me with peace, Lord. May the conditions not deny my love for you . . . I am ready to die, though missing my family. To live is Christ. To die is gain . . . I will trust in God though he will slay me, yet will I trust him, he is the way, the truth, the light."

As his final hours approached, Turner's body was shutting down; but it was as though his spirit was opening up. All the questions, all the doubt and anger seemed to dissolve like so much morning mist on that unnamed lake. What remained was the unbreakable bedrock of belief.

"*God loves (unreadable word) Love Dad, Mike,*" the last legible line reads. A boulder could crush his legs; it could not crush his faith.

And then, 10 days after he was pinned, Mike Turner's journal goes silent.

In the flurry of days that followed Diane's initial call for help, a "hasty team" traced Turner's itinerary. Retailer REI faxed in the crack pattern for the size 13 Asolo hiking boot Turner wore, so searchers could look for prints. Posters went up at trailheads, in every storefront from Pinedale to Lander. The Turner children collected names from trail-head registers and matched them with phone numbers off the Internet. Carloads of volunteers from Turner's congregation converged on the Wind Rivers to help. "We've never had a search like this one in terms of the family and friends being so involved and so helpful," Holgate says. "It was obvious from the start that this guy was loved and respected."

But even with all of those eyes out there looking, clue after clue led nowhere. And time was running out. More than 70 percent of lost victims found alive are discovered within the first 48 hours. Of those who don't survive, 75 percent die within the first 3 days. "I pulled Danny aside at one point," Mark Smith remembers, "and asked straight out how long someone could last out there." Holgate answered that with a traumatic injury, "you'd probably make it through the first night. You might make it through the second. The third night would probably get you." It was now nearly 3 weeks since anyone had seen Mike Turner.

On August 23, the search for Mike Turner was called off. "The case isn't closed," Holgate told the family. "We'll throw everything we have at any new lead. But for now, we've done all that we can." As the days grew colder and the first snow dusted the high peaks, is seemed that Mike Turner's fate would become a secret of the mountains. "We needed to catch a break," Holgate says.

And then they got one.

Five days after the search was called off, Turner's dog Andy walked out of the wilderness led by a pair of hikers who had seen the posters at the trailhead. Wet, footsore, and 20 pounds lighter, the dog was exhausted but not hurt. He was taken to a veterinary clinic and rested while searchers and the family regrouped. "Andy being found alive opened up a whole new realm of emotions for me," Diane says. "I was hopeful but still trying to be realistic."

On August 31, more than a month after Mike Turner had set out and 23 days after his family had expected him at Big Sandy, a search team set out on one more trip into the Wind Rivers, hoping Andy would lead them to some answers. That same day, Jeff Stewart, a hiker from San Diego, was making his way along the edge of the unnamed lake near the Brown Cliffs on a 9-day cross-country hike with a route eerily similar to Mike Turner's. Intent on his footing in the loose rocks, Stewart glanced up and, 50 yards away, saw what appeared to be a man sitting up in the rocks. "I had seen the posters at the trailhead and knew they were looking for someone," he says. "So I called out, 'Hey, are you all right?' There was no answer. I knew there wouldn't be." Stewart already knew who it was.

On September 3, just as the search team prepared to drop off Indian Pass onto Knife Point Glacier with Andy in the lead, their radio crackled to life. It was Danny Holgate: Turn around, he said. A hiker had walked into the Sublette County Sheriffs office carrying a wallet. It belonged to Mike Turner.

The coroner performed an autopsy and filed a report showing that Mike Turner had died sometime on August 11, the same day the first helicopter carrying Danny Holgate lifted off to begin the search.

More than 3 years after her husband's death, Diane Turner sits in the family room of her home in Caldwell, Idaho, gently holding a thin, red spiral notebook, the journal of Mike Turner's "Wander in Wonder." Daughter Jill, who was just starting college when the search began, is now engaged to be married; Ben is a freshman in college; Katie, a junior in high school, plays volleyball. Andy goes on fewer hikes these days, but he still smears the patio doors with his nose trying to get in or out. "Oh, if he could only talk," Diane says with a sad smile.

"It was only this spring," she says, "that I began to finally see things not through the filter of Mike's death." There is still pain and tears and questions. But there is healing, too. "We knew an extended solo hike could be dangerous, but I've always believed that to live fully sometimes involves risk," she says. "Our Christian faith points us towards a life of courage."

One year to the day after Mike Turner was to complete his hike at Big Sandy trailhead, his family and a small group of friends returned to the Wind Rivers. They hiked the same torturous trail; Diane carried her husband's ashes on her back. In a private ceremony deep in the heart of the Wind River Range, Mike Turner's ashes were given to the winds over Island Lake, the spot that had filled his soul with its "amazing beauty." That night, while walking alone on the lake's edge, Diane Turner looked down to notice millions of stars reflected in the still water, as if heaven were glancing at itself in a mirror. "It was perfect," she remembers, "the beauty of God's heaven reflecting in the beauty of God's wilderness."

It was the kind of moment Mike Turner would have loved.

The Last Days of the Mountain Kingdom

by Patrick Symmes

Patrick Symmes traveled from Kathmandu into Nepal's Rolpa district in May 2001 to attend a rally of more than 10,000 communist rebels.

I t is in the nature of communist revolutions, many scholars have noted, to screw up a good cappuccino. Lying on the hotel bed my second morning in Kathmandu, I find that the medicinal properties of caffeine have assumed heroic proportions in my jet-lagged brain. There was airport Nescafé in New York and London, anemic hotel java in New Delhi, and watery airborne muck everywhere in between. Now, all I really want from life is some strong coffee.

While I wait for room service to deliver the cure, I try the phone number one more time. I've dialed it for a day with no results. The telephone system in Kathmandu is inexplicable. I can't tell if I'm getting no connection, or no one is answering, or I'm dialing the wrong number.

If someone ever does answer, that person is supposed to know where the guerrillas are. The insurgents, elusive revolutionaries from the hills, call themselves Maoists. Nobody paid attention when this hard-line faction of communists declared a "people's war" back in 1996. The guerrillas were almost without weapons, and did little more than organize propaganda rallies for poor farmers in Rolpa district and other remote western zones of Nepal. But they've earned a reputation for severity—banning alcohol, cutting off the hands of hashish dealers, and forcing village gamblers to eat their decks of cards. And last September the revolution entered a new, militant phase. A thousand guerrillas appeared from nowhere to blast their way into Dunai, the remote western town that served as the gateway for Peter Matthiessen's trek into Inner Dolpo in *The Snow Leopard*. The pace of attacks has picked up since then: This April the Maoists stormed two remote police outposts—known here as POPs—in the western towns of Rukumkot and Dailekh. The posts were overrun at night by hundreds of guerrillas hurling homemade hand grenades in human-wave attacks. Seventy police officers were killed, some of them executed after they had surrendered. On July 7, another 39 were killed in three simultaneous attacks in Lamjung, Gulmi, and Nuwakot districts, west of Kathmandu. Smaller skirmishes are now a weekly event, as the Maoists drive the government out of whole swaths of the countryside, stripping the dead and the prisoners of rifles, ammunition, and shoes. With up to 5,000 full-time fighters, and as many supporters in part-time militias, the biggest problem the Maoists face is having more recruits than equipment.

Most Western tourists and trekkers, including the 40,000 Americans who visit Nepal each year, have dodged the sharp edge of this unsheathed war. But that grows harder every day. In February, a Chinese development worker, the first foreigner, was injured when Maoists raided a dam project to steal dynamite. Still, in Kathmandu, there is denial.

I punch the digits on my phone, and this time someone answers. "Sorry, sir," the voice replies in trembling, terrible English. "No Maoists." He doesn't know what I'm talking about, he's never heard of the Maoists, there's nobody here by the name I'm asking for. I leave a message and hang up. A couple of minutes later, there's a knock on the door. It's room service with the cappuccino, which smells of everything good. I take one sip, and the phone rings.

It was then, with the heavy cup still in my hand, that words began to drift toward other meanings, that reality began to melt into new and unstable forms. Like Alice, I'd swallowed a potion that would take me into a Wonderland, a kingdom of retrocommunism unlocked by secret handshakes and punctuated by thousands of clenched fists. Time would now flow backward, the 21st century giving way to Year Zero, Boeings yielding to bows and arrows, video night in Kathmandu becoming firelight in mud huts. The forecast for the glorious future would look a lot like 1950.

It is the same voice on the phone, but different. His English and his attitude have suddenly improved. "You want to meet the Maoists?" he asks. Voices argue in the background, and then he announces that it is time for a journey. He can't say what kind of a journey it is, whether it will be to the east or the west, into the Himalayas or down to the subtropical plains. He can't say how long we will be gone. He won't even tell me who he is.

I write down an address. "You must be there in 15 minutes," he says.

This is impossible, but we try. I run downstairs, rip photographer Seamus Murphy from the lunch table, throw money at the front desk, and we walk out with only the clothes we are wearing, spare socks, and the contents of our knapsacks.

The taxi creeps through the crushing traffic of Kathmandu, swerving around bicycle rickshas and sacred cows sleeping in the stream of Toyotas. We turn along the Royal Palace, a Himalayan Elsinore surrounded by spear-point fencing that serves not to keep danger out, but to trap it inside. (The massacre of the royal family is less than two weeks away.) Our driver turns down Durbarmarg; we cross a bridge, enter a neighborhood that foreigners never visit, and are dropped on a busy sidewalk, 20 minutes late. I watch the passing stream of humanity, sari-clad shoppers and topee-topped deliverymen, students in jeans and dusty construction workers in sandals. They are remnants of a Nepal that is already fading away.

A young man in a tan shalwar kameez—a Pakistani-style long shirt over pants—steps out of the traffic. His eyes are burning in his brown face, and his smile is a trick. "Hello, sir," he says. "Come with me." Without waiting, he folds back into the flow of people, walking fast.

The rabbit hole opens up, and we, soon to be followed by the entire nation, fall in.

They definitely need some new astrologers at the royal court in Kathmandu. It was the seers of the spheres, casting their ancient divinations and decoding the celestial motions, who laid the trap. They calculated that the heavens were not in alignment for a royal wedding. The crown prince had picked the wrong bride. The auspicious date and the harmonious mate were still years in the future. The queen listened to them too closely—or, some say, they listened to her too closely—and rejected her son's plan to marry his girlfriend.

Intrigue is the Nepalese national pastime, factionalism the country's historic curse. Crown Prince Dipendra's bride-to-be, Devyani, and Queen Aiswarya were both members of the most powerful political clan in Nepal, the Ranas, who ruled the country from 1846 to 1951 in an inherited dictatorship that allowed the royal Shah Dev family to retain the crown. But the Ranas long ago split into rival branches, and Aiswarya could not stomach her son's choosing from the wrong side of the family tree.

On June 1, 29-year-old Dipendra—popular heir to the throne of the world's only Hindu kingdom, inheritor of the Lost Horizon—did something that was, the astrologers admitted later, not foreseen in his charts. He reportedly drank some scotch, smoked some hashish, and then committed regicide, patricide, matricide, fratricide, sororicide, and finally suicide. Shortly after being ejected from a family dinner for drunkenness, Dipendra returned with a submachine gun, an assault rifle, a shotgun, and a pistol, and killed everyone he could, beginning with his father, continuing through most of the royal household, and ending with himself. When it was over, ten people were dead.

Like Hamlet, the crown prince seems to have been driven to violence by the inbred madness of a rotten kingdom. Like Ophelia, the star-crossed young royal killed himself at a pond in the palace garden. But you don't have to look to Shakespeare for analogies: Nepal's own history is littered with examples of blood on the crown, including a spectacular 1846 massacre, instigated by the queen, that cut down more than 30 members of the elite.

Still, the murdered king had seemed the very model of a modern minor monarch. Birendra Bir Bikram Shah Dev, a descendent of the original Gurkha prince who conquered and united Nepal in the 1760s, had been educated at Eton and Harvard, and became absolute monarch at age 26 upon the death of his father, King Mahendra, in 1972. Unlike his father, who had dissolved Nepal's first constitutional government in 1960, imprisoned most of the dominant Nepali Congress Party leadership, and banned all political activity, Birendra was a relatively liberal ruler, the glue that held together this country of 23 million people—a patchwork of 60 languages and a score of ethnic groups—as it opened to the outside world.

The political system, however, remained tightly restricted until 1990, when street demonstrations forced Birendra's royal hand. He cemented his popularity by assenting to democracy—albeit a system where weak prime ministers are squeezed between an unaccountable monarchy and a parliament of cynical, corrupt coalitions. Democracy has now given birth to 92 registered parties, among them 15 "legitimate" communist parties that have often overlapped in coalitions, and even names. The Kathmandu phone book currently lists the Nepal Communist Party (United Marxist Leninist)—the main opposition in parliament—as well as the Communist Party of Nepal (Marxist Leninist), the Nepal Communist Party (Democratic), the Nepal Communist Party (Masal), and its rival-by-one-letter the Nepal Communist Party (Mashal). All of them despise the Communist Party of Nepal (Maoist) for abandoning the electoral process in 1995 to go underground.

Despite the patina of modernity in Kathmandu, the country still suffers the aftereffects of isolation. High-caste Hindu Brahmans and Chetris of Indian descent, called Aryans, control the government, the economy, and much of the best farmland, while low-caste farmers and untouchables are marginalized. Almost half the country's people, including the Sherpas, are "tribals," mountaineers of Tibeto-Burmese descent, usually Buddhist or animist in their beliefs. There are long memories here, and hill people resent that Hindus arrived centuries ago as refugees, only to impose their culture, alphabet, rulers, and religion.

"It is a country made of groups that have long histories of suspicion toward each other," says Joe Elder, director of the Center for South Asia at the University of Wisconsin, Madison. "The farther you go out from the Kathmandu Valley, the more people insist that they are Gurung, or Tamang, or Magar, not Nepalese."

Modern geopolitics plays out along parallel lines. Never conquered by the British, Nepal swelters in the economic and political shadow of India, the regional superpower. Since the enemy of my enemy is my friend, Nepal has reluctantly turned to China. The realpolitik issue for China is Tibet. As long as Nepal clamps down on its tens of thousands of restive Tibetan exiles, Beijing supports Kathmandu, not the Maoists.

Squeezed between giants and pricked by overpopulation, deforestation, and corruption, many resentful Nepalis are vulnerable to conspiracy theories. ("In my experience, there's at least one conspiracy theory for every person in Nepal," Elder notes.) Ideologues who promise a war on "class enemies" and the satisfaction of ancient grievances find willing listeners. The Maoists' elusive leader, Comrade Prachanda (Nepali for "fierce"), constantly denounces the country's Hindu Brahman leaders, despite being a Hindu Brahman leader himself, and has whipped up nationalist paranoia with predictions of an imminent Indian invasion. Most of the time, however, Prachanda leaves the talking to the guerrillas' media-savvy second-in-command, Baburam Bhattarai, an Indian-educated architect fond of gassy vows to "hoist the hammer-and-sickle red flag atop Mount Everest."

The explosion of all these tensions came not with the royal massacre, which left the nation in stunned silence, but three days later, when—as in Hamlet—the dead king's brother, 55-year-old Gyanendra, assumed the throne in a ceremony whose very haste prompted suspicion. Many Nepalis did not believe—would not believe—the official verdict that the massacre was the act of a single, drug-addled prince. It was a double cross by factions of the Rana family; it was a coup plot by India and the CIA; it was Gyanendra, who, conveniently absent, used his despised son Paras to orchestrate the killings. Comrade Prachanda, rumored to be hiding in India or London, issued a statement calling the carnage and its aftermath "a serious political conspiracy." On June 4, thousands of demonstrators, fronted by communist students, took to the streets. Fourteen curfew violators were shot and wounded by police. Two editors and the publisher of *Kantipur*, a Kathmandu daily, were arrested after publishing an anti-royal article by Baburam Bhattarai. The Maoists launched a string of symbolic bomb attacks, dynamiting the house of the unpopular prime minister, Girija Prasad Koirala, and the chief justice of the supreme court, who led the dubious investigation into the massacre.

When King Birendra, his skin painted pink with tikka paste, was cremated on a funeral pyre, the old Nepal went up in flames with him.

The Maoists are perhaps the only beneficiaries of this national nervous breakdown, with thousands of men and women scattered in the hills, lodged in remote base camps in Rolpa and Jumla districts, settled in small villages down on Nepal's flat southern *terai*, or living over the next ridge somewhere near the Tibetan border. At a time when the entire nation is disarmed by events, the Maoists are bristling with weapons; as the government founders in discord, the guerrillas are laying out five-year plans; while Nepal's archaic social order crumbles under corruption, the insurgents spread hyperrational fantasies of a cultural revolution that will wipe the slate of history clean. The rebels already operate in a third of the country; they will only expand, thanks to the bloody discrediting of the ancien régime.

Despite the evasiveness of our Kathmandu contacts, we gather that there is going to be a big rally somewhere in the foothills. Although the guerrillas don't carry around copies of Mao's Little Red Book, they have adopted the Great Helmsman's essential strategy: using the countryside to encircle the cities. They have chased away the national police and established broad *aadhar ilaka*, or base areas. They have set up "people's courts" and village councils in a few places, but now they are going to declare a new shadow government at the multidistrict level, their biggest step so far. Our role, apparently, is to attend the rally and spread their propaganda.

We're not surprised, therefore, to find ourselves driving westward on the Prithvi Highway that first day. If the Maoists have a homeland, it is a cluster of five districts—Rukum, Rolpa, Salyan, Jajarkot, and Kalikot—in the midwest, a jagged, densely cultivated hill country dominated by the Magar ethnic group, far beyond the tourist orbits of Annapurna and Pokhara. We head out in a taxi—a Korean microbus—crowded with Seamus, our Maoist guide, our driver, and me, plus three Nepali men who turn out to be stringers for Kathmandu dailies. Still unsure of our destination, companions, and prospects, we keep our eyes focused on the countryside, the dry-season rice paddies decorated with tumbledown huts.

We turn south before reaching Gorkha, a region immensely popular with trekkers—and, increasingly, with Maoists. Although the guerrillas have ignored tourists so far, the U.S. Embassy cautions Americans against visiting Gorkha and 16 other districts, from Kalikot in the far west, to Sindhuli, east of Kathmandu; it restricts its own staff from traveling in Jajarkot, Kalikot, Rolpa, Rukum, and Salyan. With Maoists operating in 60 of the country's 75 districts, trekking companies like Geographic Expeditions and Snow Lion Expeditions have canceled or rerouted some excursions.

Not far from Buddha's birthplace of Lumbini, we pass a troop of rhesus monkeys waiting impatiently for the wheels of our taxi to split open the unripe fruit they have deposited on the asphalt. We overtake two long files of teenage soldiers, a 600-man battalion of the Royal Nepalese Army marching westward, clutching automatic rifles. So far the army has stayed in barracks while the demoralized, poorly trained national police have done all the fighting. King Birendra had been reluctant to escalate the conflict, convinced that negotiations were preferable. Within a few weeks of Birendra's death, however, Gyanendra would verify his conservative reputation by proclaiming a draconian National Security Act, permitting the arrest of anyone, anywhere, without any explanation. For now, the soldiers we pass, and the guerrillas we are heading toward, are all blissfully ignorant of the approaching storm.

By dawn the next day we leave behind asphalt and turn up from the flat *terai*. The first thing we see is a cardboard effigy of despised prime minister Koirala dangling from a lamppost: We are in contested country now. We swing up and over the Mahabharata mountains and pick up the Bheri River valley. Our leader, another Kathmandu supporter of the guerrillas, is sweating inside a down vest; he never removes his hat, dark glasses, or the earphones of his cassette player. With rigid discipline he gives no explanations, offers no answers, names no destinations.

The taxi driver, on the other hand, is a verbose fraud. The deeper we get into hostile territory, the more he quivers with fear. He invents a series of imaginary breakdowns, pulling over at any pretext to announce that it is "impossible, sir" to continue. Each time, after crawling under the van for inspections, I shame him into pushing on, but when he begins surreptitiously pumping the gas and brake pedals, ascribing the van's lurching to "clutch broken, sir," I drag him from behind the wheel and start driving myself.

The correspondents are equipped for the mountains in slacks and loafers. They speak Inspector Clouseau English, and pander to us all day with a stream of preposterously false declarations about the terrain, the travel time, and the villages we pass. If you like dust, bumps, bad food, sweaty seatmates, misinformation, near misses with trucks, and Bollywood music, the road trip has its moments.

We rattle down washboard roads and ascend toward the middle hills of the Dhaulagiri Himal. We pass a few POPs, outposts where frightened cops hide behind sandbags, and in the late afternoon we reach a nameless, straggling village where policemen stand on the roofs, scanning the valley. We check into a smoke-filled bunkhouse, and at five the next morning, under an icy half-moon, set off again. After dawn we try to sneak past the capital of Rolpa district, a heavily garrisoned town called Libang. We disembark, somehow manage to convince the authorities that we are just a badly confused trekking expedition, and continue on foot, leaving the road—and electricity, the government, and the taxi driver—behind.

After a couple of hours, we step along a swaying footbridge high over a green, boulder-strewn stream and find a tattered red flag with a hammer and sickle snapping in the breeze. "We are now entering area of topmost Maoist influence," one of the correspondents explains—the *aadhar ilaka*, the home of the revolution.

One more nameless river valley and we trip lightly across a second cable bridge to find an unarmed woman in camouflage sitting at a picnic table, watching the bridge. She pays no attention to us, and we march quietly on, turning left beneath a "Martyrs Arch"—a cement gate dedicated to the 2,000 guerrillas and civilians the Maoists say have been killed in the war so far. Within the hour we are waiting in a farmhouse while messengers are sent. A handful of curious men appear, loitering outside the hut, reluctant to come in. A couple carry astonishing muskets obsolete since the American Civil War. One has a pistol, but most are unarmed. They are wearing flip-flops.

Incredibly, these losers are the guerrillas.

There are three rules of travel in the Maoist heartland. Sitting in the safe house, we are briefed by the leader of the ragtag squadron, a 42-year-old former school principal who speaks fine English. He is an ethnic Gurkha and goes by the nom de guerre of Sanktimon, after the hero of a cartoon on Indian television. Sanktimon means "strong man," but it's not for his muscles. "It is because I am strong in ideology," Sanktimon offers with a wide grin. He explains the route we will follow and then the rules: (1) No taking pictures without permission. (2) No going to the bathroom without a guard. (3) You must give a speech.

Within hours, Seamus will disregard the first rule completely; the second one proves deeply problematic; the third rule is one I immediately reject.

We gloss over these disagreements and seal the deal with an exchange of *lal salaams,* a revolutionary slogan that means "red salute" and is always accompanied by a clenched fist. We quickly march off in single file, crossing more paddies and then heading up through a beech forest onto a switchbacking trail that becomes, eventually, the steepest surface I have ever climbed. Hours later we reach a razor-thin, foggy ridgeline at 5,000 feet. The slopes are stacked with terraces even here, the paddies no wider than a single ox. Nepal's population has tripled since the 1940s, and the relentless search for arable land has increased deforestation and erosion massively while still not producing enough to eat. Exclusively agricultural, western Nepal is nonetheless a net importer of food. Hungry, impoverished peasants are easy recruits to the Maoist cause, with its promise of a government by, for, and of the small farmers.

Sometime after dark, the sky explodes with rain, and we tumble into a puny hamlet where dozens of guerrillas wait in huts. These are real Red Army troops, main force soldiers in neat camouflage uniforms. They carry Lee-Enfield .303 rifles, relics from World War II but state of the art compared to the flintlocks carried by our patrol.

In a dark, smoky room we eat with the soldiers, wolfing down rice and lentils with our fingers. Comrade Strong Man won't answer questions about the movement, its ideology, or his own position within the group—"I am just someone," he says, dismissing my questions. The only foreign correspondent they've seen before, he says, was a dyed-in-the-wool communist from *The Revolutionary Worker,* the weekly newspaper from Chicago, and Strong Man assumes we're here to cheer the revolution on. He is thrilled to host fellow travelers and promises to find two spoons for "the gentlemen comrades" by the next meal. Out here, spoons are still in the future, and metal of any kind is so rare that even plowshares are made of wood. In the soft light of the cooking fire, surrounded by men clutching ancient weapons, we seem to be regressing toward the Bronze Age.

We sleep packed elbow-to-ass amid a dozen snoring guerrillas. At 2 a.m., I am jolted awake by a shower of blows. The guerrilla on my left is twitching in the grip of a nightmare. I lie on the stone floor, staring at the ceiling until 5 a.m., and then we are hiking again.

In meeting the Maoists, we've achieved exactly what most visitors to Nepal have been hoping to avoid. Although few foreigners have heard much about the guerrillas—thanks to a suppressed local news media and a see-no-evil tourism industry—the two groups are already beginning to meet on the remote mountain paths that they share. Some trekking groups have bumped into Red Army patrols, who have pressed them to "donate" binoculars and sleeping bags to the revolution, but in most incidents the guerrillas and hikers have passed without speaking.

The real squeeze is happening back in Kathmandu. In March of last year, many foreign-owned businesses were approached by guerrilla representatives demanding money. Speaking on background, to protect his business, the head of one major American trekking company explained it as "a choice between operating here or holding to your ethical standards." Like several other foreign outfitters, he paid $1,400 to ensure that the Maoists left his clients alone.

Funding the very revolution that threatens you may seem self-defeating, but taking a stand against corruption in Nepal is like pissing up a rope. Extortion was once the privilege of the royal family, but since democracy arrived, in 1990, there are many more hands in the pot. Foreign aid funds evaporate; trekking fees earmarked for irrigation projects and reforestation are siphoned off. Until the practice was exposed in 1995, Queen Aiswarya received three million rupees annually from the oil monopoly and a rake-off from all foreign aid that passed through her powerful Queen's Coordinating Council. The weak do what the powerful teach them: Traffic policemen shake down motorists, and beat cops hit up restaurants for protection money.

By this standard, the Maoists are quite reasonable. They send neatly written, personalized letters to hotels, businessmen, teachers, NGOs, and even government offices requesting the payments. In typical Nepali fashion, they will negotiate the price. The business of extortion has now become so lucrative that the country suffers from a plague of fake Maoists. A group of tourists rafting in the Chitwan nature reserve was robbed last year by "guerrillas," but an American diplomat told me that, of the four to five such encounters reported by tourists so far, only two involved genuine Maoists. In an effort to fight this corruption of their corruption, the Maoists began issuing receipts on official revolutionary letterhead, but they had to abandon this effort when—also in typical Nepali fashion—fake receipts were rushed into circulation.

Pervasive government corruption has become the single greatest source of support for the guerrillas. "Look at Kathmandu," says Barbara Adams, a textile expert living here since the early 1960s. "Most of the palaces were built with corruption money, taken from development funds and foreign aid. It's an aid mafia, literally." Originally from New York, Adams knows the inner workings of the Kathmandu elite better than almost any foreigner, having been the *kanchi swasni*— "unofficial wife"—of a prince in the 1960s. She still has the Sunbeam Alpine sports car given to her by King Mahendra's brother.

Like a surprising number of people in Kathmandu, including intellectuals, members of parliament, and even army officers, Adams is eerily sympathetic to the Maoists in the hills. She believes they are patriots, fighting against a corrupt order. They actually care what happens to the majority of Nepalis, who can't read and have no electricity. She quotes a Nepali friend: "We're all Maoists now; there is no alternative."

But the lack of alternatives is the very problem. King Birendra was quietly sending signals to the Maoists, who praised him and sent condolences on his death. The new government is a cipher, but will likely take a harder line to protect its wealth and position. Even a Sunbeam-driving sympathizer can see that every day that passes without a solution makes things worse. Like the Shining Path, the Khmer Rouge, and Chairman Mao himself, the more the guerrillas fester in mountainous isolation, the more paranoid and intolerant they become. "The longer this goes on," Adams notes, "the harder the Maoists will get. And the next thing you know, we'll have a Taliban."

• • •

We summit one of Rolpa's infinite peaks, and suddenly we're looking down on the site of the rally. It is a broad, rounded spur the size of several soccer fields, reaching out over a deep valley. We hike down, pass beneath another Martyrs Arch and find a half-dozen huts and a long schoolhouse—the hamlet of Babhang. A battery-powered public address system is lashed to poles, and a packed-earth platform with chairs awaits the speakers. After only a few minutes, there is the sound of chanting in the distance.

They come in village by village, spilling down into the rally with unfeigned hoopla. Sixty from one hamlet, 30 from another, 40 from a third, a stream of desperately poor, excited people waving their fists in the air. The men wear bland homespun skirts or worn-out tracksuits; the women dress in saris of royal blue, emerald green, earthen reds, and otherworldly purples. Within minutes, a second column begins to stream over a high peak in the distance. As they spot the rally site, men discharge their blunderbusses in thundering blasts that echo back and forth in the hills. A third column appears, snaking steadily up from the valley floor, hundreds more carrying banners and blasting off their own guns in reply.

The largest guerrilla rally I've read about featured 700 people; within an hour there are a thousand here, and then twice that, delegations from 52 villages across Rolpa. They march in crude military lockstep, barefoot or in blown-out sandals, and arrive chanting call-and-response slogans ("Communist Party of Nepal, LONG LIFE!" and "Marxism-Leninism-Maoism, LONG LIFE!"). Perhaps 200 Red Army soldiers wait, stonefaced. They've got Enfields—like the canvas sneakers on their feet, captured from the national police—and wear counterfeit Lowe Alpine backpacks. Comrade Strong Man appears from time to time to shout, "Here are the masses! The masses are coming!"

Village bands arrive, tooting on horns and banging drums. A group of black-clad boys dances into the rally, bells jangling on their ankles, and girls from the remotest peaks, who walked three days to get here, giggle and cover their faces at the sight. Every few minutes another black-powder gun detonates, launching a huge doughnut of smoke into the sky.

By noon there are 4,000 people, and still they pour in. A village militia arrives from some other century, clutching bows and carrying quivers of neatly fletched arrows, chanting, "No to feudalism!" Next is an entire girls' soccer team armed with blue tracksuits and muskets. Student groups traipse in with neat flags, and associations of untouchables, and women's groups chanting, "Murder and rape must stop!" The Maoists can sound progressive: They vow not only to fight police corruption, but to punish spousal abuse and hunt down rapists, while recruiting women guerrillas and political cadres. Likewise, they challenge the ancient caste system, which is nothing but racism, and the untouchables are among their most eager recruits.

Five thousand, six thousand, eight thousand people. The crowd fills the entire ground, each group parading under the Martyrs Arch with chants, and then marching to an assigned spot where they collapse into densely packed clusters. They open their umbrellas to make shade and light up chillum pipes, little chimneys of tobacco and marijuana casting puffs of smoke over the scene. There's a flurry of excitement when a government helicopter circles (high) overhead, scanning the rally, but they might as well read it in the papers: The Nepali journalists are busy taking notes, and their dispatches will hit the Kathmandu front pages in about four days. ("MAOISTS DECLARE ADMN, VOW TO FIGHT ARMY.")

Strong Man spots me taking my own notes. "You are preparing your speech," he announces. No, I remind him, I won't be giving any remarks. He seems disappointed but counters with the good news that two spoons have been found. A young guerrilla spoon-bearer is assigned to serve us lunch.

In midafternoon, with 10,000 peasants packed onto the spur, the propaganda starts. The main event is the declaration of the shadow government in Rolpa and several adjacent districts, and the new leaders of the revolution's first official government are invited to step forward. There are 19 of them, a cross-section of the movement itself—a few tough Magar peasants from Rolpa, much like the attendees at the rally, but also an ambitious student leader from Kathmandu, and several older professional communist politicians. Comrade Strong Man turns out to be Rolpa's new representative of "the intellectuals." Invoking the name of the almighty Prachanda, he delivers a 30-minute speech about the teachings of the leader they follow but never see; after him the new vice-chairman gives a speech, and after him the district's new top man, Chairman Santosh Buddha, gives an amazingly dull, hourlong talk. A typical politician, Buddha is lofty and affected, and seems to have practiced looking thoughtful in a mirror. Despite the sunshine, he preens about in a gray Gore-Tex coat, the only one at the rally. Seamus and I call him Chairman Gore-Tex behind his back.

My speech is a huge hit, although I have no idea what I said. With dusk approaching, Strong Man drags us onto the platform for a ceremonial welcome. Chairman Gore-Tex pins us with red ribbons and smears a thumbful of pink dye between our eyebrows, the traditional tikka blessing. As he lays a garland of lali guras flowers around my neck, he explains that these red blooms grow only at high altitude— "like the revolution." I try to run for it, but it is too late: They push me at the microphone.

The second I open my mouth ("Greetings to the people of Rolpa district") the crowd starts giggling. In a region where even radios are an unknown luxury, most of them have never heard a foreign language, and my brief clichés about peace and justice are buried beneath a rolling wave of laughter. After a *lal salaam* and a pathetic clenched fist, I slink offstage to a ragged cheer. I'll never survive my Senate confirmation hearings now.

I'm replaced by another speaker, and then another, on through dusk, politicians, newly appointed cadres, the women's representative, and then, in the dark night, a string of guerrilla officers, hard men in camouflage speaking hard words about "taking on" the army in a coming war.

By 10 p.m. all 10,000 Maoists—armed men and women, kids and babies—simply lie down where they are, some sleeping, others smoking, everyone wrapped tightly in shawls against the mountain chill. I head for the alfresco bathroom, trailed by the usual guerrilla guard. This time I'm ready. Hidden in my backpack, I've found a handful of chemical light sticks, and I break a green one and give it to him. He's never seen one before and rushes off in delight to show it around, leaving me in peace. The beam of my flashlight illuminates the bushes around me: wild cannabis, the source for Nepal's hashish industry and one explanation for the laughter during my speech.

Back at the hut, my guard sits in a circle of Red Army men, their faces glowing green from the soft chemical light. One of the guerrillas throws an arm around me and says, "Good speech." The valley still echoes with the words of the Red Army's top officer, Comrade Lifwang. "War is a challenge," he says. "Without war, nothing can be changed." So many military terms here are borrowed from English that I can follow along as he describes a battle just days ago, in eastern Nepal. He tells of the first platoon attacking the police. He pantomimes a police helicopter circling overhead, trying to relieve the besieged POP, the machine finally chased away by rifles cracking in the night. The second platoon comes forward, and finally the POP is overrun. Victory for the revolution. I pass out.

By first light there is not a single person left on the field. I wander over the barren saddle of the mountains, wondering if the 10,000 chanting peasants were a dream, but the proof is on the ground, the dust still imprinted with the shapes of their missing bodies.

The guerrillas' philosophy too is ghostly. So far we've had a propaganda massage without getting to ask any questions ourselves. Finally, at 10 a.m., with cold clouds blowing in, I am summoned to the schoolhouse, where the entire gang is assembled for a press conference. Gore-Tex, Strong Man, some Maoist schoolteachers, and several vice-flunkies are lined up on benches.

I sit on my bench, scuff my feet in the dirt, and finally ask the question I should have asked the crowd yesterday: How many people must die? The guerrillas like to cite the Shining Path as their fellow travelers in the Maoist cause. I point out that 30,000 people have died in Peru, without a Red victory. If that many people die in Nepal, will the revolution still be justified?

Yes, they all nod immediately. The true face of the revolution at last. "To protect a whole thing," a schoolteacher says, "a part can be damaged. It is the rule of nature."

Comrade Strong Man elaborates: "A big part of the people here believe it is not necessary to solve Nepal's problems with violence." He brushes aside this natural reluctance. "We clear their mind of this idea," he says. "The people's war is necessary."

They dismiss offers of peace talks from the government, tricks designed to fool the people, weaken the country, and deliver it to the control of India. Ominously, Gore-Tex vows a "protracted war in rural areas," and "armed urban rebellion," the first hint of a guerrilla war in Kathmandu.

They descend quickly into jargon. They are for dialectical materialism and against reactionary power. Chairman Mao's Cultural Revolution, in which mobs beat "class enemies" through the streets, was good, and will be imitated as soon as they come to power. Colonialism, feudalism, imperialism, capitalism, and revisionism are all bad. Peasants are good and politicians are bad. On this animal farm, four legs are good and two legs are bad.

Their policy about foreign tourists is clear: The more, the better.

"Not any foreign person is to be disturbed," Gore-Tex announces, as Strong Man nods. They actually invite trekkers to visit their areas—with permission—because they believe Westerners will be seduced by Maoism and spread the revolution to Europe and America. It's a Red Tourism offensive. "We will inspire them to flourish the same movement in their country!" Strong Man boasts.

Strong Man presents me with several pages ripped from his notebook. This document begins with an error-riddled manifesto—"the C.P.N. (Moist) is guided the ideology of Marxism-Leninnism-Maosim against the reactionary power of Nepal which is preserved by Indian expansionis and world imperialist"—and continues with an executive summary of the press conference, which bears no relation to any of the questions I asked.

> Q. *How do you face Royal Army.*
> A. *We will face it with the power of the people.*
> Q. *How do you forward the production.*
> A. *We forward it with the help of people.*
> Q. *How do you bring about indigenous society.*
> A. *We bring it according to Lenin's ideology.*
> Q. *How do you forward Negotiation with the government.*
> A. *We are fighting total war.*

As we talk, an early tendril of the monsoon season blows in, a thick, blasting rain of tropical density and high-altitude chill. We exchange endless good-byes in the dripping hut, while guards are found to escort us out of the base area.

During the wait, Strong Man teaches me the secret Red Army hand-shake (fore-fingers, pinkies, and thumbs meet in a triangle; then rotate on the thumbs into a soul shake). A dozen guerrillas crowd around to give me the shake. Overwhelmed by emotion, I hand out the remaining light sticks.

In a sopping-wet ceremony, Gore-Tex drops more flowers around our necks and rubs more tikka on our foreheads. He gives all of us, including the Nepali journalists, sealed airmail envelopes. I naively assume that these contain a letter, or a certificate, or some propaganda, and stuff mine into my pocket, ready to get moving. As I walk out the door, I notice that the Chairman's Gore-Tex coat has soaked through completely. It's as fake as he is.

The descent is a hallucination. We set off into howling rain, speed-hiking hour after hour in a downpour. We're still wearing our lunch clothes from a week before; our raingear consists of garbage bags. We trudge through mud, ford streams, and cross cliffs on slate paths two feet wide. At times the guerrilla walking point disappears into fog and mist. Landscapes open abruptly, and worlds disappear between glances. There are few people on the trails. A herder driving goats and cows stands still and looks askance; in one barefoot hamlet, we draw the entire population in a shy, silent crowd. A patrol of Red Army soldiers hustles past, without even a lal salaam. Bells tinkle in the distance, and strange howls float down from the slopes. One long day, and we are out of topmost Maoist country. Climbing now with night coming on, we hit the road and hitch a ride into Libang.

At some point in here I drag the crumbling, soggy envelope from my pants pocket, slide a finger down the seal, and discover that it contains money. Not a letter, not a certificate, not a propaganda flyer, but a bribe. About $5 worth of rupees. Now I'm as dirty as everyone else in Nepal.

Alice wakes up from her dream, and time begins to move forward again, bringing with it small signs of the depressing realities that grip present-day Nepal. In Libang, I meet Chairman Gore-Tex's nemesis, Harikrishna. He's the government's chief district officer for Rolpa, a conceited, high-caste politician who shows up an hour late, awash in flunkies. Although he can't even visit most of his guerrilla-controlled territory, he insists that the Red Army rules by fear alone. "They have no support," he tells me, cleaning his nails with the tip of a key.

We meet a 75-year-old refugee, Ratibhan Oli, one of hundreds of people the Maoists have chased out of their base areas. These are the "revisionists," people who won't, for one reason or another, toe the party line. And at a mud-floored boarding school the same day, 300 students assemble on the parade ground to hear me, at the insistence of their teachers, give another speech. Staring at their upturned faces, beneath guard towers, I am at a loss. Should I tell them to pay no mind to communist dingbats and court astrologers? Should I point out that the Maoist revolution will inevitably turn inward and eat its children, like every revolution everywhere?

I can't think of a damn thing to say.

Another day of brutal road travel and a prop plane back to Kathmandu. In the terminal, I spot a plastic box for donations to the Red

Cross and shove the remaining rupees, the Maoist bribe money that we didn't spend on Fantas, through the acrylic slot.

Soon the king will die. Kathmandu, like the countryside, is already seething, as if by premonition. There's another general strike on, one in a series that has paralyzed transport and turned the city into a ghost town. For days we wander avenues so quiet that the holy cows are confused by the lack of traffic and moo in despair. Without the pollution of tailpipes, the fresh mountain breeze is a reminder of an old Nepal. But the empty sidewalks and shuttered cybercafés of Thamel also look like another Nepal, some future place where the Maoists have come to power and dispersed the modern world with a harmless cultural revolution, emptying the city like the Khmer Rouge with good manners.

There are Nepali journalists who predict just such a Maoist takeover, but that worst-case scenario is unlikely. The army will deploy, the old guard in Kathmandu will rally to defend itself, and India, China, and the United States will stir themselves from indifference. "The Maoists are a real problem," says University of California, Berkeley professor emeritus of political science Leo Rose, a leading Nepal expert. "But it's hard for me to see them overthrowing the present government. What are they offering? They don't have any achievements or accomplishments. My own guess is they'll be an irritant, a problem, but not an alternative."

It is more likely that the Maoists will be undone by their own quest for ideological purity, by their faith in a violence that, as they themselves admit, is not supported by the Nepali people. The U.S. Embassy in Kathmandu argues that there may be as few as 2,000 hard-core communists, and that, as an American diplomat there told me, the "masses" backing the Maoists "are really ordinary people more disgusted with circumstances than Maoist in ideology." Their support for the guerrillas is "wishful thinking in a desperate situation," as Nepali political scientist Vijaya Sigdel puts it. But the more the Maoists expand, the quicker the people will learn that opposing a corrupt government is not the same as supporting a fanatical insurgency. Nepal can still evade the dark garden of Maoist dreams, but the exceptional kingdom is already losing its distance from the world, becoming instead a troubled, unexceptional place.

In the last days of the old Nepal, it is lovely to walk the strike-bound streets or roll about town in rickshas, pausing to watch aimless bands of students and communists march listlessly through the city, lifting their fists, occasionally tossing a brick. There's something wonderfully feeble about the scene. Perhaps the Maoists' grim ferocity will yet founder in the traditional incompetence of Nepali politics. There is always the hope of farce, rather than tragedy.

I stop around the royal palace a few times, but nobody is allowed to visit. The Gurkha guards in puttees and plumed hats shoo me away, and I have to settle for looking through the fence at the lush grounds, the pine trees, and the ornamental gardens.

In a few days the king will be dead. Long live the king.

When the Whip Comes Down
by Topher Donahue

Climbers are drawn from all over the world to Patagonia's soaring rock towers—even though the region's treacherous weather patterns make any Patagonia expedition a gamble. Topher Donahue and partner Jared Ogden took their chances in November, 2001.

I t started with a phone call in November from Jared Ogden. "Any chance you could go to Patagonia? It'll be my last trip for a while:" He was about to enter a more demanding and important challenge, fatherhood.

Jared and I had done only one climb together before, but it had tested us thoroughly. It was a first ascent in the deep, dark Black Canyon. Clawing our way out, hours past sunset, after hanging on for some of the most stomach-churning pitches either of us had ever done, our energy had been 100 percent positive, and the manner in which we played the game seemed compatible. Now we decided to roll the dice on a short trip to the Fitzroy region of Argentina, hoping for even one good day, to go big.

In late November we got off the bus in El Chalten, the small town at the trailhead to the area, to find the foothills covered in snow. Locals said they had had an exceptionally stormy month. We cringed, but from earlier trips, I knew that being ready for anything—from bouldering to yoga, ice climbing to reading, studying Spanish to cragging on the flanks of the giants—is the only sure way to have a great time in Patagonia. Otherwise, given the land's legendary storminess, it is too easy to get carried away by monomania, a tendency directly proportional to the number of days spent in a tent or snowcave. Would you rather fail attempting your dream objective, or succeed on whatever is in condition? Patagonia forces an answer to the dilemma. Many Patagonian veterans tell stories of fruitless focus on an objective for months, and then, in the last days of their trips, opening their minds to all options, and bagging fantastic spires.

We had one existing complication. On the bus ride from the airport in Rio Gallegos, a bus had left with our bags, but not us. Pike Howard, a friend from Colorado, was on board and tried to get all our bags off, but the bus driver kept the one full of food. The next day the driver denied that the bag had ever been there. It had been our first hint of the desperate poverty of most of the Argentine people. Pike kindly sold us some of his food, I had some that I'd brought from home, and we bought some in the expensive market of El Chalten, but our money was running out. The cheapest things in town are lamb and polenta, so we bought a lot of each. Raw meat doesn't keep too well, so ultimately we'd find ourselves fueled by polenta and pasta. "Fast and light" took on a whole new meaning: we'd fast, and then go home light.

We opted to hike into the range at the first sign of a calm day and try to go mixed climbing if the rock was too frosty for anything else. Most climbers hire horses to carry gear to the basecamp at the scenic Poincenot Camp, a three-hour walk from the trailhead. The other strategy is to ferry loads during the frequent periods of bad weather in order to maintain fitness and save money. The human-powered approach had always worked well for me until this time, when, after we'd spent two days carrying heavy packs, the sky cleared and the wind stopped. The clear, windless sky is like a whip, and we arrived at our basecamp with tired legs and backs only to find its lashes driving us out of bed at 2 a.m.

Two hours later, beads of sweat ran from my forehead into my gaiters, and words like, "skis . . . snowshoes," ran through my mind like a stuck record as we pushed sore legs in and out of post holes in the snow. The glacier had not yet hardened into a summer snowpack and we found ourselves sinking above the knee for most of the 4000-foot approach. What should have taken four and a half hours took eight and a half. We arrived in the cirque on Fitzroy's east side at 1 p.m. completely wasted and doubtful of even being able to climb easy terrain.

In any other mountain range we would have waited until the next day, but missing a day of good weather in Patagonia will haunt you for the rest of your life. With binoculars we could see ice lacing almost every crack in the cirque. A soaring line of ice ran unbroken for 1700 feet to the ridge between Aguja Mermoz and Fitzroy, so we stashed the rock shoes, pulled out the ice screws, and started climbing.

Thin ice runnels, often narrower than shoulder-width, ran uninterrupted up steepening corners of perfect granite. As we gained altitude the sound of the wind ripping over our heads went from a quiet hiss to a distracting roar, but the face was protected from the wind, and the climbing was five-star. We reached the ridge at 8:30 p.m. A face steeper than the one we'd just climbed dropped off the other side. Our eyes teared in the powerful gusts, inspiring the name *Padre Viento* (Father Wind) for the route. We savored views of obscure spires and the continental icecap that stretched from below us for 40 miles to the Pacific Ocean, acting as a freezer for violent incoming Pacific storms.

Our summit wasn't really the top of anything. It was merely a notch in a long, broken ridge that culminated to the right with the Mermoz, and far to the left with the massive bulk of Fitzroy, but we were thrilled to have climbed to the end of such a stunning line. The combination of the approach, pumper pitches up to WI 5+ and M6, rappelling into darkness, and recrossing the glacier put us past the 24-hour mark and into an energy deficit that would dog us for the next three weeks.

Señnor José Cuervo helped us celebrate the good fortune of making the trip a success in the first week, but 36 hours later, the whip cracked again. Another posthole session took us to the base of an improbable-looking line of ice on the Indian-headdress-shaped east face of Aguja

Guillamet. Jared led over the bergschrund and onto a bulge of over-hanging slush. For nearly an hour he got pumped stupid trying to get over it, his only protection two ice screws that wiggled in their holes. Eventually, by drop-kneeing against the rock and swinging like John Henry, he reached the solid-looking blue ice above. Unfortunately we were too late, and water cascaded around us as well as behind the vertical sheet of ice we'd hoped to climb. Jared rigged a dubious V-thread and down climbed carefully.

Back in camp, a single hello from Señor Cuervo sent us spinning while we ravaged our meager food supply. The ongoing debate of what to try next ranged widely. "Where's the *Potter-Davis* go?" Jared asked me of a new line on Poincenot.

"Who are Potter and Davis?" I asked jokingly, as we both knew the first ascentionists well.

"I think they're Harry Potter and Miles Davis," Jared answered, conjuring up an image of the youthful magician and the ancient (in fact, late) musician swapping leads on a Patagonian spire.

Rock climbing was still out of the question after a couple of days of snow, rain, and cold, so we decided to give the ice line on the Guillaumet one more try.

A bivy on the glacier put us at the beginning of the ice at first light. A cold, clear night had turned the slush into climbable ice, and we moved past our very low highpoint quickly. To our right, the terrain dropped off for 6000 feet to the desert lowlands and glacier-fed lakes. To our left, Fitzroy's mile-high North Pillar dwarfed every peak on that side of the massif. Thin ice and tricky mixed climbing set the stage for the next 12 hours. As we had on the Mermoz, we opted to leave the packs behind, and go for the 1800-foot face with some energy bars in the pocket and a water bottle on the harness.

"Hey," said Jared. "When we get home let's preach how the new style is pack-free climbing. We can write articles about how using a pack virtually guarantees success and takes the adventure out of climbing."

"Yeah, we can belittle anyone who ever carried a pack up a mountain! We can seek sponsorships, claiming to be practicing a purer form of the sport." We laughed until one of us happened to glance up at the next pitch, a melting runnel that sobered us right up.

For six pitches in a row, whichever of us followed would reach the belay and say with stunned honesty, "Wow! I'm glad I didn't lead that!"

The quality of the climbing kept us moving, but each section was so daunting that we never once uttered the momentum-gathering phrase, "It'll go!" At one point we followed the same runnel for 1000 feet. It ranged in width from three feet to three inches, and in places the angle tipped past vertical. On one pitch, the ice actually stayed smooth at 95 degrees without forming icicles or pillars. Desperate stemming against smooth rock and drop kneeing like sport climbers got us past the hardest sections while our forearms, biceps, and calves competed for delivering the most crippling cramps.

I watched Jared's front points to get an idea how hard it was going to be seconding. The harder the climbing, the more accurately he placed them. I knew a section was going to be desperate when he was setting his points without the slightest scratch or double-thrutch. Five pitches of M7 and four other burly ice pitches made for the most sustained long mixed climb either of us had ever done. At the ridge, another granite notch stopped us cold with smooth stone on either side. While summits in Patagonia are like nowhere else, our willingness to consider possibilities that ended on ridges had rewarded us with two mixed climbs that I'd thought only existed in my wildest dreams. Setting anchors down another face presented us with a rare problem in Patagonia: If we had another opportunity to climb, we were running low on equipment.

We named the route *The Gambler*, in honor of the state of mind anyone has to be in to take a climbing trip to Patagonia. We slept in an abandoned snowcave long into the daylight hours, cringing like vampires at the sunlight reflecting into the cave. In a moment of exhaustion-induced stupidity—aided, I can at least say, by quickly approaching black clouds and rain—we decided to bring all our equipment down to basecamp because we felt sure the good weather was ending.

The next day dawned clear and calm, and the whip stung. This time it sent us on the long walk to the Torre Valley in hope that the windward west side of Fitzroy and its satellite spires, Poincenot and Saint Exupéry, would be free of ice and snow and allow dancing in rock shoes. Eight hours later we were lost on the Torre Glacier, crawling over piles of glacial rubble, infinitely more wasted and wishing we could stick the perfect weather in our pockets and save it for later.

We finally found the Polish camp directly between Fitzroy and Cerro Torre, and passed out quickly. Morning brought rain and clouds enclosing the Cerro Torre group. We opted neither to climb nor wait, and instead walked another eight hours back to the trail-head at El Chalten, arriving wasted, of course. It's easy to take weather patterns personally, and with global warming a reality, maybe we should. It felt as if the weather had a bad sense of humor, because the next day was perfect.

We found ourselves toting full packs back to our original basecamp, Poincenot Camp, wondering how much more of a whipping we could take. "I guess we gotta just keep going!" became our mantra. Our motivation was much greater than our strength, because although we intended to try Fitzroy's East Pillar, one of the longest climbs in the range, we barely drug ourselves up the shortest route on the smallest spire, Aguja de la S.

To our immense relief, a couple of days of dubious weather gave us a break. We used the second cloudy day to carry anything we didn't need out to El Chalten because the end of our trip and the end of our food were both two days away. We devoured another lamb shank while frying polenta, flour, and potato flakes into funky patties to take along for lunch if the weather gods gave us another chance. To our amazement, our last possible day to climb was reasonably clear at midnight, so we mustered the juice for another 4500-foot approach to the base of the half-mile-tall east pillar of Saint Exupéry, one of the most artistically shaped spires in the area, with an angular twin summit. Only the granite giants surrounding it keep Saint Exupéry, just south of Fitzroy, from being one of the planet's most legendary spires.

Our lactic-acid-packed legs demanded that we leave anything not absolutely necessary behind. Over the years, Jared has completely over-dosed on hauling loads while climbing some of the biggest walls on the planet, so when it comes to leaving things behind he's manic. He wore just a single light sweatshirt under his Gore-Tex, and would have ditched everything else if I'd let him. He'd drilled out his hexes and cut every extra scrap of material off his pack and clothes. We talked about drilling out our carbon-fiber ice tools to really save some weight.

We had no route information, so we just picked the best-looking line and started climbing. The high pressure was crumpling as we started up the initial 800-foot mixed couloir. The upwind edges of the clouds were sharply chiseled, while the downwind edges smeared across the sky like paint brushed with water. The wind ripping over-head and around the spires sounded like a jet engine, and kept us scur-rying like scared rabbits.

As we climbed higher, the roar of the wind grew louder, but the corner system we ascended protected us well. "It feels like we're dancing with the devil!" said Jared wide-eyed as we moved past the point where we should have turned around. I remembered vaguely and completely inaccurately that the line, the East Pillar, was graded 5.10. Wearing packs containing our mountain boots, we swapped leads up increas-ingly hard and dripping wet dihedrals, trying to believe it was no harder than 5.10. A month later we found out it was probably the first free ascent, as the climb had been graded 5.11 A1. Now we know why it felt like 5.11+ in a waterfall; it was.

Fantastic corners of sharp-edged granite tempted us onwards, and soon we were within sight of the summit. Rapidly swirling clouds and rogue gusts buffeted us as we zigzagged along a devious line of least resistance. In one place we followed an arching hand crack along the edge of the spire. Although the line was still protected from the main force of the wind, I could reach out and put my right hand into the air current. It was like sticking a hand out the window of a car doing 80 miles per hour.

It was pure coincidence that we were on the summit at the precise moment the tempest pounced. If the weather window had slammed shut 10 minutes earlier, instant retreat would have been mandatory. In the time it took Jared to follow 50 feet of 5.2 to the top, it started snowing heavily and without a pause we shifted into rap mode. As we descended, the snow turned to rain and soon the wall was running with slush, filling every gap in our clothing with icy motivation. We pulled the ropes like men possessed, trying to stay warm. Jared was shivering so hard he could barely tell me how much he wished he hadn't left his insulated jacket behind. He was too cold to feel solid going first, so rigging the anchors became my task. Soon we were leaving behind cams, slings, and biners in the race against hypothermia and darkness.

Just as we reached the glacier and dusk reached us, the sky exploded with flashes of lightning. We coiled the ropes in a frenzy, and started across the soggy glacier, burning muscle for fuel. Jared went into overdrive hoping to get warm and to cross the crevasse field in the last fragments of light. I fell over trying to keep up with the adrenaline-jacked figure breaking trail in front of me, while flashes of lightning illuminated the monstrous spires and glacial chaos around us. We collapsed on a rock at the end of the snow in complete darkness, but another flash showed us how far we had to go and we staggered onwards.

A waterfall we had forded easily on the way up now appeared out of the darkness, and sent a new wave of adrenaline through our haggard nervous systems. It had grown in the storm to four or five times its original size, and the rocks we'd hopped casually across 20 hours earlier were completely submerged in raging whitewater. We discussed following the cascade down, but felt sure at some point we would be cliffed out, and forced to reclimb the talus. Before committing to an all-night ordeal, I thought we should rope up and try our luck in the torrent. Since it was my idea, I guessed I should volunteer to go first. Jared tied himself to the biggest boulder around, and sat down to belay. I tightened the cuffs of my jacket and gloves.

A slippery slab and stemming move across the first of the white-water put me face to face with the main current. I stuck a ski pole into the water to test the force, and it almost knocked the pole from my hand. Between thoughts of madness and backtracking, I noticed a sub-merged boulder halfway across the waterfall. I grasped onto the vision that I could dive to the boulder, then swallowed the metallic taste of fear, and jumped. Rather than try standing on the rock, I grabbed it in my arms. I stuck the water dyno and clambered into a crouch like a spastic torrent duck, then jumped again for the shore. My feet landed in whitewater, but the momentum carried me onto the slabs on the other side. I found a cluster of flakes to wrap the rope around and belayed Jared across the waterfall, pulling in rope at the cadence of his headlamp's movement.

We ate the last of our polenta patties, and fell into a sort of walking coma while negotiating the last couple of hours through loose talus to our basecamp. We didn't warm up until the following day while hiking out for the final time. Back in town, we learned that as we'd guessed, the two ice climbs, *Padre Viento* and *The Gambler*, had been first ascents, and the lightning storm that pummeled us on the final descent was the first lightning anyone could remember since the 1970s. Getting to experience one of the most unusual seasons in Patag-onian history made us feel extremely lucky.

We sold some gear in El Chalten, so instead of passing a 16-hour lay-over in the parks and streets of Buenos Aires, we were able to afford a room. And that was our luckiest break of the trip, because on the tele-vision in the hotel, every channel broadcast live coverage of the rioting taking place a few blocks away. We stayed in our ninth-floor room, watching out the window as people marched in the streets below, shouting. Office workers nearby threw reams of paper out of windows to drift in the wind and add to the chaos. We wondered if we would get out of the country safely.

Witnessing Argentina's economy, which at the end of 1999 had been the seventh-largest in the world, unravel made me wonder about the fate of the largest economy in the world, the good old U.S. of A. Between October and December of 2001, unemployment in Argentina had risen from 15 percent to nearly 30 percent, and the president resigned. On December 19, while we'd been fighting swollen rivers and fatigue on Saint Exupéry, the Argentine government had declared a state of siege and retreated to guarded offices while public violence escalated. On the television we watched footage of a McDonalds being pillaged and burned, government vehicles torched, and crowds trampled by police on horseback.

We left for the airport early, in a taxi with a driver who kept constant radio contact with other drivers to know which streets were safe for travel, and made it through the city along roads clouded with smoke from burning cars and looted buildings. A few days ago we had completed one of the hardest mixed climbs in Patagonia, and it meant absolutely nothing.

from Climbing Free
by Lynn Hill and Greg Child

Climbers ordinarily rely on artificial aids to climb the Nose route up Yosemite's 3,000-foot El Capitan. Gifted female climber Lynn Hill (born 1961) in 1994 tried to climb the route relying only on natural holds. Here, with help from climber and writer Greg Child (born 1957), she tells the story of that attempt.

A fter my career in climbing competitions, I returned to my roots as a rock climber, and I headed back to the cliffs that nature had made. After succeeding on Masse Critique, I knew that if I expanded my vision of what was possible, I could probably do an even harder climb. But rather than directing my efforts toward climbing a route of a higher technical grade, I wanted to expand my capacities on climbs with sky above my head and space below my feet. The idea of combining a high level of technical difficulty on a climb of big-wall scale began to take shape in my mind.

On one of my visits back to California in the early nineties, I met up with my friend John Long. While talking about climbing and my future plans, John said, "Lynnie, you should try making the first free ascent of the Nose on El Cap. It's one of the last great problems in American free climbing."

Of course! John was right. This was just the kind of challenge I was looking for. The Nose route follows the most prominent line right up the center of the biggest granite monolith in Yosemite Valley, and is perhaps the most famous big-wall route in the world. Climbers had been trying to free it for several years, but a few sections of the wall presented immense difficulty and had stopped all comers cold. Although it had been years since either John or I had done the route, we both remembered clearly that the crux problems consisted of thin cracks and delicate face climbing. John pointed to my fingers and said, "Those little fingers of yours will be the secret weapons on the Nose."

With my background as a traditional climber, combined with all my experiences on various types of rock over the years, I realized that this would be the perfect challenge.

A year passed, in which I shuttled back and forth between America and my home in France. Then, in 1992, I happened to cross paths with Hans Florine, who casually asked me if I would like to do a one-day speed ascent of the Nose with him. Hans was one of the leading speed climbers of the day. In competitions he often won the crowd-pleasing speed events in which two climbers race each other, and the clock, up a wall of moderate difficulty, hitting a bell at the end of their route to signal their arrival at the final hold. Hans had transferred that ability onto the rock, and the pure crystalline granite of the Nose had become his playground. By August 1992, Hans had made seven ascents of the route, and I had confidence in his ability to figure out the best strategy in solving time-consuming maneuvers like the King Swing pendulum. Speed ascents of the Nose are not done in the same style as free ascents because they involve a mixture of free and aid climbing techniques— an "anything goes" approach. To climb nearly 3,000 feet of El Cap granite so rapidly, a climber generally uses aid to pull past difficult sections. Though we clocked a time of eight hours and forty minutes, my main objective was not about speed. As we raced up the wall, I tried to imagine what it would be like to try free climbing past the notorious Great Roof, as well as the other sections that had never been free climbed. By the top of the route, I knew that I had indeed discovered a magnificent challenge. Perhaps I would never succeed in free climbing the Nose, but being back in Yosemite on one of the most beautifully sculpted cliffs on earth would be worth an effort as grand as the route itself.

The first climber to put serious effort into free climbing the Nose was a Californian named Ray Jardine. A space-flight mechanics system analyst by profession, Jardine had spent his free time living in Yosemite between 1970 and 1981. With his thick beard and horn-rimmed glasses, Jardine looked like an eccentric professor, but his powerful physique and his mind-set of pushing the limits of climbing difficulty by adopting new tactics made him a controversial figure among Yosemite climbers, some of whom did not agree with his style. Jardine drove the grades of crack climbs into the 5.12 range, and later he pushed grades even higher when he made the first ascent of the Phoenix, a 5.13 crack. To achieve this he ignored the prescribed styles of the day, and it was Jardine who first brought the issue of hang dogging to public attention. Jardine's creativity in finding ways to make harder climbs possible led him to other innovations such as the piece of gear he called the Friend, an ingenious spring-loaded device designed to expand inside a crack. He eventually sold the design to a British company and these camming devices have been so successful that nearly all climbers use them today, in one derivation or another.

In 1981 Jardine decided that a free ascent of the Nose would be his masterpiece climb, and for four months he set about trying to accomplish it. But instead of coming away with a masterpiece, Ray Jardine created a great controversy—some say an atrocity—over which he ultimately left Yosemite and stopped climbing.

Jardine did not call the route he wanted to free climb the Nose. He referred to the general area of rock around this section of El Cap as the Southwest Buttress, and he envisioned a route that he called Numero Uno that would link together sections of the Nose with new lines or with parts of an adjacent aid route called Grape Race. The result, he hoped, would be a route up the great face that went entirely free. Before him, climbers like Jim Bridwell, John Bachar, and Ron Kauk had freed the most obvious cracks on the Nose. What remained to be freed were several sections of aid climbing and pendulums (where a climber rigs up gear to swing across a blank section of rock), the Great Roof, and a few other wildly steep sections of climbing near the top. Jardine found featureless rock just before the famous King Swing pendulum that connects the upper and lower sections of the wall. Looking through a telescope set up in the meadow, he noticed a row of holds heading toward another crack system, on Grape Race. If he could just span this 35-foot section, he would be able to overcome the first of the major obstacles in freeing the Nose.

"After several days of working on the traverse, I determined that it was a lot harder [than 5.11—a grade that was at the upper end on the scale of difficulty in those days]. So I bought a cold chisel," Jardine told writer Eric Perlman in a *Rock and Ice* magazine interview in 1995.

Using logic that most climbers find hard to justify, Jardine "tooled" several holds into the rock by striking the chisel with a hammer to chip away small edges for his fingers and toes. The traverse he manufactured allowed him to climb sideways across the rock into Grape Race. The difficulty was 5.12a. Without chiseling, many climbers, including myself, believe that the traverse may have been possible, but at a much higher grade. Jardine has since admitted he was appalled at his own workmanship, because the holds he created stood out as being blatantly man-made.

"Was I committing a moral injustice or making a little bit of history?" he asked rhetorically in his interview in 1995, adding, "My vision was for a moderate route up the Southwest Buttress of El Cap. I wanted to make it not of the highest standard but of the highest meaning. After I realized that enhancing face holds was not the way to go, I quit the project—I knew its time had not yet come. Progress demanded that the route go free, but I lacked the technology to contrive the necessary holds."

Though Jardine's vision may have been ahead of its time, he failed to recognize that the spirit of free climbing is about adapting one's personal capacities and dimensions to the natural features of the rock, not the other way around. Jardine left Yosemite in 1981, leaving the Nose to be freed by others.

It was not until 1991 that two talented free climbers, Brooke Sandahl and Scott Franklin, resumed the challenge. They free climbed across Jardine's traverse to make progress far up the wall, but the Great Roof stopped them. When they arrived underneath the Great Roof, they discovered that it was soaking wet and therefore too difficult to try climbing without aid. The following year, Brooke returned to Yosemite to continue his effort with Dave Schultz. Though they failed to free climb two key sections of the route, their vision helped pave the way for someone to come later and make the first all-free ascent of the Nose. Their most significant breakthrough was the new free variation they created on the last pitch, up the spectacular overhanging headwall where Harding had spent fourteen hours placing fifteen pitons and twenty-eight bolts on the last day of his historic first ascent of the route in 1958.

Returning to El Cap felt like coming home, I realized as I headed up the wall on my first attempt to free the Nose, in 1993. Some twenty years had passed since my first view of this grand monolith, when I had come on a camping trip to Yosemite with my family. Later it had been a rite of passage when I struggled my way up the Nose with Mari and Dean in 1979, climbing the route using aid during our three-day ascent. Then, thirteen years later, I had made a speed ascent with Hans Florine in just over eight hours. Now, at age thirty-three, my mission was to free climb every inch of this legendary 3,000-foot rock formation.

My partner was a British climber named Simon Nadin, a tall man with a soft voice and a sunny-faced complexion, whom I had met at a World Cup competition in 1989. That year, Simon had entered his first competition; by year's end he was the first World Cup champion in the history of the sport. I felt at ease around Simon and respected his understated personality. As a climber, he had bundles of natural talent. In addition to being a good sport climber, Simon was used to doing bold, naturally protected routes in England. Simon, like me, had served an apprenticeship in traditional climbing style as opposed to sport climbing alone. When Simon and I had had a chance encounter at Cave Rock, on the shore of Lake Tahoe, we discovered our mutual desire to try to free climb the Nose. Though Simon had never climbed a big wall, I trusted him to be my partner on this towering cliff where swallows and peregrines swooped. Within an hour of our meeting, Simon had postponed his return flight to Britain. Five days later, we were already two-thirds of the way up the wall, sleeping on a ledge beneath the Great Roof.

We woke up on our bivy ledge 2,000 feet above the ground with the first rays of light spilling into the valley. As we looked down from our perch, the giant pine trees on the valley floor appeared like small heads of broccoli. Despite our airy position and bright sunshine illuminating the day, I didn't feel a sense of lightness. Getting to this point had taken us two days, and now, on our third day on the route, the force of gravity was weighing on us heavily. We were twenty-one pitches up the wall, and we had climbed eighteen hours without pause the previous day, finally quitting at midnight. The fatigue from all that free climbing, and the backbreaking work of dragging up two ropes, a heavy rack of gear, and a cumbersome haulbag, made us wake feeling tired and fuzzy-headed. As I looked at the Great Roof looming above my head, I felt my swollen hands throb with each beat of my heart.

The Great Roof pitch begins with a corner shaped like an open book with a crack at its center. The rock to either side is smooth, and the width of the crack at times pinches down to a quarter of an inch. The corner rises straight up for about 100 feet, but then it begins to tilt to the right, leaning over until it becomes a large roof shaped like a breaking wave of granite. To free climb it, a climber must surf sideways on smooth, featureless rock with his or her fingers jammed into the crack above. We knew this was one of the longest pitches of the entire route and its impressive architecture appeared unrelenting in its continuity. To make matters worse, the intensity of the midsummer heat radiated from the rock, making our skin ooze with perspiration.

"It looks like you get the first shot at leading the Great Roof," I said, handing the gear over to Simon. We had been swinging leads all the way up the wall.

"I guess I'll give it a try," he said softly in his adorable English accent.

Simon looked graceful as he cruised up the first three-quarters of the pitch, lay backing and jamming his way up the crack that split the center of the right-facing corner. But just before arriving under the Great Roof, his progress came to a distinct halt.

Simon slumped, his weight onto the rope and shouted down to me, "The crack is too thin. I can't even find a way to hang on up here."

Watching such a talented climber become increasingly frustrated with each unsuccessful effort, I couldn't help but share his sense of disappointment.

"You might have a better chance at this pitch than me," he shouted before lowering back down to the belay and turning the lead over.

This was the section that John had in mind when he pointed to my small fingers and said they would be my secret weapon. Ironically, my height of five-foot-two is often a shortcoming on the most difficult face climbs, where there are inevitably moves with long reaches between holds, but on the Great Roof it appeared that the tables were turned and perhaps my small size would be an advantage.

When I arrived at the first difficult section below the roof, I immediately understood why Simon was having such a hard time hanging on. Though I was able to wedge my fingertips into a few small openings in the crack, the face on either side was utterly devoid of features to stand on. At one point, the only edge of rock I could use to stand on was located at shoulder height and I needed to make a powerful kick just to get my foot up onto this hold. Underneath the roof itself, I had to duck my head down inside the curl of this granite wave, while wedging two fingertips of each hand straight up into the crack above my head. In order to keep my feet from skating off the smooth surface of the rock, I needed to maintain a perpendicular angle with my feet pressed flat against the vertical wall below. Moving from this rock-surfing position involved strenuous yet delicate tai-chi-like dance steps to coordinate finger moves and foot shuffles. After trying countless combinations of hand and foot sequences, my strength and concentration were nearly spent. I knew it would be possible to free climb this pitch, but I wasn't sure I would have enough strength to do it that day. I didn't have the luxury of coming back another day, nor did I have the energy to refine the sequence any further. My only hope of free climbing this pitch on my next try was to perform each move with as much grace and finesse as possible. I lowered down to the belay to rest before giving it my best effort.

After a twenty-minute rest, I started up again feeling surprisingly strong and fluid. But as soon as I began the most difficult series of moves, my timing was off and my body position faltered. I thrust my fingertips into a small opening in the crack just as my right foot popped off the face. In the next instant, I was airborne, then the rope caught my fall and I swung sideways into the corner. I hung on the rope, panting, with 2,000 feet of air below my feet, and then I lowered back to Simon.

"One more try. I'll do better next time," I said, voicing my mantra of hopeful determination.

While I rested, a team of Croatian climbers passed us. They moved quickly, climbing in traditional aid style. Down on the meadows I noticed that the pines were casting long shadows. We had limited energy and daylight left. Either I would make the first free ascent of this pitch on my next try, or we would have to abandon our all free attempt and finish climbing to the top.

While resting at the belay, I looked across the valley at the face of Middle Cathedral. On its mottled wall I noticed a play of shadows form the shape of a heart. I have always noticed the symbols around me, and this heart on stone reminded me of the values that have always been most important in my life and in climbing. My own development as a climber has been an extension of the experiences, passion, and vision of others. For me, free climbing the Great Roof was an opportunity to demonstrate the power of having an open mind and spirit. Though I realized that I could easily fall in my exhausted state, I felt a sense of liberation and strength knowing that this was an effort worth trying with all my heart. I had a strong feeling that this ascent was a part of my destiny and that somehow I could tap into that mysterious source of energy to literally rise to the occasion. I said nothing to Simon of my private thoughts, and when I returned to the roof, I realized that this was the moment of truth.

This time, as I began the most difficult sequence of moves, I could feel my strength waning, but willpower alone seemed to fuel me past the move where I had fallen on my previous attempt. Inches before the end of the traverse, my foot slipped off the face again and I began tipping backward. Because I had crunched my body into a tight and awkward position under the roof, my head butted into the ceiling above me, unexpectedly steadying me. I propelled myself onward, extended my right arm as far as I could, and shoved my fingers into a small slot. I composed my breathing for a moment, then focused on making a few final moves onto the belay ledge where one of the Croatian climbers stood staring at me wide-eyed. He had just witnessed the first free ascent of the Great Roof and he was as surprised as me at what had just taken place. Simon shouted up some words of congratulations, then came up the pitch using aid.

Simon didn't need to say anything for me to understand the disappointment he felt in having failed to free climb the Great Roof himself. Years later, I read an interview in which Simon spoke about his feelings watching me free climb the Great Roof that day:

"One more attempt was all the dwindling light would allow. I tried hard to stay cheery and not upset Lynn's concentration. Dejected that I had failed at the first obstacle, the consolation of just doing the Nose wasn't enough. Lynn's free ascent of this pitch was inspirational. She had been on the edge, feet popping off several times but somehow summoning up enough reserves to complete it."

The hard climbing was not over yet, though. There was one more pitch above Camp Six called the Changing Corners that had never been free climbed, and it had a reputation among the few who had tried it for being "reachy," meaning that the key holds were far apart. I knew that there was a good chance I would not be able to find an alternative way to make it past this blank section of rock.

Sensing that Simon needed a bit of cheering up, I said, "I think you'll have a much better chance of free climbing the pitch above Camp Six.

Brooke told me that this section involved a long reach with virtually nothing in the way of intermediate holds. There's a good chance that you'll be able to free climb it and I won't. If that's the case, we may be successful in making the first free ascent of the Nose as a team."

In retrospect, I don't know if my comments inspired or intimidated him. Simon merely nodded with a look of mixed emotions as he prepared to climb the next pitch. We climbed a little higher that evening, finally bivouacking on the ledge at Camp Five.

The next morning we organized our gear and shared our last food: one-half of an energy bar and one date each. We started ahead of the Croatian climbers, and it was Simon's turn to lead up a difficult pitch called the Glowering Spot. It turned out to be a horrendous way to start the day. This pitch follows an incipient crack to the left of a grass-filled corner that throws the climber into a frenzy of technical stemming and shallow finger jams. Rated 5.12d, and protected by small wired stoppers that are tedious to wiggle into the crack, Simon was grunting with fatigue by its end. As I climbed up behind him, struggling to stay on the rock without slipping, one of the Croatians appeared behind me, aid climbing upward, right at my heels.

Having climbed twenty-eight pitches, we arrived at Camp Six at eleven-thirty a.m., tired but hopeful of being able to continue our free ascent. Brooke Sandahl had already tried to free climb the pitch above us a year earlier by deviating to the left of the original line, up a steep face, then back right across a blank section of rock. I went up first to check out the crux moves and was quickly discouraged. Getting across the crux section involved reaching out to a tiny hold a full arm-stretch away, with nothing on the sheer face below to stand on. Taller climbers could stand on a small crystal of rock on the face, but this hold was located so low down on the face that I wasn't able to reach the crucial hold with my arms spread apart in a nearly iron-cross position. After a few tries, it was obvious that the mechanics necessary to make this move were not going to work for me. Simon went up next. Though he was able to make it past the first reachy move, he was stopped by the next section, which involved an acrobatic jump to the right. After a few tries, he too determined that the moves were too difficult in his tired condition.

As a last resort, I tried climbing up the original line that nearly all climbers had followed for the previous thirty-five years. This way climbed a shallow, flaring corner to our right. The walls to either side of this feature were smooth, and little in the way of a crack split the corner itself. The climbing was desperately hard and our spirits had been withered away by hunger and fatigue. We had only a few hours of daylight left to make it to the top, so we reluctantly decided that we had no other choice but to abandon the all free effort. We had made a valiant effort to free climb this route, but a mere 10-foot stretch of blank rock had foiled us.

Over the next few days, which I spent at a family reunion in Idaho, I thought of the moves that had stopped us. Getting up those few feet had seemed so improbable, but after considering the possibilities from a fresh perspective, I was convinced that it was worth giving it another try

The following week I returned to Yosemite with my friend Brooke Sandahl, a talented and passionate climber with an understated manner who turned out to be an ideal partner on this landmark ascent. Brooke revealed to me that when he was a young boy learning to climb with his father, he had looked at pictures of the Nose route and thought, *One day I'm going to free climb that route.* Brooke was eager to try it again himself. We hiked nine miles to the top of El Capitan, rappelled down to the pitch above Camp Six, and set to work on this enigmatic section of climbing. Brooke focused on trying his own face climbing variation; I focused on climbing the original line. Climbing up this corner demanded an ingenuity of movement that I had rarely ever encountered. We spent three days working on this pitch, and by the end I had pieced together a sequence of moves that went together like a crazy dance. I had invented a wild tango of smears with my feet, tenuous stems, back steps and cross steps, lay backs and arm bars, and pinches and palming maneuvers. Ironically, instead of being stopped

by the reachy variation, I discovered that the original route turned out
to be much better suited for a person of my body dimensions.

September heat dogged us, but I was able to climb this pitch with
only one fall. Brooke was not successful on his variant, but seeing how
close I was to success, he was keen to join me in our effort to make a
free ascent of the entire route from bottom to top. When we returned
to the Nose a few days later, we were well stocked with food and
water, and we both felt a sense of harmony in this magical place.
When we arrived at the Great Roof, I went up once to familiarize
myself with the moves, then made a successful free ascent on my first
try. Next Brooke gave it a try for the first time since his ascent in 1991
when the crack was soaking wet. Though he felt it was possible for him
to free climb this pitch, he knew that it would be too hard to do that
day, so we continued climbing up to our bivy ledge at Camp Five. At
the end of the same day, I led the Glowering Spot pitch while I was still
limber from the day's climbing.

The morning of our final day, I woke up on the ledge at Camp Five
and opened my eyes to look straight up the giant dihedral at the last
several hundred feet of the climb. There, above, was the Changing Corners pitch that would make or break our free attempt. I had just
dreamed that I had free climbed this pitch, and I felt a strong sense of
excitement about what was soon to unfold. The weather was cool and
I felt relaxed.

Brooke put me on belay and I started up knowing I would have to
link the complex set of moves together exactly the way I had imagined
them over the past several days. To get up the Changing Corners section, I had worked out a maneuver involving a bizarre contortion that
seemed like a disappearing act. Using a carefully coordinated sequence
of opposite pressures between my feet, hands, elbows, and hips against
the shallow walls of the corner, I turned my body 180 degrees around.

"That looks like a contortion only Houdini would make up,"
Brooke yelled up as I spun around from my double-arm-bar contortion. When I reached the belay I felt a tingle of disbelief run through
me. Though we had several pitches to go, none were as hard as this

one. Rating the difficulty of such a pitch is almost impossible. Even after having done it, I would say the most accurate grade would be to call it "once, or maybe twice, in a lifetime." I rated it 5.13b/c, but it could have just as easily been rated 5.14b. Scott Burke, who spent 261 days over a three-year period in an effort to free climb this route in 1998, was quoted as follows in *Climbing*: " 'There are no holds,' he said, claiming difficulties of 5.14b. If his grade holds, The Nose sports one of the hardest free pitches in Yosemite and in America and ranks as the hardest free climb of its size in the world."

Brooke shouted up a stream of congratulations, then he turned serious. "Looks like a storm, we better punch it all the way to the top today."

A dark wall of clouds was rolling in overhead leaving a few rain-drops in its wake. Nothing is more miserable than being caught in a rainstorm on El Cap. It takes only minutes for the cliff to become a sheet of water and for hypothermia to set in.

The last pitch before the summit was one of the most exciting pitches I've ever done. With nearly 3,000 feet of exposure to the ground on an overhanging wall with 5.12c face climbing at the lip of a bulge, this was a spectacular way to conclude such a monumental climb.

Brooke and I bivouacked on the summit, curled around a campfire next to Mr. Captain: a venerable old juniper tree that was gnarled from centuries of lightning strikes and winter blizzards. The storm passed by and the evening sky was bright with stars and a fulsome moon. We huddled around the fire, relishing its warmth, laughing and reliving the most powerful moments of our climb. I felt a rush of emotion knowing that the combination of both of our dreams and efforts had led us to this historic moment. Though Brooke had climbed all but two sections free, he admitted that he was glad not to have completed the entire route free. He felt that free climbing every pitch would have taken away some of the mystery of this great climb and might have left him with a sense of emptiness about what to do next. But that night as we fell asleep under the bright stars, we both felt a sense of completion—as though everything we had ever done had led us to this summit.

from The Gloves

by Robert Anasi

Robert Anasi (born 1966) started boxing in his twenties to keep in shape, but put off entering the Golden Gloves tournament until he was 33—his last year of eligibility.

The single preliminary round for featherweight novice fighters would take place at St. Catherine's Church in Franklin Square, Long Island, a few miles outside Queens and one town away from Busdriver's home of Lynbrook. The church lay in a small business district surrounded by suburban sprawl, like a fat man's skeleton. Inside, Catherine offered a benediction from an aisle alcove. Across the aisle, a bearded male saint carried what appeared to be a framing square. The narthex walls bore holy water ewers surmounted by intaglios of stylized doves and a statue of the Virgin. An enormous crucifix with a straining Christ filled the wall above the chancel.

That night's card also included further preliminary rounds for 147- and 165-pound open fighters (who went through more rounds because there were more fighters in those divisions). In the church basement, the fighters waited to be processed. We were told to strip down to our Skivvies and then lined up for the scale. I looked at the undraped bodies around me, most darker, although I was far from the only white. Some of the boxers looked like boys: narrow shoulders, shadow muscles, smooth faces (I saw the angel-faced Puerto Rican kid I'd almost fought in Yonkers). Others looked like men: mustaches, cabled arms, prison ink. There would be terrible mismatches tonight.

Certain of the open boxers had competed in area tournaments and shows for years; these old hands greeted one another and narrated their recent battles. In general, however, the boxers stood silent, apart from the boxing people: the judges, referees, officials and trainers. The majority of these had been around New York boxing for decades, in some cases for their entire lives. They chatted under the fluorescent lights, the event a social outing with a competitive edge, a Kennel Club meet or flower show.

I waited in line and watched the scale, an electronic contraption, with a red digital display. The boxers stepped on and off, toes creasing on the tile. The vision returned of me jogging up and down on the pavement, wearing three pairs of sweats and two borrowed sweaters. My warm feet met the cold metal plate, and my number came up: 126.3, reported by the official as 126 and transcribed in my book as the same. I had made it. Time for a water transfusion and the energy bar. Then it was off to the doctor, with his blood pressure cuff and penlight. A few questions, the cursory exam and then "Good luck." I wondered if they ever disqualified anyone. Doubted it.

Artificial limbs? Right this way.

Multiple personality disorder? Go get 'em, champ.

A commotion erupted behind me. I turned to see a swarthy man step quietly from the scale as his trainer argued with the official.

He's not one twenty-five, said the official. He's one twenty-seven and a half. And I want you to keep quiet.

The trainer looked sulky but said nothing. He had shouted, "One twenty-five!" as his fighter stepped on the scale, fooling no one. The number was recorded as 127 ½, and they admitted the fighter. The weight allowance was three pounds, not two, after all.

Jeans and T-shirt restored, I sat and munched my energy bar. I went to the bathroom. I peered into the auditorium. Doubt surged and ebbed in me, as it had before my other fights. I told myself I could draw some teenage killer who had been boxing since the age of five. A junior De La Hoya with a hundred stripes on his record. Yet, unlike in past fights, I could quell the fear by telling myself that I had been in with pros, with amateur champions, and that my opponent would be young and feeling the same doubt, but without my years to balance him. I knew I had a solid chin (I hadn't been off my feet once with Milton) and six months of serious training behind me.

I sidled over to the U.S. Boxing table and made out the list of fighters in my class, my name printed there at the top. Only twelve novice featherweights had registered and passed their physicals, twelve for the entire tournament, meaning that two wins would put me in the Garden. Fifteen years earlier there would have been twice that, and forty years earlier, twice that again. Bill Butterworth, the videographer of New York City amateur boxing, has told me that when he started shooting the Gloves in the mid-eighties, an average prelim had thirty bouts. Now a good night would bring half as many; every year the tournament took up fewer column inches in the *Daily News*, where once the call "Support Your Battling Paperboy!" bannered the back page.

I sipped a diet cola to elevate my caffeine level into its normal range, and an unfamiliar trainer glared at me.

Are you fighting tonight? he demanded.

Yes, I answered.

Well, you shouldn't be drinking soda.

But it's diet, I said in my defense.

I don't care.

I shrugged my shoulders. Another bad omen? I wondered about the taboo on cola and hoped it wouldn't make a difference in the fight.

Stella and Laura had arrived together and stood before me. I was glad they had come.

There's only twelve guys in my class, I said, so somebody's going to get a bye.

But you *want* to fight, said Stella, who always did. I wasn't so sure. I did and I didn't. The tournament was already two months old. I'd been waiting a long time. It would not do to sit there in hope of a bye. It would weaken me. I had to convince myself that I had traveled those many miles to shatter the bones of my enemies.

Oh, yeah, sure, I said.

I looked up to see Milton bearing toward me.

They got a match for you, he said. He pointed across the room at the swarthy man from the scale incident.

I took a breath; I had crossed over.

His book says three fights, but . . . Something's not right about this, Milton said enigmatically, and stalked away.

I shifted my gaze toward the opponent. A rugged fellow who could have been thirty. Stubble darker than Milton's, chest fur up to his Adam's apple. Face scarred, bridge of the nose crushed flat. He wore the gaudiest pair of boxing sandals I had ever seen, a neon yellow and green, coming almost to his knees. Across the room, I noticed Milton leaning over the officials' table, speaking forcefully to the pleasant-faced blond woman who arranged the matches. She seemed the person least likely to have that job. Milton had claimed he held her in his pocket, and every show he played her with his contentious charm. I sat chewing my lip. There would be no escape tonight.

I went to the bathroom. At the sink, I waited as an older black man, wearing the U.S. Boxing laundryman white, shoveled water at his mouth, then spewed it across the sink and floor with shuddering hacks. As I watched him hawk and spit, he stood back, gesturing for me to use the sink.

I can wait, thanks, I said.

No, I'm gonna be a while, he said. I just had surgery for cancer, and they took out my saliva glands, so I got to do this every couple of hours. I'm still learning how to swallow.

Scar tissue seamed and charred his throat, loose flesh dangling. I looked at the water dripping from the sink ledge and puddled on the floor.

That's okay, I said. I'll wait.

I left the bathroom and stared into the church. People filed into the nave and filled the seats, shrinking the room. As I watched, a red manifold curtain slid over the enormous crucifix to shield the Son of Man from the brutal proceedings to follow.

Back in the annex, Milton's agitation continued. He muttered urgently into his cell phone and strode about the room. There was a sense that he was always about to perform some sleight of hand that would cost you your wallet.

Now he bore toward me, still discoursing into his cell.

This guy is a ringer, Milton said. He's got a hundred and fifty fights.

One hundred fifty fights? I said. That was a championship number, an Olympic number, the number of amateur fights a Hearns or Ali would have before turning pro. Maybe three other amateurs in New York State had that many amateur fights.

So am I going to fight him? I said, and wondered if I sounded shrill. I fingered the Golden Gloves shirt I'd been issued, blue with gold lettering.

That's what I'm trying to take care of right now, Milton said.

Milton left to join a conference that included the officials, the other fighter's trainer and the other fighter, whose face was no longer calm.

What's the matter? Laura asked.

I don't know, I said. Milton told me that this guy had a hundred and fifty fights.

Laura didn't appear surprised.

I *knew* something was up with him when he came in. I noticed him right away. He was just too calm. And then those sandals. The sandals definitely gave it away. They're tournament shoes.

I looked again at his Day-Glo dogs. A man who wore those would have to be supremely confident.

As Milton returned, Laura departed, the Arctic between them. The cell phone still clutched Milton's ear.

What the hell is she doing here? he said. So I found out all about this guy. He's Turkish. Had a hundred and fifty fights. Took a bronze in the Euro Cup.

How do you know?

I been around this game for a long time, Milton said. When he strolled in, I knew he didn't have no three fights. Just by how he walked across the room. I could see he was comfortable. He was too relaxed. I said, "This guy has to have more . . . This guy has to have

had more than three fights." Three fights? I'm like, "Nah, no way."
Still, even after I found out about his record, I was going to let him
fight us, but . . .

I considered the aplomb with which Milton regarded "us" fighting
Mr. 150 but let it pass. Milton had learned the fighter's nation of origin
from his trainer ("Oh, where is your guy from?"). When the trainer
denied previous boxing experience ("three fights"), Milton had taken
another approach.

So after I found out where he was from, I called the Turkish
embassy. I figured, he came over here, right? So they must have some
record of him somewhere.

You called the Turkish embassy?

Yeah.

And they told you about his career?

Well, they told me some, and then he started talking.

Why?

Well, when I started pushing with the questions, he got nervous and
spilled his guts. He would have said anything not to get thrown out of
the tournament. I'm telling you. This is going to be the talk of the
Gloves this year, just you watch.

So, am I going to fight? I ask.

They're trying to make a match for you now.

So they *were* out to get us. Will's loss, Julian's disqualification . . . We
didn't stand a chance. I didn't need any more proof and prayed for a
bye. It would be fine to relax and watch the competition, live to fight
another day. Yet the absurdity also relaxed me. I couldn't do worse
than 150 fights.

Milton's return put an end to my hopes.

They got someone for you. He pointed. Mexican kid.

My eyes followed his finger to a solid-bodied man with a perfectly
spherical head, the roundest head I had ever seen. A Mexican was a
misfortune. Mexicans were inevitably tough, practically indestructible.
Their national boxing style had developed in response to the small
stature of the typical Mexican man. Almost any non-Mexican boxer

would be taller, so Mexicans did not jab, just slipped and launched titanic hooks. The Mexicans followed you, taking three punches to give one, boring forward. A Mexican would not give way. After handing me my Gloves shirt, Milton vanished, and I was left to consider my fate.

So they finally made a match for you, Laura said, smiling. You're going to be great.

I took a breath and sighed it away. Laura pressed a bottle of cold water to my forehead.

It's going to be all right, she said. You know, Mike Tyson used to cry before his fights? I couldn't believe it when I heard. I mean, Mike Tyson.

In my case I thought tears unlikely, putting me one up on Tyson.

This feels good, she said, placing the water bottle against my neck. Relax.

Milton returned.

Laura, why don't you go somewhere else? he said, snatching the water bottle from her hand. Why don't you go upstairs?

Can I have my water bottle? she said. Milton presented it.

Don't tell me what to do, Laura said.

I rolled my eyes at them and leaned against a pillar in the middle of the room. They stood there, glaring at each other.

Hey, guys, I said, *I'm* the one who's supposed to be fighting.

Laura walked away.

Dumb broad, Milton groused. What was she doing holding the bottle on your neck? She's going to make you cold before your fight.

Having banished Laura, Milton disappeared again. I changed into my shorts and was left alone in the almost empty room, the weight of the fight stacked upon my chest sixteen stories high. The matches made, everyone had departed to watch the action, and Milton was somewhere among them. Absenteeism was Milton's usual MO at bouts. If you wanted to find him, the one place *not* to look was anywhere near his fighters. There were too many people for him to talk to, too many angles to work. Over the years the team had become resigned to his behavior. "That shit can get on my nerves sometimes,"

Julian said once, "but let Milton go do whatever. The one thing I ask is, just wrap my hands before you take off, you know? Do whatever, but just wrap my hands first. Sometimes he don't even do *that*." My own hands remained unwrapped.

My opponent sat with his trainer and seconds (I recognized the trainer as the owner of the Yonkers gym where I'd almost fought Angel Face). They sat close, talking and staring over at me. The trainer was skinny and shifty-looking, with drooping mustaches and a narrow goatee, a type you see sauntering out of a pawnshop or strip club at four a.m.

To cast off the weight, I decided to loosen up. In the shadow of the big pillar, I swung my arms and circled my waist, then took a stance and started throwing punches. As I moved, I noticed that Goatee had risen from his chair and sidled around the pillar to compass an angle on my movements. I stopped. As I looked at him, he stared nonchalantly in the other direction, the portrait of a pimp on a thoughtless Sunday stroll. I moved farther behind the pillar. A few minutes later I noticed that he had drifted in the same direction. I stopped again. He stared into the distance.

Julian saved me.

Come here, Bob, he said. He held up his hands for me.

Jab, jab. That's good. One-two-three; one-two-three. All right. It's show time, baby. Let me see the four. Good. I *know* you're ready. You about to take this kid out. Come to the body, right away. Boom, boom. He won't be expecting it. Body shots. At least, that's what I'd do.

Julian was always so modest with advice, never commanding, merely saying that in a similar circumstance, he would choose a particular action. We didn't have much time to get warm, though.

Milton ran in. We're up next, he said.

One match away, and my hands still weren't wrapped. Milton wore his usual black warm-up suit and black jacket, looking sardonic, sinister and a little dissipated. As he wrapped, then taped my hands, he couldn't get over the Turkish incident.

That was some funny shit, he said, looping gauze around my hands. Everyone's going to be talking about that. You watch.

Yo, he said to Julian, a hundred and fifty fights.

One hundred fifty fights? Julian answered. He stood behind me, his thick fingers kneading my neck.

That's what the little motherfucker had.

So did he get thrown out?

No, they pushed him up to open. Let him beat Peña's ass.

Who we fighting? Julian asked.

Milton pointed out the Mexican with an elbow.

I'm telling you, that's gonna be the talk of the Gloves. That's one for the books.

In street clothes Julian loomed bigger than he did in the gym. He wore a pinstriped dress shirt untucked, which made him seem even wider.

Then the gloves were on my hands, and a *Daily News* robe was tugged over them. I didn't need the robe, but I appreciated it. Another election and anointing. Then the official was there with his clipboard, calling my name. He was a tall brown-skinned man with bony wrists and a natty salt-and-pepper beard. He squeezed the gloves and looked me over.

No earrings, nothing?

Nothing, I said (an earring could catch on headgear or glove and tear through an earlobe).

Your trainer is wearing an earring.

My trainer wears a lot of things, I said, which meant nothing at all.

On my way to the ring I heard the pleasant-faced official complaining to the Turk's trainer. I just can't understand how you can do that and feel good about yourself.

I understood. It was boxing. Anything you could do to gain an advantage. I barely recalled the incident, having moved to a different plane. The Turk was a very long time ago.

The Mexican stood just in front of me on the stairs at the annex entrance to the hall, wearing his gold shirt with blue lettering. His trainer, Goatee, pointed at him and shouted to a woman holding a video camera. "The next Golden Gloves champ. Just you watch." Another of the officials, an older, demitoothed Puerto Rican I saw at every show, exhorted the Mexican in Spanish. Then he smiled and

tousled Mexico's cropped hair. What were they, related? None of the
U.S. Boxing was patting *me* on the head.

At the equipment table in the corner near the stairway, Milton made
a request.

Suede, he said to the equipment manager, meaning suede headgear.

Sweat? the man answered in a heavy accent.

Suede, Milton said.

Sweat? the man responded again.

No, Milton said. *Suede, suede, suede.*

He lifted a helmet by a dangling chin strap and waved it in the air.
The man gestured toward the ring and shrugged. Suede was in use. I
would wear vinyl.

Drawn forward, down the aisle, conspicuous, a fleeced lamb. I wondered if I looked tough. I *had* to look tough. I didn't *feel* tough. I started
to hate whoever had put me in this situation. I started to hate . . . the
Mexican. Drawn forward, down the aisle with my little entourage. "Go
back," the officials said. Confusion. The Mexican's group, just ahead,
snaring with mine. Signaled to proceed again. Up the stairs to the ring
apron, sucked through the ropes. Don't go through the canvas, Bob. I
would not be shamed before hundreds of people.

Across the ring, my opponent limbered up, making a half bend, followed by an oscillation of the shoulders.

Bernabe Guerrero: from Mexico by way of a Yonkers boxing club.

Twenty-four years old.

A construction worker who "burned with a passion for boxing."

He had real boxing polish, there in the shoulder shake, in the way
he kissed his gloves and raised them high when his name was
announced. Very pro. Guerrero was distorted with muscle, his arms
layered and curved, skin with a metallic density. His wide jaw gave him
a shark smile. He stood about three inches shorter than I did (and, I
would soon discover, had a shorter reach). All my protein powder and
skim milk had paid off.

In my corner, Julian instructed me in boxing etiquette. "Bob, walk
out to the referee," he said, at the appropriate moment. "Bob, lift up

your gloves now," when my name was called. I was glad to have Julian there, a tower at my back.

Blue, hey, Blue. Blue! wafted to my ears from the judges' table.

Bob, they want you, Julian said, and I looked down at them. I was blue.

Blue, how do you pronounce your last name? they asked. I told them. "Ann-uh-see. Ann-uh-see." The announcer still got it wrong.

At the bell I came out fast. I had resolved to start fast. In my other fights I had started slowly and gotten clobbered. Bernabe extended his glove for a courtesy touch. Suspicious, I tapped his glove and immediately threw a left, which missed. I followed with a few light jabs and some long hooks, avoiding any sort of commitment. Bernabe rushed at me behind a wild hook, which also missed. I sidestepped and hit him with a counterhook. The momentum of my hook, added to his rush, sent him stumbling into the ropes. The referee stepped between us and rubbed Guerrero's gloves against his chest, an action taken whenever a fighter's gloves touch the canvas to cleanse them of foreign matter that might have adhered to them, matter that could abrade the face of the other boxer. Guerrero wasn't hurt, but it was definitely my punch that had made him stumble. An argument could have been made for giving him a standing eight, but I didn't make it.

As the round progressed, Guerrero pushed forward and I backed away. Most of his punches fell short, but I felt the wind from his rainbow hooks. I had two inches of reach on him, at least, and the advantage of fighting someone with shorter arms became obvious. Those of his straight punches that did connect were exhausted at the end of their trajectory and had little force. On my side, I countered well, especially as he tried to get out of range after punching (the boxer with shorter arms must constantly put himself at risk in order to attack). Twos and threes, I remembered Julian's advice, twos and threes.

As Guerrero and I faced each other, he reminded me of a solid, ferocious Puerto Rican kid I had sparred at Revolution, the same build and standing in the same posture, stance a little open, exposing torso and head. I remembered hitting the kid with an uppercut at that range and decided to try the same with Guerrero. The punch dropped spang on the point of his chin. Delighted, I did it again, with the same gratifying result. Then I released the uppercut as he bore straight in, and it thumped against his chest. I kept pushing the button and whacking Guerrero, like a child with a new toy. It was one of the most thoughtful things I had ever done in the ring.

Meanwhile, I couldn't believe that I wasn't getting hit more and, when I did get hit, that it didn't hurt. I'd passed more grueling tests a dozen times at the gym. Whenever Guerrero forced me toward the ropes, I sensed them at my back and shifted away. It was a subtle movement that I didn't even realize I was making, the unconscious conditioning of hundreds of rounds of sparring. Guerrero allowed me the space to escape into the open; our boxing remained polite and technical, something that I didn't expect and that suited my style.

The bell came as a surprise also. I couldn't believe the round had gone so swiftly. Guerrero had cooperated with me by staying on the outside and trying to box. I sat on a stool in my corner with Julian and Milton over me.

Well, you won that round, Milton said, but there's a few things you need to work on. Try to wait on him a little more, slip and then come back with a hook. You're killing him with those fives, but you got to follow it with a three.

Julian sprayed water over my scalp and told me to relax.

You're doing good, Bob, he said. Keep the pressure on.

At the bell I jumped and ran out into the ring.

In the second round, Guerrero tried to press, weaving forward in a crouch with his gloves close to the sides of his head. I missed him once or twice as he weaved, and his sweeping hooks rebounded from my shoulders and arms. I made him pay, though, scoring with counters and forcing him back. The round settled into a pattern of back-and-forth exchanges. I pitched fives whenever I could, and he still didn't adjust for them, every five landing solid. As he rushed in, I bowled another, but my arm somehow tangled with his. His forward motion snapped my arm back at the elbow, and I suffered a jolt of intense pain. I forgot about it immediately—thank God for adrenaline—but I didn't throw another uppercut for the rest of the fight.

In our most grueling exchange, we parked directly in front of each other and slugged. Guerrero landed the better blows at first, but I kept hitting. He finally sagged back, and as he did, I jolted him with a left to the jaw. His knees buckled and he staggered three steps sideways. I didn't see the weakness, and the referee didn't step in with a standing eight. It was probably my best chance for a knockdown, but I didn't follow. An experienced fighter would have tested him to see if he was really hurt, but I didn't have the eyes for it (I noticed his stumble only later, watching the videotape). Winded from the exchange, I stood facing him for a few moments. Then he recovered and attacked, standing in front of me until I scored with two good body shots. The bell surprised me again and it was back to my corner.

Well, I thought you won that round too, Milton said, but you got to remember the combinations. Don't throw just one punch. Use the dunh, dunh-duhs. Keep sticking out the jab; the jab can score points. You're doing great. You're hitting him hard without even trying.

On the stool, I rent the air with gasps that didn't bring my body enough oxygen. I felt enfeebled, on life support. Julian sensed my exhaustion and gave instruction.

Bob, lift up your hands. Lift them up. Now take a deep breath. You're doing all right. Breathe. You got this kid. One more round.

I remembered the exhaustion I'd felt the last time I sparred Joey. His pressure had drained me. In my regular sparring, I hadn't maintained this intensity; the competition hadn't pushed me to it. By the end of the rest minute, my breathing had slowed, and I felt ready to continue. The referee walked over to order Milton from the ring.

Seconds out! he barked. (Through the early days of British pugilism, the seconds actually stood near the boxers as they fought.)

As I stepped forward, a chill slashed across my back. Milton had emptied the water bottle on me, and water drenched the canvas. The referee grimaced and shook his head. Milton pushing the boundaries, once again.

Round three went slowly and ill for me. Guerrero's pressure was rewarded. Now when I was backed into the ropes, I could not shift away. Guerrero slipped more smoothly, and my twos missed over his head. He still wasn't scoring clean, but I was no longer able to drive him off. Milton's pullback worked for me, drawing my head out of danger, the big hooks brushing my nose. Whereas, in the first two rounds, I had moved faster than clock time, in the third I dragged through a syrupy nightmare. I clinched for the first and only time in the fight, leaning on Guerrero's shoulders until the referee separated us. I'm really tired, I thought, then: He must be tired too. That reassured me (he didn't try to wrestle out of the clinch). Still, he kept throwing, and a hook finally landed flush on the side of my head. I rolled with it and heard the crowd's exclamation (feeling the crowd noise as a physical presence, the cheers and shouts jostling my body). After the blow, I slid along the ropes, and what seemed like an instant later (it was full seconds on the videotape) another hook burst on my chin. It was the hardest punch I had taken, and I bounced back against the ropes. The punch angered me and stirred me from a defensive inertia.

I'd better start throwing, I thought, or I could get a standing eight.

Later I was glad that the referee had the temperament not to interfere, that he "let us fight," because if he could have given Guerrero an eight-count in round two, he could have given one to me after the second hook.

I started punching again and we remained in front of each other, banging until the round ended. The ovation was enormous, a swelling embrace as we trudged back to our corners.

Well, you lost that round, Milton said as he cut the tape from my gloves and pulled them off my hands, but if they gave you the first two, you got it.

I walked out jaunty and a little confused. The referee lifted our arms to the same grand applause. The boxing people approved of us.

When the announcement came, " . . . for the gold corner," my knees sagged. It was only a physical reaction. I was too stimulated to feel the pain of the loss then.

from Black Livingstone
by Pagan Kennedy

William Sheppard, a charismatic African-American Presbyterian missionary, was 24 in 1890, when he left New York for the Congo. Pagan Kennedy's (born 1962) biography of Sheppard describes the missionary's attempt to find the elusive Kuba people.

The most famous missionary of Sheppard's boyhood had been David Livingstone. Wandering through the outback accompanied only by a few Africans, the British hero had collected specimens, made maps, and searched for the source of the Nile. Livingstone rarely bothered to preach or hand out Bibles to the Africans; in fact, the so-called missionary failed to make a single convert—except among the English. In a series of best-selling books, he celebrated the grandeur of the continent and the essential decency of the Africans themselves. "If one behaves as a gentleman he will be invariably treated as such," he believed. Denouncing the Arab slave trade, he lectured his fellow Europeans that they had a duty to bring the "three Cs" to Africa—Christianity, commerce, and civilization. As naive and culturally insensitive as this plan sounds now, Livingstone had a point: He wanted to see Europeans invest in Africa rather than feast on it.

Sheppard followed the Livingstone model. He treated the missionary job title as an umbrella under which he could pursue his multifarious ambitions. Explorer, big-game hunter, celebrity speaker, fund-raiser, art collector, anthropologist. He would excel at roles that were closed to nearly every other black person of his day.

But in the 1890s, the era of Livingstone was drawing to a close. The empty swathes on the map had been filled in, and now Westerners were settling the interior of the Congo as traders, bureaucrats, preachers, and teachers. Soon there would be no need for explorer-missionaries at all.

More to the point, the last the thing the Presbyterian Church wanted to do was fund lavish expeditions into the wilderness. Every year, the Foreign Missions department issued a newsletter that listed success in exact figures, divided up into categories and columns. If the format looked suspiciously like a corporation's annual report, that's because in a way it was. Charity donors would want to know how many churches had been built, how many schools founded, how many persons aided by medicines. But by far the most important figure was how many converts had been made.

Saving souls, the most crucial part of Sheppard's job description, was a task for which he was ill-suited—literally. In a group photograph from 1909, his colleague William Morrison wears a dark woolen jacket, cravat, and battered black hat; he's dressed for the mundane duties of teaching and preaching and desk work. Sheppard, on the other hand, has costumed himself as a cowboy-explorer in a blinding white suit, Panama hat, and lace-up boots buffed to a high shine. He poses with his chest puffed out, one hand on a hip. He looks ready to hunt, not preach.

In 1892, when his partner's death left him suddenly in command of the Presbyterian station, Sheppard needed converts desperately. The church might close the Congo mission entirely unless they saw some results.

But when it came to dressing Africans in cheap calico cloth and forcing them down on their knees to pray, Sheppard was profoundly ambivalent. He had too much respect for Africans to strip them of their culture and teach them to imitate Americans.

Had he wanted converts, he could have found them within easy preaching distance. The ex-slaves and refugees who had settled on the

Presbyterian plantation belonged to the Luba/Lulua tribe. This bedraggled and deracinated people, who'd been scattered all around the Kasai region by the slave trade, bore an uncanny resemblance to early Christians. Fleeing from slave traders, exiled from burned villages, forced to labor by the Free State, orphaned, widowed—the Luba had nowhere to go besides missionary stations. In years to come, they'd flood to the Presbyterians in such numbers that the missionaries would have to turn many of them away.

Sheppard could have hunkered down in Luebo and tended to these unfortunates, setting up a school, a church, and a health clinic. Had he done so, he would have become like many of the missionaries who followed him, social workers who taught orphans to farm and preachers who translated English hymns into the Luba dialect.

Instead, he modeled himself on Livingstone. He wanted to open the door to Africa's secret places so that the next wave of missionaries could follow.

Of course, by 1892, most every door in Africa was already open, at least a crack. That's what made the Kuba people so special. They had refused contact with the West. For nine years, Europeans had been battering at the gates of the Kuba kingdom, without success. Whoever did find a way into the forbidden city would be hailed as a great Christian *and* a brilliant explorer. He would pave the way for future missionaries *and* he would prove his own genius. It was a challenge worthy of Livingstone himself. Sheppard would take it.

Hours after he learned of his partner's death, Sheppard burst into action. He gathered Africans from the plantation and made his pitch: He needed a party of men to join his search for the elusive Kuba kingdom. "We may all be marching to our graves," he warned the men who stood before him. Nine were sufficiently devoted to him to volunteer. A day later, he and his men packed up and headed down a sandy path into the jungle. They possessed no map or guide, only an idea: In remote parts of Africa, roads tended to run between markets, zigzagging around to accommodate traders. Rather than trying to plot the entire route to the forbidden city, Sheppard would hop from market to market, posing as a wanderer who hoped to buy food for his men. He would approach the city in the manner of a sailing ship, tacking back and forth against a headwind.

That first night, the group camped in a Kete village, joining the locals for evening festivities around their fire. What a strange vision they must have been. Sheppard led his men in singing "We Are Marching to Zion," a hymn about a city of God that could be reached on foot. Their hosts reciprocated by carrying drums and ivory horns from their houses. Soon, dancers swirled around the flames of the fire under a red moon that sat in the sky like a poppy. The villagers cavorted all through the night. What with revelers tripping over their tent ropes, drumbeats shaking the ground, and goats rooting around in their possessions, Sheppard's footsore men hardly got any sleep.

After a few days, Sheppard sidled up to the village chief and asked how to get to the next marketplace. The chief refused to tell, explaining that the king had decreed such information should be kept from foreigners. "I dare not disobey him."

So, Sheppard wrote, "I slipped out of the village quietly and stood in the road at a place where three paths met. By and by I saw a man starting out to the marketplace. I stepped out and followed him without asking any questions, making a mark so my men could come after me."

In this next town, he ingratiated himself by buying quantities of eggs. Perhaps aware of his hidden agenda, the people presented him with yet more food, goats, and chickens that kept his men stuffed and stuck in the campground. "I knew we couldn't dispose of all that food in one day, so I concluded to have a sit-down for four or five days; but the food rolled in without abatement."

Generous as they were, the villagers refused to reveal the path to the next market. So Sheppard tried a new approach: He pleaded that he and his men needed eggs. They'd managed to eat every last one in the vicinity—wouldn't his hosts consent to take one of Sheppard's men to the market, on an innocent errand of egg-buying?

His ploy worked. The villagers consented. Sheppard's man learned the way to the next town, and soon enough, the little band sneaked off and continued meandering toward the heart of Kubaland.

Sheppard used the egg trick over and over. "Day after day we moved along this way . . . We did nothing but buy and eat eggs," he wrote, joking that in villages well stocked with chickens, the plan backfired. You want eggs? the people would say. And then they would drag out baskets full of them. Once, Sheppard had to gobble thirty before he could beg his hosts for more.

Eventually, when the expedition reached the town of Ngallicoco, the villagers would not offer help. At night, a town crier strode through the streets, announcing that no one should give directions to the strangers.

Still, Sheppard's luck held. He struck up a friendship with a fellow traveler, a Kuba man who offered to take him along on the path to the next village. "I was delighted, knowing that this man had full knowledge of [the king's] edict and yet cordially invited me to his town."

The next leg of the journey would be different from the other hops between villages. The travelers would be entering Kuba territory, the first of the towns in the sprawl around the capital. Like a pawn jumping into a strategic square on the chessboard, Sheppard would be one step closer to checking the king.

The village was called M'boma, and here he got stuck again. The egg trick would not work, of course. Nothing, not even hard cash, would persuade the locals to show him the way. Sheppard despaired. Every day he lingered in M'boma, he risked drawing attention to himself and bringing down the king's wrath. For almost a month he paced before his tent, watching for an opportunity.

Finally, it came. Some travelers emerged from the forest and announced themselves to be the king's ivory traders. Sheppard slunk off and found his most trustworthy volunteer, N'goma, one of the servant boys from the Lower Congo, now grown into a man. N'goma was as much a foreigner in Kuba country as Sheppard. Still, he—carrying a spear and wearing a loincloth—would attract less attention than his pith-helmeted boss.

"Follow those men's tracks in the soft sand," Sheppard instructed N'goma. "Make a cross mark in all of the off trails. . . . I will follow your trail at once with the caravan."

The plan would only work if the next few days continued to be dry—even a brief downpour would wash N'goma's marks away. As Sheppard led his men through the maze of paths, watching for the crosses drawn by a toe in the sand, his luck held. So did the weather.

After they'd walked for two days, the woods opened out, spilling Sheppard's men into a marketplace in the middle of a town called Pish aBieeng. Amid the tall Kuba people, parading about in their elegant drapery, Sheppard spotted wiry N'goma. He was buying—what else?—eggs. Perhaps the young man hoped to use Sheppard's favorite ruse to get to the next village.

For N'goma had lost his quarry. The traders had noticed him following, and in the middle of the night they'd pulled out of Pish aBieeng, leaving not so much as a footprint to tell where they'd gone.

As Sheppard's men massed in the village, and the local people began to understand the missionary's intent, they grew terrified. "If the king hears you are here all our heads will come off," they said, pleading with him to leave their town.

Should Sheppard stay and risk the lives of these strangers? Or should he retreat, which would be tantamount to giving up? He settled on the awkward compromise of camping in the jungle—close to the village but not technically in it.

Once again he'd been beached. He had no idea how to get any closer to the capital. To pass the time, he pulled out a two-year-old edition of a newspaper he called the *Daily News*, probably the *London Daily News*, most likely purchased before he left Europe. Its presence here in the jungle was somewhat miraculous—for two years it had survived the ravages of the white ants that had eaten up nearly every other piece of paper.

The words on the yellowed pages must have spoken to him like messages from another world: news stories about political debates, reviews of theater shows that had long since closed, advertisements for a new box camera from Kodak and a strange contraption called the phonograph. It would have reminded him of the wonders of London: thundering trains, ladies' eyes flashing under ostrich plumes, the smell of coal smoke, the leaden shine of the Thames and the Houses of Parliament lit up golden in the wash of a winter sunset. And Lapsley beside him, Lapsley fussing with the foreign coins and eager to visit Livingstone's grave.

How far away all that must have seemed on a sweltering morning in the Kasai outback. The clothes that hung on Sheppard's back had grown gritty with sweat. He had not shaved, and could only bathe in an improvised fashion. It had been months since he'd spoken to anyone in English.

So he paged through the moldy newspaper, trying to lose himself in the imaginary city, London two years ago, bursting with luxuries he could have never explained to the Africans around him. Perhaps he was reading an article about the new spring hats or a recipe for coq au vin when the screams began.

The village had erupted into noise and motion. Voices sobbed, moaned, begged for mercy. People were crashing past him into the woods. From between the trees, Sheppard could just glimpse the soldiers who had marched into town, a band of men in feathered hats and kilts, brandishing knives.

"Now hear the words of [the king]," one of them proclaimed to the fleeing people. "Because you have entertained a foreigner in your village, we have come to take you to the capital for trial."

Sheppard lifted himself out of the chair and strode in the direction of the soldiers. The leader, over six feet tall, bronze-colored, half blind, regarded Sheppard haughtily with his good eye. This was N'toinzide, one of the king's sons.

In his ragged white suit, Sheppard must have been an odd vision. These Africans had never before seen a man clothed head to toe, his legs encased in "bags," his feet hidden inside contraptions that dangled string, his face half hidden under a kind of roof. The stranger stood tall enough to stare into the prince's single eye.

"The chief of this village is not guilty," the stranger insisted. "He . . . told me to go away, . . . and I did not." Furthermore, he said, no one had helped him find the outskirts of the capital. He'd figured it out for himself. If the soldiers wanted someone to blame for his presence here, well then, they'd have to convict him and him alone. He was the guilty one, not these hapless villagers.

"You are a foreigner and you speak our language?" the dumbfounded prince replied. He spoke with a foppish lisp, for his two front teeth had been removed, according to Kuba fashion. Then he swaggered away, conferred with his retinue, and led them off in the direction of the capital.

After the soldiers had disappeared, the village fell silent. People huddled in groups, hardly bothering to move. Someone explained to Sheppard the exact manner in which they would be killed. Their necks would be stretched over bent saplings, and when the executioner swung his sword, their heads would fly into the air and land at the feet of a delighted crowd of aristocrats.

Sheppard couldn't eat. A piece of chicken on a banana leaf, a fried plantain cut up into yellow coins—these things made as little sense to him now as jokes without punch lines. Why bother to choke down food he'd never have a chance to digest? Why bother to do anything?

They were all corpses-to-be, everyone in this village, right down to the youngest Congo boy, Susu, who had been with Sheppard for almost two years now. Soon their bloody heads would fall with the hollow sound of hail.

The prince marched back to the palace and briefed the king: The intruder spoke the Kuba language, knew the secrets of their geography, and wore the strangest clothing he'd ever seen.

Intriguing news indeed. King Kot aMweeky called a meeting with his advisers. He reclined on two slaves—as a demigod, he was forbidden to touch the ground, could not come in contact with anything as mundane as dirt, and so must be cushioned by warm human flesh. The advisers wore the dress costume of the Kuba aristocracy, later described by the ethnographer Emil Torday:

> All men wore the kilt, very like that of the Highlanders; . . .
> a leaf-shaped knife about a foot long with a beautifully
> encrusted handle stuck in the belt on their right hip; in
> front a long pocket of skin, from which the hair had not
> been removed, dangled like a sporran; their heads were sur-
> mounted by a conical cap of lace-like fibre, fixed to their
> hair by needles ornamented with a miniature bell.

The men conferred. King Kot aMweeky needed to strengthen his hold on the throne, in order to keep power away from the many rival clans that vied to control Kubaland, and to awaken even more terror and awe in his people. What could be a better addition to his entourage than a ghost—or even better than that, the ghost of a long-dead king? The advisers decided then and there that the stranger would be called "Bope Mekabe," and that he'd be introduced as a reincarnation of one of the ancient kings.

As one ethnographer has noted, Kuba oral history contains no record of a "Bope Mekabe"—which is all the more reason to assume that the king and his advisers came up with the story during a brainstorming session. They may not have believed that Sheppard was a ghost, but they knew a political opportunity when they saw one. A royal ancestor come back to life in order to endorse King Kot aMweeky—it was a brilliant political move.

One day Sheppard had been a condemned man, and a few days later the prince's delegation marched into town and declared him royalty. "You need not try to hide it from us any longer. You are Bope Mekabe who reigned before my father and who died," the prince told him.

"His spirit went to a foreign land; your mother gave birth to it, and you are that spirit."

Now, rather than sneaking through the mazelike paths of the jungle, Sheppard promenaded beside the prince, marching to the capital behind an honor guard.

Giddy with his good luck, he was also overcome by the beauty of the land around him. He described the jungle they marched through as a place of fairy bowers and grottos. "Festoons of moss and running vines made the forest look like a beautifully painted theatre or an enormous swinging garden." Above, someone had strung what appeared to be hornet's nests through the trees. Even these charms to ward off invaders, filled with poisoned arrowheads, had a festive look to them, like a string of Chinese lanterns.

And then he caught his first glimpse of the city itself, spread out before him on a vast table of land above forests of cultivated palm trees. As he marched through the gate, he knew he'd entered a place unlike anywhere else in Central Africa. Emil Torday gives us some idea of the scene that must have opened up before Sheppard:

> Stepping out of a lovely grove of palm trees we faced a long street, at least thirty feet wide, as straight as an arrow. It was bordered by oblong huts, each standing alone at an equal distance from its neighbors; they were all the same shape and differed only in their walls, which were made of mat-work [sic] ornamented with beautiful designs in black. . . . The houses were as spick and span as if they had just been finished; the road was swept clean. Though the day was still hot the village was busy as a hive. . . . The very children were bent on some task, some working the smith's bellows.

As they passed a guard post, hundreds of Kuba urbanites swarmed around Sheppard, pressing against each other to get a glimpse of the spirit king. Prince N'toinzide led Sheppard through the crowd to a house—a high-ceilinged place with walls made of cleverly woven screens—and presented it to him as a gift. Sheppard's men were shown to their own quarters. Their goats and chickens were led away, to be cared for until Sheppard required them. Strict sanitation laws prevented anyone from keeping sheep, dogs, ducks, pigs, or chickens within the walls of the city.

The next morning, Sheppard woke to the ringing of horns and a commotion of people scurrying around the town square. Today would be his debut—his first ceremonial meeting with the king—and he was dismayed that he had nothing better to wear than a suit "that had once been white linen," with the broad-brimmed pith helmet and the white canvas shoes. His men, too, rooted around for something fancy to put on. One of them donned a necklace made out of string and a brass button, only to be told that he had to remove it, because brass and copper ornaments were reserved for the king.

In the city square, to the beat of drums, a crowd of thousands gathered before a horseshoe-shaped stage. Seven hundred women—the king's wives—preened and jostled each other around rugs of leopard-skin and an ivory throne. The crowd parted, and a carriage made its way through the river of people, an elaborate hammock inlaid with cowrie shells carried by sixteen men. They installed the king on his throne, careful to keep his feet from touching the ground.

Torday, who visited the capital in 1908, a decade and a half after Sheppard, described it this way:

> A comparison with Japan, in the middle of the last century, is forced on one's mind, [except that the Kuba king] was the Shogun and the Mikado in one person. . . . [He represented] the living link that alone can join [the Kuba people] through the chain of his one hundred and twenty predecessors to Bumba, the founder. The spirit of Bumba lives in every one of them; it is the life of the living, the memory of the dead, the hope of the future. . . . Any

weakening of [the king's] power, every affront to his dignity sends a tremor through all.

If the king died, the majestic ceremony of the city would turn into cacophony: Aristocrats would plot against each other; royal heirs would be assassinated in droves. Eventually, a new king would be installed, and the city would return to its calm. The king represented order.

Kot aMweeky's hair had gone white—Sheppard estimated him to be about seventy-five years old—but he'd lost none of the vigor of youth. "I judged him to have been a little more than six feet high and with his crown, which was made of eagle feathers, he towered over all." He wore blue cloth studded with cowrie shells, which gleamed so white that they hurt Sheppard's eyes, and a dusting of camwood powder from toe to ankle.

The king reached out a hand to Sheppard and proclaimed, "Wyni"—"You have come." Sheppard, who had already mastered the niceties of Kuba court manners, bowed and clapped, then gave the appropriate response: "Ndini, Nyimi"—"I have come, King."

Reaching toward his belt, the king pulled out a knife, its blade snicking against a hilt. The weapon gleamed, a foot long. The king turned it so that the hilt protruded toward Sheppard. "In the red halls of the Kuba royalty, this has been handed down for seven generations," he announced. "It is now yours."

And then he invited Sheppard to join the entourage on stage, the royal family and the army of wives. Dancers strutted into the square, whirling and ducking. Singers called out choruses. Drums and orchestras played. One by one, the seven sons of the king performed military ballets, leaping about as they cut the air with their knives.

Sheppard kept stealing glances at the king. The old man was absorbed in the entertainment, laughing sometimes at a particularly clever bit of footwork. After perhaps an hour, Sheppard screwed up his courage and leaned toward the throne. "I understand, King, that your people believe me to be a [Kuba] who once lived here," he whispered.

The old man turned to him, beaming. "True."

There was no way to put it delicately, so Sheppard blurted it out: "I want to acknowledge to you that I am not a [Kuba] and I have never been here before."

At that, "the king leaned over the arm of his great chair and said with satisfaction, 'You don't know it, but you are *muana mi*, one of the family.'"

"They knew me better than I knew myself," Sheppard joked. The more he insisted that he was a foreigner and a missionary, the more smug the Kuba grew. Having been reincarnated in a land across the ocean, they allowed, he might be discombobulated. He might have forgotten his true identity and his real name. But at least he hadn't lost his ability to navigate the secret paths of his own country. At least he hadn't forgotten the customs and manners of the palace.

They had a point, for no matter who Sheppard said he was, he conducted himself exactly like a reincarnated member of the Kuba elite. He made friends with his new "brothers," most especially Prince Maxamalinge, who feted Sheppard with a lavish dinner party; the two men became close enough that, a decade later, Maxamalinge would become a fixture in the Sheppard household.

Most important, Sheppard handled the king like an old pro. "I was rather careful not to ask him too many questions," he said later. He learned to cough when the king coughed; he clapped after every sentence; he talked in the strange, low voice he'd observed other courtiers using around Kot aMweeky. In fact, Sheppard proved to be so deft a politician that he might have been able to take the throne, had he wanted to. A few years later, when Kot aMweeky finally did die, Sheppard was looked upon as a serious contender, despite his frequent protests that he had no connection to the royal family. Had he been a different kind of man—say, a fellow like the bounder in Kipling's "The Man Who Would Be King"—he might have ruled hundreds of thousands of people and commanded untold wealth.

So why not agree to become Bope Makabe, prince, magical spirit, and Kuba sophisticate? Sheppard had found a far more alluring role for himself. He would be the Kuba's documentarian, bringing back to America evidence of their grandeur. To this end, he hurried around with notebook in hand, observing the city's inhabitants and recording details of their myths, customs, clothing manufacture, child-rearing practices, laws, and civic behavior. He collected piles of art, from stunning velvet cloth to witty pieces of pottery. Fifteen years later, Picasso would shock Europe with *Les Demoiselles d'Avignon*, a painting that incorporated West African masks. The revolutionary work helped give birth to cubism—and eventually, to a European love of African art. But in Sheppard's day, the pieces he gathered would have been regarded as curios, far less valuable than the ivory tusks that the Kuba used as doorstops.

Despite his lack of training in anthropology, Sheppard somehow guessed the significance of what he saw in the Kuba capital—"their knowledge of weaving, embroidering, wood carving, and smelting was the highest in equatorial Africa," he asserted. Later scholars would prove him right. According to Jan Vansina, the region's most eminent ethnographer, Sheppard had stumbled into the last of the stately courts in Central Africa, kingdoms that hundreds of years before had rivaled the courts of Europe in technology and culture.

But in the nineteenth century, few people knew about Africa's grand past. In anthropology books, engravings of African and European skulls sat side by side, offering "proof" that the owners of the former had tiny brains. Scientists described the peoples of the Congo as hardly human. "Lord Mountmorres states that he saw in the vicinity of Avakubi a more primitive and simian type of Pygmy than the Babbute," reads one anthropology book. "These [people] he first took to be a group of chimpanzis [sic], springing from branch to branch, and stopping from curiosity to look at the intruder in exactly the same way as do the larger apes."

Sheppard had stumbled onto proof not only that the Africans were fully human, but that they could be as elitist and tradition-mad as Westerners.

• • •

Like feudal Japan or the Europe of the Middle Ages, Kuba society was one of high formalism. About half of the men who lived in the capital had a title—and with each aristocratic office came unique insignias, names, hats, rituals, privileges, and philosophies. You might be, for instance, a provincial governor; with that office came a white oxpecker feather, a copper hat pin, a special wooden staff, and tiny bows to wear under your shoulders. These accoutrements spoke volumes about your position in society, your family, and your history.

Ethnographer Torday described one such provincial minister: "Isam-bula N'Genga did not look down on the common people any more than we look down on a fly crawling across a wall. The rabble did not exist to him; I am quite certain that their voice never reached his ears. . . . He did shine like a diamond in the sky; groomed, oiled, combed to perfection, he would walk down the street, slowly, his staff over his shoulders and his hands negligently slung over its ends. . . . When I asked him a question he would just wave his hand towards one of his courtiers—that was that fellow's department!"

The Kuba's household possessions—stools, boxes, pipes, and cups—were as ornate as the city's aristocrats. Lapsley had observed that even the least of their utensils was plastered with designs. Vansina noted that the Kuba learned to carve the way children in Europe learn to read. The best artisans had developed methods unknown outside of the kingdom—drilling tiny holes in shells, creating detail work with copper inlay, making velvet out of palm fiber, weaving fabric into pom-poms and wavelike folds. The artists delighted in trompe l'oeil, visual puns, sight gags: They made pots that balanced atop human feet and carved clay cups so that they appeared to be woven out of basket material. For those in the know, the pipe bowls lampooned the faces of famous people, much the way political cartoons caricature politicians.

Kuba dynastic history—ancient kings and the stories surrounding them—was also a favorite theme. On a hilltop in the city, four statues represented the Kuba's founding fathers. The most important of the ancestral kings, Sheppard noticed, held a game on his lap that resembled a checkerboard.

Indeed, the checkerboard was a fitting symbol for the city itself. Sheppard described the streets as a grid, but beyond that, the city's extreme cleanliness, the origami folds of its social classes, the complicated decorations on every wall, and its draconian laws, gave it the atmosphere of a life-size game. The citizens moved in ballet-like harmony. After lights-out at about nine o'clock, the entire town went dark. Only the king could flaunt the law—behind the walls of his palace, seven hundred wives sang him to sleep. In the morning, prisoners scurried out to clean the streets and pull up weeds. Every family had to sweep the public way in front of their house every day.

Aside from the king, the Kuba were monogamous. "A young man sees a girl whom he likes; he has met her in his own town or at some other, or perhaps at a market place or a dance. He sends her tokens of love, bananas, plantains, peanuts, dried fish, or grasshoppers. She in turn sends him similar presents," Sheppard noted. He praised the Kuba as moral people, with a high sense of duty to their own families and their city.

The Kuba were so well behaved it was downright eerie. Sheppard's description of one man's death captures the essence of what is so beautiful and also so disturbing about Kuba culture:

> [A man named] Nnyminym took to his bed. . . . I visited the patient; also treated him, but Nnyminym grew weak and was moved from his bed to a mat on the dry ground. . . . [One day], earlier than my usual time for calling, his wife sent for me, saying that Nnymmyrn was dead. . . .
>
> I found the family bathing him and putting on his burial clothes [even though the man was alive].
>
> I remarked, "You are hasty, I fear, in dressing him for burial."
>
> But the wife remarked with grief, "No, he will be dead soon."

When they had fixed his hair, shaved his face and shoulders, anointed his body with palm oil and adjusted his legs back under him, they all sat in a semi-circle. . . . This was all done in a businesslike way. . . .

The wife asked in a calm, gentle tone, "What of your debts are unknown to us?"

Nnyminyn answered calmly, "I have settled all my debts; but listen, I will tell you the names of those owing me." And without effort, he called name after name as his wife broke small pieces of bamboo for each name. These pieces of bamboo were kept and the debts collected after death.

Now and then Nnyminyn in his sitting attitude looked at his hands growing pale, watched the heaving of his breast, looked at his family and friends before him, drew a long breath as though very tired, and actually watched death steal his life away. As soon as his eyes were closed a scream went up from his wife, and the rest of his family joined in.

The Kuba had an enviable bravery. They faced death squarely, performing a ritual around it as profound as a tea ceremony.

And yet this dignified grief could turn murderous. Anyone not displaying sufficient sorrow might be accused of witchcraft and forced to drink poison. The "witches" were almost always women of low caste.

Sheppard recounts the following story to illustrate how one family's grief could spin out of control and turn into a witch trial:

A child died suddenly in the town. The wise men said, "It is bewitched."

So they rushed through the street, crying out, "Where is the witch? Where is the witch?"

They saw an old woman sitting alone in a house. Some cried out "There is a witch." They seized her. She said, "No. I am no witch."

> . . . They dragged her to the poison house; gave her
> poison; she drank it, and in a little while was seized with
> pain, but could not throw off the poison, fell down and
> died in agony.

Witchcraft ordeals and divination existed side by side with the kind of
legal proceedings more familiar to us: courts, juries, trials, sentences.
For the Kuba, the poison cup was a kind of DNA test—scientific evidence of guilt or innocence. If you drank the poison and lived, you
were proved innocent. But Sheppard regarded the poison cup as
nothing less than the African version of lynching. He became dis-
traught when the victims staggered through the streets, vomiting up
bile or dying in contortions.

Nor would he look the other way when it came to human sacrifice.
Though they did not trade in slaves, the Kuba used captive men and
women to ornament their funerals. "The burying of the living with the
dead [is] far beyond [what the Kete do], who only bury goats with their
dead," the king once bragged to Sheppard. "Our kind of people," he
seemed to be saying, "aren't so cheap as to send our loved ones off
with a smelly pack of animals." The king's own mother had glided off
to the afterlife with a thousand servants in tow.

Weeks after he arrived, Sheppard confronted the king about the
poison ordeals and funeral sacrifices, arguing for human rights "in the
strongest language." It was the first time he had violated court protocol,
had dared to challenge the divine authority of the king. But instead of
beheading Sheppard for his insolence, King Kot aMweeky only laughed;
he took the foreigner's suggestion as a joke. Had Sheppard traveled to
King Leopold's palace and argued that the Congolese deserved to run
their own country, he might have received a similar response. The idea
was simply beyond the pale, too absurd to be a threat.

It was a different matter entirely when Sheppard began to weave his
magic spells.

One day, Sheppard's servant was observed sprinkling foamy powder
into a stream. A few hours later, a tornado whipped through the city,

flattening several houses. Kot aMweeky was furious. Only kings—and the spirits of kings—could create storms like that. Sheppard must have caused the cyclone with that bubbling powder; he'd been showing off with his high winds; he'd been spitting rain down onto the palace. And for what purpose? To steal the throne? To stir up a storm of political unrest?

At noon, two court messengers showed up at Sheppard's house and told him his presence had been demanded at the palace. Sheppard stood before a looking glass and brushed his hair, then shrugged on his coat. He followed his escorts along the streets, through a succession of gates, and into the cool darkness of the palace.

The king's face twisted when he saw Sheppard. "What caused that storm?" Kot aMweeky demanded.

Sheppard offered some sort of meteorological explanation—the rainy season, weather patterns in the Kasai, high pressure systems.

He might as well have poked the king with a stick. Eagle feathers flailing, neck cords bulging, Kot aMweeky screamed out his accusations: Sheppard had brought that storm down on the city. Sheppard would have his head lopped off.

The missionary froze—terrified, tongue-tied.

And then he found himself speaking in a tone you might use to croon to a baby, a voice he'd heard all around the palace, a Kuba way of talking, the only known antidote to the king's tantrums. He borrowed it for the occasion. He put it on like a velvet hat.

"It is true, King, my people were at the creek, but they were washing my clothes and it could not cause a storm," he said. "They used in washing what we call in the foreign country 'soap,' and it caused the whiteness and foam on the water, but it is something innocent and cannot cause a storm." The moment had passed. Even the king had grown bored with his own tantrum. "Well, don't have your clothes washed anymore," he snapped.

Sheppard left the palace and emerged into the pounding heat of the day, shouts of leapfrogging children, smells of peanuts drying in the market, the drone of the snake charmer's horn, ladies chatting in a doorway, the whole parade of ordinary life around him. Later, he joked about how anxious he'd been in that palace, wondering whether the king would take off his head. He needed his head, as "it is the only one I have."

But as Sheppard stumbled back to his quarters that afternoon, he probably could not see much humor in the incident. Soap flakes, gunshots, a bit of brass worn on his clothing—any of his Western habits could be misinterpreted as a political statement and lead to a death sentence.

Kubaland must have reminded him of the American South. In both places, his survival depended on his ability to play-act, to go under a false identity, to hide his true impulses and feelings—and most important, to stay on the good side of men who could easily kill him. Of the many explorers who could have wandered into Kubaland, Sheppard was uniquely equipped to live through the experience. His years in America—where he'd had to step into a variety of roles, from the "son" of a white dentist to the leader of a black church—had taught him to be a shape changer. Sheppard was a whirlwind of smoke and air and glitter, a dazzling sideshow of a man who could cough like a Kuba courtier or preach a sermon to a Virginia congregation. But the cost of such stupendous adaptability must have been high. Who was he under all the different masks and costumes?

It was soon after the storm, and his near-execution, that Sheppard decided he'd had enough. After several months in Kubaland, he wanted to return home with the tremendous artifacts and notes he'd collected—for surely he would be celebrated for the coup.

But leaving would be no easy matter. First he asked the king point blank whether he might be dismissed. "Oh no," Kot aMeeky said, "you must stay with us."

Sheppard visited the palace several more times: "I told [the king] that I loved him and his people, and that it was a real pleasure to live in his town, but that his [Kete] subjects at Luebo were looking for my return. . . . The king replied . . . that he wanted me to remain with him and not to return again to Luebo."

Finally, Kot aMweeky relented and granted Sheppard a leave of absence: "You may go and remain a year."

In his negotiations, Sheppard did not forget his duties to the church. He convinced the king to grant him nine acres of land in the center of town on which he could found a mission station. Perhaps Sheppard eyed that lovely green field and imagined children running across it, and his future wife Lucy leaning against a doorway of a cottage—for she still waited for him back in the States, and he planned to bring her here as soon as he could.

He carried so many artifacts out of the city that his men had to walk single file, like porters struggling along one of Stanley's old trails. For years, the Belgians had been attempting to get into this kingdom and plunder it, to carry out ivory, rubber, and gold. Sheppard took art instead—what would later become one of the most valuable collections in the world.

"The parting with King Lukenga was touching. He was king, but he had a kindly heart," Sheppard wrote, suddenly forgiving Kot aMweeky for his moods. "The king furnished us with two guides and his royal mace for safe conduct. Hundreds of men, women and children followed us out on the plain, waving, singing and shouting a farewell."

As Sheppard traveled back to Luebo, he reveled in his freedom, away from the intrigues of court and the whims of the king. In small villages, he shared meals with farmers and hunters, humble people who called him simply "Sheppate."

One night, he gathered with some villagers around a leaping fire. They told him of the jackals and leopards that stalked the woods; how the people stayed up late at night in the safe circle of firelight, entertaining each other with stories to pass the time. They asked Sheppard about his own country, questions that must have struck him as refreshingly honest after all the subterfuge of the capital. "How do you get to the foreign country?" they wanted to know. "What do you eat?"

They laughed at some of his answers, for the place he described seemed a fairyland.

"When I tried to tell them that we had a season of the year that . . . got so cold you could walk over streams without breaking through, and that some of our houses were taller than a palm tree, they incredulously shook their heads," he wrote.

Did he also tell them that across the sea, in a palace far taller than any palm tree, a king paced around his throne room, plotting their fate? Did he break the news that they were doubly cursed by kings, not just their own but also Leopold?

Most likely not. That night, as the cups of palm wine went from hand to hand, and people leaned against each other, enjoying the scratchy sound of tired voices, Sheppard's far away home must have seemed far away indeed. He was, that night, a man born in the land of the dead, come across the sea to this place of light, before this snug hearth, to tell his tale. He was Bope Mekabe.

acknowledgments

Many people made this anthology.

At Thunder's Mouth Press and Avalon Publishing Group:
Thanks to Will Balliett, Neil Ortenberg, Susan Reich, Dan O'Connor, Ghadah Alrawi, Maria Fernandez, Mike Walters, Paul Paddock, Simon Sullivan, Linda Kosarin, Sue Canavan and David Riedy for their support, dedication and hard work.

At The Writing Company:
Nate Hardcastle and Nat May did most of the research, with assistance from Kate Fletcher and Taylor Smith. Mark Klimek and March Truedsson took up slack on other projects.

At Shawneric.com:
Shawneric Hachey oversaw rights research and negotiations.

At the Portland Public Library in Portland, Maine:
Thanks to the librarians for their assistance in finding and borrowing books and other publications from around the country.

Finally, I am grateful to the writers whose work appears in this book.

permissions

bibliography

The selections used in this anthology were taken from the editions listed below. In some cases, other editions may be easier to find. Hard-to-find or out-of-print titles often are available through inter-library loan services or through Internet booksellers.

Anasi, Robert. *The Gloves: A Boxing Chronicle*. New York: North Point Press, 2002.

Beller, Thomas (editor). *Before and After: Stories from New York*. New York: W.W. Norton & Company. (For "The Numbers" by Bryan Charles.)

Boukreev, Anatoli; translated by Natalia Lagovskaya and Barbara Poston. *Above the Clouds: The Diaries of a High-Altitude Mountaineer*. New York: St. Martin's Press, 2001.

Donahue, Topher. "When the Whip Comes Down". Originally appeared in *Climbing Magazine*, August 2002.

Finkel, Michael. "Thirteen Ways of Looking at a Void". Originally appeared in *National Geographic Adventure*, September/October 2001.

Fletcher, David. *Hunted: A True Story of Survival*. New York: Carroll & Graf, 2002.

Hill, Lynn with Greg Child. *Climbing Free: My Life in the Vertical World*. New York: W.W. Norton, 2002.

Kennedy, Pagan. *Black Livingstone: A True Tale of Adventure in the Nineteenth-Century Congo*. New York: Viking Press, 2002.

Moffett, Mark W. "Bit". Originally appeared in *Outside*, April 2002.

Price, A. Preston. *The Last Kilometer: Marching to Victory in Europe with the Big Red One, 1944-1945*. Annapolis, MD: Naval Institute Press, 2002.

Rennicke, Jeff. "I Cried Aloud for You". Originally appeared in *Backpacker Magazine*, June 2002.

Salak, Kira. *Four Corners: Into the Heart of New Guinea - One Woman's Solo Journey*. New York: Counterpoint Press, 2001.

Souhami, Diana. *Selkirk's Island: The True and Strange Adventures of the Real Robinson Crusoe*. Orlando, FL: Harcourt Brace & Company, 2002.

Symmes, Patrick. "The Last Days of the Mountain Kingdom". Originally appeared in *Outside*, September 2001.